· E P O C A ·

THE RIVER OF SAND

· EPOCA ·
THE RIVER OF SAND

CREATED BY
KOBE BRYANT

WRITTEN BY
IVY CLAIRE

GRANITY STUDIOS
COSTA MESA, CALIFORNIA

Dear Kob-Kob and Gigi,
You continue to inspire us every day.
Here's to dreams that never die.
We love you for now, forever, and for always.

Love,
Viski/Mommy, Natalia, Bianka, and Capri ♥

To Kobe,

who loved stories, inspired wonder,

and conjured a world of magic and delight.

And to Gigi,

who inspired this story and so many more.

—*Ivy Claire*

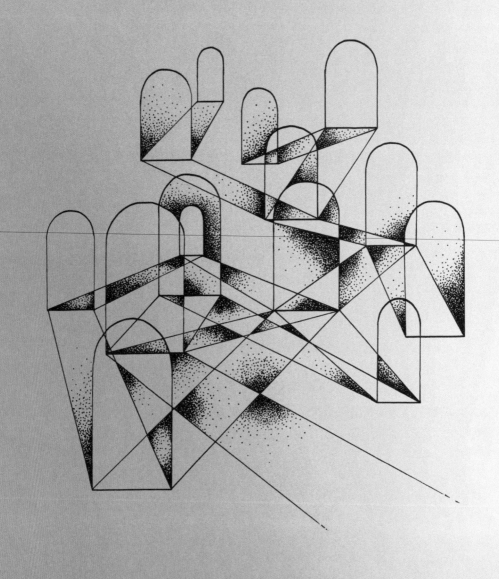

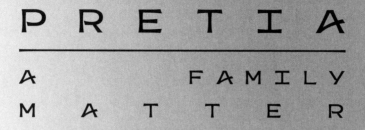

1

PRETIA

A FAMILY MATTER

"ON YOUR MARKS. GET SET. GO." PRETIA opened the door of the van and sprang out before the vehicle had come to a full stop.

Her feet hit the ground for a split second before she raced off.

"Pretia!"

She ignored her parents' voices. The only thing she cared about was being free, moving, stretching her legs.

Behind her she heard another set of feet hit the ground.

"Catch me if you can," Pretia called.

"Pretia, wait!" Rovi cried.

"Not a chance," Pretia hollered. There was no way she was waiting or slowing down, and Rovi knew it.

For a week they had been cooped up in the royal caravan with her parents as Pretia's family conducted the end-of-summer ceremonial tour of Epoca's holy sites and her relatives' palaces. For seven days, she and Rovi had been forced to behave, sit still, and shake the hands of hundreds of strangers. For seven days she'd had to plaster a tight smile on her face while people from all over the country paid their respects to her—bowing to the Child of Hope. Pretia had worked hard not to roll her eyes at the name. For seven days, she had been forced to act as if the most exciting thing in the world was that one day she would rule Epoca.

For seven days, she had not been allowed to run.

But that was over now. This was the last stop: Ponsit Palace, the seat of House Relia, her mother's ancestral home. Ever since she could remember, Pretia had spent part of her summers here with Queen Helena and Uncle Janos. Unlike the wide-open spaces at Castle Airim, a complicated maze of narrow corridors and secret rooms made up Ponsit Palace. She loved exploring its host of complex rooms and hallways that twisted and coiled, ending in switchbacks and dead ends. There were hidden passages and tunnels all over the building. It was possible to get lost for hours and then find yourself in the exact opposite place from where you expected to be.

This year the trip would be a short one. She only had one day to show it all to Rovi. Tomorrow, along with her uncle and her cousin Castor, they would depart for Ecrof. Pretia didn't want to waste any time.

"Hurry up," she scolded Rovi as they raced up to the gates.

An orange late-afternoon sun hung over the squat, square collection of buildings with stocky purple columns spread out across the hilltop. The guard swung the gate open for Pretia. He didn't even have time to bow before she blasted past him, Rovi in pursuit.

As they sprinted up to the palace, Rovi called, "Is it true that someone once got lost in this palace and was never found?"

"Maybe," Pretia cried over her shoulder. "Let's find out!"

They were breathing hard when they bounded up the short flight of stone steps that led to the lowest of Ponsit's many colonnades.

"It's too bad we only have today to explore," Pretia said. She had entered the grand door of the palace and darted to her right down a narrow corridor that led off the main hall. She took two fast turns and was quickly inside the maze of hallways. "There's so much to see," she said.

"*See?*" Rovi said. "I can barely *see* anything at all."

He was right. The corridor was dim. But that was the fun of Ponsit. You were often in the dark. "You'll get used to it," Pretia said. And ran off again.

"Wait," Rovi called.

Pretia didn't listen. She took two more turns, leading them deeper into the palace.

Rovi kept pace. Pretia turned left, then right, then left again. She thought they were heading toward the outermost of the palace's many courtyards, but she couldn't be sure. After four more left turns, they hit a dead end and had to double back.

Twice they wound up at the same dead end before Pretia figured out a route that returned them to the original corridor.

"You weren't joking," Rovi said. "This place really *is* a maze."

"Let's hope we don't get lost," Pretia said.

"No kidding," Rovi replied. He sounded anxious.

"Let's go," Pretia exclaimed, dashing off in the opposite direction from where they had begun.

"Hold on," Rovi insisted.

But Pretia had raced ahead again. She made three quick turns, then found herself in a small sanctuary she'd never seen before. She pulled up short. There was a bowl for a ceremonial flame, but it was cold and filled with ash. Pretia ran her fingers across the bowl. They came up black. She glanced around. A chill ran through her—was this an altar to Hurell? She searched for some indication of whose shrine she was in, whether it might belong to the Fallen God, but before she could find any, she heard her name echoing through the halls.

"*Prrreeeeeettttttiaaaaaaa.*"

Rovi sounded panicked.

"In here," Pretia called.

"Where's here?"

"I'm right over . . ." she began again. But it was no use. "Stay where you are. I'll come to you."

Rovi kept calling her name. Pretia turned left. His voice grew fainter. She turned right. Louder. Right again. Fainter. Left. Louder. Right. Louder. She staggered down a short flight of steps, following the sound of Rovi's voice. He was nearby . . . somewhere.

She was standing in a dark, cool room. The only light came from a single flame at the far end.

"What is this place?"

She nearly jumped out of her skin. Rovi was right behind her. He sounded scared.

Pretia blinked and rubbed her eyes, adjusting to the dark. "It's a crypt. They're all over the palace. It's nothing to worry about."

"Is—is that someone dead?" Rovi extended a finger toward a stone coffin with a frieze of a Realist queen on it.

"She probably isn't in there. Epocan royalty are usually hidden way belowground where no one will find them and their jewels or whatever they were buried with. If there's anyone in that box, it's probably a servant."

"Can we get out of here?" Rovi asked.

"Lead the way," Pretia teased.

Rovi stayed rooted in place.

"I thought you were famous for your fancy footwork," Pretia added, poking her friend in the ribs.

"I need to see where I'm going," Rovi said, jumping at her touch. "These walls make me claustrophobic. It's like the maze is blocking my grana. I can't even guess which way to turn."

Pretia shuddered at the thought of something muting her grana, the gods-given talent that allowed her to excel at sports.

"Okay," she said. "I'll lead." Rovi followed her as they twisted and turned, finally arriving in a small sanctuary. "This place is such a puzzle," Pretia marveled.

"It's more like a trap," Rovi muttered.

"When you get used to it, you'll love it," Pretia promised. And off she ran once more.

They wound their way through the corridors. Soon Pretia was out of breath, but she pressed on.

"Pretia," Rovi panted behind her, "you know where we are, right?"

"Sort of," she replied. She did and she didn't. Three more turns to the left. Two to the right. Then she bumped against a wall. Rovi crashed into her.

"Never mind," Rovi said. "You clearly have no idea."

"Don't worry," Pretia said. "Someone will find us . . . eventually."

"Who? When?" Rovi replied. "We're supposed to go to Ecrof *tomorrow*. We can't miss the ship."

"You don't actually think we're going to be stuck in here all night, do you?"

"I don't know what to think," Rovi groaned. "We've been in this maze forever."

"Well," Pretia replied, "then we need to keep going."

Rovi sighed.

"We'll be fine," Pretia assured him. But truth be told, she was getting a little worried. She'd never been lost for so long in Ponsit. They would find their way out, though. They had to. "Trust me," she added.

"I do," Rovi said.

Her best friend's vote of confidence put an additional spring in her step, making her sprint faster and faster through the twisting halls. They bumped into walls. They doubled back. Pretia's heart began to race. What if Rovi was right? What if they were really and truly lost?

Deep breaths, she urged herself. *Deep. Breaths.*

And then they stumbled out into the fresh air. Pretia looked up to see the vault of the blue sky overhead.

"Whoa!" Rovi gasped.

"Just look at you two." Pretia was startled by the sound of her cousin Castor's voice. "You're acting like something was chasing you through the halls." Then a look of gleeful amazement broke across his face. "Wait. Were you *lost*?"

"Of course not," Pretia retorted.

Pretia found Castor annoying, and he could be a bully, but she often felt sorry for him. After all, she was the Crown Princess of Epoca, heir to both House Somni and House Relia. No matter whether her mother's house, the Realists, or her father's, the Dreamers, came out victorious in the next Epic Games, she would rule Epoca. And Castor—well, he was always second-best to Pretia, always made to watch from the sidelines as honors were bestowed on her. She tried to remind herself of that when he was being particularly irritating. Like now.

"You *were* lost," Castor taunted. "I recognize the panicked expression on your faces."

Now that Pretia had caught her breath, she was able to see where they had emerged from the maze: the Games Pit, which was exactly where she wanted to be. The pit—a rectangle with a circular track carved into it—was surrounded by four stone walls from which steep stone bleachers rose on all sides. Unlike the famous Athletos Stadium at Castle Airim, whose track and playing field felt accessible, when you were in Ponsit's Games Pit, you felt trapped by the seating that loomed above.

There were rumors that during the time of Hurell, when many Realists had been lured to follow his dark rule, the Games Pit had been used as an arena for deadly sports battles. Athletes—or rather, prisoners—were forced to compete while spectators towered overhead. But those times were long gone, and now it was where the best athletes of House Relia trained in private.

"What is this place?" Rovi asked.

"It's a track," Castor replied.

Rovi glanced around nervously. "It feels more like a jail."

"That's because it's a *secret* track," Castor said snidely. "It's just for the use of people who live in Ponsit. And I've been using it all summer to train for the Junior Epic Games."

Pretia felt a jolt of excitement. This year wasn't any normal school year. In a couple of months, the Junior Epic Games, the second most important sporting event in Epoca after the Epic Games, were set to be held. Representing your house and your academy was the highest honor a young athlete could receive. The Junior Epic Games were considered to be a prediction of which young athletes would go on to illustrious careers and even Epic Glory.

"You seem pretty confident that you'll qualify," Rovi said.

"I have a good coach," Castor retorted. "My dad."

Pretia and Rovi exchanged a look. That certainly *was* an advantage. Not only was Pretia's uncle Janos their formidable Head Trainer at Ecrof, he was also one of the best athletes Epoca had ever produced.

"We've been training, too," Pretia said.

"Good for you," Castor replied. "But I'm sure it's not very hard to get chosen for the Star Stealer team."

Pretia didn't have to look to know that Rovi's cheeks were blazing with anger at the mention of the gang of outcasts he'd been part of in Phoenis.

"Oh whoops," Castor said, "Star Stealers aren't *allowed* to compete in the Junior Epic Games. None of the Orphic People are."

"Like you know anything about the Orphic People," Rovi said. "You're too busy locked up in a palace to have learned the first thing about anyone who isn't a fancy Realist or Dreamer."

Pretia glanced down at her shoes. The same could be said for her. She, too, knew little about the Orphic People except that they were made up of gangs of street kids in different cities who were neither

Dreamers nor Realists and therefore castaways. Their names differed from city to city, and they were usually considered harmless because they were children. No one knew—or no one told Pretia—what happened to them when they grew up.

"I know enough to be sure that no Star Stealer or Sun Shooter or Moon Grabber or whatever else you're called is ever going to compete in the Junior Epic Games," Castor retorted.

"Luckily, I'm not a Star Stealer," Rovi snapped. "I'm a Dreamer."

Castor laughed. "As if that's any better."

Pretia sighed. Less than a minute after they'd encountered each other, the boys were already at one another's throats. It was going to be a long year if they kept this up, especially with spots on the Junior Epic Squad at stake.

"How about we settle this on the track," Pretia suggested.

Castor hesitated.

"Unless you have a problem with outsiders using your *secret* track, Castor," she added.

"It's not that," Castor said quietly.

"What is it, then?" Rovi asked. "I thought you said you'd been training all summer. Are you afraid?"

"I'm not afraid of you," Castor said. Then he looked at Pretia.

"You're afraid of *me*?" Now it was Pretia's turn to laugh. "Why?"

Castor glanced nervously from side to side. "You're not going to do that thing if we race, are you?"

"What thing?" Pretia asked.

"Splitting yourself."

Pretia took a deep breath. "Why?" Last year, when her grana had finally come, she'd learned that she had a remarkable and unique talent for splitting herself. In a tough competition, she could often watch herself divide in two and see her shadow self race on ahead and accomplish amazing feats she wouldn't otherwise have imagined possible.

"I want to race you fair and square. That's all," Castor said.

"It *is* fair," Rovi said. "It's not cheating. It's her grana."

"I'm just saying that if you want to race here on my track, don't split yourself," Castor said.

Pretia was suddenly dying to race her cousin. Except for the last week, she and Rovi had been training hard all summer with the exact same goal—to represent Ecrof at the Junior Epic Games. It was basically all they had thought about from the moment they left Ecrof three months ago. And, although it was true that it was easier for her to beat Rovi when she split herself, she often managed to do so without releasing her shadow self. If she could beat Rovi, she could certainly beat Castor, splitting herself or no. Still, it bothered her.

"Let's go," she said to Castor. "I'll try not to scare you."

"And I'll try not to embarrass the Child of Hope with how badly I beat her," Castor boasted.

Pretia reddened. "Don't call me that."

Castor stepped up to the starting line. "Whatever you say, Child of Hope. I bet you have no *hope* of making Junior Epics."

Rovi jumped in before Pretia could reply. "And I bet Pretia can make Epic Elite and compete in the Junior Epic Games even without splitting herself," Rovi said.

"Doubt it," Castor said. "Go!"

He took off. Pretia and Rovi followed. They raced around the track, once, twice, three times, their feet in lockstep. Pretia crossed the finish line a split second before the others.

"Pretty good for a princess," Rovi teased.

"Yeah," Castor panted. "Pretty good for a princess."

"I'm not just a princess," Pretia called back, surprised that the boys had united in teasing her. "And I'm not the Child of Hope. I'm a future Junior Epic Champion."

"Then show me what you got," Rovi answered. And with his

trademark fast footwork, he reversed course and began racing in the opposite direction on the track.

Castor cupped his hand over his mouth and called after him, "Not bad for a Star Stealer!" He sounded impressed, which also surprised Pretia.

"You two better catch me if you're going to make the Junior Epic Team," Rovi said.

"Don't worry," Pretia replied, racing toward him. Castor kept pace. Once more, they sprinted around, with Pretia now in the lead.

All summer, she'd only had Rovi to race. She was now so used to running against her friend that it had become routine—the same patterns, the same races repeated over and over. But now with someone else in the mix, the competition felt real. It was exhilarating. She wondered if Castor, who had been alone at Ponsit all summer, felt the same about having her and Rovi to compete with.

These thoughts distracted her, and Pretia fell behind the boys. Rovi had picked up his pace, and Castor stayed with him. Pretia would have to scramble if she was going to catch them. They were pulling ahead of her.

But she had no intention of letting them win. She was just going to let them *think* that victory was theirs.

Rovi and Castor were now a whole turn ahead of her.

"You're going to have to do better than that to make Junior Epics, Princess," Rovi called.

"I wouldn't want you to strain yourself, Princess," Castor echoed.

It seemed the only thing the two boys could agree upon was teasing her.

But Pretia wasn't worried about them beating her. She didn't care about Castor's dislike for her talent. He wasn't the boss of her.

Rovi was fifty yards from the finish, Castor on his tail. Pretia took a deep breath and then relaxed as she watched her shadow self sprint away, closing in on Rovi and Castor, running faster than her physical body ever could. Pretia's shadow self moved without anxiety or doubt. It didn't worry about her performance, the crowds, the results. It simply ran.

She passed Castor first, then Rovi a few steps before the finish line. She watched herself beat the boys. Then her physical body made it across, and her shadow self collided back into it and disappeared, leaving her whole again, doubled over and panting from her effort.

Rovi staggered after her and collapsed. "I knew you were going to do that. I knew it. It's almost not—"

Pretia held up her hand. "Don't tell me it's not fair."

Rovi bit his tongue. "You're right," he said. "It's totally fair. You have to use whatever grana the gods gave you, right? But boy, wait until Vera sees how much you've improved over the summer."

Pretia smiled at the mention of her other best friend. "If I know one thing about Vera Renovo," she said, "it's that she's trained harder than all of us combined. And she's probably improved more."

Rovi laughed. But Castor's face was sunken in a scowl.

"You cheated," Castor said.

"Excuse me?" Pretia replied.

"You said you wouldn't do that," her cousin moaned.

"I didn't say anything except that I'd try not to scare you," Pretia said. "Sorry," she added with a smile, pleased that she'd unnerved her bossy cousin. "Go again?"

"Sure," Castor said. "But play fair this time."

"I'm not breaking any rules, Castor."

The kids readied themselves on the starting line. Rovi counted down. On "Go," they took off. The three were even at the second turn. But Pretia could feel herself starting to lag. At the third turn she was several paces behind Castor and Rovi. She needed to dig deeper.

And just like before, the moment she *needed* to excel, her shadow self broke away. She watched her shadow sprint ahead. As her shadow self passed Castor, Pretia's physical body felt a jolt. Castor had flung himself onto her shadow self, trying to restrain her.

Pretia's entire body shuddered with the sensation of someone scraping her soul. But her shadow self didn't seem to mind. It didn't even slow as Castor held tight, his arms wrapped around her middle. Then, to her amazement, Pretia's shadow self hoisted her cousin onto its back, and without missing a footfall, accelerated to the finish line ahead of Rovi.

Pretia felt the curious collision as her selves reunited. Her shadow self had dropped Castor, who lay on the track, staring up at her in astonishment. "What just happened?"

"I think Pretia *carried* you across the finish line," Rovi said, "and still beat me."

"But—" Castor began. "I don't understand. How did you do that?"

"I don't know," Pretia admitted. She was pretty stunned.

"If you don't know, then it's got to be cheating," Castor said.

"Why?" Pretia asked.

"Because you don't understand what you can do," her cousin said. "It's dangerous."

"There's nothing dangerous about it," Pretia said, helping him to his feet. "I was just giving you a friendly lift over the finish line."

Castor was eyeing her sullenly. "I don't like it."

"I'm sure if I had chosen to represent House Relia, you'd have no problem with me splitting myself," Pretia said.

"That's exactly right," boomed a voice across the Games Pit.

Pretia looked up to see her imposing uncle Janos standing on the stone bleachers. She was torn between rushing to greet him and staying where she was, remembering that the last time she'd seen her uncle he'd been praying to Hurell, the Fallen God. Or at least that's what she thought he'd been doing. As the summer stretched on, she'd become less sure.

"If Pretia had chosen House Relia," Janos continued, "we'd be thrilled by her talent. And one day she might compete for the Realists. She has every right to choose whatever team she wants to compete for. At the moment, she is a Dreamer, and an impressive one. You, too, Rovi Myrios. It seems you've learned some discipline over the summer."

Rovi shuffled his feet and muttered something under his breath.

"I'm very impressed with both of you. Castor, you and our fellow Realists have your work cut out for you. Now let's see you race again."

Pretia had had three months to wonder about her final encounter with Janos at Ecrof. Eventually, she'd decided to take what he'd said to her at the time at face value—there were indeed things in her world that were beyond her own understanding. In fact, there were things about *herself* that she failed to comprehend. First of all, her position as the Child of Hope, the only royal born to both a Dreamer and a Realist parent. And second, the fact that her powerful grana allowed her to do something—split herself—that was only ever spoken about in rumors and legends.

"On your marks, get set, go!" Janos blew on the wooden whistle he always wore around his neck. This time Pretia didn't wait until Rovi and Castor had nearly beaten her to split herself. She did so right from the start, beating them both by a full three seconds. It felt amazing.

"Wow," Rovi said when he joined her across the finish. "Just *wow*."

"Yeah, wow," Castor said, although with slightly less enthusiasm than Rovi.

"Pretia!"

She looked up at the sound of her name. Her mother stood in

the stone bleachers next to Janos, her arms folded across her chest. Pretia waved.

"Isn't she awesome?" Rovi called. "She destroyed me in that last race!"

The queen ignored Rovi. "Pretia," the queen called again. "Come up here immediately."

"One more race," Pretia replied.

"Yes, Helena, I'd like to see my best second years race again," Janos said.

The queen turned and gave her brother a cold stare. "Janos, I need to speak to my daughter immediately. No more races." The queen's voice was firm and had an unfamiliar edge to it. "Pretia, get up here immediately."

Pretia looked at Rovi and shrugged. Even Castor refrained from teasing her about being summoned by her mother. "See you at dinner. It's in the Hall of Logic. Castor can show you." Then she climbed the steps to join the queen.

Pretia was out of breath after the short, steep climb to where Queen Helena stood. "Did you see that?" she asked. "I totally crushed the boys."

"I saw," the queen said. "I don't like it."

"When I win?"

"When you split yourself."

"What!" Pretia said, horrified. "That's the best part."

"It makes me uneasy," the queen said. "It attracts attention."

"Even Janos thinks it's amazing," Pretia said. "And I'm on the opposite team."

Her mother began to ascend the steps out of the stadium. Pretia followed. "My brother doesn't always have his priorities right. And, Pretia, let me remind you, you are not on any team."

Pretia stopped walking. "Is this because I chose House Somni for my time at Ecrof and not your house?"

"No," the queen said without turning around. "It is because of who you are. You are both Dreamer and Realist and therefore *do not* have a team. You are the—"

"Child of Hope," Pretia grumbled.

"I don't like that tone," Queen Helena warned.

And I don't like that all anyone cares about is that I will rule Epoca one day, Pretia thought to herself. *I don't care about ruling or uniting houses or being the child of anything.* But she knew better than to say those things out loud.

"Sorry," Pretia said. "It's just all anyone ever talks to me about is something that's going to happen when I'm older instead of what's happening this year—the Junior Epics. I know I'll have state responsibilities soon. But this is my life *now.*"

They had arrived at the upper level of the palace. "I've asked your father to join us in your rooms," her mother said, ignoring her explanation.

"Why? Wh-what's going on?" Pretia stammered.

"We'll discuss it when we're all together." And before Pretia could object or ask any more questions, the queen headed straight for Pretia's quarters, finding them with zero difficulty. She'd grown up in this palace, after all.

She held the door open for Pretia and stepped inside. Pretia followed her and sat on the bed, feeling as if she was in trouble for something she didn't know she'd done. She racked her brain but came up with nothing.

Her mother sighed. "Pretia, you certainly have an impressive talent. But I don't think it will serve you well."

"Why not?"

The queen put a hand on Pretia's shoulder. "Once you unleash your grana, you will most certainly be chosen for the Junior Epic Games."

"But—but isn't that the point?"

Queen Helena glanced at the door. "Where *is* your father?"

"I don't understand—" Pretia began, but she was interrupted by the arrival of King Airos.

He took one look at Pretia and rushed to hug her.

"Do you know how much better she is than those boys out there in the Games Pit?" the queen asked, looking at Pretia's father.

"I suspected," he said. "In fact, I just heard that you *carried* your cousin across the finish line."

"Part of me did," Pretia admitted.

"You see?" Queen Helena said. "She's exceptional. She's bound to be chosen for the Junior Epic Team, and then it would be her duty to compete."

"What's wrong with that!" Pretia demanded.

The king and queen exchanged a look that filled Pretia with anxiety.

"We've learned that the Junior Epic Games are going to be held in Phoenis this year, as planned," King Airos said. "We were hoping they'd relocate it."

"Why? Phoenis is great! That's where Rovi's from—at least when he was a Star Stealer. I guess technically he's from Cora Island. But in Phoenis he'll have home-field advantage."

The king took a deep breath. "The Star Stealers are exactly what's wrong with Phoenis."

"What do you mean? They're harmless."

"That's what Rovi told you," the queen said.

Now her father sighed. "That's how I've always liked to think of them," he admitted. "We've given them the benefit of the doubt until now. But there have been rumors."

"Serious rumors, Pretia," the queen added. "The Star Stealers have been rising up. They've been revolting against the authorities. You have to understand that gangs like Rovi's pose a serious threat to Dreamers and Realists, since they don't adhere to our rules."

"They're just kids!" Pretia exclaimed.

"There have been incidents," the king explained. "Small riots. We're afraid that they might try to stage something at the Junior Epic Games to challenge our authority. The Junior Epic Games set the stage for the Epic Games, which allow us to maintain peace in Epoca. They are a perfect setting for an attempt to undermine our centuries of tradition and rule."

"In the last few months, the authorities have had to deal with them frequently," the queen added.

"It's happened before," the king said. "The Junior Epic Games will bring a lot of attention to Phoenis. This could give the Star Stealers the platform they need to make a serious stand."

"But Rovi has always told me all his gang ever did was steal what they need to survive. That's it."

"The Phoenician guards have been trying to control the situation," the king continued. "But there are too many concerns."

Once more Pretia looked from one parent to the other. "What kind of concerns?"

"For your safety," her father said slowly. "Which is why your mother and I have decided you will not be allowed to participate in the Junior Epic Games this year."

Pretia flopped back on the bed. She couldn't even find the words for how angry she was. She bit her lip to restrain her anger. She knew showing her rage wouldn't help her cause.

Her parents sat on either side of her. "Pretia, we are also going to have to forbid you from going to Ecrof," the queen said, stroking her hair sympathetically.

Pretia felt a sick dread rise in her. "Why?"

"Cora Island is one of the few places in Epoca where things are slightly beyond our control," the king explained. "As you know, it was once one of the holiest sites in our land—the magical last home of the gods."

◆

"I know," Pretia said impatiently. Her anger welled up inside her.

"The only way to get to Cora is by means of Ecrof's ship," the king continued. "Not even your royal parents can reach you there. When you are on Cora, anything that happens is out of our hands."

Pretia stared at her father uncomprehendingly. "So—so what? What do you think is going to happen?"

"If you display your talent for splitting yourself, you'll undoubtedly make the Junior Epic Squad," Helena said. "Then, by Epic ordinance, you will have to compete. There will be nothing we can do to prevent you from traveling to Phoenis. As you know, it is each citizen of Epoca's duty to do whatever it takes to represent their house in Epic competitions."

Pretia rolled over and buried her face in a pillow. "Except mine," she muttered. She felt tears sting her eyes.

"There is more to life than sports," the king said in his kindest voice.

"No, there isn't," Pretia insisted, lifting her head from the pillow. She caught her parents exchanging a worried glance.

"Ruling Epoca is more important than sports," the king said. "You are going to be a distinguished and unique ruler."

"I'm eleven," Pretia cried. "I don't want to rule anything. I want to compete."

"In time, that will change," the king said.

"Don't count on it," Pretia said.

"Your birth is exceptional in all of Epoca. You are destined for greatness," the queen said.

"But not *Epic* greatness," Pretia said. All her parents ever thought about was ruling, ruling, ruling. They had never been serious competitive athletes. They had no idea what the rush of competition felt like.

"I'm sorry," the king said. "Maybe things will be different in four years at the next Junior Epics."

Pretia glared defiantly at her parents. She took a deep breath and leveled her voice. "If I don't go back to Ecrof *this* year, I'll fall behind, and I won't make the team in four years, either."

"And perhaps that is for the best, too," Queen Helena said. "But what concerns us now is this year. And *this* year, it is unsafe for you to participate."

"We love you too much to allow you to take such a risk," the king said.

"And we must all put Epoca above our happiness," Helena continued. "Since you are to rule one day, this is a lesson you must learn."

Pretia was too upset to speak. She was almost too upset to breathe.

Her mother stood up and placed a kiss on the top of her head. Pretia watched in disbelief as she left the room.

Her father remained at her side. "One day this will just be a distant memory," he said. "You can't imagine it now, but someday you'll forget all about this disappointment."

Pretia bit her lip so hard it nearly bled. There was no way she would get over this. Ever.

"And, Pretia," her father added, "I'm impressed by how you handled this news. Some children would have burst into tears and raged. But anger gets you nowhere. You showed remarkable restraint, and you behaved nobly. You behaved just like a princess."

Pretia tried to find comfort in her father's words, but inside she felt like anything but a calm, noble princess. And anyway, a *princess* was the absolute last thing she wanted to be.

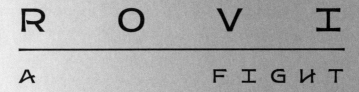

2
ROVI
A FIGHT

OF COURSE, THE DIRECTIONS CASTOR HAD given Rovi to his room were purposely vague, and he got lost several times before eventually finding his way. Rovi couldn't understand Pretia's enthusiasm for the palace. The mazelike layout of Ponsit made his throat constrict and his heart beat too fast. He couldn't breathe or focus in the labyrinthine rooms. He found that when he was enclosed in the walls, unable to see around corners or understand the layout of the terrain, his grana couldn't guide him as it usually did. He felt helpless and lost.

When the dinner bell rang, it filled Rovi with panic. What if he couldn't find the Hall of Logic? What if he got lost in the corridors and missed dinner? What if he wound up starving in the maze?

He twisted and turned through the palace. Twice he nearly gave up and returned to his quarters—not that he was convinced he could find them again. But suddenly he burst into a room in which the most impressive array of food he'd ever seen was spread out.

The Realists were known for their seafood, and it seemed as if everything in the entire ocean—lobsters, crabs, towers of mussels, glistening fish in a wild palette of colors from silver to orange—had been laid out on a table so long Rovi couldn't see from one end to the next. He filled a plate and sat down across from Castor, the only familiar face in the hall.

Suddenly a gong sounded, announcing the arrival of the king and queen. Everyone stopped eating to acknowledge their presence. Pretia followed her parents at a distance, keeping her eyes fixed on the ground. And when she finally took her seat next to Rovi, he could tell she'd been crying.

He sensed tension in the air amid the royal family. But family matters were none of his business, he figured, so he kept his focus on his food.

Pretia, however, wasn't eating.

Rovi kicked her under the table. "What's wrong?" he whispered. She didn't reply.

"Pretia?" he tried again. "What's wrong?"

"Everything," Pretia muttered.

Servers filled the adults' glasses with wine and the kids' with Spirit Water.

Castor leaned toward his cousin. "So, is my father right? Are you considering switching to a winning team and joining the Realists?"

"I'm not considering anything," Pretia said dully.

Rovi studied her, wondering what could be bothering his friend.

"Then again, maybe you should stick with the Dreamers—you might not even make it if you had to try for one of the Realist spots," Castor continued. "Too much tough competition."

"Who cares about Junior Epics?" Pretia said.

Rovi couldn't believe his ears. An hour ago, Junior Epics were *all* Pretia cared about.

"I do," Rovi said.

"Yeah, me too," Castor said, giving her an incredulous look.

"Well, good for you guys," Pretia said.

"Didn't we spend all summer training for the Junior Epic trials?" Rovi said.

"I guess we wasted all that time," Pretia snapped.

"Training isn't wasteful," Castor said, catching Rovi's eye. The boys exchanged a glance.

What's going on? Rovi wondered. He was getting along with *Castor* better than with Pretia.

"Forgive me for not caring about a dumb competition," Pretia said. Then she hunched her shoulders and stared down at her plate.

The king cleared his throat. "Speaking of Junior Epics, Janos, I'm still wondering if you might consider petitioning to relocate this year's games, considering the situation in Phoenis."

Phoenis? Rovi's ears perked up and his heart leaped. This was the first he'd heard about Junior Epics being held in the city where he'd lived before attending Ecrof. He could just see himself marching into the stadium as a hometown hero. His fellow Star Stealers would be shocked—not just shocked: impressed. He smiled inwardly at the thought of Issa, his best friend and the leader of his old Star Stealer gang, watching him compete in the Junior Epic Games as a member of House Somni. He instantly redoubled his commitment to training harder than ever. He was going to make that team. He was going to be a Junior Epic Athlete.

"Airos," Janos replied, "the Junior Epic Games will be held where they have been scheduled to be held for the last four years. The committee has been working tirelessly to ensure that everything is in order."

"Reports say that everything *isn't* entirely in order," the king said.

"I can assure you, as a member of the committee," Janos replied, "that when it comes to preparations for the games, everything down to the smallest detail has been taken care of. And the problem to which you are alluding is under control."

"What problem?" Castor asked.

Rovi looked to Pretia for an answer. She returned his look with the darkest stare he'd ever seen. What had *he* done?

"But as far as safety goes, perhaps Phoenis is not the right place at the moment," King Airos pressed.

"Airos, you are the ruler of Epoca," Janos said. "You know how much pride each region takes in hosting our various Epic events. You wouldn't want to deny the people of Phoenis the chance to showcase their city, would you?"

"I am merely suggesting that perhaps this is not the year for them to showcase their city," Airos replied.

Rovi looked from the king to the Head Trainer, trying to make sense of the conversation.

"There's nothing to worry about," Janos said.

The king stared into his wineglass. "I hope you're right."

"I am," Janos replied heartily. "I'm expecting our squad to bring great glory to Ecrof."

Rovi watched Janos give Pretia a meaningful glance. "What do you say, Pretia?" Janos said. "Are you prepared to bring glory to the academy should you be chosen?"

Pretia pushed her food around on her plate. "I won't be chosen," she muttered.

"That's not the attitude I expect from one of my students," Janos said.

Pretia shrugged and said something under her breath that Rovi couldn't make out.

A troubled look passed across Janos's face. But he quickly brushed it off. "Airos," he said in a loud and confident voice, "these Junior Epics are going to be the best in Epocan history. Our young athletes will excel and thrive."

"Well, in that case," the king continued, "all I can ask is that you take special care of all of your students."

Janos's brow furrowed. "As always, I take care of *everyone* under my command."

"Well, there's one student you won't have to worry about," the queen said.

Pretia shot her mother a reproachful glance.

"Not you, dear," Helena said. "Rovi."

Rovi's heart fluttered, then sank.

"And why is that?" Janos asked.

"Well," the queen continued, "since Rovi is a Star Stealer from the Sandlands, he should of course have no trouble looking out for himself in Phoenis."

"Was," Pretia said loudly. "Rovi *was* a Star Stealer."

Rovi could feel his cheeks flush.

"I'm not sure what that has to do with anything," Janos replied.

"Oh, I'm sure you do," the queen said meaningfully, "since it's the *Star Stealers* who are disrupting the peace."

"What?" The word was out of Rovi's mouth before he had time to restrain it. He knew better than to barge into conversations involving the royal family, but he couldn't help himself.

"Yes, Rovi," the king said, "I'm sorry to say that the Star Stealers have been rioting, causing trouble for the Phoenician authorities in advance of the games."

"But that's not," Rovi shouted, before lowering his voice, "...true."

"It is," the queen said. "Quite true."

Rovi looked down at his plate. His food wasn't as appealing as it had been before. In fact, he didn't really feel like eating at all.

"Rovi is a Dreamer," Janos said firmly. "And a promising one. At Ecrof, we are hoping he does both his house and the academy proud. Whatever he was or did in the past disappeared when he boarded the boat to Ecrof. Should he be chosen to compete, he will do so as a Dreamer. His past won't enter into it, nor will it be advertised. What's more, I can assure you both," Janos said, looking from the king to the queen, "the games are as safe this year as they have been in the past."

"Apparently not," Pretia muttered, glowering at her dinner.

"Come on," Rovi whispered to Pretia. "You don't believe that, do you?"

She returned his question with a cold stare.

They spent the rest of the meal in silence. Even Castor remained quiet, chastened by the tension at the table.

Finally, the meal ended. Rovi sighed with relief. Now he and Pretia could escape and he could find out what was bugging her. Surely she couldn't be mad because of some rumors about Star Stealers. But without waiting for him, Pretia bolted from the hall.

Rovi rushed after her. He lost sight of the princess as she turned down a hallway.

"Pretia," he called. "Wait!"

He could hear her footsteps up ahead. He ran, turning left and right, hoping to find her. Then, as he rounded a corner, he crashed smack into his friend. They bounced off each other and fell to the ground.

"Leave me alone," Pretia said, picking herself up.

"What did I do?"

"Just go away."

Rovi looked around. "Where do you want me to go? I don't know anyone here. I barely know where I am."

"Can't you just go to your room or something?"

"Tell me what's wrong and I'll leave you alone," Rovi said. "Tell me what I did."

"It's not what you did. It's what your friends did."

"What friends? You and Vera are my only friends."

"Not us. Your old friends in Phoenis. They're ruining my life."

Rovi could feel the anger stirring inside of him. "What do you mean?" he asked slowly.

"Your friends are the reason I'm not allowed to return to Ecrof to try out for the Junior Epic Games," Pretia snapped. "They have threatened the Junior Epic Games and Epoca. Or at least my parents think so."

"Wh-what?" Rovi stammered. "That can't be right." Too many conflicting emotions were crashing into him at once—anger at Pretia for what she was suggesting, heartbreak on her behalf, sadness that his best friend wasn't coming back to school with him, worry about the Star Stealers.

"Apparently my parents think it's too dangerous for me to compete in Phoenis, and they're worried if I go to Ecrof, I'll make the team and then by Epic Code I'll be compelled to compete." He could sense that Pretia was near tears. "So you and Vera and even Castor better enjoy yourselves while I'm sitting by myself back at Castle Airim. I'm sure by the time you all get to Junior Epics you'll have forgotten all about me."

"No," Rovi said. "Never. I'm sure your parents will change their minds."

"They won't," Pretia said. "Your friends have already done enough damage."

Any pity Rovi had felt for Pretia evaporated. "Stop talking about Issa and the gang. You don't understand the first thing about them."

"I know they stole my Junior Epic Games."

Rovi's anger was boiling over. "This is the first time I've ever heard you sound exactly like a spoiled princess."

"Well, that's all I am and ever will be—a princess. The boring Child of Hope." And with that, Pretia turned and fled, leaving Rovi fuming in the hall.

He listened to her steps disappear. He understood she was angry. But what she had said about his friends was horrible. He thought of Issa and the gang who had taken him in when his father died. No one who lived in the acceptable world dominated by Dreamers and Realists understood Star Stealers or the other Orphic People in different cities. They were just kids with no place in Epoca—outcasts who survived on their own until they grew up and had to flee Epoca or turn themselves over to the authorities and work in the sand or salt or silver mines. They were kind, and they were loyal to one another. They were more talented than other people realized. It wasn't just the kids with parents and Grana Books who had skills.

What's more, there was no way the kids on the streets of Phoenis were causing the trouble the king and queen described. Riots? Star Stealers never drew attention to themselves. Ever.

Rovi glanced around at the horrible halls of Ponsit Palace. The place gave him the creeps—the crypts, the maze, especially the terrible Games Pit. And now his best friend had turned on him.

More than ever, Rovi couldn't wait to get to Ecrof. He couldn't wait to start training and make the Junior Epic Team and leave all of this behind. He would show the world—especially this stuck-up royal family—what a former Star Stealer could do.

3

PRETIA

A DECISION

PRETIA DIDN'T LOOK BACK OVER HER SHOUL-
der as she left Rovi in the hall. She knew she'd been cruel. It wasn't
Rovi's fault that the Star Stealers had ruined the Junior Epic Games
for her. But still, they had. And there was no changing that.

She ran fast, weaving through the corridors. She darted this way
and that until she found herself in the High Sanctuary, where lanterns with blue flames burned in honor of her deceased Realist relatives. The room smelled of smoke. Dust swirled in the flames' light.

On the wall, the names of the royal family were inscribed. Next
to each one who had competed in the Epic Games or the Junior
Epic Games, a small, golden E was etched. Pretia had always imagined that one day one of those E's would appear next to her name.
But that dream had just died. Without Ecrof, she'd never receive the
training she needed to make it to the Epic Games. And her parents
seemed set against her having a life in athletics at all.

Her dream of Epic Glory was over before it had even really
begun. She could just picture her life from now on: one boring royal
duty after another. No more sports. No more Ecrof. No more friends.

She glanced around the High Sanctuary to make sure she was
alone. And when she was certain that it was just her and the ancestral

flames, she fell to the floor and allowed herself to cry where only her deceased relatives might see.

She was trying to stop her tears when she heard footsteps. Pretia glanced around, looking for a hiding place.

It was too late. A long shadow stretched from the top of the stairs across the room.

"Pretia?"

She froze. What was her uncle doing here?

Janos stepped into the room. "I had a feeling I'd find you in this place." In the flickering light from the ceremonial flames, Pretia could see her uncle's concerned smile. "Your parents told me about their decision. They would like you to go find them."

"I'll be seeing enough of them next year when I'm stuck at Castle Airim," Pretia grumbled.

"Ah, yes." Janos rubbed his beard. "That does seem rather extreme."

"*You* think it's extreme?"

Janos put a hand on her shoulder. "I do."

"So why didn't you say anything?" Pretia asked. "Why didn't you tell them?"

Her uncle sighed. "Pretia, there are areas in which I may contradict the king and queen. There are things I can stand up to my big sister about. But how they raise their child is not one of them."

Pretia made herself into a tight ball, pulling her knees to her chest and pressing her head down into them.

"My sister is extremely stubborn and very protective of her daughter," Janos said gently.

"Yeah," Pretia said. "I know."

"Maybe overprotective."

"Well, she's the queen and she can do whatever she wants," Pretia said bitterly.

Janos lowered himself to the floor and sat beside Pretia. "She may be the queen, but you're the princess."

"I still have to do whatever my parents say," Pretia said. "All they care about is the fact that one day I'll rule Epoca. But, Uncle Janos, I don't want to rule *anything*." She couldn't believe she'd said it aloud. "All I've heard since forever was that one day I'll be the head of House Somni and House Relia and that I'm the Child of Hope, whatever that means. I don't care about that. I don't. All I care about is the Epic Games."

Janos took a deep breath. "Have you tried to talk to them?"

"Sort of," Pretia said. Then she dropped her chin. "Not really. There wasn't much to say."

"Or was there something to say and you didn't say it?" Janos suggested.

"I'm not sure," Pretia admitted.

"You know, favorite niece, I chose sports over statecraft. Sports are where my grana is strongest. But I *do* know a thing or two about ruling. After all, before you came along, I was next in line to lead House Relia."

Janos was right, of course, but Pretia had trouble imagining him at the head of House Relia instead of running Ecrof.

Her uncle drew a deep breath. "And what I know about ruling is that, while it is both wise and essential to listen to the counsel of others, ultimately the decision about what to do comes from within. That is what makes a leader's grana exceptional—a king's or queen's or even princess's. A great leader listens to others but also takes her own counsel. A great leader can look within herself to make a difficult decision. And when that leader makes a decision, she must stand behind it and stand up for herself."

"What do you mean?"

"As future Queen of Epoca, people are going to try and tell you

33

a thousand different things. They are going to advise you and tell you what to do. Some will do so with wisdom and kindness. Others will do so for their own agenda or even to hurt you. But your grana will guide you to the right decision."

"I hope so," Pretia said. But even if her grana guided her, her parents had the final say until she was older.

Janos scooted around so they were sitting face-to-face. "Pretia, I'm going to ask you a difficult question—you don't have to answer right now. Do you think that your staying away from the Junior Epic Games is in the best interests of Epoca and our people?"

"I—I don't know."

"Do you think the people want to see their princess and her remarkable talent or not?"

"I'm not sure."

"Think about it," Janos said.

"But even if I went, it's not like I'd be on your team. I chose House Somni."

Janos smiled. "That's all right—we are always on the same team. You'd still be representing Ecrof. And more important, you'd be representing my family. Our family. And that is important to me. You may have chosen the Dreamers, but you are also my blood. Realist blood is strong. I see it in you. Others do, too. You could be the star of the games."

She gave her uncle a confused look. "But I can't go to the Junior Epic Games if I don't go to Ecrof and try out for the squad."

"Let me rephrase." Janos cleared his throat. "Do you think it is in the best interests of the people of Epoca for their princess *not* to try to represent her house and her country at the Junior Epic Games?"

"Wait," Pretia said. "You think I should go to Ecrof even though my parents forbid it? And then . . . then try to qualify for the Junior Epic Games?"

"I think you should do what your grana guides you to do."

"But—but—" Pretia stammered. Too many thoughts were crowding her head at once.

"Favorite niece, once you are selected as a Junior Epic Athlete and your name is on the team roster, it becomes your duty to represent your house. There's nothing anyone can do to keep you from the team—not even your parents."

"But they told me I can't go to Ecrof in the first place."

"And I'm telling you to be your own guide. You are a girl of many strengths. I don't think your parents quite understand that. You might not even understand it yourself yet. Follow your grana, Pretia. It will show you the right thing to do."

"How?" Pretia asked.

"That is up to you. I have my methods. You need to discover yours."

"I mean how would I get to Ecrof without my parents knowing?"

"Aha," Janos said, a spark in his emerald eyes. "The van leaves quite early tomorrow in order to make the long overland journey to the harbor back in Helios. I think there might be a little space in the back where you could sleep until it sets off."

Pretia opened her mouth. But Janos held up a hand to silence her.

"I'm not telling you what to do. Only you can decide for yourself." He wrapped his hand around hers. "If you stay, I will know it was what your grana led you to do. All I ask is that you think about my question."

"I will," Pretia assured him. Then she flung her arms around her uncle. There was no one on earth whom she loved more at that moment.

When her uncle had left, Pretia remained on the floor of the High Sanctuary. She lay back and stared at the gap in the ceiling through which paper lanterns would eventually carry her relatives' ceremonial flames up to the gods on Mount Aoin.

◆

How in the world was she meant to search within herself? Where was she supposed to look for answers? Was that what Janos was doing when she thought she had seen him praying to Hurell? Was that his form of turning inward? If so, what was hers?

She closed her eyes and tried to decide what to do.

Could she disobey her parents?

Could she run away to Ecrof?

Could she compete in the Junior Epic Games without their blessing?

If she did those things, how mad would her parents be? Would they ever forgive her?

Even more confusing was her uncle's question—what was best for Epoca? Staying or going? Being a princess . . . or a princess and an athlete? Or maybe just an athlete! That last one was impossible. She would always be the princess, no matter what. But how could her parents, of all people, forbid her from competing? How could they forbid *sports*? It was so unfair.

Pretia tried to grab each question as it flew past. But her mind was churning with a mixture of excitement and anxiety. She tried to search deep within herself. All she found was chaos and confusion.

She took a deep breath and stood up, facing the ceremonial flames. "What should I do?" she asked aloud.

The flames simply flickered in response.

Pretia shook her head. The flames couldn't give her the answer. But there was something that might.

She raced down the stairs from the High Sanctuary and rushed down the twisting corridors. She made it to her room without getting lost. She closed the door quietly so no one would hear her return. Then Pretia began to dig through her official Ecrof duffel for her Grana Book.

Pretia sat on her bed. The moon cast a silver light through the window. She clutched her Grana Book in both hands and said aloud,

"Should I go to Ecrof so that I might represent my house at the Junior Epic Games, or should I obey my parents and stay home?"

Last year, at Ecrof, she'd struggled to learn how to interpret the images in the book. Pretia had always figured that part of this difficulty stemmed from the fact that she was half Dreamer, half Realist. Dreamers were open to a wide range of interpretations, while Realists often demanded literal answers. She could always feel the two inclinations warring within her when she considered the images in her book.

Now she kept her eyes closed and cracked the book slowly. Her fingers brushed across a few pages until one felt right. She opened the book wide and laid it flat on the bed.

By the light of the moon she could see that the image was of a road that twisted and turned dramatically between two mountains. At the road's vanishing point there was a golden flame. The mountain on the left side of the page was lit by pale daylight—it sat under the pastel-blue sky of early morning. The mountain on the right was shrouded in darkness and had a deeper purple hue. At the vanishing point, the flame lit up the sky in an explosion of golds and oranges.

The interpretation hit her like a punch in the stomach. Pretia slammed the book shut. It couldn't be right.

Go to Ecrof. That's what the picture told her.

She opened it again and stared at the picture. She looked for an alternative way to read the image, but she knew what it implied. The feeling inside her was strong. Her mind was clear. She felt exactly as her Granology teacher, Saana Theradon, had told her she would when she understood an image in her book perfectly—the same feeling Janos had said she would experience when she learned to consult her grana in matters of state.

But Pretia wanted to be sure. So she did what Saana had taught her to do in class—she broke down the image into its components and interpreted them one by one and then all together.

The mountains were easy. They were her parents—the purple

mountain, her Dreamer father and the blue, her Realist mother. And the road was leading *away* from her parents to a golden fire. She traced her finger along the road. She could see it now. She *was* the road. She was movement. She should move. And if she did, victory would be hers.

But Saana had cautioned her to consult the entire picture, not just the parts that seemed relevant or interesting or easy. And the road itself posed a problem.

The road was twisty rather than straight, which Pretia understood to mean difficulty and challenges. Hadn't her parents just thrown up a challenge? Then there was the golden fire at the end of the road. The color signaled to Pretia that Junior Epic Victory would be hers. But the fire told her that it would be hard-won and come at a serious price.

Pretia squinted at the page. She was fairly confident in what she saw. But she was also aware of something else. More than anything, she wanted to go to Ecrof and later to Phoenis. Regardless of what her book said, regardless of what Janos had suggested might be good for Epoca, she wanted to go.

Pretia shuddered at the thought. Maybe she shouldn't go. Maybe the price was too high. Perhaps her parents were right. Her safety was at stake. Maybe she should just suck it up and face her boring destiny of Epocan history and statecraft.

She closed the book. But the image remained in her mind. It was emblazoned on the backs of her eyelids if she blinked. She had her answer. The book said *go*. The question now was would she, could she, do what it said?

4

R O V I

A   R E U N I O N

ROVI SKIPPED BREAKFAST, WHICH WAS A DIF-
ficult decision. But he had no interest in running into Pretia or her
parents. He didn't need anyone reminding him about his old life as
a Star Stealer or hinting that Star Stealers were the problem with
Phoenis—and he didn't want to think about the fact that if he were
chosen as a Junior Epic Athlete, his past would probably be hidden
from the public.

He was the first to arrive at the van. It was early and the sky
was still dark. He had to wait nearly an hour before Castor and
Janos appeared. To Rovi's surprise, Janos held out a bag filled with
pastries.

"An Ecrof student cannot skip meals," the Head Trainer said.

"Thanks," Rovi said, stunned by the Head Trainer's kindness.
His stomach was growling.

Before Rovi took the food, he reached for his duffel to lift it into
the back of the van.

"Allow me," Janos said, swooping in to lift Rovi's bag.

Rovi gave him a startled look. Janos wasn't in the habit of helping students.

"You'll have to work enough when you get to Ecrof," Janos

explained with a small smile. "Get settled and enjoy your breakfast. I understand you have the appetite of two boys."

"Okay," Rovi said uncertainly, climbing into the van.

Castor followed as Janos took a seat next to the driver, and they were off.

Dawn was only a suggestion at the horizon as the van rolled away from the palace. Rovi didn't bother to glance over his shoulder. He wasn't sorry to leave the palace behind. Pretia, on the other hand, was a different story. Their last exchange had been ugly. One day she'd probably regret her words. At least he hoped she would. Despite their argument, he missed her. He couldn't imagine being told he couldn't go to Ecrof. And he couldn't even begin to think about explaining to Vera why Pretia was missing. He knew Vera would be as devastated and angry as he was.

Rovi settled back in the seat. It was a ten-hour journey to the port—ten hours that he'd have to play nice with Castor or risk Janos's anger.

When the van passed the gates, Castor looked back. "I can't believe my uncle and aunt *actually* forbade Pretia from coming," he said. "I mean, something serious must be going on."

"Why are you looking at me?" Rovi asked.

"I'm not," Castor said. "All I'm saying is that if it's dangerous for Pretia, maybe it's dangerous for me, too."

Janos turned around and looked his son directly in the eye. "It will only be dangerous for you if you make the team."

Rovi tried not to laugh.

Castor quickly shook off his dad's rebuke. "It really is too bad, though," he said to Rovi.

"What?" Rovi asked.

"Pretia might be a total weirdo, but she *was* a winner. House Somni really needs her at the Junior Epics."

"We'll be fine," Rovi said.

Castor laughed. "Dream on. Get it?"

"Yeah, I get it. I'm not laughing."

"Of course, what she can do isn't exactly natural," Castor continued. "Doesn't that worry you?"

Rovi shut his eyes and yawned, hoping Castor would take the hint.

"That's what everyone's been saying all summer. Do you know anyone else who can split himself?"

"You mean, split *herself*?" Rovi asked. "No."

"And you don't think that's weird?"

"I don't," Rovi replied. "I think it's special."

"So you think it's fair that Pretia can always beat you? That she can use this talent to win no matter what?"

"Yeah, I do. She's not cheating. It's her grana. We're supposed to use our grana for sports. And she doesn't always beat me. But when she does, I don't mind."

Castor looked at Rovi as if he were the stupidest kid in Epoca. "There's the spirit," he said. "It's fine to lose, right?"

"I care about my team winning," Rovi said. "That's what matters."

"Well, that won't happen now," Castor said.

Rovi balled his hands into fists, then sat on them. It was promising to be a long drive. In fact, it was promising to be a long year at Ecrof if Castor continued like this, especially without Pretia around. Pretia always had the right words to stand up to Castor—Rovi only had anger.

He could think of one way to escape Castor's taunts, though. If Rovi was selected for Junior Epics and Castor was not, they would be separated for a good part of the year. Well, two ways: if Castor was selected and Rovi wasn't, that would work, too. But that was a far less appealing solution.

Rovi figured he had a decent shot at the squad. Members of Ecrof's Epic Elite Squad were automatically taken to the Junior Epic

Games, but many of them had graduated, which meant there was plenty of space for newcomers.

Last year, he'd been selected for his house team for both Dreamer and Realist Field Days, so he was already ahead of his classmates. Vera would be his biggest rival without Pretia there. Rovi was sure Vera had spent her entire summer doing nothing besides training for the team.

This should have made him happy, but instead it filled Rovi with a feeling of loss. He, Vera, and Pretia had grown into a tight trio, their friendship sealed by their incredible adventure in the sunken temple of Hurell at the end of last school year. How could Pretia miss out on all the fun this year? She was the glue that held him and Vera together. What's more, she was the one who'd saved the school from the strangler fig tree that had been stealing the students' grana. This year, Pretia would have finally been able to openly use her remarkable talent for splitting herself and lead the Dreamers to victory.

That was his and Vera's job now, he figured.

He heard Castor give a smug sigh. "I guess it will be up to a Star Stealer and a Replacement to help Team Somni," he said, reading Rovi's mind but putting his own snarky spin on it.

Rovi opened his mouth to reply, but before he could, he heard a loud rustling from the back of the van. Several of Castor's bags came flying forward. A small duffel knocked him on the head. The bag exploded, showering Castor with clothes.

"Why don't you think I'm making the Dreamers' team, Castor?"

Rovi turned. "Pretia!" he exclaimed.

Castor frantically pawed away the clothes covering his face while at the same time trying to turn and see what was happening at the back of the van.

More bags flew forward as Pretia sat up. Her black hair was messy and her face was creased with sleep. "Packed enough, Castor?" She plucked an undershirt off his head.

"What are you doing here?" Rovi asked.

"Going to Ecrof," Pretia replied. "Isn't that what we're all doing?"

"But—but—but . . ." Rovi stammered, unable to complete his thought.

Castor was staring at his cousin openmouthed. "You stowed away," he said. "The Child of Hope stowed away?"

"Looks like it," Pretia said.

Then both boys turned to Janos. Rovi expected to see the Head Trainer's trademark glower. But to his surprise, Janos was laughing.

"Well done, Princess," Janos said. "Very well done."

"Wait," Castor said. "You knew about this?"

"No," Janos said. "Not exactly. But I am glad to see you, Pretia." He lowered his voice, making it stern. "Although, now that you are aboard my van, I must remind you that you are no longer a princess, but an Ecrof second year. And I expect that from now on you will begin to obey all rules your elders set out for you." This last admonishment was delivered with a smile. "You will not run away on my watch!"

"Of course not, Uncle. Why would I do that?" Pretia said, climbing over the seats to settle next to Rovi.

"I can't believe you're here," he said when she'd gotten comfortable.

"I had to come," she replied. "I just couldn't miss out on a chance at the Junior Epic Games. And I couldn't imagine you at Ecrof without me. I'd miss you too much." She looked down at her lap. "Rovi— I'm sorry for what I said back at the palace. You know, about Star Stealers. Whatever is happening in Phoenis isn't *your* fault."

"I don't believe *anything* is happening," Rovi said. He simply couldn't imagine the Star Stealers causing the kind of trouble the king and queen had described. If anything was happening, someone was causing trouble for the Star Stealers and not the other way around.

"My parents definitely think so," Pretia said. "I hope they're wrong."

◆

"You'll see," Rovi said defiantly. Then he shot a meaningful look at Castor. "Star Stealers are the last people you need to worry about."

"I'm sure you're right," Pretia agreed.

Rovi found that it was impossible to be mad at Pretia when she had risked everything to return to Ecrof and to support House Somni. "You'll see when we get to Phoenis," Rovi said. They slapped hands.

"Here's to dreams that never die," they chorused.

"Great," Castor grumbled. "Now I have to listen to two Dreamers talk about their stupid house all day."

"What's wrong with that?" Pretia asked. "Dreamers are the best." She grinned. "Everyone knows that."

With Pretia next to him, Rovi felt like the ten hours to the harbor flew past. It was late afternoon when they arrived at port. The ship was waiting, having just returned from dropping the third-year students at the academy. The green-and-gold Ecrof flags flapped in the wind.

By the time they stepped off the van, Janos had slipped from his unusually jocular and kind mood into his customary stern persona as Head Trainer of Ecrof.

"Hurry and join your class," he said. "We're late as it is."

They were the last to board the ship. The minute Rovi, Pretia, Castor, and Janos climbed aboard, the ropes were untied and they pushed out to sea.

Pretia stared back at the land. "For a while there, I really thought I wasn't coming."

"Not coming?"

Rovi felt a hand slap his back. He turned and saw Vera standing behind them.

"You guys were late, obviously," she said, "but I didn't think there was a possibility of you not coming *at all*."

Vera was sweating as if she'd been exercising. Her long, puffy waves of hair blew out behind her in the wind. She looked even fitter and stronger than she had three months ago. Her dark skin was tanned and glossy, presumably from extensive, hard workouts under the strong sun of Alkebulan, the distant land where her family lived.

Pretia took a deep breath, preparing to fill her friend in. "Vera, you're not going to believe this. My parents *forbade* me to come, but I consulted my Grana Book."

"And it told you to run away?" Vera sounded incredulous.

"Sort of," Pretia said. "You know how Grana Books work. There was an image of a road running between two mountains. I am the road. The mountains are my parents. The road meant movement, escape. It meant *running*. And running means sports. So I had to come." She paused. "I wanted to come more than anything in the world. I know my parents are going to be furious. But there's nothing they can do now that I'm on the ship." Pretia paused again. "At least I think there isn't."

"Why didn't they want you to come?" Vera asked.

Pretia explained how the king and queen worried about her making the Junior Epic Squad and the potential danger that lay in wait for her in Phoenis.

"Danger!" Vera scoffed. "That's ridiculous. Four years ago, I went to watch Julius at the games in Mount Oly, and there were guards everywhere. It was the safest place in Epoca."

"That was the year Julius won eight medals!" Rovi exclaimed.

"Don't sound so impressed," Vera said. "I'm going to top that. In fact, I'm going to set the new record for the most Junior Epic Medals."

"If you break your brother's record, that *would* be epic," Pretia said.

"My brother doesn't hold the record," Vera said.

Rovi and Pretia exchanged a look. It was a well-known fact that Julius Renovo was the most decorated Junior Epic Athlete of all time, breaking a record once held by Janos Praxis himself.

"Listen," Vera said, "I spent all summer reading up on Junior Epic history."

"Of course you did," Rovi said.

"Well, that and training," Vera added. "Just because it's summer, you can't let up."

Pretia tried not to laugh.

"When I wasn't training, I did a lot of reading on the Junior Epic Games. I always thought that Julius had won the most Junior Epic Medals. But that's not true. There was someone else: Farnaka Stellus."

"That's a funny name," Pretia said.

"It's a Sandlander name," Rovi corrected her.

"Anyway," Vera prattled on, "this Farnaka Stellus turns out to have won more medals than Julius. Julius won eight, but Farnaka won nine." She looked from Rovi to Pretia. "Nine!" Vera repeated. "Can you believe that?"

"Seems like a lot," Pretia said.

"Totally," Rovi added, trying to match Vera's enthusiasm. The wind had picked up as they sailed away from the port. He gripped the railing of the ship when it dipped into the furrow of a wave. Some of his classmates whooped with delight while the boat rocked and swayed.

"It *is* a lot," Vera continued. "But not unattainable. I'm going to break Farnaka's record. Most of his medals came on the field, but three were in the pool." Vera began to list events so quickly that Rovi couldn't keep up. "Maybe I won't do the exact same events. But I'm going to get the same number of medals or more."

"You'll have to be chosen first." The kids looked up to see that Nassos and Myra, two of the Realists in their class, had joined them at the railing. Myra looked as if she'd grown a foot over the summer and towered over Pretia and Vera.

"Luckily you're a Dreamer, so you have a better shot," Myra said. "It's less competitive for you guys."

"You know," Vera said, "historically, Dreamers hold the edge in the Junior Epic Games. In fact, House Somni has won eighty-five more Junior Epic Medals than House Relia. And Dreamers and Realists have a pretty much equal chance of making the team overall."

"Dork," Nassos said.

"Being a Junior Epic Athlete isn't just about competing. It's also about knowing your history," Vera retorted.

"I don't think history is going to help you win medals," Myra said.

"You never know," Vera replied. "After all, several of the best Junior Epic Champions went on to become leaders of state and—" Before she could finish, Myra and Nassos walked off. "Well, clearly *they* aren't going to break Farnaka's record," Vera said as she watched them go. "But when I—"

"We get it, Vera," Rovi said.

"When I win those medals," Vera continued, determined, "I'm not going to be forgotten like Farnaka Stellus was."

The boat dipped again, knocking the kids into one another.

"*You* haven't forgotten him," Pretia said. "Obviously."

Before Vera could tell them any more about her new obsession, Janos's whistle sounded across the deck. Immediately the boat was filled with the clamor of kids rushing to gather before their Head Trainer. Rovi surveyed his classmates. Like Myra, several of them had sprouted over the summer. Others looked stronger and more mature. He wondered if he had changed without noticing it in himself.

Janos blew his whistle again to summon a straggler—Leo Apama had become entangled in a coil of rope as he'd tried to cross the deck. "Leo," Janos said, "this is an inauspicious start to your return to Ecrof."

"Sorry," Leo muttered.

"I'd imagine that this year would be of exceptional importance to you, Leo."

Leo stared at the Head Trainer blankly. The ship hit a wave. Leo toppled forward.

"Or perhaps you don't care about being selected for the Junior Epic Squad and representing your school and your house in your home city?"

"The Junior Epic Games are in Phoenis this year?" Leo said, his voice an excited squeak.

Janos clapped his powerful hands. "Indeed!"

A ripple of excitement ran through the kids as they took in this information.

"But before you get ahead of yourselves, keep in mind that this year, you return to Ecrof with knowledge, and with knowledge comes responsibility to yourselves, your houses, and your teammates. You are no longer recruits, but second-year students."

Virgil's hand shot in the air. "That means we can use the pool!"

"Among other things," Janos said. "You will learn more about this school year during the Placement Ceremony. Our first term will be different from last year's because of the Junior Epic Squad trials. Training for trials will start soon. So enjoy this ride. It will be one of your last leisurely days." And with that, he left them.

Everyone started talking at once. Leo was babbling most furiously of all. "I can't believe it's Phoenis. It's the *best* place in Epoca."

"It's lucky you live there, then," Castor said.

"Why?" Leo asked.

"Because you've already seen it. And there's no way you're making our team." Castor and Nassos slapped hands.

Leo frowned at him.

"We'll see what happens," Leo said. "No matter what, I bet Phoenis is going to host the most incredible Junior Epic Games ever. The city is amazing."

"Yeah?" snapped Cyril, a Dreamer from the Rhodan Islands who had an islander's dislike for the Sandlands. "How is it so amazing? Isn't it just a big, hot desert?"

"Well," Rovi began, since he, too, had lived in Phoenis. But Leo cut him off with a dismissive wave of his hand.

"First of all, there's the Tile Palace, which is completely covered in bits of mirror and tile and glows at sunrise and sunset. Then there's the smaller Moon Palace at the edge of the desert. That one glows white."

"There's also the Alexandrine Market," Rovi said.

Leo looked at him. "The Alexandrine Market?"

"Yeah," Rovi said. "People travel from all over the Sandlands to buy and sell there. It's the biggest in the land."

"No one wants to visit a dirty market when they can visit the Royal Baths, the Crescent Stadium, and the Temple of Arsama, a tomb for all the ancient rulers of Phoenis."

Rovi stepped back from the group. The places Leo had listed were indeed the most wondrous in Phoenis, or so he'd heard. But all of them were strictly off-limits to Star Stealers, and except for his one misadventure in the Royal Baths, when he'd challenged a Realist boy on the diving board, he'd never visited any of them.

"What's the Temple of Arsama?" Adira asked, her headscarf flapping in the light wind.

Leo puffed out his chest, happy to be the center of attention. "The Temple of Arsama is one of the holiest sites in the Sandlands. It stands at the center of Phoenis, at the base of a great pyramid that rises higher than even the Tile Palace. It's where the most famous Sandlander kings and queens from the time of the gods are buried. All their treasure is down there, too, as well as some treasure that our current nobles want to keep safe."

"They keep their treasure in an old tomb?" Virgil asked.

"It's the safest place in Phoenis," Leo continued. "But the Moon Palace is my favorite. It stands alone out at the edge of the desert and—"

Rovi slipped away before he had to hear any more. His Phoenis was not the Phoenis that belonged to boys like Leo. They never came down into the Lower City. They never dangled their feet into the river Durna. They never slept under the Draman Bridge or were chased by the guards in the Alexandrine Market. Boys like Leo lived a finer life, filled with comforts Star Stealers couldn't even dream of. Boys like Leo belonged to a totally different, more refined Phoenis. Rovi wondered which city he'd see when he returned.

He wondered where he belonged now.

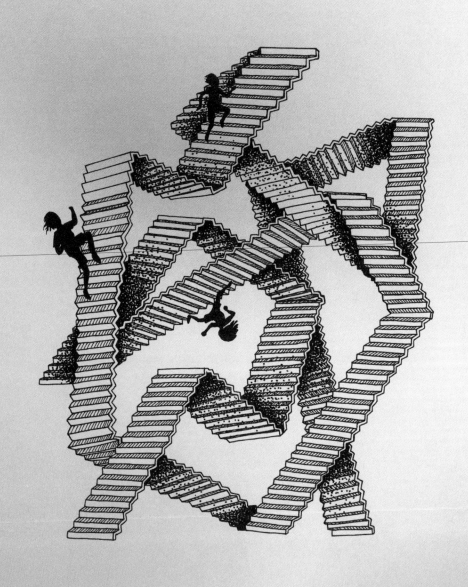

5

PRETIA
A RETURN

THE NEXT MORNING, PRETIA LEANED OVER the ship's railing, letting the salt spray sting her face. She opened her mouth, and the wind flooded in. The early-dawn sun glowed pink and orange on the horizon back toward the mainland. She took a deep breath, as if she could swallow the air and sea. She wanted to feel more free than she did. But she couldn't shake the worry that her parents would send someone after her, even though they said it was impossible. They were the king and queen. Surely they would try something. Her eyes scanned the lapis water for a boat filled with royal guards, a caravan come to return her to her parents. But the Ecrof boat was alone on the rolling waves.

No matter how confident she was in her decision to return to Ecrof, she *had* defied her parents. She had run away and put sports above Epoca and above family. No doubt there would be consequences. Eventually, she suspected, she would have to pay the price for what she had done.

"You're nervous, Pretia."

While she had been looking the other way, Janos had joined her at the railing.

"Should I have left them a note? That was careless, wasn't it?"

"Yes, Pretia, you probably should have. But I sent word from the port at Helios that you had stowed away. Your parents know where you are. It's too late for them to do anything about it," he added with a wink.

"They are going to be so angry," Pretia said.

"And with me, too," Janos said. "I hope you think your decision was worth it."

"For the chance to be a Junior Epic? Definitely."

"You will have to confront them at some point. You know that, don't you?"

Pretia couldn't meet her uncle's eye. "I know," she said quietly. The thought made her cringe.

"Spend the next months figuring out how you will handle that when it happens. And training your hardest so that you have something to show for your disobedience." He ruffled her hair. Pretia glanced over her shoulder to see if anyone had witnessed the familial gesture. But they were alone on deck.

When Janos left, Pretia closed her eyes so she could sink into the feeling of the boat cutting through the waves. She took several more deep breaths, reassuring herself she had done the right thing. But something deep inside her kept nagging—her motivation for running away had been selfish. Janos had been talking about what was best for Epoca. But she knew she'd done it for herself, not for Epoca. Still, she wouldn't admit that to anyone else.

When she opened her eyes, this last anxiety flew from her mind. In front of her was majestic Cora Island, rising from the sea. How could she not have come? How could she have missed returning to school and to this wondrous place, which she loved better than anywhere else in the world?

Cora Island was even more beautiful than Pretia remembered—the towering cliffs, the sparkling blue water, the white sands. As the small boats rowed her and her classmates to shore, between the ancient gates that loomed over the harbor, she couldn't keep her eyes from wandering toward the cave that once led to the fallen Temple of Hurell. To her surprise, the cave opening was no longer there. Boulders had fallen, filling the entrance. She breathed a sigh of relief.

Once on shore, Janos directed the second years to the far end of the beach. "You'll find the stairs to campus right behind that jetty," he said, pointing across a line of rocks that led from the beach into the water.

"Stairs?" Adira asked.

"Unless you prefer the long climb like the new recruits," Janos replied.

Adira shook her head and, quick as a shot, headed for the jetty, followed by the rest of the class.

Pretia was stunned. The moment she scrambled over the rocks, she looked up to see a flight of stairs cut into the cliff. How had she overlooked these in her explorations of Ecrof?

The climb was steep, but much easier than last year's precarious scramble up the goat path. In fifteen minutes, they'd arrived at Cora's plateau. They didn't even have to cross the Decision Woods. In fact, they were to the west of the Panathletic Stadium. They could see the TheraCenter and the Halls of Process directly in front of them.

"Wow," Vera said, "too bad Julius never mentioned these stairs when he shared some of Ecrof's secrets with me."

"If we'd taken these stairs last year, there would have been no Placement Ceremony, and you wouldn't have become a Dreamer," Rovi said.

"True!" Vera said. "Race you to the Temple of Dreams." She was poised to tear off in the direction of the Dreamers' dorms.

"Wait," Rovi said, pulling her back. "There's something I want to see first." He was looking in the direction of the stadium. "The tree."

Racing could wait. Pretia also wanted to see the tree—one of the Four Marvels of Epoca. She was proud to have saved it last year

◆

from being poisoned by the deadly strangler fig that had been turning it sickly black.

"You go, Rovi," Vera said. "Let us know how it's doing." She had her hand on Pretia's arm, trying to pull her toward the Temple of Dreams.

Rovi had already taken off in the direction of the stadium. Pretia started to follow.

"Pretia, wait," Vera said.

Pretia turned. "What?"

Vera bit her lip. "Nothing," she said.

"Race you to the tree, at least?" Pretia urged, then darted after Rovi.

"You're on," Vera replied, following.

Pretia and Vera arrived at the center of the stadium just behind Rovi. The Tree of Ecrof stood in the middle of the track, as always. It had sprouted up and out. It was taller, its trunk wider, its leaves shinier and more silver. It seemed to glitter in the perfect sunlight that always graced Cora Island.

"It looks amazing," Vera said.

"Even better than last year," Rovi added.

Pretia's eyes ran up the trunk to the top.

"Want to climb it?" Vera asked.

"No way," Rovi said. "From now on I'm only admiring the tree from a distance. Last year I had enough of trees to last me a lifetime."

"But I want to *do* something," Vera moaned. "We've been cooped up on that ship forever. We've lost valuable training time."

"We were only on the ship for one night," Pretia said. "That's hardly forever."

"It is when you're training to make the Junior Epics," Vera said. "Every moment counts."

"We know," Pretia and Rovi chorused.

The recruits weren't set to arrive at Ecrof until the next morning, which gave the second years a day to relax and explore. Adira and Virgil, both divers, went in search of the pool that they hadn't been allowed to even see their first year. Castor and Myra joined a baseball game that was taking place on the main field.

Rovi busied himself stuffing as many snacks from the vending machines into his mouth as he could.

"Is that how you plan to spend the afternoon?" Vera asked.

"Um, yeah," Rovi said. "I missed these machines."

"You missed *vending machines*?" Pretia said. "I should have told the cooks at Castle Airim you preferred a junk food diet."

"This isn't junk food," Rovi mumbled through a mouthful of Power Snacks. "It's heaven."

"Well," Vera said, retying one of her shoes, "while you two are busy bickering over details, I'm going to train. I'm not waiting until tomorrow."

"Vera," Pretia groaned. "We just got here."

"That attitude didn't win Farnaka Stellus all those medals," Vera said. "I guess I'm practicing alone?"

Pretia looked from Vera to Rovi. All she wanted to do was hang out in the Temple of Dreams. But then she thought of what she had risked in coming to Ecrof, and what was at stake. If she didn't make the Junior Epic Squad—if she didn't win Junior Epic Glory—all was in vain. She had to make that team. She had to. "I'm coming," she said.

Vera's eyes lit up. "Great!" she said. "There's something I wanted to talk to you about."

Pretia checked that her own Grana Gleams were tied tightly. "Cool," she said. "Catch you later, Rovi."

Rovi crinkled the wrapper of his last Power Snacks package. "Hold up. I'm coming, too."

"Whoa," Vera said.

◆

"What?" Rovi asked.

"It's just—" Vera began. "When did you become Mr. Dedication?"

"You think you're the only one who wants to make Junior Epic Squad?"

"Fair enough," Vera replied, heading for the exit.

"So where are we going?" Pretia asked. "The Infinity Track?"

"Even better: the Infinity Stairs. I heard about them from my brother before . . ." She trailed off.

Pretia could have finished the sentence for her. *Before I became a Replacement and was reclassified from House Relia to House Somni and Julius stopped talking to me.*

"He shared a bunch of stuff about Ecrof with me that he shouldn't have on the condition that I not explore it or talk about it until I was allowed to. And that's now."

She led them across campus to the main gymnasium. As recruits, they had only been allowed to train on the outdoor fields, the Infinity Track that hovered over campus in a different location every day, the obstacle woods, and the Panathletic Stadium. But there were dozens of other buildings around campus that were now available to them, from the hidden pool (wherever *that* was) to the massive Main Gym.

They burst through the gym's doors. In front of them were three basketball courts side by side. Over their heads were three levels of indoor tracks reaching up to the ceiling. Countless machines that measured abilities and taught skills that Pretia didn't understand surrounded them. There were off-road simulators, wind runners, rain machines, muscle-memory machines, and hundreds of other things that flashed and beeped.

Rovi stopped in front of an off-road simulator and pressed a few buttons. "This would be amazing for steeplechase," he said.

"Come on," Vera said, tugging his arm. "Forget the machines."

They followed her to the back of the gym. "I think the stairs are around here somewhere," she said, yanking on a few closed doors until one of them opened.

They were standing in a dark room. At the sound of their voices, lights came to life.

A huge staircase rose in front of them.

"Now what?" Pretia wondered.

"Now we race," Vera replied. She beamed.

The three kids stepped up to the bottom stair. "On your marks," Rovi said.

"Get set," Vera added.

"Go!" Pretia shouted.

Off they went, up the stairs. Rovi was the first to the top. He put up his hands in victory, but as he did, the staircase curved and a new flight of steps appeared. Vera pushed past him into the lead.

"Don't slow down," Pretia called, chasing after Vera.

Every time one of them reached the top of the stairs, the staircase mutated. It grew or doubled back or became so impossibly steep that their noses touched the step in front of them as they climbed. Once it even bent into a figure eight.

After one particularly steep flight of stairs, Rovi collapsed on a landing. "Hold on," he said. "I need a break."

To Pretia's surprise, Vera fell down next to him. "This is exhausting."

"But weirdly fun," Pretia said.

"One more race?" Rovi suggested.

When they'd recovered, they discovered that the stairs had returned to their original form, and it was simple enough to descend to the level where they'd started.

"I guess that's what happens when you stop for a while," Vera said.

"It's always easier going down," Pretia said.

Rovi wiped his brow. "You can say that again."

"Okay, final race," Vera said.

◆

"How do we know when it's over?" Rovi asked.

"When the stairs take us back to the ground, that's the end. Whoever gets off the stairs first wins."

Together they all drew a deep breath—and away they went. Rovi led first. But then the stairs turned a loop-de-loop and Pretia pulled ahead. When the stairs switched to a sharp descent, Vera overtook her. Vera extended her lead when the stairs turned into a ladder, so steep they couldn't run but had to climb, using their hands.

Pretia could feel a deep burn in her calves. Her lungs stung. Rovi had come to a standstill, too worn-out to continue. But Vera seemed to be climbing effortlessly. She was going to win—and win easily—unless Pretia did something.

In an instant, she was watching herself accelerate away, flying up the ladder, passing Vera and coming to a last landing from which the stairs plunged dramatically. She raced down, down, down to the ground.

As always, Pretia felt the curious collision when her two selves reunited.

Vera arrived on the ground a moment later. "Wow, Pretia, that was . . . something." There was a strange note in her voice.

"Sorry," Pretia said.

"If you think that was something," Rovi called, "you should have seen her do it while carrying Castor and *still* beating me."

"Seen her doing what?" Vera asked.

"Castor tried to stop my shadow self by jumping on its back. But my shadow self just carried him," Pretia explained with a laugh.

Vera let out a loud giggle. But then her face grew concerned. "So are you going to do that all the time?"

"I don't know. It's a game-time decision. And sometimes it's not even my decision."

"Does it always work?" Vera wanted to know.

"I think it works best for simple things like running. It's harder for complex sports like tennis. And I haven't tried it in the water, but—" Then Pretia stopped talking. "Oh, Vera, Farnaka's record!"

"What?" Vera asked.

"You're worried that my grana will prevent you from breaking Farnaka's record. But you shouldn't be. I'm not even interested in—"

"That's not what I'm worried about," Vera said. "I can take care of my own performance. It's something else."

"What is something else?" Rovi had reached the floor.

"Nothing," Vera said.

"I think I heard the hunting horn for dinner while you two were busy racing," Rovi said breathlessly.

"Is food all you think about?" Vera asked.

"I bet Farnaka Stellus never skipped a meal when he was training, right, Pretia?"

Pretia ignored Rovi's joke. "Vera, what were you going to say?" Pretia asked. She was certain something important had been on the tip of Vera's tongue before Rovi interrupted.

"Nothing," Vera replied, and set off toward the Main Gym.

Pretia hesitated before following. "Are you sure?"

Vera paused and looked over her shoulder. "It can wait."

She held Pretia's gaze for a moment, her mouth open as if she was about to say more. Then she continued out the door.

After dinner that night, Pretia climbed into the bed across the room from Vera's. Her entire body ached from their race on the Infinity Stairs.

"I think I like the stairs more than the Infinity Track," she said.

"Mmmmmm," Vera replied.

"Vera," Pretia said, "it seemed like you were holding back earlier. What did you want to tell me?"

But there was no answer. Vera was already asleep.

As exhausted as Pretia herself was, she wanted to check her

◆

Grana Book one last time before turning out the light. She reached over and took her book out of her backpack. Then she sat cross-legged on her bed and closed her eyes. "Will my parents be disappointed in me?"

She flipped the pages until one felt right. When she opened the book, it showed a ship on a turbulent ocean with a shoreline in the distance. She smiled. The road would be hard, but the outcome would be positive if she was as steadfast as a ship. And with that, she closed her eyes and slipped away to sleep.

The next morning, Pretia tried to sleep in. She had one more day of total freedom at Ecrof, one more day before the Trainers would start bossing and instructing, correcting and ordering. But before she'd even opened her eyes, Vera was already yammering about the Infinity Track. "We can't waste a second," Vera said.

While Pretia dressed, Vera summoned Rovi. She handed both of them a few snacks, then marched them to the track.

"Okay," Vera bellowed. "Let's moooooove."

Pretia and Rovi exchanged a startled glance.

"I said MOVE!" Vera had started doing jumping jacks. Then she dropped to the ground and executed twenty push-ups. "Warm up, you two."

Rovi and Pretia dropped to do their push-ups, but Vera had already moved on to squats.

"Vera, you're going to destroy us before we race," Pretia gasped after a set of high-knees.

"Then you'll need to train harder," Vera said.

"Come on," Rovi moaned. "Let's race."

"Not yet," Vera said. "One set of mountain climbers, one of star jumps." Pretia couldn't help but notice that she sounded pretty tired herself. Pretia and Rovi were drenched in sweat by the time the routine was over.

"I can't believe that was the *warm-up*," Rovi panted.

"I'm done and we haven't even started," Pretia replied.

During the races, Pretia sometimes won without splitting herself. But often she needed her special talent to beat her friends. Each time she used it, Vera eyed her strangely.

After several of these looks, Pretia stopped Vera from getting in the starting blocks. "Is something wrong?" she asked.

"No," Vera said.

"Are you *jealous*?" Rovi teased.

"No," Vera insisted.

"Does it make you uncomfortable?" Pretia asked, remembering how Castor had reacted back at the Games Pit in Ponsit.

"I'm not *uncomfortable*," Vera replied.

"So, what then?" Rovi demanded.

"It's nothing," Vera muttered. "Let's just race. I need to work even harder when Pretia splits herself. So that's good for me."

Pretia paused before crouching in the starting blocks. Something was obviously bugging Vera. But when Vera said, "Go," Pretia shook it off and got down to the serious business of training.

Vera insisted on so many races, Pretia's legs turned to jelly, her feet went numb, and her lungs felt scorched. She could barely walk away from the track.

By the time lunch was over and the hunting horn blast sounded, summoning the school to the Panathletic Stadium for the Placement Ceremony, it was all Pretia could do to drag herself to the bleachers.

"She's going to kill us before school starts," Rovi whispered when Vera was out of earshot.

"I know," Pretia said. "My legs are on fire."

"I think I'm going to be sick, my stomach muscles ache so badly," Rovi groaned. They looped their arms around one another and helped each other to the stadium, where they joined the ranks of the Dreamers.

What a change to be seated in the stands for the Placement Ceremony instead of stumbling through the woods uncertain of what was about to happen. The recruits looked wide-eyed as they emerged from the woods one by one, blinking as they encountered the grand stadium festooned with blue and purple banners celebrating each house. Pretia loved seeing their awed expressions as they caught sight of the magnificent Tree of Ecrof for the first time. She watched as Satis Dario, the kindly Visualization Trainer, handed each newcomer a tracksuit in his or her house colors.

"Did we look like that?" Rovi asked.

"Like what?" Vera replied.

"Confused," Rovi said.

Vera shaded her eyes, watching the most recent recruit enter the stadium. "I'm sure I did," she said. She was making small comments as each recruit appeared, dismissing many of them for some weakness only she could see.

"Vera," Pretia began. "What did you want to tell me earlier?"

But Vera shushed her. "I'm concentrating."

Rovi tapped Pretia on the shoulder. "Vera's sizing them up," he said in an exaggerated whisper.

Suddenly Vera was sitting up straighter, her eyes lasered on the latest recruit to appear.

"Eshe Sonos!" Vera exclaimed. "I *know* her."

Pretia peered across the stadium at the new recruit. She looked like Vera but with a slightly darker amber complexion. Her puff of wavy dark brown hair was pulled into a large bouncing ponytail. She had the widest smile Pretia had ever seen.

"She's from my town," Vera continued. "She's . . . she's . . ."

"She's the competition," Rovi provided.

Vera wheeled around. "I didn't say that."

"You didn't have to," Rovi said. "You're staring daggers at her."

Just then, an explosion of purple Dreamer fireworks lit up the sky, and Eshe ran to sit with House Somni.

"Hi, Vera," she said, squeezing into a spot on the bench below Vera's and Pretia's feet. "So, you really *are* a Dreamer. I'd heard, but I didn't believe it."

"Believe it," Vera said.

"I mean, that's just the coolest thing ever," Eshe continued.

"Is it?" Vera asked.

"To be on the same team as Vera Renovo is a dream come true," the young recruit gushed.

"You bet it is," Rovi teased.

Vera rolled her eyes. "I don't know about teams this year," she said. "This year it's every athlete for herself during Junior Epic trials. And that matters a lot more than a silly house cup."

Eshe did not take the hint. "Well, it will be amazing to compete with you in the Junior Epic Games, then."

"You think you're getting selected for the Junior Epic Squad?" Vera said.

Eshe smiled brightly. "Why not?"

Vera rolled her eyes again and returned her focus to the newly arrived recruits.

Pretia leaned over and whispered in Rovi's ear, "I think Vera's met her match."

"For sure," Rovi replied.

When the last recruit arrived and had been placed, Janos announced the house captains for the year. The captains accepted their sashes and returned to their seats.

"Now," Janos bellowed, clapping his powerful hands to summon the students' attention. "Normally I would proceed to tell you about our two Field Days, which are the focal points of our school year. And indeed, we will have Field Days later. However, this year is—"

"JUNIOR EPIC GAMES!" chorused a group of fifth, sixth, and seventh termers who'd been around for the last games four years ago.

"Right," Janos said. "Which means this year we do things differently."

A ripple of excitement passed through the bleachers. Soon it had turned into a roar.

"First things first," Janos said, holding up his hands. "The Junior Epic Games are going to be held in less than two months' time in Phoenis. Ecrof will be sending a squad of thirty athletes who will join contenders from the other seven elite academies. As you know, our Epic Elite Squad has already secured their places on the team."

Vera bristled at the mention of the Epic Elite Squad. She had made the squad last year, but Janos had left her off the team, relegating her to an alternate, supposedly to give her time to mature. At least that had been his stated reason. Vera suspected otherwise. Since she hadn't been officially named to the squad and hadn't been allowed to train with them yet, her spot on the Junior Epic Team was not guaranteed.

"There are eight returning Epic Elites this year who've booked their spots. This leaves twenty-two spots on the team. Both Epic Elite alternates will have to try out this year. Two spots on the squad are reserved for more divers. If an athlete qualifies in both the pool and the track, that does not free up another spot. In that event, we will take fewer athletes. The total number of athletes from either house may not exceed two more than the opposite house. If the balance between the teams is uneven, it will be adjusted."

Janos waited for a wave of chatter to pass through the students.

"At the Junior Epic Games, you will compete for your house. Our Dreamers will compete alongside Dreamers from all over Epoca. Our Realists will compete alongside Realists from all over Epoca. Junior Epic Glory will be given to the house with the most medals. Individual Epic Glory will be granted to individuals who medal even if their house is not the winner. Overall Junior Epic Individual Glory—the most prestigious prize any young athlete can aspire to—will be given to the athlete who wins the most individual medals."

Pretia stole a glance at Vera. Vera's jaw was set, her eyes blazing with determination.

"And finally, the academy whose students take home the most medals is awarded the Junior Epic Cup. Therefore, you will compete with and against your fellow students. You will strive to shine on your own. And you will fight for your house . . . but also for Ecrof."

A cheer exploded from the students at once, followed by the Ecrof fight song. Janos let the song finish before demanding silence.

"Now," he said, "in the interest of selecting and training our best team, regular classes are canceled for the first two months of school. There will only be Junior Epic Conditioning, all day, every day. You will train for the two arenas of sport in the Junior Epic Games: track and field and swimming and diving."

"So these new recruits are going to get to use the pool their first year?" Virgil grumbled. "Unfair."

"In six weeks, we will hold trials," Janos continued. "The swimming trial will be an individual medley showcasing all four strokes. Diving will be a single dive from the springboard and platform. And track-and-field competitors will be selected by means of a decathlon—ten events spread out over two days to determine our best athletes. After the team members are selected, they will depart for Phoenis immediately."

The stadium broke into a clamor. "The squad will be away in Phoenis for a month. During this time, Ecrof business will continue as usual under the guidance of our best Junior Trainers. When the games are over, the squad will return to campus and resume training as normal."

"But it won't be normal," Rovi whispered in Pretia's ear. "How can anything be *normal* once you've been to the Junior Epic Games?"

◆

Janos clapped his hands. "Go!" he bellowed. "Prepare yourself for the tasks ahead."

All at once, the students got to their feet. Adira passed close to Pretia. "I guess we know one member of the team," she said.

"Vera?" Pretia asked.

Adira snorted like Pretia was beyond silly. "You. Do you know anyone else who can split themselves? Janos might as well have said there were only twenty-one spots available."

"Who knows," Pretia replied. "I've never tested my grana with water sports."

"That's a relief," Virgil said. "I don't need anyone taking my spot as a diver."

"So you're not trying out in the pool at all?" Adira asked.

Pretia shrugged. "I hadn't really thought about it."

Virgil and Adira exchanged a glance, then looped arms and walked off.

"All of Vera's training nearly killed me. I can barely stand," Pretia said. "I'm going to soak in the TheraCenter."

"Me too," Rovi added.

"I'm going to do a few more laps around the track," Vera said, trotting past them.

"Vera, come on," Pretia groaned. "Your legs will fall off."

"You heard Janos," Vera replied. "We have less than two months to become the best we can."

"I don't think he meant for us to train nonstop," Pretia said. "Haven't you ever heard of recovery?"

Vera's eyes flashed. "No."

"Me neither." They all turned to see that Eshe Sonos had joined their group. She gazed at Vera with a look of admiration and determination. "So where are we training?" she asked.

Vera rolled her eyes. "We?"

"I mean, since your friends are too lazy, I figured we could train together. You and I."

"The Infinity Track," Vera said through gritted teeth, and trotted away, Eshe at her side. The moment they were far enough away, Rovi and Pretia doubled over with laughter.

"The look on her face—" Rovi said. "Those two are totally made for each other."

"I didn't think the world could take another Vera," Pretia agreed. "But I'm glad Eshe is going to train with her. My legs are like jelly!"

Gingerly and with much effort, the two of them made their way to the TheraCenter.

That night, Pretia was asleep before her head hit the pillow.

She didn't dream. She didn't move. She just slept.

Until—

"Pretia?"

Pretia rolled over. She groaned and rubbed her eyes. Vera was standing over her, a sheen of sweat gleaming on her forehead.

"Don't you dare tell me you need someone to train with you right now. You need to get some rest."

"No," Vera said.

"Thank the gods," Pretia said.

"But I do need to talk to you about something."

"Now? Can't it wait?"

"Not really," Vera said. "I've been trying to talk to you alone, but it's been hard."

Pretia sat up. Vera *did* have something on her mind. "What is it?"

Vera looked concerned. "It's about your grana and what you can do." She swallowed hard. "While I was home this summer I overheard some stuff I shouldn't have. From Julius."

"Like?"

"Julius is too old for this year's Junior Epics. But of course he's going to be there, since he's basically a hero after his last Epic Games. I mean, he won more medals in his first senior event than Janos did at his age." Vera's voice was sour as she talked about her brother.

"Whatever," she continued dismissively. "Here's what's important. Julius is going to be at the Junior Epics, since he's the most decorated Junior Epic Champion except for—"

"Farnaka Stellus," Pretia said with a groan.

"Right," Vera said. "Anyway, he's not simply going for the Parade of Past Champions. He's also going to lead a protest."

"Against the Star Stealers?"

"No," Vera said. "Against you."

Now Pretia was wide-awake. "*Me?*"

Vera's eyes slid away as if she couldn't look at Pretia directly. "Because of your grana. He thinks splitting yourself gives you an unfair advantage."

"What?" Pretia cried. "It's not *unfair*. That's just how my grana is!"

"*I* know that. But Julius is a very popular athlete. He never lets me forget it. He's circulated a petition, and a lot of people, mainly Realists, have signed it. They're going to try to forbid you from splitting yourself in competition."

Suddenly Pretia felt sick. "Can they do that?"

"Who knows," Vera replied. She wiped the sweat off her forehead. "I just wanted to warn you."

Pretia had no idea what to say. "Um, thanks." She hoped she at least sounded somewhat relaxed. In truth, her mind was racing. A protest? If her parents knew about this, they'd double down on their prohibition against her going to Phoenis.

"Don't worry," Vera said. "I'll have your back no matter what happens."

Pretia's heart beat fast. "What do you think is going to happen?"

"I don't know," Vera said. "Julius and his friends will make some noise and try to cause a scene. But the Dreamers will support you. And your uncle will, too, probably."

"Janos is totally on my side," Pretia said. "Which is weird because I'm on the opposite team . . . but I guess he doesn't care about teams when it comes to family."

"So, you have nothing to worry about," Vera said. "Realists can be total bullies."

"Yeah," Pretia said, thinking once more of Castor. He was a Realist *and* a bully—and he also didn't like her talent for splitting herself. She could easily see him joining Julius's protest.

"Plus," Vera said, "you're the princess. You can totally stand up for yourself."

"I don't know," Pretia said. The idea of drawing attention to herself and staking her claim to use her grana made her uneasy. "I'd rather show them on the field." She'd leave the big statements for her parents. She preferred to hide behind sports.

"Hopefully that's all you'll have to do," Vera said brightly.

Pretia looked at her friend. "Why didn't you tell me this earlier?"

Vera hesitated. "I didn't want to say anything in front of Rovi or anyone else."

"Why not?" Pretia asked.

"I don't know. It just seemed private."

"Let's hope it stays that way," Pretia said. "Let's hope there are no protests."

"And if there are, we'll show my brother and his silly friends exactly how great you are," Vera declared. She wiped her forehead again. "I need to shower."

Pretia was still awake when Vera returned from the shower. She watched her change, not into pajamas like a normal person, but into a fresh set of training gear, and climb into bed.

"Vera," Pretia whispered across the dark room, "it doesn't bother you when I split myself, does it?"

"No," Vera said sleepily. "I love it. It forces me to train harder."

Vera was certainly the only person in all of Epoca who would have given that answer.

Pretia stayed awake for hours staring at the moon. This was the second time in four days she'd been told there was something wrong with her grana. The second time she'd been urged to keep it in check. It had even made her mother uncomfortable. She tossed and turned, unsure of what to do—unsure if there was in fact anything she could do.

Maybe she shouldn't have come to Ecrof. Maybe she shouldn't be using her grana. Maybe, despite what she'd *thought* she'd seen in her book, her fate was not to be an athlete but a ruler. But she'd come all this way. She'd risked her parents' anger. Now she had to make that team and show everyone what she was made of and what she could do. She had no choice but to prove herself on the field.

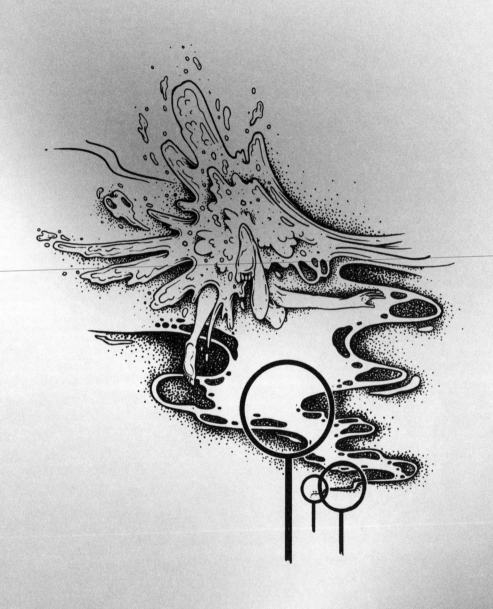

6

R O V I

A MEMORY

ROVI WAS USED TO EXHAUSTION. HE'D SPENT many years on the streets of Phoenis, jolted from his sleep by any number of disturbances—wagons passing by on the Draman Bridge above where his gang camped, someone or something falling into the river next to his pallet, the snores of his fellow Star Stealers, the shouts of the Phoenician guards shaking him awake, telling him and his gang to move on. He'd been kept awake by hunger, by heat, and by the odd cold spell for which he wasn't prepared. Too many nights to count, he hadn't slept at all, watching the sun set over the Tile Palace to the west and rise above the Moon Palace to the east. He had been so tired that he didn't remember what it felt like to be well rested.

The tired he felt now, at Ecrof, was something different. In the first weeks he'd trained harder than he'd ever imagined.

He trained using weighted vests and ankle and wrist weights. He trained uphill. He trained in wind machines.

He did sit-ups. Push-ups. He did all sorts of plyometric exercises— box jumps, side-to-side jumps, jump squats, and squat thrusts.

He ran relay races. Half marathons. Full marathons.

He did hurdles. High jump. Long jump. Triple jump.

He ran until his lungs felt like they might explode. He jumped until he worried his calf muscles would snap. He sprinted until his thighs burned.

He ached in his bones, his joints, his lungs. After a day's training, Rovi could barely lift his fork to his mouth—and that was saying something for him. He could hardly climb the stairs to his room.

Toward the end of the second week of term, he lay on his back during a break from track practice in the Panathletic Stadium and listened to Cleopatra Volis, who had been promoted to Head Athletic Trainer, as she listed their next activities: ropes courses, followed by wind sprints, then a short-distance run to cool down. After a quick break there would be resistance training.

He closed his eyes briefly and opened them to see Cleopatra squatting next to him. "Let's have a little chat, Rovi," she said. She sounded stern. "Walk with me."

With a groan, Rovi stood. "Am I in trouble?"

Cleopatra didn't reply as they walked away from the track. "I see you're working hard, and believe me, I am pleased. It's quite a difference from last year."

"Isn't that a good thing?" Rovi asked.

"It would be . . . if I didn't know that you can work harder," Cleopatra said.

"What?" There was no way he could give any more on the track or anywhere else.

"It's great that you're happy for your friends when they beat you. That is an admirable quality. But you also need to be tougher on yourself." Cleopatra paused to make sure she had his full attention. "It should hurt to lose."

"It does," Rovi said, massaging his hamstrings, still burning from the last race.

"Not in your legs, Rovi. It should hurt in your heart. I'm not telling you to be a sore loser. I'm just asking that every time you lose, you pledge to work harder."

"I don't know if I can work any harder," Rovi groaned.

Cleopatra reached out and pressed a finger into Rovi's stomach. "Listen to what's in here. If your core, the seat of your grana, tells you that you can do no more, then fine. But I think your body will give you a different answer."

When she walked away, Rovi flopped on his back next to the track. He put his hands on his belly where Cleopatra had just touched. He could smell oleander and grass. His legs felt heavy. His feet ached. Cleopatra was wrong. He was already pushing himself to his limit.

Then he took a deep breath. And when he did, he felt something press against his hands—an electric current, a reserve of energy that he hadn't noticed before. Hardly knowing what he was doing, he leaped to his feet ready to race again. There *was* more he could do. There was another level he could reach.

"Castor," he called, "let's do this."

"Let's do what?"

"Let's race," Rovi called.

"I need a break," Castor said. "Why don't you ask Pretia? I'd love to watch her beat you again. Even if she has to do that thing she does."

"Are you sure, Rovi?" Pretia asked. She looked uncertainly at his wobbling legs.

"I am."

They lined up, and Cleopatra counted them down. Rovi's feet were on fire. He felt as if his legs were going to give way. If Pretia split herself, there was nothing he could do—but he had to try.

Like the last race, at the final turn, he sensed her about to blow past him. "Dig," he urged himself, "dig."

And as if they had a mind of their own—which it sometimes seemed that they did—Rovi's feet accelerated. They barely touched the track. In fact, they didn't touch the track at all. He was gliding. He was flying. He was moving faster than he'd thought possible. He reached the finish a millisecond after Pretia. He had almost caught her. He had almost beaten her, even though she'd split herself. He fell to the ground utterly exhausted.

"Whoa!" Vera squatted down next to him. "I've never seen you run so fast."

Rovi couldn't talk. He closed his eyes. He breathed deeply, taking in the grassy, salty scent of Cora Island, the smells of his childhood. Despite his exhaustion, he smiled. His father would have been proud of his effort. Then he heard Cleopatra's voice above him. "You see, Rovi Myrios. There is always more to give."

That afternoon, Rovi could barely walk to the pool for swim training. All he wanted to do was soak in the baths at the TheraCenter. But he knew he'd get in serious trouble for skipping practice. And this year more than anything, he wanted to avoid trouble.

Rovi didn't excel in swimming. He found the water soothing, but when he tried to swim competitively, it made him feel clumsy, heavy, and graceless. After only a few days of swim practice, he had lost hope that the water would yield to his grana. Despite this, he loved the pool because it was perhaps the most miraculous place in all of Ecrof—and *that* was saying something.

The pool was hidden underground far beyond the main sports fields, to the west of the campus, deep inside a craggy collection of low hills. The entrance to the pool area was down a winding, damp staircase that led to a dark tunnel, which eventually opened into a massive subterranean cavern. The walls dripped with water. Voices echoed and bounced around the cave. High overhead, a hole in the cavern's roof let in the sun or the moon or the stars—depending on the time of day—making the water catch their dancing reflections.

Each time Rovi saw the pool, it managed to take his breath away. The water shimmered blue. There were natural waterfalls and a bubbling hot tub fed by a hot spring. Slides had been carved into the cavern walls, slick with water that sent you flying into the pool.

Dozens of lanes divided the pool for different distances, with a shallow end for doing underwater sprints. There were all sorts of diving boards attached to the towering cavern walls. Bleachers were built into the side of the cave on one end. On the opposite was another flight of steps that led deeper below the earth to a viewing area under the pool, where instructors could get another angle on the swimmers' strokes.

Rovi barely had the energy to change into his swimsuit. Nassos and Cyril, the Rhodan Islanders, had already dived in and were swimming like dolphins. Vera was doing her best to keep pace with them. Far above his head, he could hear Adira and Virgil up on the highest diving board, getting ready to turn an impossible number of flips and twists.

Lavinia Lux, the compact, muscular Head Swim Trainer with blue eyes the color of the sea, clapped her hands for attention, then instructed everyone to warm up with ten lengths. Rovi dove in, thrilled with the cool water rippling against his skin. He swam hard, as hard as he could. But he couldn't help noticing that at each turn, he fell farther and farther behind his classmates.

When the warm-up was over, they all hauled themselves out onto the pool deck. Rovi trailed the rest of his classmates. He rolled onto his back, staring at the distant roof of the cavern.

"Nice effort, Rovi," Lavinia said.

But it didn't feel nice. It felt pathetic.

Rovi pressed his hands into his abdomen where Cleopatra had told him his grana was centered. He felt nothing. Was it possible he was giving his all and failing? That hurt worse than anything.

"Okay," Lavinia said, gathering the students. "Today we are doing Sea Lion Obstacles. Of course, you'll never do anything like this in a real swim meet, but it's good to push past what is normal. To train yourself to go above and beyond what will be required."

Adira's hand shot in the air. The entire class knew what she was going to ask before the words were out of her mouth, Lavinia included.

"No, Adira," the swim instructor said with a smile, "you can't just dive instead. You have to complete the whole practice before there is free time for the exercise of your choice."

Adira made a face. "Fine," she said.

"All right," Lavinia continued. "The idea of this is sort of like hurdles, but in the pool. You'll swim two at a time and do one length of butterfly, but on every fifth stroke, you have to pull farther out of the water and dive through one of the rings without touching the edges. There are ten rings. Each time you touch one, a second will be added to your finish time. If you miss a ring entirely, you'll be disqualified."

Rovi watched as rings rose from the bottom of the pool.

Nassos and Cyril slapped hands. "You and me," Cyril said. Although the boys were from opposite houses, their superiority in the pool had bonded them.

"What about me?" Vera asked.

"I don't know," Pretia said, mock-serious. "I heard Eshe crushed it in her heat this morning. Are you as good as she is?"

Rovi wanted to join Pretia in teasing Vera about her first-year doppelgänger. But he was too preoccupied with the task ahead. He didn't want to embarrass himself. He didn't want to finish last—or worse, be disqualified.

Lavinia paired them up. Rovi was drawn with Leo—two Sandlanders swimming against each other. They were the last to swim.

When Lavinia blew her whistle, Rovi was fast off the diving block. He felt sleek and swift as he crested through the air, finding the best aerodynamic path into the water. His grana could do that, at least. But when he hit the water, he was at a loss. He counted strokes as he approached the first ring—one, two, three, four. Then he pulled himself out of the water, preparing to clear the ring. But he was too early. The ring was still a stroke ahead of him. He crashed back into the water, but not before seeing Leo easily clear the ring.

It was like he was back in the maze at Ponsit Palace. He couldn't rely on his grana to help him. Rovi felt blocked—not entirely helpless, but certainly hindered. He made it through the first ring and the second. By the third he'd almost caught Leo. He was working hard. His grana didn't guide him through the pool, so he had to pay particular attention to where he was and when he needed to arc through a ring. This was costing him time. Leo pulled ahead at the fourth ring. Rovi gritted his teeth. He drove his hands as hard as he could through the water. He kicked his feet. But when he pulled out of the water for the final ring, he'd mistimed it. He dove right in front of it, plunging back into the pool, missing the ring entirely. He was disqualified.

Slowly he swam back to the end where his classmates were gathered on the deck and sat on the edge of the pool. "You lost to Leo," Virgil snickered.

"It doesn't matter who he lost to," Myra added. "His time would have been last anyway."

Rovi extended his legs in front of him and leaned forward, touching his toes and pressing his nose to his knees, pretending he was stretching instead of hiding his fury.

"Too bad the Star Stealers aren't allowed their own Junior Epic Squad," Castor said. "That's the only way you'll make the swim team."

Who says I want to make the swim team? Rovi thought. He preferred to compete on land.

"From what I've heard, the Star Stealers aren't going to be allowed much of anything anymore," Leo said.

Rovi looked up. "What do you mean?"

Leo, clearly emboldened by having defeated Rovi, cleared his throat. "You haven't heard? They are trying to expel Star Stealers from the city. All summer, the Phoenician guards were rounding them up."

◆

Rovi felt his stomach tie into a knot. "Why? What did the Star Stealers do?"

Leo shrugged. "I guess they want to clean up all the riffraff from Phoenis before the Junior Epic Games. Or maybe they're just tired of having thieves on the street. Anyway, the Star Stealers started rioting."

"Star Stealers don't riot," Rovi protested. "And they aren't thieves."

"Then what are they?" Leo asked.

"They—they're . . ." Rovi couldn't find the right words. "My friends."

Leo crossed his arms. "Are you a Dreamer or a Star Stealer?"

"A Dreamer," Rovi answered without thinking. But that didn't mean that he'd forgotten his old friends.

"Doesn't sound like it," Leo snickered.

Rovi didn't want to hear any more. He dove back into the pool and let himself sink all the way to the bottom, trying to escape his anxiety about the friends he had left behind in Phoenis. His old gang was closer to family than anything he had in the world. But not even the soothing water of the underground pool eased his mind. He needed to find someone who might know about what was going on back in Phoenis.

The Halls of Process were cool and dim, as always. Rovi stepped into the quiet corridor. He was overcome with relief to be away from his fellow students and the pressure of competition.

Since the non-sports classes—Visualization and Granology— were canceled until after the Junior Epic trials, Rovi had seen next to nothing of Satis Dario, the Visualization Trainer, during the first weeks of the term. Satis had always been kind to Rovi, ever since he'd scouted him from the streets of Phoenis. He had also been a close friend of Rovi's father, Pallas Myrios, before Pallas had his grana stolen. But none of these was the reason that Rovi wanted to find Satis after swim practice.

Rovi took a deep breath and exhaled, relaxing into the solitude of the building. There were two classrooms in the Halls of Process. In between them was a small door that most students never noticed. Rovi knew this door well. It led to what had been his father's office when Pallas Myrios had been Ecrof's Visualization Trainer.

Rovi paused at the door for a moment, and when he did, he heard a noise from within. Without thinking, he turned the handle and opened the door.

The room had been completely rearranged since he'd been there last year. All the clutter left behind by Pallas had been organized. The shelves were filled with neatly labeled storage boxes. The myriad machines that Pallas had left in disarray were lined up along one wall. The long desk in the center of the room where Rovi's father used to work late into the night conceiving new methods and gadgets for visualization was free of clutter.

Sitting behind this desk was the squat Visualization Trainer, Satis Dario, his bald head shining in the sunlight streaming in from one of the freshly washed windows.

A broad smile broke over his face when he saw Rovi standing in the doorway. "Rovi! You've grown tired of all that training and decided to take a break with some visualization?"

"I—um—no," Rovi sputtered. He suddenly felt terribly guilty for completely ignoring the practice of visualization. Had he offended Satis? Had he done a disservice to his father?

Satis's face fell. "Are you upset about the office?"

"Upset?"

"That I took over your father's laboratory?"

"Not at all," Rovi said. He looked around some more. "It looks great in here. Maybe some of this stuff can help me train for the Junior Epic Games."

Satis stepped out from behind the desk. "I like the way you're thinking, Rovi. Imagining that something is going to happen is the first step toward ensuring that it *will* happen. What sort of visualization do you want help with?"

"I—er—I'm not here about visualization, actually." For the second time in less than two minutes, he felt he'd let Satis down. "I mean, I know I need to practice it, but I have a question about something else."

"Well, take a seat, then," Satis said, pulling out a stool for Rovi. Rovi did as instructed.

"What can I help you with?" the Visualization Trainer asked.

"Did you scout the new recruits this year?" Rovi said.

Each year the ceremonial Scrolls of Ecrof were opened to find the names of the new students. Then Ecrof scouts were dispatched all over Epoca to determine whether these students were a true fit for the academy.

"Yes," Satis said. "But I can't tell you anything about the scrolls or the scouting process." The scrolls were a mystery even the Trainers didn't understand.

"I know," Rovi said. "But did you scout in the Sandlands again?"

"I did."

"Did you—" Rovi began. "Did you see any Star Stealers?"

"Well," Satis said. He drummed his fingers on his knee. "I wasn't looking for them. As you know, it's unprecedented for a recruit to come from a gang of Star Stealers or from any of the other Orphic People. You are the one and only in the history of Ecrof."

"But did you see any Star Stealers? They're always around."

"Rovi—"

Rovi didn't let the Trainer finish. "At the Alexandrine Plaza. By the river Durna. That's where my group hung out. Or other places, like the catacombs. The desert fountains. You must have seen them."

"I didn't," Satis said slowly.

"So it's true what Castor and Leo have been saying?"

"I can't imagine that anything Castor and Leo have been saying is one hundred percent true," Satis said.

"They say the Star Stealers have been doing something bad and that they are being rounded up."

Satis looked concerned. "I admit there may be some truth to that, but I'm not sure exactly what it is. I've heard rumors of some sort of dispute between the Star Stealers and the Phoenician officials. I don't know the circumstances. But it does seem as if the Star Stealers have been gathering in large numbers."

"More than one gang together?"

"I don't know the details," Satis said.

"But that *never* happens. They wouldn't do that." Star Stealer gangs kept their distance from one another in public out of a sense of mutual self-preservation. Too many Star Stealers in one place attracted attention and made life difficult for all of them.

"All I can tell you is what I heard."

"I just . . . I can't stop thinking about my old gang. My Star Stealer brother Issa, especially. He's the toughest, smartest kid I know. And he saved me when my dad died. If anything happened to him—" Rovi stopped talking abruptly, swallowing the lump in his throat and wiping the tears away from his eyes.

"I remember Issa," Satis said. "I watched you two together for several days while I scouted you. He seemed to love you very much."

Rovi could only nod.

"And he took great care of you."

"He was—he is the best Star Stealer leader," Rovi said.

"Which is why," Satis said kindly, "unless you have specific knowledge that something bad happened to Issa, you shouldn't worry about him. He seemed to me like someone very capable of taking care of himself."

"Okay." Rovi nodded. Issa *was* resourceful and strong.

Satis's hands flew to his desk, and he began to fiddle with some fabric strips strung together with copper wire. "There is something I should tell you, though. I have heard that the Star Stealers are afraid to be seen in the open on the streets of Phoenis, so they travel underground as much as possible."

"Underground?"

"They use the tunnels left behind by the River of Sand."

Like everyone else, Rovi knew that the River of Sand was one of the Four Marvels of Epoca. It was once a mighty flow of quicksand that the gods used to travel across the Sandlands to mainland Epoca. The river originated deep below the streets of Phoenis and emerged into the desert, connecting the Sandlands to the rest of the country. But when the time of the gods ended and they left for Mount Aoin, the people of Phoenis dammed the river because it was thought to be too powerful for humans to control in the gods' absence. There were other rumors, too—ones that were only spoken of in whispers. Some said that the River of Sand had been a creation of Hurell when he was still one of the blessed gods.

For years, Rovi had heard stories about the maze of tunnels left behind by the river—about thieves and criminals who camped in them. He'd heard rumors about kids getting lost down there and never being seen again. He'd even darted into them to escape the Phoenician guards once or twice, and each time he had, the tunnels had terrified him. He knew that somewhere a small portion of the River of Sand still flowed. There were rumors that the Phoenician guards had the power to turn it loose to clear the tunnels. He also knew that there was a siren that would warn the city's residents if the river broke free on its own. He'd heard this siren tested before, and it made his blood run cold.

Rovi opened his mouth to ask more questions, but Satis held up his hand. "I am sorry that I don't have more answers for you, Rovi. I hope your friends are all right."

The thought of Issa and the rest of his gang of Star Stealers, whom Rovi had left behind without a goodbye, made him choke up a little.

"And speaking of the Junior Epic Games," Satis said, "I have something for you."

The Trainer went to one of the well-organized shelves and opened a box. He took out a strip of thick fabric cut like a headband and handed it to Rovi. The fabric was black on one side and gold on the other.

"Is that a new kind of Mensa Crown?" Rovi had learned to master Mensa Crowns in Visualization the previous year, and had become pretty good at projecting an image of himself playing a sport into the air above his head.

"No, it's a Memory Master."

"Did my dad invent it?" Rovi asked, taking the fabric from Satis.

"He did."

"What does it do?"

"If you wear it when you train, it records your movements so you can play them back in your head later and study them. You put it on with the gold side touching your forehead to record and flip to black to replay."

"Thanks," Rovi said, taking the headband.

"Give it a try," Satis said. "The competition for the Junior Epic Squad is going to be fierce."

"I will," Rovi replied, although he didn't like using gadgets for visualization, preferring instead to rely on his natural talents. He turned the band around in his hands. "Promise," he added, more to himself than to Satis. He vowed once more to do anything possible to get to Phoenis and return a hometown hero.

He'd make Issa proud—and show him just how far he'd come.

◆

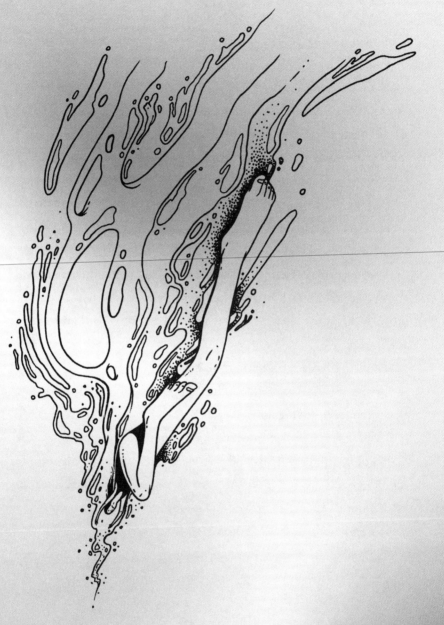

7

PRETIA

A WARNING

THE NIGHT BEFORE THE JUNIOR EPIC SWIM trials, the Dreamers' cafeteria was filled with nervous electricity. Even Adira and Virgil, who were normally thick as thieves, seemed to be keeping their distance from one another.

"You're not diving, are you, Pretia?" Adira said as Pretia passed by on her way to sit with Rovi.

"I wasn't planning on it," Pretia replied.

"Are you sure?" Adira asked. She sounded incredibly anxious. She was fiddling with the edge of her headscarf, twisting it around her fingers.

"Have you ever even seen me dive?" Pretia asked. She figured that was enough of an answer. Not once had she participated in diving practice.

She found a seat next to Rovi. The only other occupant of his table was Virgil. As soon as she sat down, Virgil said, "You're not diving, right? Or anything like that?"

"Anything like what?"

"Like, you know, doing things that aren't your thing, just because."

"Just because *what*?" Pretia tried to hide the irritation in her voice.

"Because you can," Virgil snipped.

"Are there things I should and shouldn't do?" Pretia asked.

"Yes." Virgil stood and grabbed his tray, knocking into Rovi. "Diving." Together Pretia and Rovi watched Virgil march over to Adira's table and slam down his tray.

"I've never even attended a single diving practice," Pretia said. "Do they actually think I'm suddenly going to start diving?" She had signed up for swim trials, but diving didn't interest her at all.

Rovi looked at her strangely. "Well, they think you can do any-thing you want."

"That's ridiculous."

"But it's sort of true."

"It's not like I can magically do everything just because I can split myself. It's not like that at all." Her talent was causing more and more trouble each and every day. No one understood it. In fact, there were times when Pretia herself barely understood it.

"What do you think will happen if one of those two makes the diving team and the other doesn't?" Pretia said, glancing at Adira and Virgil, who were making a big show of not talking to each other.

"It's going to be ugly." Rovi stuffed a huge spoonful of rice into his mouth. When he was finished chewing, he put down his spoon and looked at Pretia. "So are you going to try out for the team?"

"The diving team?" Pretia threw down her fork. "You think I'm going to get up on a diving board for the first time and just hope my grana helps me execute some kind of miraculous somersault? It doesn't work that way. I can't just do whatever I want, whenever."

As far as she could tell, splitting herself required a very specific balance of things—confidence, desire, calm, and focus. Sometimes when her motivation was low, she couldn't manage to step outside herself. Sometimes when she was distracted, it didn't happen either. The times she could do it, of course, were the crucial ones, when winning was essential both to her personally and for a greater good. "I'm going out for swimming and that's all."

"All I'm saying is that every time you've split yourself, you've beaten me," Rovi said. "It doesn't bother me. But I understand why they're worried."

"I don't *always* split myself." Did everyone think she could win medals just by turning up? Pretia's heart sank. No matter what she did or what happened to her, she was always different, singled out for either the accident of her mixed heritage or her royal birth or her intense grana. "They must hate me," she said glumly. Maybe she should have stayed home. Maybe ruling Epoca would have been easier than dealing with her classmates.

"I think they're more afraid of you than anything else."

Somehow that was worse. Pretia was torn between horror and grief. There was no reason to *fear* her. She had a talent for splitting herself, which meant she could win races when she did so. There was nothing scary about that.

"Well, everyone except Vera," Rovi added.

Pretia smiled. "Vera says my talent makes her work harder. She thinks she can beat me and everyone else no matter what." Pretia glanced around the cafeteria. "Speaking of Vera, where is she?"

"She was in the Hall of Victory when I came down," Rovi said.

"Again?" Pretia asked. For the last month Vera had been spending every spare moment staring at the pictures and memorabilia of famous Dreamer athletes.

"I bet she's still there," Rovi added.

Pretia picked up her tray. "I want to see how she's feeling about tomorrow."

"All right," Rovi said. "I'll see you later."

She returned her tray to the kitchen and exited the cafeteria, aware of dozens of eyes on her, assessing her, judging her, envying her. A group of recruits were whispering over their trays. They fell silent as Pretia passed. "What?" she said. There was no answer.

"What?" Pretia repeated.

Eshe lifted her head from the cluster. "They want to know if it hurts when you split yourself," Eshe said.

Pretia locked eyes with her. "Would it matter to them if it did?" She held Eshe's gaze for another moment, enjoying her speechlessness, before turning on her heel and striding out of the cafeteria in search of Vera.

Vera was exactly where Rovi said she'd be, staring at a picture hanging on one of the marble walls of the Hall of Victory.

Pretia reached out and tapped her on the shoulder. Vera jumped, obviously startled.

"Sorry," Pretia said.

Vera's eyes were wide, an excited smile on her lips. "It's him!"

"What? Who?"

Vera jammed her finger against the glass protecting the photo. "There."

"I can't see anything with your finger in the way," Pretia said.

Vera removed her hand.

The picture showed the opening ceremony at what Pretia assumed must be the Junior Epic Games about twenty years earlier. It was a group picture of the entire Dreamer squad from all the academies wearing official Epoca Dreamer tracksuits from that year's games. She peered at the smudge left behind by Vera's finger and saw a slender teenage boy with a mop of dark hair falling over his brow. He had the complexion of a Sandlander and was shorter than his teammates.

"Who's that?" Pretia asked.

"That," Vera said, "is Farnaka Stellus."

Pretia scanned the caption on the wall below the photo. It identified none of the athletes by name, just the year and location of the Junior Epic Games in Hydros.

"How do you know?" Pretia asked. The boy looked like a lot of the other Sandlander kids in the photos on the wall.

"Process of elimination," Vera said. "I found him twice." She moved to another similar group picture of older athletes at the Epic Games held in Phoenis two years after the previous photo was taken. "There," she said, pointing at the same face, slightly aged. "I can identify every single person in these photos but this one." She jammed her finger into the glass again. "That Junior Epic photo is of the year I read about, when Farnaka set the Junior Epic Medal record."

"I thought you said he didn't compete in the Epic Games," Pretia said.

"That's what I *thought*," Vera agreed. "But he did. That's him, right there. Look."

Pretia glanced at the Epic photo. The guy Vera was pointing at certainly did look a lot like the person in the earlier, Junior Epic photograph.

"But he's not in any of the record books as an Epic Athlete. Only a Junior Epic," Vera said.

"Maybe he got injured."

Vera paused, considering this. "That would make sense. But I'm certain this is the guy with the Junior Epic record. And he's the one I'm going to beat."

"Well, if that's the plan," Pretia said, "you better take it easy tonight. It's a big day tomorrow."

"Wrong," Vera said. "There's something else we need to do."

"Please, please don't say training," Pretia begged.

"Not training—visualizing. I borrowed two Mensa Crowns from Satis so we can visualize our swim trials. Let's go. I think the common room is empty."

"Vera, come on," Pretia pleaded. "Give me a break."

"We don't have time for breaks," Vera insisted.

Pretia knew better than to argue with her friend. She only hoped that Vera would be so distracted by her own visualization that she wouldn't notice Pretia's exhausted mind drifting off.

In the morning, the Temple of Dreams was unusually silent. Vera had disappeared before daybreak for whatever last-minute preparation she felt she needed. Pretia walked down the halls. Her housemates were absorbed in their pregame preparations. Some were visualizing using Mensa Crowns and other devices. Some were listening to music. Others were in deep consultation with their Grana Books. Best friends were keeping their distance, eyeing each other mistrustfully, as if a smile might cost them a spot on the squad. No one spoke over breakfast.

Eventually the hunting horn sounded, summoning the students to the pool. Pretia slipped into a long line of stone-faced Dreamers heading for the trials. They were joined by a throng of Realists who were equally serious and silent.

Pretia loved the pool. She loved the way it seemed to appear magically when you least expected it, when you thought you'd descended too deep into the cavern and had somehow become lost. She loved the towering walls that kept the water perfectly cool and the echoes that bounced around the massive room. But today it did nothing to soothe her.

When everyone had assembled, Janos blasted his whistle. The kids fell silent. "Lavinia will explain how our trials work," he said. "I ask only that you compete with grace and dignity. Honor yourself and your house, and respect your competitors."

Then Lavinia stepped forward. "In addition to our Epic Elites, we will be taking ten swimmers to Phoenis. Those trying out will be divided into heats of ten. The race is an individual medley—a lap of each of the four swimming strokes." A murmur rippled through the stands. Lavinia held up her hand for silence.

"The top five in each heat will progress to a following round. Then five from following heats will progress until we are down to ten swimmers. Three heats to show us your stuff. When we are done with swimming, we will move to the end of the pool for diving. Since two of our Epic Elites are diving in Phoenis, we only have room for two more divers on the squad."

"Stop reminding us," Adira groaned.

Pretia didn't pay much attention to the rules for those trials. She had no intention of trying out for diving.

Of the roughly one hundred Ecrof students, eighty had signed up for swim trials. The Epic Elites, of course, were exempt. Some of the older students had grown too specialized in sports besides track and swimming to revert. Others had physical challenges that allowed them to excel in certain areas but prevented them from taking to the water. And some, like Rovi, understood that they had little chance of making the team and didn't want to waste their energy.

The names of the eighty students were put into a hat and drawn into eight races of ten. Pretia found herself in a heat with Myra. They were to swim fourth.

Pretia put on her swimsuit and her long swim coat that enveloped her like a sleeping bag to help her stay warm and went to chat with Rovi, who was sitting close to the pool. He reached into his backpack and pulled out a few packages of Power Snacks. "So do you think she's going to do it?" He gestured at the pool with his snacks. Vera was on one of the starting blocks, ready to race.

"I think she'll make the team," Pretia said.

"What about breaking the record held by the guy no one's ever heard of?" Rovi asked.

Pretia watched Vera touch her hands to the block. "Seems difficult. But who knows. When Vera's determined to do something . . ."

"Let's hope so," Rovi said. "We'll never hear the end of it if she doesn't make it."

The race started. Vera cut through the water like a seal, graceful and elegant. Her strokes were controlled. She didn't waste any energy. Pretia felt a little sorry for the swimmers in her wake, Vera was so far ahead. After two lengths she had already dusted the competition. On the backstroke she put another half a pool length between herself and the second-place finisher. "Whoa," Rovi said, "if she keeps this up, what's his name's record doesn't stand a chance."

Despite the statement she'd made in the pool, Vera clearly wasn't pleased with her victory. She toweled off quickly and marched away to cool down and prepare to swim again.

After Vera, Nassos was the only member of the second-year class to make it out of his heat until it was Pretia's turn. When she'd finished a brief warm-up on the pool deck, she took to the starting block. The water welcomed her when she dove in. She found her rhythm, and her breathing came easily. At the wall, her turn was efficient. At the end of two laps she felt herself tire but reached down for another reserve of energy. When she touched the wall after her final lap, she was surprised to see she'd finished second.

As she pulled herself out of the pool, she felt the entire school staring at her. She knew they were wondering why she hadn't split herself.

She did her best to ignore these questioning looks and just went about her business of cooling down.

The first round of heats concluded. Forty students moved on. Cyril had also qualified for the next round.

Rovi joined Pretia on the pool deck where she was keeping warm. "Only two more rounds," Rovi said, slapping Pretia on the back. "You got this."

"We'll see," Pretia said. She felt confident, but she knew not to be complacent.

Vera's heat went first again in the next round. Everything seemed to go wrong from the start. She slipped off the board, resulting in a graceless and inefficient entry that cost her time. Instead of refocusing her energy, she seemed to panic, chopping at the water with uncharacteristically frantic strokes. Rovi and Pretia got as close to the water as they could, chanting Vera's name.

Vera's struggle was evident. She was swimming desperately.

"What if she doesn't make it?" Pretia whispered.

"Come on, Vera," Rovi shouted.

Pretia cupped her hands over her mouth. "Let's go, Vera," she cheered.

Vera touched the wall and threw off her goggles to look at the clock, then heaved a frustrated but relieved sigh. She'd squeaked into fifth place by a split second. She was into the final round.

Then it was Pretia's turn. This time when she dove, her movements felt clunkier. The water felt like a burden, something she had to battle. She pulled through it like it was mud. She could sense several of her competitors ahead of her, and could tell she was losing ground. She tapped the wall and surfaced. She, too, had finished fifth, but barely. It hardly felt like a victory.

Nassos, Cyril, Vera, and Pretia were the only second termers to make it to the final round of twenty that would determine the team.

Pretia found Vera recovering in the whirlpool. Her face was stern and stony. "Don't," she said when she saw Pretia.

"Listen, I struggled, too. You're going to have to relax and let it go," Pretia said.

"Let what go?"

"You can't be perfect every time," Pretia continued.

"Not *all* of us can split ourselves, Pretia," Vera snapped.

Pretia's eyes widened in anger. "For your information, I'm working just as hard as you are. I haven't split myself once today," she said. "But maybe I should."

Vera punched the water, then exhaled sharply. "I'm sorry," she said. "Do whatever you need to do to qualify." Then she dunked her head, letting Pretia know the conversation was over.

There was a long break before the final heat, to allow for recovery.

Pretia wrapped herself in her warm jacket and watched as Vera emerged from the whirlpool, where she'd been soaking her muscles, and started to pace nervously. "I can't even visualize," she said to Pretia as she passed by.

"Maybe that's because you're ready," Pretia said. "Maybe your mind already knows what it needs to do."

"Maybe," Vera said. She sounded less certain than usual.

A blast from Janos's whistle echoed off the cavern walls. Vera snapped to attention. "Showtime," she said.

Vera and Pretia got on their starting blocks for their final heat. They were drawn next to each other. To Pretia's surprise, Eshe had also made it to the last round. Before they bent down, Pretia reached out and took Vera's hand. "You got this," she said.

Vera met her eye. This time she looked like her old self. "I know."

The starter's bell rang. Pretia was off the block in an instant. She felt confident and in control. She breathed effortlessly. The water enveloped her, cool and silken. She felt like she could shape it as she wished. But she could sense something else as well, a current in the pool that was carrying her forward.

Pretia allowed this current to take her. The water moved her. It was as if she had to exert no effort at all.

And then it happened. Without her bidding. She watched herself swim away. She pulled away from Vera and Eshe. She passed three powerful seventh-year swimmers.

She watched herself move into the final turn.

Then she saw Vera pop up and take a breath and notice what was happening. She saw her friend lose her rhythm.

Pretia's heart sank. She hesitated. She couldn't take Vera's place on the team. She couldn't be the one to trample Vera's ambitious dreams. She had to restrain her shadow self. She had to pull herself back. She let go of her drive to swim her best and in an instant her selves collided, not up ahead where her shadow self was preparing to win the race, but farther back in the pool, where the physical Pretia had been left behind.

She finished last.

Vera had finished fifth.

Eshe was fourth.

Pretia climbed out of the pool and hugged her friend.

"What happened?" Vera asked. "You were . . . You were . . ." she stammered.

Pretia wouldn't let her finish. "You did it," she cried. "You made it! You're going to the Junior Epics."

Vera beamed, but then the smile vanished. "But you didn't," she said. "You . . . lost." She gave Pretia a funny look. "You were winning and then you lost. You shouldn't have done that."

"What do you mean?"

"Is this about what I told you? About Julius? Are you afraid to split yourself?"

"No," Pretia said. She wasn't going to tell Vera the truth about why she'd lost the race.

"You shouldn't worry about splitting yourself," Vera said. "Even if Julius leads a stupid protest. I mean, I get how you feel. Everyone looks at me strangely, too—at least every *Realist*. They think I'm some sort of freak for turning out to be a Dreamer."

"You are *not* a freak. You're the most talented athlete I know," Pretia said.

"That's how I feel about you," Vera said, beaming. "And you need to use that talent! Even if you had beaten me, I'd have your back," she continued. "Do what you have to do from now on. Promise?"

"Promise," Pretia agreed. She told herself there would be a time when she had to rely on her shadow self, and she would draw on her remarkable grana then. But she wouldn't use it to deny her best friend.

Despite Vera's encouragement, though, a lingering doubt was forming at the back of her mind. Was there truly something wrong with her power, something scary like Castor had suggested back at Ponsit? Something worth protesting?

◆

8

R O V I

A TRIAL

ROVI SLID ON THE MEMORY MASTER AND pushed it into place on his forehead. Then he lay back on the ground under the Tree of Ecrof. Each time he used the device, he felt as if his father were with him, watching over him and helping him.

The first day of track trials had arrived. He had a few more hours to hone his skills—ten skills, in fact.

That afternoon's events were pole vault, high jump, discus, shot put, and javelin. The 100-meter sprint, the hurdles, the 400-meter sprint, the 1,500 meters (the Epic Mile), and the long jump were scheduled for the second day. It was the first day that had Rovi worried.

He looked up at the shimmering leaves of the tree, wishing his father could see how healthy it was. If only his father could somehow know that Rovi had played a major part in saving the very tree Pallas Myrios was falsely accused of trying to kill. It was too bad his father never knew that he'd been restored to being a Dreamer, and hopefully a celebrated one.

Rovi closed his eyes. He needed to concentrate on the moves recorded by the Memory Master. He needed to revisit and absorb every last moment to prepare, if he was going to return to Phoenis as a hero of House Somni. Rovi's best chance of escaping his past as a

Star Stealer was making the team, and he was determined to do so.

Once more Rovi ran through the discus event on the Memory Master, watching himself spin and let go at the perfect moment. After discus he moved to shot put and then to javelin.

He watched himself go through the javelin again. He could feel his muscles mimicking the recording in the headband. He felt himself let go. He watched the javelin fly. It seemed good. But was it good enough? His grana was strongest in his feet, guiding him across obstacle courses and around tracks with hardly any input from his mind. It allowed him to jump well, perfectly judging where he needed to plant himself to take off in any of the jumping events. But his grana was less helpful with throwing. He could throw decently, but he knew his skills didn't match up to those of his older and stronger classmates. He was especially concerned about the competition from a few of the older girls, who were surprisingly slight but through some remarkable combination of talent, timing, and coordination could hurl the discus and the shot twice as far as Rovi.

Focus. His mind was wandering. He needed to stay within the activities recorded by the Memory Master and not worry about outside things. He squeezed his eyes shut, willing himself to concentrate and not panic. He had to master his fears.

Once more he ran through the javelin. Then discus. Then shot put. And then again.

"Rovi?"

His eyes snapped open. Pretia stood over him. In fact, the entire stadium was filled with kids. How long had he been lost deep inside the Memory Master?

"Were you asleep?" Pretia asked.

"No," he said, leaping to his feet. "I was training."

"Well, it's game time," Pretia said. Her matter-of-fact tone made Rovi's heart race faster.

All around him, his fellow competitors were warming up. Rovi took a few laps at a slow pace before Cleopatra Volis blew her whistle, silencing the students. "The rules for this are simple. The ten athletes with the best cumulative score go to Phoenis. All scores count. That said, if your scores today are so low we don't believe you can make them up tomorrow, you will be dropped."

At this Rovi's heart sank even further. Why did all the throwing events have to come today?

"First is the shot put," Cleopatra announced. "We will throw by class in age order. Seventh years first. Your scores will be posted on the leaderboard." She pointed to the middle of the field where a large board bearing all the students' names was standing in front of the magnificent Tree of Ecrof. "My suggestion is not to focus on your score or that of your competitors. Focus on your own performance. Seventh years, you have twenty minutes to warm up."

"Why can't it just be a mile or a steeplechase?" Rovi grumbled.

Of course, it had to be Vera who overheard him. "Because the decathlon is the most challenging test of all-around skill. It's said that the athlete who wins the decathlon at the Epic Games is the nation's greatest athlete. In the Junior Epic Games, Farnaka Stellus—"

"I don't want to hear any more about Farnaka Stellus," Rovi moaned. He stormed away to visualize in the hopes that he could summon some new throwing power he hadn't felt before.

He flopped down again in the shade of the Tree of Ecrof and closed his eyes. But the peace he'd found earlier wouldn't come. His mind wouldn't settle. He couldn't see himself throwing that shot any more than he could imagine himself flying.

In no time Pretia was at his side. "I'm fine," he said before she even had time to ask.

"It doesn't look like it." She lay down next to him. "It's amazing," she said.

"What is?" Rovi groaned. His pulse was racing, his palms were sweating, and his stomach was doing double-flips. Nothing felt amazing.

"The tree, silly," Pretia said. "Look."

Rovi squinted upward.

"I mean *really* look. It's so beautiful."

Rovi exhaled. He felt his tense body loosen slightly as he peered up into the towering canopy of the majestic tree. The branches made the sunlight into spiderwebs, and the leaves were glittering with their strange silvery light. The tree was lush and thick.

"We did that, Rovi. We saved the tree."

"I know," he said.

"Well, that's got to be more difficult than anything you have to do today, right? Something really deadly could have happened in the cavern with the strangler fig last year," Pretia continued. "We risked everything to save the school and ourselves."

"And you could have lost your grana," Rovi said, remembering his best friend trapped inside the deadly tree.

"Or you could have fallen in the cavern," Pretia added, reminding Rovi of the terrifying moment he lost his nerve when hanging from a tree branch over a deadly fall. "After that, today will be a walk in the park."

"Maybe," Rovi said. "But I'm not ready. I thought I was, but I'm not." Rovi could hear the anxiety in his own voice. His mind was racing. What if he didn't make the team? What if he let his father down? What if everyone thought he was a Star Stealer forever?

"You've got this," Pretia said. "You've been working so hard."

Rovi stopped and whirled around so they were face-to-face. "What does it feel like?"

"What?"

"When you split yourself."

Pretia glanced around as if someone might be eavesdropping. "It's like nothing else. When it happens, it just happens."

"I know that. I'm asking what it *feels* like."

"Well," Pretia said slowly. "It feels like . . . like I could be any-where watching myself compete. As if it's not me competing."

"I wish it wasn't me competing," Rovi said.

"That's not true. You want to do this."

"I want to go to the Junior Epics. I don't want to go through the trials."

"You're thinking too much," Pretia said. "It's just throwing and running and jumping."

"I guess," Rovi grumbled.

"You've done all these things hundreds of times."

"I mean, with Issa and my Star Stealer gang, yeah. We were always running away from the guards and jumping over things in the market. That's not the same."

"It sort of is," Pretia insisted.

"No—" Rovi began. But then something occurred to him. He held out his hand, imagining it contained the heavy, round shot. He thought of its weight. "You know, sometimes Issa and I would steal stuff from the market and get chased by the guards. Then the safest thing to do was to throw whatever we'd stolen as far away as we could so it wouldn't be associated with us. It's kind of like—"

"Shot put," Pretia finished for him. "You see, it *is* the same. Just imagine that you and your friend—"

"Issa."

"That you're throwing something to Issa."

"Okay," Rovi said. The idea was taking shape in his head. "We got a moonfruit once, a heavy one. I had to throw it to him far over the heads of the guards."

"Exactly. Just imagine that and you'll be fine." Pretia gave him a high five. And together they went to line up.

But they weren't in the stadium; they were in the noisy Alexan-drine Market in Phoenis. And the voices of Rovi's fellow students cheering each other on—those were the peddlers calling out their wares and the Phoenicians haggling in return.

Someone was calling his name, but Rovi didn't turn, didn't blink. He kept the vision in his head.

He and Issa had stolen the moonfruit, a dense purple globe imported from the chilly Winterlands, when Rovi was first taken in by the Star Stealers. As Rovi had palmed the fruit, three Phoenician guards had descended on him at once. He'd dashed through the market, not wanting to lose the prize. Then he'd caught sight of Issa far across the plaza. With all his might, he'd thrown the moonfruit to his friend. It had flown—sailed—right into Issa's waiting hands. As he caught it, Issa had raised his free hand in the Star Stealer salute, arm extended toward the sky, palm up, fingers together as if plucking a star from the heavens. Then he'd taken off, luring the guards after him.

Again, Rovi heard his name, but he still didn't break stride. He didn't even know who was talking.

"What's with him?"

As if from afar, he heard Pretia answer, "He's in the Sandlands."

Over and over, he ran through the memory until it was time to throw.

When he took the shot, it wasn't a heavy ball but a moonfruit. He didn't heave it across the field but across the Alexandrine Plaza. When he was done, he raised an arm straight up to the stars as Issa had done.

He heard his classmates applaud. He didn't look at his result. He just hurried away from his schoolmates. Next was discus. He needed to create a new memory.

For discus he conjured the image of when he'd stolen a rich, fatty chop from the best butcher in Phoenis and thrown it to Amrav.

For javelin he imagined spearing a fish in the river Durna.

Pole vault and high jump were slightly easier for Rovi. But still he kept up his mental game, imagining he was escaping from the

Phoenician guards by catapulting himself onto the second-story arched walkway around the Alexandrine Plaza.

Only when he'd finished his final event did he check the leaderboard. Of the eighty students trying out, Rovi sat in twenty-fifth place, one spot ahead of Pretia, and one behind Castor. Vera was comfortably in tenth place.

It wasn't a total triumph, but better than he'd expected when he entered the stadium that morning. And his best events were yet to come.

Pretia and Vera babbled excitedly as they headed back to the Temple of Dreams. Rovi kept his distance. In twenty-four hours, the trials would be over and he'd be on his way to Phoenis if and only if he stayed within himself. And to do that, he couldn't afford any distractions. He needed to keep away from his fellow Dreamers. He needed to stay in the mindset of a Star Stealer.

Star Stealers did things that were forbidden.

Star Stealers played by their own rules.

While everyone else was at dinner, Rovi snuck into the hidden pool just as he'd once snuck into the Royal Baths back in Phoenis. He cooled himself in the water, then loosened his limbs in the natural whirlpool. When he was done, he darted to the Temple of Dreams, entered the kitchen through a back door, stole leftover food, and snuck back to the empty Halls of Process. He knew he couldn't risk his old hideout in his father's lab because it was now Satis's office. Instead, he stretched out in the dim interior of the Granology classroom and napped until the bedtime horn sounded.

He knew exactly where he needed to sleep—outside, under the stars. He would flop down below the Tree of Ecrof and pretend its towering canopy was the Draman Bridge over the river Durna, below which he'd slept during his years as a Star Stealer. For one more day he'd inhabit the mind of a Star Stealer. And when he was done—if all went according to plan—he'd once more resume life as a Dreamer, more confident than ever.

When he woke in the morning, all doubts about his performance had left his mind. Rovi was ready. Five events and he was going to nail each one of them. He didn't need to win every one, but he needed to be solid.

He entered the cafeteria to find the atmosphere even tenser than the day before.

"Where have you been?" Vera asked. "Everyone's looking for you."

"Preparing."

"Did you sleep outside? Because I hear that some athletes—" Vera said. But Rovi cut her off with a raised hand.

"You know when you're so ready to do something, you don't need to talk about it anymore? That's where I am."

Vera rolled her eyes. "Whatever you say, Rovi."

"I'm sure you're ready, too," Rovi said. "You just need to calm down."

"That's the worst advice ever!" Vera sounded furious.

"It isn't," Rovi said. "Just trust me."

He ate a decent breakfast. He changed into a fresh set of gear, headed for the track, and didn't listen to the chatter about the twenty students who had been dropped for the final day of trials.

Rovi had a single goal, a sole focus as he entered the stadium. He was there to do his best. And if he did, he would make the squad. He couldn't worry about others' performances. He could only take care of himself.

He ran the hurdles as if he were leaping over peddlers' blankets at the Alexandrine Plaza.

He did the long jump as if he were leaping as far as he could into the river Durna.

He ran the 400 as if he were being chased by Phoenician guards from the Upper to the Lower City.

He did the 1,500—his best event, the Epic Mile—as if leading the guards on a chase from the Tile Palace in the center of Phoenis to the Moon Palace at the edge of the desert.

By the last event, he had moved up the leaderboard into the top twenty along with Castor, Pretia, and Vera. The other students were giving him space. He heard his name spoken in whispers. He could feel the speculation mounting.

The twenty leading runners would be split into two heats for the marquee race: the 100. There was so little separating them that each of them still had a chance to make the Junior Epic Squad.

Rovi was drawn in the second heat.

He did everything he could to stay within himself. But his excitement was building. He was so close. The first group of runners, including Vera, positioned themselves in the starting blocks.

If he ran well, he would make it. He would represent House Somni. One race, just a few seconds long, would determine his chance at Junior Epic Glory. He could almost see it. Now his mind began to spin. He could feel himself pulled back to the present. No longer was it possible for him to maintain the illusion that he was leagues away in Phoenis preparing for one last mad sprint from the guards. He was at Ecrof. He was in the Panathletic Stadium. He was about to run the most important race of his life.

The first heat was over in a flash. Vera had outsprinted her opponents. Rovi watched her cross the finish line and try to restrain her joy that she'd almost definitely made the squad.

He stepped up to the line. He was drawn on an outside lane— less than optimal. Pretia and Castor were in the middle.

Frantically Rovi tried to organize his mind. He tried to take himself out of the race. He tried to put himself in Phoenis or anywhere else that would distract him from the importance of what was about to happen. He tried to conjure the image of Issa standing near the finish line urging him on.

The starter's horn sounded.

Rovi abandoned his imaginary pursuits and threw his faith in his grana, depending on it to lead him. He took off quickly. His gait was even, his strides smooth. But everyone else was running well, too. He knew without looking that Pretia was going to step outside of herself. This was her event, after all. And he knew better than to check in on his competitors. He'd made that mistake last year in his first race of House Somni, when he'd looked over his shoulder to see how far ahead he was and lost his lead.

Nevertheless, without looking, he could feel what was going on around him. He could sense it. And he knew he needed to push himself harder.

He had a few more strides. That's all. One last effort.

And then he saw him—his father as he'd been before he had his grana stolen. His father racing around the Panathletic Stadium with Rovi, letting Rovi win, encouraging him. His father, the important Dreamer he'd once been, not the messy Somnium addict Rovi had known at the end.

That's all it took. Rovi found that final reserve to take him across the finish line.

When he slowed to a stop, he doubled over, hands on his knees. Castor was next to him. They'd finished neck and neck.

Rovi was almost too afraid to check the board. He felt his heart in his throat. He was about to check his result when he was tackled by not one but two bodies. Pretia and Vera pulled him down, and together, all three rolled around on the track with excitement, a tangle of arms and legs. It took Rovi a moment to figure out what was happening.

"We made it!" Pretia and Vera chorused.

"We?" Rovi said when he could talk. "We?"

"Yes," Vera said. "The three of us."

Rovi turned at the sound of a voice outside their group of three. Eshe Sonos had her fists in the air. "We *all* made it! And Vera and I are the only athletes to be selected for track *and* swimming."

Rovi and Pretia laughed. "Of course," Rovi said. "That's so perfect."

Eshe and Vera glanced at each other. "What's so funny?" Vera said.

Eshe also looked confused. "I don't know."

Rovi felt as if his chest might explode with joy. "I need to see for myself," he said, disengaging himself from his friends to go look at the leaderboard.

Vera was in third place. Pretia in sixth. And Rovi Myrios, a former Star Stealer, in tenth. He was going to the Junior Epic Games. He threw his fists in the air and let out a loud whoop.

Then he noticed Castor staring at the board, too.

Rovi dropped his fists and looked for Castor's name. There it was, right below Rovi's. Number eleven.

"Sorry," Rovi said. "You *almost* made it."

Castor, for once, was silent. He hung his head. Rovi could see tears at the corners of his eyes. Suddenly he didn't feel like celebrating. Suddenly he actually felt bad for Castor. Imagine coming that close and failing. Imagine falling short in front of your father. Rovi felt a stab of pain in his heart.

Now Janos was blowing his burled-wood whistle. The students assembled in front of him. Rovi watched Castor slip off to the back.

"Congratulations, Junior Epics," Janos bellowed. "As you can see from the leaderboard, we have an impressive team heading to Phoenis. And as you can also see, there are two students who qualified both on the track and in the pool, Eshe Sonos and Vera Renovo. You two are the pride of both Ecrof and Alkebulan."

Eshe held up her hand for a high five that Vera was slow to return.

"Overachievers cost me my spot," Castor grumbled. "It's not fair they get to compete in both track *and* swimming."

"It's not a question of fair," Eshe said. "It's a question of talent. Right, Vera?"

◆

Rovi tried not to laugh as Vera rolled her eyes dramatically and attempted to detach herself from Eshe.

"I'll tell you what else isn't fair," Castor snapped. "Pretia and her *talent*. It's ridiculous that she's even going to Phoenis, since she won't be able to split herself when she gets there."

"What do you mean?" Rovi asked.

Castor glowered at him. "You'll see."

"Quiet!" Janos said. "Junior Epics, you will return to your houses and pack your things. We depart for Phoenis tonight."

"Tonight!" the entire team chorused at once.

Rovi blinked. It was happening. And it was happening fast.

The selected Dreamers raced toward the Temple of Dreams. Virgil, who'd made the diving squad, babbled about the new dive he was going to debut in Phoenis. Cyril and Nassos had both been chosen, too, giving the second-year Ecrof class the highest number of Junior Epic Squad members.

Vera chattered incessantly the entire way back to the Dreamers' house, anticipating what events she needed to get selected for at the games in order to win the most medals. Rovi stayed quiet, thinking about bringing honor to the Sandlands and to the memory of his father.

He would show the world he was a Dreamer once and for all.

And yet he hadn't simply been a Dreamer during the trials. Without the memories of his life as a Star Stealer, he'd never have succeeded in making the team. His past was part of his history. But he feared he would have to put that past behind him when he returned to Phoenis.

9

PRETIA

A CHALLENGE

BEFORE NIGHTFALL, THE STUDENTS CLIMBED into two boats and were rowed to the ship. Janos, Satis Dario, Cleopatra Volis, Lavinia Lux, and Sonya Pin, the diving coach, were already on board.

"Welcome, Junior Epics," Janos said. "Get ready for the most exciting adventure of your lives. We will sail for the coast of Chaldis, then drive overnight through the Sandlands and on into Phoenis. Try to relax and get as much sleep as possible."

The ship pulled out of the harbor, then swung northeast, away from Cora. Pretia shaded her eyes and stared toward the western horizon where the sun was dyeing the water pink and orange. She felt a hand on her shoulder. She looked up and saw her uncle.

"We expect great things from you," he said, beaming.

"Even though I'm competing for the rival house?" Pretia asked.

"You are also competing for Ecrof. Don't forget that."

"What about my parents?" Pretia said. "What if they try and stop me?"

"Ah," Janos said. "I was wondering if you would ask."

"What if they show up? What if they forbid . . ."

Janos put a second hand on her opposite shoulder and turned

Pretia away from the ship's railing. "Pretia, I acknowledge their concerns about why they didn't want you to compete. But you must understand one thing. Nothing would bring more disgrace to Epoca now than if they withdrew their daughter, the Child of Hope, from the Junior Epics."

"I hate that name," Pretia grumbled.

"In this case I think it will serve you well. Imagine if the Child of Hope were publicly removed from the Junior Epics. That would give the people the opposite of hope. Your name has been submitted by Ecrof and will be announced officially when we come to port tomorrow. You need to take pride in that."

"I'm trying to."

A dark look clouded Janos's face. "I don't like your attitude, Pretia. We expect our selected athletes to carry themselves with the confidence that comes from being selected. It is your duty to be confident in each and every thing you are going to face in Phoenis. This includes your parents, in the event that they grace the games. Can I trust in you to do this?"

"Yes," Pretia said. "Yes, you can." A wave of regret crashed over her at the mention of the king and queen. The way she had betrayed her parents by defying their wishes and running away still nagged at her.

"I've written to your parents again, to tell them about your selection. I'm sure they will be proud."

"Even though I ran away?"

"Even though you ran away. You will have to face them someday, however. Probably sooner than you'd like."

"I'll just prove myself on the field."

Janos shook his head firmly. "That won't be enough. You need to explain to them your reasons for defying them, not simply by winning medals but by demonstrating that your reasons transcended a self-indulgent desire to compete."

"And I can't just do that by winning?"

"Another athlete would be able to rely on her performance to make a statement. But your parents will require more than that. They have staked so much on your birth. You owe it to them and yourself to articulate why you felt you needed to represent Ecrof and the Dreamers at the Junior Epic Games. When you are able to do that, you will fully understand who you are."

Pretia's heart sank. The idea of facing her parents filled her with anxiety. They were so confident that they knew who she was and why she existed.

"My parents think my only purpose is to bring a new hope to Epoca."

"And you don't feel that way?" Janos asked.

"No," Pretia muttered. "But it's so hard to contradict them."

Janos let out a great laugh. "You have already contradicted them, with your actions. All you have to do is back it up with an explanation."

Pretia shuddered. Her reasons were selfish. She couldn't tell her parents that. She couldn't tell her parents anything.

"Don't worry," Janos said kindly, "your parents will understand. You have distinguished yourself in a very elite field. They will recognize this. Remember, you searched deep in yourself before you chose to come to Ecrof this year."

Pretia couldn't meet his eye. She *had* looked deep inside herself. But she knew she'd run away to Ecrof simply because she'd wanted to, not because of any important or profound reason. She just couldn't imagine a life without sports.

"Favorite niece, you will need to do it again to continue to find the confidence in your decisions. You bring a special talent to the games, and I cannot wait for the people of Epoca to witness it."

"Not everyone feels the same way," Pretia said.

"That is because not everyone understands. People often fear what they don't understand, right?" The ship hit a wave and bucked,

◆

knocking Pretia into her uncle. "For instance, I believe you witnessed me doing something last year that you didn't understand. Isn't that right?" He stooped to catch her eye when she looked away from him.

Slowly Pretia nodded. She remembered her final encounter with Janos at Ecrof last year, when she'd seen him standing in front of a bust of Hurell, the Fallen God, praying over a large ceremonial flame. At least, she thought that's what she'd seen.

"There is more to every story, Pretia. Just like there is more to you splitting yourself than some incomprehensible power that makes you a better athlete. You see, Hurell, before he turned, was closest to the Realists—more than any other god. He embodies our principles. We understand that only through embracing suffering can we rise above it. We are a practical house. We accept the reality this world presents." Janos's voice grew stern. "Things are not always easy. You already know that. To make peace with the suffering we will encounter, we must elevate and praise it, not allow it to control us. Do you understand? We are guided by our fears into strength."

"Sort of."

"Embrace what most scares you. Relish the pain that comes your way and it will cease to be pain. These were the lessons of Hurell. And don't be quick to judge or fear what you don't understand, because you would not want others to do that to you. Keep these things in mind and you will do well in Phoenis and beyond, favorite niece."

"I'm your only niece," Pretia reminded him, as she often did.

"And you are also one of my star athletes," he said. "Try to enjoy the voyage. The games will consume you soon enough."

Janos's words soothed Pretia. She joined her teammates in races up the masts and in diving contests when the boat anchored in the late afternoon. She raised her voice to the stars for the Ecrof fight song before bed and slept dreaming not of her parents' anger as she'd worried, but of racing around a track in the Sandlands in front of a massive crowd who didn't care that she was the crown princess.

In the early morning, the shoreline of Chaldis was already visible on the horizon. By the time the squad had finished breakfast, the ship's crew was dropping anchor, and a long boat had rowed out to carry everyone to the port.

Chaldis was at the eastern edge of the Sandlands, a bustling port town filled with commerce and transport. There were boats laden with imports and exports, as well as ferries to the islands and even mainland Epoca.

Two luxurious vans with fully reclining sleepers were waiting outside the harbor. The kids clambered on, followed by the Trainers. Pretia pressed her nose against the window and watched Chaldis pass by—a busy, crowded city of small cobbled streets, colorful markets, and clay-colored buildings with purple and blue turrets.

Soon they were on a long road that led from the city into the desert. The rich, yellow sand rolled away in all directions. There were flat areas and areas made up of hundreds of small hills. The wind had carved small textured ripples into the sand that gave the illusion of thousands of black lines. At night, the setting sun dyed the sand orange, then umber, until it was swallowed by shadow.

In the morning Pretia was woken by the van's wheels rumbling over a rough patch of road at the same time that she felt someone grab her arm and tug excitedly. "Wake up!"

Pretia rubbed the sleep from her eyes. Rovi's face was inches from her own and he was chattering excitedly as he pointed out the window. "Look quick or you'll miss it," he exclaimed.

Pretia glanced out the window, her vision still blurry with sleep.

Her eyes settled just in time for her to catch a glimpse of a magnificent palace crowned with white and silver domes standing at a distance in the desert.

"That's the Moon Palace," Rovi cried.

"We're here?" Pretia asked groggily.

"We're here!" Rovi confirmed.

Pretia yawned, momentarily wishing to go back to sleep. But then she saw the city emerging in front of her. Her mouth dropped open.

Phoenis rising from the desert was unlike anything she'd ever seen before. The city was golden—a bright hill shining in the brilliant desert sun. All around it was a wall. Beyond the wall was the city, with its neighborhoods stacked on top of one another until they rose to a plateau.

"Up there," Rovi said, pointing toward the highest point, "that's the Upper City. That's where the Temple of Arsama and the Tile Palace are. Down here, where we enter, is the Lower City, which is not as nice, of course. But that's my old home. Back when, you know, I didn't have a real home."

The Lower City seemed nice enough to Pretia. More than nice. It was stunning. There were golden buildings everywhere, or buildings that looked made out of gold.

"It's the crystals in the sand that make them glitter like that," Rovi explained when she asked. "If you get caught as a Star Stealer, you get sent to make sand bricks. The worse your crime, the longer you have to stay away and make bricks. It's not so bad, really. Eventually they send you back to the streets."

"Were *you* ever caught stealing?" Pretia asked.

"Never!" Rovi replied proudly. "I was too fast. I was one of the few Star Stealers who never got caught. That's why they called me Swiftfoot."

The van rumbled through the wondrous chaos of the Lower City. Purple and blue silk fabrics fluttered everywhere. All around were small temples, crowded markets, and people cooking delicious-looking food in outdoor stalls.

Slowly they wound their way up and up through the narrow streets, which gave Pretia time to look at everything. There were street performers and musicians, artists creating sand paintings, and living sculptures. They passed through gates, now and then catching sight of the river below.

Rovi leaned over Pretia and pointed out the window. The van was rolling over a bridge. "Down there by the river is where my old gang camps," he said. He craned his neck. "That's weird."

"What?"

"I don't see any sign of the camp. Even when we clear out during the day, there's usually some cooking stuff or blankets or—" He half stood in his seat to get a better look, then toppled into the window.

"Maybe they moved," Pretia said. Her mind was elsewhere.

They were approaching the Upper City, and she began to see banners advertising the games, expressing support for House Somni and House Relia and praising the eight elite academies, including Ecrof.

Pretia's excitement began to grow. This was actually happening. She was going to compete!

The van rumbled over a massive bridge and passed through an ornate gate decorated with a mosaic of hundreds of thousands of glittering tiles. They were in the Upper City.

Pretia gasped at the sight of so many tiles everywhere. The entire city seemed be awash in color, glinting and glimmering in the bright sun. She widened her eyes to take in the vaulted horseshoe arches stacked atop one another, crowned with blue and purple turrets. There were patterns and designs everywhere, wonderful symmetries and stars made out of millions of shimmering tiles.

Pretia pressed her nose harder into the window to get a better look.

"If you think this is something, just wait until you see the Tile Palace," Rovi said.

"I can't wait," Pretia said.

The van had reached the plateau of the Upper City, which was much wider and vaster than Pretia had thought from below. Up top she could see that the city stretched out of sight in all directions, but from where she was sitting, neither of Phoenis's most famed land-marks, the Tile Palace or the Temple of Arsama, were visible.

From the angle of the fiery sun, Pretia could tell they were head-ing west. Everywhere she looked she saw signs of the upcoming games. Vendors were selling T-shirts for the rival houses and also the rival schools. There were imitation medals and trophies, flags, scarves, stuffed Realist Owls, and plush versions of the Dreamer Peg-asus. Paper vendors hawked programs and brochures.

The van slowed to a stop at the foot of a towering arch that was blocked by a massive iron gate. The driver leaned out and conferred with a guard who wore a bright red hat. The guard nodded and waved at someone out of sight. The large iron gate began to lift, and the van rolled through.

Pretia heard the gate fall into place behind her, but she didn't look back. She was too entranced by where she was: the Junior Epic Village.

The van headed up a straight road that divided the village in half. One side was decked out in blue, the other in purple. There were young athletes everywhere, running, jumping, stretching, spinning, and flipping.

"The competition," Vera said, leaning over Pretia to look out the window.

"We'll crush them," Eshe said with a grin.

"But they're also our teammates," Pretia said. "We're mainly competing for House Somni."

"Sure," Vera said. "But for ourselves, first and foremost."

"Vera, that's terrible," Pretia said.

"It's true, though," Vera said. "And anyway, the more I win, the better it is for the Dreamers and Ecrof. I mean, you're going to do whatever it takes to win your events, right?"

"Of course," Pretia said. "Why wouldn't I?"

Vera lowered her voice. "Because I suspect you restrained your-self at swim trials."

"I had my reasons," Pretia muttered.

"Don't worry about some silly protest," Vera said.

"Vera," Pretia said, "I'm here to win, and I'll do exactly what it takes to win."

"No matter what?"

"No matter what," Pretia assured her.

The van stopped. Janos, who had been sitting up front, stood. "All right, Team Ecrof. Welcome to the Junior Epic Village. This is a haven for athletes and athletes alone. No one from Phoenis or elsewhere can enter. No family members. No fans. Not even former athletes. This is your sanctuary away from the games. And you will obey the rules of the sanctuary. The girls will never trespass into the boys' tower and vice versa. All room doors are to remain unlocked at all times. No outsider visitors. No contraband. No sneaking around." Then he narrowed his eyes, taking in each student in turn. "No Dreamer will enter the Realist Village and no Realist will enter the Dreamer Village. Do you all understand?"

Murmurs of assent rippled through the van.

"Now, before we get out, I need to educate you about the Junior Epic Code," Janos continued. "No Ecrof athlete has ever violated this code. And no athlete of mine will be the first. If you do, you will be expelled both from the games and from Ecrof."

Pretia glanced at Rovi and Vera and saw identical horrified looks on their faces.

"Never are you to leave the athletic village or the venues. You are here for sports and only sports. This is not a place for your opinions and ideas. You compete. You win or you lose. You do it again. You are in Phoenis for the glory of sport and Epoca and not for your personal agendas. Am I clear?"

"Yes," the team chorused.

"When we exit this van, Dreamers and Realists will part ways, coming together at the various ceremonies and on the field and in the pool. You will have ten days to train and acclimate, followed by the opening ceremony and the parade of past Junior Epic Champions—something to which I imagine you all aspire."

Pretia could feel Vera literally vibrating with excitement at the mention of this parade.

"Good luck," Janos added. "Train hard. Compete harder. Honor your house, your school, and yourselves. And remember, never violate Junior Epic Code. Now go with grace!"

A cheer erupted as the kids rushed off the van. It had parked on a broad public concourse that divided the two sides of the village, which perfectly mirrored each other. The purple-festooned Dreamer enclave was to the left. The Realists went to the blue half of the village on the right.

Pretia, Rovi, Vera, and the rest of the Ecrof Dreamers headed for the welcome center, where they were assigned to one of two residential towers—vaulted structures that closely resembled traditional Phoenician architecture and rose higher than the rest of the village.

Pretia couldn't believe the extent of the village, her home for the next month. It was a literal city, with walkways and causeways, kiosks, an indoor and outdoor dining hall, a health center, a natatorium for swimming, a track for training, a media center for press conferences, a visualization center, a grana temple, and a quiet grove. At the center of it all was a scoreboard. Pretia paused in front of this when they passed. There were three categories: total medal count, academy medal count, and individual medal count. Right now, all of these stood at zero, evenly divided between House Somni and House Relia, the eight elite academies, and the entire pool of competitors, all of whose names were listed on the board.

There were athletes everywhere in the village, most of whom were wearing their school colors. Pretia proudly displayed her Ecrof green-and-gold-silk tracksuit as she strode to her tower flanked by her friends.

The Dreamer fight song blasted from speakers designed to look like Phoenis's signature turrets. Banners whipped and waved, welcoming the students. Pretia's heart swelled. There was a bounce in her step. She was a Dreamer. She was from Ecrof. She was here to win.

Vera and Pretia were in the West Tower, Rovi in the East. They said goodbye and promised to meet for lunch.

The girls took the stairs, up and up to a room on the top floor, where they found their names on the door. Vera rushed to the window. The view over the marvelous Junior Epic Village and into the heart of the Upper City of Phoenis was spectacular. "Look," Vera exclaimed.

Pretia followed the path of Vera's finger. A golden pyramid rose into the sky, its tip nearly puncturing the perfect blue heavens and pointing directly at the burning orb of the overhanging sun.

"The Temple of Arsama!"

The temple was remarkable, but something else had captured Pretia's attention. "Vera, check out what's on the beds."

Vera turned. Her eyes lit up. "Our gear!"

Together the girls tore into the huge duffels. Singlets and tank tops and running shorts and socks and tracksuits and jackets and hats and wristbands and swimsuits and swim caps and headbands and T-shirts and even several pairs of sneakers all in Dreamer purple spilled out. There were more clothes than they could imagine using in a year, let alone a month. Each item had that year's Junior Epic insignia on it—the Temple of Arsama in golden thread—as well as the Ecrof crest. Printed on the back of all the tops were their names: Praxis-Onera and Renovo. Even the sneakers bore their initials.

Vera seemed speechless for once as she sifted through the piles of gear, holding up each item like a holy relic.

The girls changed immediately, pulling on matching T-shirts and sweatpants. They laced up their sneakers and put on wristbands and headbands just for fun.

At the bottom of each bag they found a piece of paper listing the

◆

fifty events at that year's Junior Epic Games. Next to each event was a small box.

"We're supposed to check off the ones we want to compete in," Vera said. She grabbed a pen, and her hand flew wildly down the page.

"How many are you choosing?" Pretia asked.

"Well, I need ten medals," Vera said, tapping her pen on the paper. "And since there's a risk I won't medal in every event, I need to compete in at least thirteen to be safe. Possibly fifteen. And since I won't be selected for every event I choose, I figure I might as well mark . . ." She paused, clearly counting something out in her head. "Twenty."

"Twenty!" Pretia said.

"It's just enough," Vera said. "What about you?"

"I don't know." Pretia stared at the paper. She was good at sprints and jumping.

"Let's do a few together," Vera urged. "For sure the 4x400 relay. That's an important one, and I think it comes last. Four athletes on a team all from the same academy."

Pretia checked it.

"The marathon, too," Vera suggested. "I've heard they take the most competitors for that one."

Pretia checked it. Then she checked the 100, the 200, the high jump, and the long jump. She wrote her name on the paper.

"Let's go deliver these." Vera was already out the door. "I want to get mine in as early as possible."

Together they raced back down the stairs, passing Dreamers from other schools who were equally excited about their new gear.

Pretia felt as if she were floating. She smoothed her tracksuit jacket, making sure the Ecrof crest was clearly visible.

She could hear a few comments in passing as people noticed her name on the back of her jacket. But she only smiled and waved.

There was one thing she was certain of—she hadn't been selected for the squad because of her parents. Her parents hadn't even wanted her to be here.

Music blasted from speakers. Dreamers on the elevated walkways called down to teammates on the ground below. Everywhere Pretia turned, there were pickup soccer and basketball games. Kids were doing flips and handstands.

They found Rovi at the kiosk where they were supposed to drop off their selection sheets. He was talking to two boys from different academies whose kits identified them as coming from Aquiis, a school on the Rhodan Islands famed for training elite swimmers, and from Dynami on Mount Oly, renowned for middle- and long-distance runners. Like Pretia and Vera, they were all kitted out in their Junior Epic gear.

Rovi introduced his friends, Nevo from Aquiis and Max from Dynami.

"Tomorrow they're making event selections," Nevo said. He had a swimmer's build—powerful shoulders and muscular legs. His hair looked bleached by time in the sun. "What have you all put in for?"

Pretia listed her choices.

"I also put in for the 4x400," Rovi said. "Hopefully we can all race together."

"I'm sure Eshe put in for it as well," Pretia joked with a look at Vera.

"Why?" Vera asked.

Rovi just laughed, exchanging a glance with Pretia. "I applied for the 800 and the 1,500 races, too," he concluded.

"What about you?" Max asked Vera. Max was long and lean, like a distance runner, with tawny skin and startling blue eyes.

"Me? The marathon, the 400, the triple jump, the long jump, the high jump, the 100- and 200-meter freestyle and same for butterfly, the individual medley, the—"

"Whoa, whoa, whoa," Nevo said. "Do you have some sort of death wish?"

"Well," Vera said, "I'm going to break the record for most Junior Epic Medals."

"Doesn't your brother hold that record?" Max asked. "Julius Renovo is your brother, right?"

"He is," Vera said. "But he doesn't hold the record."

Pretia and Rovi rolled their eyes in unison. "Have you ever heard of Farnaka Stellus?" Rovi asked.

His new friends shook their heads.

As Vera opened her mouth to explain, Rovi nudged Pretia. "Let's explore," he said. "Or get some food."

"Yeah," Pretia echoed. "I think I've heard enough about Farnaka Stellus to last me a lifetime."

They left Vera talking to Nevo and Max and set off. There was so much to see in the Dreamer side of the village that Pretia and Rovi got turned around on their way to the dining hall and wound up on the Grand Concourse that divided their side from the Realists'.

It was like looking into a strange mirror, seeing their village reflected in an entirely different color palette. Pretia and Rovi stuck to the Dreamers' side as they walked down the wide boulevard. She could now see that both sides were lined with columns, the Dreamers' topped by their trademark Pegasus and the Realists' with owls.

"I can't believe we're here," Pretia said.

"Me neither. And I can't believe I'm back in Phoenis," Rovi said. "It's going to be so great to see my gang."

"You mean the Star Stealers," Pretia said uncertainly. She hadn't wanted to believe a word of what her parents had said about Star Stealers. But she couldn't help being nervous at the idea of meeting them. What if they were planning something dangerous?

"Yeah," Rovi said, "my friends. It's going to blow their minds when they see me race."

"Are Star Stealers allowed to watch the games?" Pretia asked.

"Well, Star Stealers aren't really *allowed* anywhere, but that's never stopped any of them, especially not Issa's gang. They're basically forbidden from the Upper City, but they'll be there. I'm sure of it."

Slightly farther up on the concourse, there was a commotion on the Realist side. A large group of athletes had congregated and seemed to be singing, dancing, and shooting blue smoke bombs into the air.

"Let's check that out," Pretia said.

As they approached they could see their rivals were holding signs. "It looks like some kind of pep rally," Rovi said.

"We should organize one, too," Pretia suggested.

"Totally—" Rovi began. But he stopped abruptly when they drew close enough to read the signs.

NOT ALL GRANA IS GOOD GRANA

REAL ATHLETES KEEP IT TOGETHER

ONLY CHEATERS SPLIT

"Is that . . ." Pretia began. "Is that about me?"

STOP THE SELF-SPLITTER

Pretia stared at the protesters openmouthed, feeling as if a hand had closed over her throat. "They want to prevent me from splitting myself."

"They want to what?" Rovi blurted.

"Vera heard about this from her brother. Julius is against me splitting myself. And so are all these people."

A strange look passed across Rovi's face.

"What is it?" Pretia asked.

"At the trials, Castor said something about you not being able to split yourself in Phoenis. He knew."

"Who else knows?" Pretia wondered. Did the spectators know? Did the authorities?

"But they can't really stop you, can they?" Rovi said.

"I don't know." Pretia felt close to tears. She wanted to turn her jacket inside out and hide her name on the back. She took a deep breath. No matter what, she wouldn't let this ruffle her, at least not visibly.

She stood up straighter. She was the Princess of Epoca. She had to face this like a noble.

The Realists were cheering and chanting loudly.

"Stop the princess!"

"Splitters are cheaters!"

"I'd never cheat," Pretia whispered.

"I know," Rovi said. "Tell them."

Pretia took an uncertain step forward. She opened her mouth. No words came out.

"Say something," Rovi insisted.

"I—I can't," Pretia whispered. What could she possibly say to change the mind of this angry mob?

"Tell them you're not a cheater," Rovi said.

Pretia cleared her throat. "I—" she began loudly, but words failed her. It was all she could do not to physically shrink back into herself. She couldn't speak. But she would do everything in her power to stand firm. "Sorry," she whispered to Rovi.

No sooner was her lame apology out of her mouth than she felt someone push past her.

"*Stop it!*" Vera had materialized out of nowhere. "Stop it!" she yelled again. "Quiet."

This only made the Realists cheer louder.

"I said *STOP!*" Vera raised her fists.

Pretia reached out and grabbed Vera's arm, trying to restrain her. "It's okay," Pretia said, keeping her voice low.

"It's not okay," Vera snapped. "They can't do this."

"Says who?" a tall Realist boy shouted. He had blond hair, alabaster skin, and the perfectly lean physique of a talented runner.

Vera put her hands on her hips and tossed her long puff of black hair. "Says me. I'm Vera Renovo."

For a moment the protesters fell silent.

Then the same kid said, "Well, Vera Renovo, your brother organized this protest. And this won't be the only one."

"Figures," Vera said, "but I don't see him here."

"He's not allowed in the village," the golden-haired Realist said. "But don't worry. He'll make his presence known."

"Who cares about Julius," Vera announced. "I'm organizing a counterprotest."

"Don't. Please," Pretia pleaded. She didn't want Vera drawing more attention to her. And she didn't want Vera risking her own games for Pretia's sake.

"Go ahead," a tall raven-haired Realist girl with ocher skin snarled. "No one will listen to you. Not even your brother cheers for you."

"You think I care about that?" Vera snapped. "When these games are over, I'm the only Renovo anyone is going to talk about. My friends and I are going to bring home victory for House Somni."

"Fat chance," the pale boy said.

"Are you going to stop me?" Vera barked.

"Do you even *know* who you're talking to?" The Sandlander girl flashed Vera a victorious glance. "That's Rex Taxus. He's the fastest athlete at these games."

Vera cupped a hand over her mouth to stifle a laugh. "You've never seen Pretia—"

Before she could finish, Rex Taxus strode in front of her. "The fastest *legitimate* athlete," he said.

Vera stared him down defiantly. "Pretia *is* a legitimate athlete."

"We'll see about that," Rex said.

From the back of the crowd of Realists, a girl's voice cried, "The

135

princess is a cheater!" Instantaneously, the protesters took up the chant, raising their fists and directing their anger toward Pretia.

Pretia told herself to be strong, to look them in the eye, and not to let them know how devastated she was inside. But she could only stand firm for so long until she felt she might crumble.

She started backing away from the concourse, back into the Dreamer Village. She wiped away the tears that were stinging her eyes. Why hadn't she been able to stand up for herself? Why couldn't she speak on her own behalf? She was ashamed that Vera could find the words she couldn't.

But no matter what, Pretia promised herself, she wasn't going to let anyone see her cry. She remembered the last thing her father had told her at Ponsit. He had been proud of how she'd behaved when her parents had broken the news that she wasn't going to Ecrof. She'd acted with nobility. She would continue to do so, no matter how painful.

Vera backed away from Rex Taxus and put an arm around Pretia's shoulder. She led her away from the protest. "Don't worry. We've all got your back." Vera swept her other arm wide, describing the entire Dreamer compound in front of them. "All of us. Every single person in this part of the village. Every Dreamer in all of Epoca, and I'm sure a few Realists, too. We all want you to do your best and do whatever it takes to win."

"Just wait until our new teammates see what you can do," Rovi added. "You're going to be the biggest star of these games."

Pretia managed a small smile. Vera squeezed Pretia's shoulder.

"Thanks," Pretia said, trying to sound reassured. But when she glanced over her shoulder at the distant protest, she was unable to shake the feeling that no matter where she went or what she did, there was something wrong with simply being her natural self.

10

ROVI

AN HONOR

ROVI AND PRETIA KNELT IN THE STARTING blocks on the Dreamers' training track. The last few days had been a blur of excitement—exploring the village, meeting new athletes, and scouting information about the competition. Rovi hadn't left the Dreamer compound once. His whole mind was given over to Dreamer Glory, Junior Epic Glory, training, and reveling in being a member of the most important junior sports team in the land.

The facilities in the Dreamer Village were more extraordinary even than Ecrof's. The track was brand-new. It could rise and fall to mimic the obstacle course of a steeplechase. It could angle uphill to increase the difficulty of training. It could record the placement of a runner's footsteps so she could revisit them later and assess if she'd taken the most efficient path. Even though he'd been training there for over a week already, Rovi still found it incredible.

All around them, other Dreamers from the elite academies were practicing for track and field. Cleopatra Volis clapped her hands, summoning all the Ecrof students.

"You all trained hard enough at Ecrof and for the last ten days here in Phoenis. It's time to start tapering your training. Don't overdo it," she said with a pointed look at Vera.

Vera and Eshe had their hands in the air at once.

Cleopatra didn't take their questions. "No exceptions. Taper training for all of you. A light workout followed by a modified version of your intended events in the morning. In the afternoon, recovery training: yoga, walking, even swimming if you're a runner. Something opposite from what you did in the morning."

Then she met each of their eyes in turn. "You are ready. Remember that. You. Are. Ready."

"Do you feel ready?" Pretia asked Rovi before they took off for a set of middle-distance laps.

He thought for a moment before answering. "Yes," he said. And it was true. He did feel ready. All the anxiety he'd felt during the trials had vanished, solidified into a core of confidence that told him he was going to do exactly what was necessary.

They placed their hands on the track, ready to take off. Rovi glanced up. Two official-looking adults, a man and a woman, were approaching them.

"On your marks," Pretia said.

"Get set," Rovi replied.

But before Pretia got to *go*, the woman coming toward them held up a hand. "Wait."

The adults wore the uniforms of Junior Epic delegates—gray pants and short tunics with the games insignia on the breast.

Rovi and Pretia stood and slowly backed off the track.

"Do you think my parents . . ." Pretia sounded near tears. She reached for Rovi's hand.

The adults reached them and the woman said, "Rovi Myrios?"

"Yes." He scanned their uniforms and, to his relief, saw Dreamer purple ribbons pinned to the side opposite the games insignia.

"We've been looking all over the village for you," the woman said.

Rovi's heart fluttered. He had begun to sweat. "Me? Why?" What had he done?

Now the officials broke out into broad smiles.

"Rovi," the woman said. "We are here to tell you that you've been chosen to carry the Dreamers' flag in the opening ceremony at the Crescent Stadium." Rovi stared at her blankly. He must have misheard. "That is, if you would like to."

"Rovi!" Pretia exclaimed.

"I'm sorry," Rovi said. "Can you say that again?"

"Rovi Myrios, you have been chosen as flag bearer for House Somni," the man confirmed. "It is a tradition in the Junior Epics that the youngest competitor from the host nation carries the flag. The flag bearer represents the bright future of the province."

"And that's me?" Rovi said. "Really?"

"You are the youngest Sandlander on Team Somni."

"But I'm not really a Sandlander," he said. He felt Pretia pinch him hard. "Well, I am, but—"

"You were recruited from the Sandlands," the female delegate said, sounding a little confused by Rovi's objection. "So you are a Sandlander, correct?"

Rovi nodded enthusiastically, trying to hide his anxiety about his background. What was it Janos had said back at Ponsit? If Rovi came to the games, he would be a Dreamer and nothing else. As much as it pained him to admit it, he was slightly relieved his past hadn't been mentioned to the Junior Epic officials. He needed to focus on his competition and not field questions about his old gang.

"Two nights from now, you will lead House Somni into the Crescent Stadium, and then you will lead us all in the Grana Prayer," the delegate continued. "Congratulations, Rovi."

Rovi's heart sank. He knew the prayer well—*May the gods grant us the fortune to compete with grace and the grana to excel beyond our expectations*—but his Phoenician was terrible. Like all Star Stealers, he spoke only a mash-up of Phoenician and the mainland Epocan tongue.

"I can't do that," Rovi said. "I don't speak Phoenician well."

"Every Phoenician speaks both Phoenician and Epocan. You can lead us in the language of mainland Epoca," the male delegate assured him.

"For real?" Rovi said.

"Absolutely," the female delegate agreed. "You are a shining star for both House Somni and the Sandlands. Congratulations," she said again.

Rovi stared at her for a second. He wasn't a Sandlander in the slightest. He was from Cora Island if he was from anywhere. He'd come to Phoenis when he was seven and had always been an outsider, an outcast. And now he was being asked to represent the city that had shunned him and his father. An objection fluttered on his lips, but he bit it back. The honor he was being given outweighed his reservations.

"Do you have any more questions?" the female delegate asked.

"No," Rovi said. "I'm excited."

"Good," the woman responded. "You certainly should be."

And with that, the officials departed.

Rovi remained by the track, stunned. "What just happened?" he said.

"Apparently you're the shining star of the Sandlands," Pretia answered.

He lowered his voice. "Do you think they know that I am—or I was—a . . . you know?"

"A Star Stealer?" Pretia said. "It didn't seem like it. But it doesn't matter. You've been chosen for an amazing honor."

Rovi was actually tempted to pinch himself. "I don't believe it."

"Believe it." Pretia beamed.

"I never—I never—I thought if anyone from Ecrof would carry the flag, it would be you."

Pretia shook her head. "No way. I've already had a lifetime of ceremonial processions. Now it's your turn."

Rovi let out a whoop. "It *is* my turn," he said, grinning. Then the smile faded. He had been restored to his former identity, which had been stolen when his father died. He was Rovi Myrios of House Somni once more. But his father wasn't around to witness this last, important transformation. He sighed. "If only my dad could see me now," he said.

He closed his eyes for a moment, trying to imagine his father's reaction—his joy that Rovi was reinstated as a Dreamer—and relief that he had been accepted by the city that had never welcomed them.

For the two days leading up to the ceremony, Rovi felt as if he were floating. All his fellow Dreamers had heard about the honor he'd been given, and instead of being jealous as he feared they might, they clapped him on the back and told him to do them proud.

"I can carry a flag better than any Realist on earth," he assured everyone.

On the evening of the ceremony, he dressed carefully in his Dreamer uniform—a purple silk tracksuit that bore his name as well as the Ecrof crest. He laced up his favorite shoes, the Grana Gleams he'd stolen from the Alexandrine Market, his last theft as a Star Stealer. His last theft ever. He looked in the mirror and barely recognized himself. He looked so different from the grubby, scrawny Star Stealer who'd made the journey to Ecrof just over a year ago. His skin was tan, not dirty. He'd filled out, grown stronger and taller. His hair was clean and had lightened. He could see both his parents in his reflection—his father's angular physique and his mother's fairer skin and hair that he remembered from the few pictures his father had of her. He was 100 percent Dreamer now.

Along with his Ecrof schoolmates, Rovi headed to the vans waiting on the causeway to take them to the Crescent Stadium. He was excited by his first chance to really experience Phoenis since he'd arrived for the Junior Epic Games.

The gate lifted for the van. Rovi stared, entranced by the glory of the Upper City, which he'd never truly been allowed to appreciate before. Inhabitants of the Lower City of Phoenis had limited access to the Upper City. And Star Stealers were absolutely forbidden to enter it. Rovi's trips to the highest parts of Phoenis had all been furtive and filled with anxiety that he might be caught.

But now he was being driven through it, a hometown hero. He could peacefully admire the turrets and tiles, the hundreds of keyhole arches and gates, the grand squares and bubbling mosaic fountains. They drove by the Imperial Hanging Gardens, which Rovi glimpsed through a golden gate, thousands of lush green plants dangling from the sky.

Unlike the chaos of the Lower City with its rabbit warren of narrow streets, the Upper City was airy and palatial. The residents moved more slowly, unhurried by the pressures of living. They enjoyed Spirit Waters and Berberian coffees on wide terraces and fanned themselves in the shade of groves of sweet date palms.

Rovi had always loved Phoenis, but the city had troubled him and caused him trouble. Now, for the first time, he could feel himself relaxing for once, enjoying the city instead of looking over his shoulder to check if the Phoenician guards were at his back.

As the van passed the remarkable buildings and historical monuments to Phoenis's glory, Rovi realized he was looking for something else among the splendor—his Star Stealer friends. He knew better than to expect them in the Upper City, but he couldn't help his eyes from skipping off into the shadows, glancing under walkways, and peeking down alleys.

The van rolled through another set of massive arched gates inlaid with hundreds of thousands of gold and silver tiles. And suddenly right in front of them was the Crescent Stadium.

Like nearly everything else in the Upper City, Rovi had only seen the stadium from the outside and at a distance. As he drew close for the first time, it took his breath away. The Crescent Stadium was a clay-colored structure with five levels of arched arcades that framed the deep blue evening sky. It looked bigger than five soccer fields and taller than any stadium in the world. Underneath it were the tunnels left behind by the redirected River of Sand. And somewhere—he didn't know where—was the quicksand river itself, dammed and restrained by ancient Phoenician architects.

Behind the stadium was the Temple of Arsama, the most holy site in all of Phoenis, its gold and bronze pyramid rising toward the heavens. Of course, Rovi had never been inside. But he'd heard enough about it to know that many famous Phoenicians were buried in its vaults and that it displayed the riches of the ancient city for visitors.

As they exited the van, Vera chatted excitedly at Rovi's side. "This is the largest stadium in Epoca," she said. "It can seat fifty thousand people and it was built before the time of grana. In fact, it's said that during the time of Hurell, the stadium was used for various blood sports. Or some secret part of it was."

"Blood sports?" Eshe had joined them. "That's not true." She looked at Rovi. "Is it true?"

Rovi had no idea. "Yes," he said. "And you can still hear the screams of the tortured competitors."

"Stop it," Eshe howled.

"It *is* true," Vera announced. "Somewhere under the Crescent Stadium is a mirror image of the entire stadium—a track that has at its center a deadly games pit. I read it in a book about the history of the Epic Games."

"Of course you did," Rovi said.

"The book said that there are all sorts of underground passageways where gladiators and animals were held before they were forced to fight to their death." Vera was talking so fast she was almost breathless. "Apparently the whole stadium is built over a system of tunnels."

"That's because of the River of Sand," Rovi said, pleased to be able to show off some knowledge of his own city's history.

"Everyone knows about the River of Sand," Vera retorted. "It was one of the Four Marvels of Epoca, but it's dried-up now."

"Not entirely," Rovi said. "A tiny part of it still flows." The look on Vera's face told him he'd surprised her with new knowledge. "Everyone knows that the ancient Phoenicians dammed it because it was too powerful. But since you're not from here, you two probably don't know that there's a small, redirected section still hidden away below us somewhere. And"—Rovi paused, drawing out his next surprise—"it could break free at any time."

"Really?" Eshe and Vera said in unison.

Rovi tried not to laugh at the identically fearful looks on both their faces.

"Well, not really."

"Where is the river?" Eshe asked.

"I don't know," Rovi admitted. "Deep underground somewhere."

"Are you *scared*?" Vera asked.

"No!" Eshe put her hands on her hips. "Of course not."

"That's all ancient Phoenician history, anyway," Vera said. "But there's Epic Games history here, too. The Junior Epic Games have been held here relatively recently, but the last time the Epic Games were held here is when Farnaka Stellus won his only medal. And that took place in *this* stadium. Which is doubly amazing."

"Why?" Rovi asked, although he wasn't that interested in the answer.

"Because he won his only Epic Medal as an adult here, and I'm going to meet him here tonight. It's perfect!"

"Meet him?" Rovi said.

"Yeah, at the Parade of Past Champions. Or were you too busy worrying about carrying the flag to remember there's a parade honoring the greatest Junior Epic Champions of all time? So Julius and Farnaka . . ."

"And Janos," Rovi added.

Pretia had caught up to them while Vera was talking.

"And Janos," Vera echoed. "They'll all be here. Tonight's my chance."

"For what?" Pretia asked.

"To meet Farnaka and to ask him how he did it. I want to find out his strategy. In four years, you're going to see *me* in that parade."

"You know what?" Rovi said. He grinned at Vera. "It's a deal."

Over a hundred Dreamers and a hundred Realists from the eight elite academies, as well as their Trainers and delegates, stood amassed in front of the stadium. An organizer was blowing a whistle, herding the different houses to different sides so that when it was time for them to enter the stadium, they would approach from opposite entrances.

When the athletes had been divided, a Dreamer delegate jumped up on a small podium and called for silence. He lifted a megahorn to his mouth and explained the proceedings.

"The stadium is filled with spectators," he bellowed. "There's not an empty seat in the house. So please follow instructions and honor House Somni. Currently, local Phoenician dancers and singers are entertaining the crowd. When that is over, the delegates will enter, starting with the Realists. As they are the winners of the last Junior Epic Games, they are honored with going first."

A chorus of boos erupted in the Dreamer camp.

"All right, all right," the delegate said. "I'm certain you will all do your best to ensure it's House Somni who proceeds first next time."

Cheers rose from the group of Dreamers.

"Then it is our turn. We will be led in by Rovi Myrios, our flag bearer and youngest pride of the Sandlands."

Rovi felt himself blush. He felt his chest swell. And to his horror, he felt tears sting his eyes. People chanted his name. They clapped him on the back. They offered high fives.

"Once Rovi has entered, our athletes will follow by each academy in alphabetical order. After you are all arrayed in your positions on the field, Rovi will say the Grana Prayer and light our Dreamer Flame. Then he will join you for the final part of the opening ceremony, the Parade of Past Champions. We conclude with this so that you are all encouraged to follow in those athletes' footsteps and aspire to their greatness. Ready?"

The Dreamers whooped.

"Here's to dreams that never die!" the delegate bellowed.

"Here's to dreams that never die!" the Dreamers shouted.

When the commotion calmed down, Rovi felt a tug on his shoulder. Pretia was beckoning him close. She pressed her lips close to his ear so only he could hear what she was saying. "Do me a favor," she said.

"Sure," Rovi replied.

"When you enter, look out for two things for me. First of all, look at the royal box to see if my parents are there. And second . . ." She paused. "See if there are any protesters."

Rovi squeezed her hand. "I will. Don't worry, Pretia."

The music in the stadium ended. Rovi could hear the announcer welcoming the Realist flag bearer, who entered to thunderous applause. Next he could hear the Realists parading in, cheering and chanting as they went.

Then it was his turn.

"Please welcome from House Somni, our Shining Star of the Sandlands, Rovi Myrios!"

His heart seemed to skip a beat. This was real.

A delegate handed him a large pole, at the end of which was a purple flag with the Dreamer Pegasus embroidered on it. Go time.

Rovi walked into the stadium, his eyes fixed on the flag ahead of him. He didn't want to misstep or stumble. But when he emerged on the field, he couldn't help but stare. The sight took his breath away. He'd never seen so many people in his life. All five arcades were filled with spectators cheering on either House Somni or House Relia. The bleachers rose and rose and rose. Flags flew. Sparklers exploded. Whistles and cheers and songs and more noise than he could have imagined encircled him. And all of those fifty thousand people were watching him.

Confidently, he marched across the field toward the raised podium. The Realist flag bearer, a small Phoenician girl, was already in place, standing next to a burning blue flame. To her left stood the athletes from House Relia.

Rovi climbed the steps to the podium. He placed the flag in a holder waiting to receive it and took the torch one of the delegates handed to him.

Now the Dreamer athletes began to arrive, one academy at a time. Rovi took this opportunity to look around again, checking the royal box for Pretia's parents and scanning the stadium for signs of protest against her remarkable talent. Neither the king nor the queen sat in the box, and from what Rovi could tell, the banners in the stadium all seemed to support the athletes.

When the team from House Somni was in position, Rovi was instructed to step up to the ceremonial flame. A megahorn was placed in front of him. He took a deep breath. For a split second he hesitated, wishing he could utter the Grana Prayer in the language of the Sandlands. But there was no time to dwell on it. "May the gods grant us the fortune to compete with grace and the grana to excel beyond our expectations," he said slowly and carefully. Then he touched the flame to the bowl. Purple flames leaped into the air.

The stadium exploded in cheers. All the Dreamers sitting in the stands leaped to their feet. The Dreamers on the field—the athletes, Trainers, and delegates—raised their fists and cheered. Rovi beamed.

He rejoined his teammates on the field to watch the Parade of Past Champions. Vera had pushed to the front of the group so she'd have a front-row position to watch the former gold medalists go by. Pretia was next to her.

"Good news," Rovi whispered in Pretia's ear. "No parents, no protesters."

Pretia's eyes widened. "Really?"

"Really!"

He could feel the tension escape from her as she let out a relieved sigh.

"And look at all those Phoenician guards," he said, indicating the first row of seats. "They aren't chasing me, for once. They have no idea I was a Star Stealer!" He was full to bursting with pride. He'd officially left his past behind. "No one does."

The sky above them lit up with blue and purple fireworks. Drumbeats echoed through the stadium, and the champions began to process. As each one entered, his or her name and number of medals won was announced with a sonic boom that nearly shook the stadium.

When Janos's name was announced, all the Ecrof students, Dreamers and Realists alike, hooted and hollered for their Head Trainer. Julius got the same reception from his former academy.

Some of the champions were so old they needed to be wheeled in. Others were in their athletic prime and bounded into the stadium. When they were all arrayed on the podium between the flames, the spectators rose to their feet and applauded—a standing ovation that lasted five full minutes.

Then the chief consul of Phoenis and the minister of sport stepped onto the podium. In unison they proclaimed, "The four hundred ninetieth Junior Epic Games are officially begun!"

Pretia and Rovi hugged each other.

"You were fantastic!" Pretia said. "You carried that flag like a pro. Didn't he, Vera?"

Vera didn't answer. She was staring at the champions on the podium. "Farnaka Stellus isn't there."

"Julius is, though," Pretia said. "That should make you proud, even if he is a Realist."

"I want to see Farnaka Stellus," Vera said.

"We should get back to the village, Vera. Don't you want to see what events you were selected for?" Pretia asked.

Vera didn't respond.

"If you're competing tomorrow, you'll need to get some sleep so you can beat what's his face's record," Rovi urged.

"Fine," Vera said. Her voice was heavy with disappointment.

They linked arms as they walked out of the stadium. Rovi glanced up at the sky. It was velvet black and scattershot with twinkling stars. A crescent moon hung overhead, giving off a luminescent silver glow. He took a deep breath, inhaling the familiar sun, sand, and jasmine smell of Phoenis. He couldn't wait for the games to begin.

As they approached the gate that would lead them back to the awaiting vans, Rovi saw a delegation of five officials approaching, heading straight for their little trio. Unlike the last time officials had approached, he felt relaxed. Everything had gone off perfectly. He was a hero of the Sandlands, and now all he had to do was represent his house as best he could on the field.

As they passed through the arch that led out of the stadium, the officials stepped directly in front of them, making Vera stumble. "Watch it," she said. "You want to injure me before the games?"

The officials ignored her. One of them, a woman with a square jaw and short black hair, spoke first. "Pretia Praxis-Onera?"

"Yes," Pretia said.

Rovi felt her tense. He, too, had grown uneasy when he heard the woman's tone.

"You'll have to come with us," the woman said.

"Why?" Pretia asked.

"Yeah, why?" Vera echoed, jumping between Pretia and the officials.

"Those are my orders," the woman insisted.

"Don't you know who her parents are?" Rovi said.

"We know exactly who her parents are," a different delegate, a towering man with dark eyes, said.

"You can't just tell her what to do," Vera said.

"Pretia, follow us, please," the first woman said. She looped an arm through Pretia's and began leading her away. Pretia shot Rovi a panicked glance. But she didn't resist.

"Her parents—" Rovi pleaded.

"This has nothing to do with her parents," the man said as Pretia was hustled away.

Pretia looked back over her shoulder helplessly. Her eyes met Rovi's.

"Let's follow," Rovi said.

Vera was already in pursuit.

They tailed the delegates as they led Pretia to a small black van and watched helplessly as she was escorted inside. Then the door closed, but not before Rovi once more saw the terrified look in Pretia's eyes. She was driven away in the opposite direction from the village.

Rovi stood frozen in place as he helplessly watched the van carrying Pretia disappearing.

"Where are they taking her?" Vera asked.

"I don't know," Rovi said. "Maybe to her parents?"

"No," Vera said. "Those were games officials, not royal officials."

"Maybe we should follow," Rovi offered lamely. It was too late. The van could have gone anywhere.

"Pretia is strong," Vera said. "She'll be able to look after herself. Plus, no one will hurt the Princess of Epoca, right?"

Rovi didn't doubt this, but he felt a sinking feeling in his stomach nevertheless. Where was Pretia being taken? And, more important—why?

11

PRETIA

A TEST

PRETIA SAT BETWEEN TWO DELEGATES IN THE small van. The windows were tinted, so she only had a dim notion of the direction in which they were headed. There were five delegates plus the driver, all of whom were staring ahead in stony silence.

She could sense Phoenis passing by outside, a nighttime blur made even darker by the shaded windows. The city felt remote and unreachable.

After ten minutes, Pretia ventured, "Are we going to see my parents?"

"No," the sole woman in the van replied shortly.

Pretia shrank back against her seat. No one else spoke for the remainder of the ride. Finally, the van stopped. The side door slid open and Pretia was led out. She tried to get a sense of where she was, but she was hustled inside a building before she got a chance to look around. From what she could tell, she was in an official Phoenician consulate or high office.

The building was imposing and cold. It was clearly closed for the day's business and felt abandoned. The delegates marched her down a dim marble hall lined with plaques and crests Pretia didn't have time to examine. Their footsteps echoed somberly—she felt as if each step was leading her toward an ominous fate. At the end of the hall, the woman with the short black hair held open a door.

They stepped into a brightly lit room. Pretia had to blink to adjust her eyes after the dark van ride and dim hall.

In front of her on an elevated platform were ten delegates dressed in the official uniforms of the Junior Epic Games with their house colors pinned over their breasts. There were five Realists and five Dreamers, ranging from extremely elderly to quite young. Along either side of the room ran long rows of elevated seats like small bleachers. These were filled, from what Pretia could tell, with all the Trainers from both House Somni and House Relia from the eight academies. She took in familiar faces from Ecrof—Satis and Janos, as well as Cleopatra Volis, Lavinia Lux, and Sonya Pin. Seeing them made her relax a little. Satis nodded as their eyes met, and he snuck her a small smile.

"Pretia Praxis-Onera, you have been summoned to the official tribunal of the Junior Epic Games to stand in judgment for your grana. Please stand before us." Pretia glanced up and saw the speaker was an imposing elderly man dressed in Realist colors seated in the middle of the tribunal. His face drooped and shook as he talked.

Pretia stepped forward. She felt tiny and insignificant. She put her hands on her knees to stop them from trembling.

"Surely she can be seated."

Pretia turned at the sound of her uncle's voice.

"This officious pageantry is unnecessary, especially given that our guest is the Princess of Epoca."

"Janos Praxis," the tribunal leader cautioned, "you know the rules of the tribunal. All athletes thought to have transgressed the rules of Epic Competition are treated the same, royal blood or not."

"Transgressed?" Pretia said.

"Quiet," the leader of the tribunal ordered. "You may only speak when addressed."

Pretia sensed movement to her left. "May *I* address the tribunal?" She recognized Satis's voice.

"Go ahead," the leader said seriously.

"I would like permission to stand with the subject," Satis said. Pretia threw him a grateful look.

"Denied," another member of the tribunal said. "Athletes must stand alone on their own two feet."

"Let us begin," the leader of the tribunal proclaimed.

Pretia felt the tribunal members staring at her. What had she done? She bit her lip, doing everything in her power not to show her fear. *I am the Princess of Epoca,* she chanted inwardly. *I will behave nobly. I am the Princess of Epoca . . .*

"Pretia Praxis-Onera," the leader said. He stared at her with watery eyes. "This tribunal is composed of the official delegates from both houses of Epoca who have been chosen to ensure that these Junior Epic Games are conducted in fairness and with grace. We oversee all aspects of the competition. Our rulings are final. Do you understand?"

"Yes," Pretia said, although she wasn't sure what exactly was happening.

The elderly man continued, "You are standing in the Phoenician High Court of Sports Fidelity. This institution was established to examine and test those who are suspected of misusing their grana or whose grana might be dangerous. And those who might be suspected of cheating by other means—through the use of illegal substances or devices."

"Test?" Pretia asked. "What do you mean?"

"I must remind you to be quiet," the tribunal leader warned her. "It has come to our attention that you possess unusually strong grana. But the strength of one's grana does not mean it is always used well or fairly. There have been complaints that your specific talents give you an unfair and unholy edge over the competition. How do you respond to these accusations?"

Pretia opened her mouth to reply, but nothing came out.

"You must have something to say?" the leader demanded.

"No," Pretia said softly. "I can't think of anything."

Now a woman on the tribunal, another Realist, with her white hair pulled into a severe bun, spoke. "Is it true that you can step outside yourself?"

"Yes," Pretia said.

"And how did you come to be able to do this?"

"It just happened when I got my grana," Pretia explained.

The woman leaned over the edge of the tribunal desk and narrowed her eyes. "Can you please tell us about that day?"

Pretia felt her knees wobble. She couldn't tell them the truth. The day her grana had come, the first day she'd split herself, her shadow self had nearly killed one of the kids at Castle Airim by accident. "Um," she said. "I—I was running in the woods and I—I—I just watched a version of myself take off and sprint ahead."

"That's all?" the woman asked.

"Yes." Pretia hoped the lie wasn't visible on her face.

Now another member of the tribunal spoke—a tiny, weasel-faced man sitting in the last chair on the right. "Have you ever considered that what you do isn't fair, given the conventional parameters of sport?"

"I thought the point of sports was to use the grana that the gods granted us to be our best selves," Pretia said.

"Not if that grana gives you an unfair advantage," the man hissed.

An outcry rose from the Dreamers' seats.

"Silence," the tribunal leader shouted. He banged a fist on the large desk. "Tell us, Pretia, can you control this talent of yours?"

"I can. Now I can," Pretia insisted, although she wasn't sure this was entirely true.

The leader blinked his watery eyes repeatedly. "And before?"

"It's like anything," Cleopatra called from the Dreamers' side. "You have to practice it to master it."

"Cleopatra Volis, consider yourself warned by this court," the leader shouted.

"I can control it," Pretia said. "Mostly," she added. It was so unfair. Wasn't the whole point of going to a place like Ecrof to learn to control your grana? Wasn't that what her friends were all training to do?

"But does it, in turn, control you?" the white-haired woman asked.

Pretia had to force herself to meet the woman's eye. "I don't know what that means."

"Can you compete without splitting yourself?" the woman clarified.

"Yes. Of course," Pretia said. "I don't always split myself. Sometimes I don't have to. Sometimes I can't."

This answer made all the members of the tribunal start discussing among themselves in low voices.

Pretia looked nervously up and down the row of adults over her head. Never had she encountered so many unfriendly faces. Never had she felt so small and lost. Maybe her parents had been right. Maybe she shouldn't have come to Phoenis. She hadn't seen anything to be afraid of from the Star Stealers, but these officials seemed scary enough.

The leader banged on the desk again. "It is the instinct of this tribunal to forbid you from using your so-called talent in these games."

Pretia felt her mind go blank. Even the Dreamers seemed against her. She thought her knees were going to give way.

"But it is also our duty to hear objections from the opposition." The elderly leader looked toward the Dreamers' seats. To everyone's surprise, the objection came from the opposite end of the room.

"Let her submit to testing," Janos requested.

"Traitor," a Realist Trainer whispered.

"You need to see her talent to understand it," Janos insisted.

The Dreamer Trainers picked up the cry. "Test her! Test her," they chanted.

A young Dreamer on the tribunal stood to get everyone's attention. "I want to see her split herself with my own eyes."

The leader banged on the desk again. "How many members of the tribunal are in favor of testing?"

"I don't understand. What are you testing?" Pretia asked.

No one responded.

The five Dreamers on the tribunal raised their hands.

Janos rose to his feet. "Let her show you herself what she can do," he insisted.

"Janos Praxis," the tribunal leader said, "if you weren't the most decorated Realist athlete of all time, I would think you were betraying your house by showing favoritism to a relative."

"Pretia's grana is a gift from the gods—it's not to be slighted," Janos said. "And I want you all to remember that Pretia isn't exclusively a Dreamer. She has chosen to be one for her time at Ecrof, but perhaps one day she will decide to come to House Relia, and if we have forbidden her talent, that will be our loss. I wonder if there would be such an outcry from the Realists if Rex Taxus had this talent."

"Rex Taxus doesn't need this so-called talent," the tribunal leader said.

"Neither does Pretia," Satis cried.

Now the Realists erupted in chatter.

"Test her, test her!" the Dreamers chanted again over the ruckus.

"Can someone please tell me what is happening?" Pretia asked. But no one heard her.

The way these adults were talking about her as if she weren't there made her feel inhuman, not worthy of addressing. Maybe she didn't even want to be tested—had they considered that? Maybe she'd rather not compete at all.

The woman with white hair raised her hand. "Test her," she said. "I'm curious."

"I'm curious, too," another Realist tribunal member, a woman about Pretia's mother's age, said. "Let's see this talent."

The Dreamers cheered.

But Pretia felt less certain than when she'd been told she couldn't use her grana a few moments ago.

"All right," the tribunal leader bellowed. "All right, all right. The decision is made. Testing will take place immediately. The Academy Trainers may now leave."

The Trainers began to depart. Satis Dario and Cleopatra Volis paused in front of Pretia. Cleopatra squeezed her shoulder. "We'll have this sorted out in no time," she said.

Then Satis leaned close so no one else could hear him. "Be yourself," he said. "Be yourself and all will be well."

Before Pretia could ask him what he meant, he'd left. And like that, Pretia was left alone in the room with only the tribunal members.

"Follow us," the white-haired lady said as the adults descended from the dais. Pretia waited until they'd all reached her level before following them out.

The tribunal members led Pretia to a room lit by lamps so bright they stung her eyes. The room was designed like a small amphitheater, with elevated benches looking down onto what seemed like a stage. On the stage were two enclosed glass chambers. One was half filled with water. The other had a moving track like a treadmill running down its center.

The adults left Pretia on the small stage and climbed into the raised seats, spreading themselves around so they encircled her.

Pretia shivered in the chilly room.

"These are grana testers. This is where our court examines any Phoenician or visiting athlete who is thought to be abusing or misusing his or her godly talent. Here we will examine *your* grana," the tribunal leader said. "Please step inside the running box."

"Then what am I supposed to do?" Pretia asked.

"Put on the Mensa Crown so we can watch your thoughts."

"And then?"

"You will run," the man replied.

"For how long?"

"We will need to see you split yourself," the leader thundered, his amplified voice echoing through the amphitheater.

"What if I can't?"

"You will run until you can," was his reply.

"But what if I injure or tire myself?"

"You will run until you split yourself," the leader insisted.

Pretia hesitated. Cleopatra had insisted on taper training, which meant she wasn't supposed to exert herself until her events. But she couldn't split herself unless she pushed herself to her limit.

"I don't—" she began to object. But then she thought better of it. If she didn't submit to this test, her games were over. And she'd risked too much for that to happen now, before she'd even competed. She'd run away from home. She'd defied her parents. She would need to meet this challenge to prove that she had been right to come to Phoenis.

Pretia took a deep breath. She closed her eyes momentarily and, once more, turned inward. *You are the Princess of Epoca,* she told herself. *Meet this with dignity.*

She was ready.

Pretia stepped into the box. She heard the door close and seal behind her. She saw the Mensa Crown on the floor. It was similar to the ones she had used in Satis's class last year to project her visualizations. She put it on.

"Where will I see my thoughts projected," she asked into a small intercom.

"You won't," the harsh white-haired woman said through the speaker. "They are for the use of the tribunal members only."

Pretia leveled her voice, trying to remain calm. "But they're my thoughts!"

"While you are in this room, your thoughts belong to the tribunal."

Pretia shuddered, but she put on the crown. Before she knew what was happening, the track began to roll and she had no choice but to run. The pace was steady, at the upper limit of a comfortable jog.

Pretia could feel the eyes of the tribunal on her, boring into her, searching and probing. She knew they were watching her every step.

She ran. Time passed at a slow drip.

"We are waiting for a demonstration," boomed the tribunal leader.

It didn't work that way, but they hadn't given Pretia a chance to explain. She couldn't split herself on a whim; she could only do it when challenged. She could do it when she needed to, not simply because she wanted to.

She wondered about her thoughts. What was the tribunal seeing? What images were flying out of her mind?

She felt the track accelerate. Now she had to sprint to keep up with it. After two minutes at 80 percent effort she flapped her hands wildly, indicating that they needed to slow it down. Eventually she felt the treadmill return to a more reasonable pace.

"Pretia, we are waiting," the leader said.

She wanted to scream at them, but the full-out sprint had stolen her voice. She thought about closing her eyes, searching deep down for her grana, looking for a way to split herself. But she didn't want to risk losing her balance and tipping off the moving track. She kept running.

She could sense the tribunal members growing impatient. She tried not to lose focus.

Just run, she told herself. *Just run and be yourself.*

But it was hard to be herself in a sealed box, jogging monotonously with a group of imposing adults staring at her, judging her

◆

every movement and seeing her every thought.

Soon her mind went blank, sinking into the dull task. And in the blankness of her mind, in the space she cleared there, rose the image from her Grana Book—the twisted road through the mountains.

This treadmill—it wasn't the road in the image in her book. Not exactly. But the image had warned her there would be difficulty and obstacles on the way to Junior Epic Glory, and the treadmill certainly presented those things. This had been foretold—this and other obstacles, Pretia supposed. She needed to relax and figure out a way to overcome this test.

This knowledge made her calmer.

But no sooner had it done so than the glass cabin filled with wind rushing against Pretia's body. She lowered her chin and shoulders, driving herself forward into the resistant gust. Her body strained as she fought against the pressure.

Her lungs burned. Her limbs felt as if they were pressing into a solid wall. Soon she could barely move at all. If the wind resistance increased, Pretia realized that she'd be flung toward the back of the enclosure.

She pressed on, using all her strength to stay upright, fight the wind, and make some progress on the treadmill so she wasn't lifted off her feet. But it wasn't working. She reached forward, grabbing the air, trying to keep herself upright.

And then she felt it happen—her shadow self emerged, pressing ahead on the treadmill, running effortlessly through the wind as her physical body stepped back. From solid ground, she watched herself move freely, smoothly, as if nothing could bother her.

Then the wind stopped. The treadmill stopped. And her two selves came back together where she stood just behind the moving track.

She stumbled as her selves collided. She heard the door unseal.

"You may step out," thundered the leader of the tribunal.

Pretia discarded the Mensa Crown and stood outside. Her lungs were scraped and raw. Her legs wobbled. She placed her hands on her knees, trying to catch her breath.

"Now you will swim," the leader bellowed.

"Wait a minute," Pretia said, her voice an exhausted whisper. "I need to recover. I can't swim right now."

"You may take ten minutes," the tribunal head conceded. "In the hall there is a dressing room. You may change into a swimsuit there."

One of the tribunal members hurried to hand Pretia a plain black bathing suit with no house or academy affiliation.

Pretia stepped off the platform and pulled open the heavy door, careful not to let her exhaustion show. When the door closed behind her, she slid to the floor. She knew from all her Ecrof training that what she should do was keep moving so her legs wouldn't seize up. But she didn't have the physical or the emotional strength to stand. She pulled her knees to her chest and rested her forehead there.

She did not want to return to the room. She did not want to swim for the tribunal. She didn't want them to see inside her mind. She just wanted to be allowed to be herself without interference and without protests.

She felt as if she were in a tug-of-war between Dreamers and Realists. A constant tug-of-war with herself over who she was and what she should do.

A knock came from the other side of the door. Pretia's ten minutes were up. Quickly she darted to the changing room, pulled on the bathing suit, and returned to the testing room.

She stood in front of a ladder that ascended to the top of the tank of water.

"Please climb up," the leader commanded. "There is a Mensa Crown hanging at the top for you." Pretia did as instructed, taking the crown from a small hook. She fitted it to her head, then slipped into the water. The water began to roil with a current that pressed against her body, providing resistance so that she swam in place, making

◆

no progress. Like before, the practice was dull and monotonous—stroke after stroke going nowhere. She wished she could make her shadow self emerge. But she couldn't. She needed a challenge for that to happen, and she feared its arrival.

She waited for the current to strengthen so she would have to fight against it, knowing that ultimately she'd have to split herself to do so. On she swam, her legs tiring, her breathing growing ragged. She felt her pace slow. How much longer did she need to do this? How much longer *could* she do this?

And then she felt something tugging at her legs. The current wasn't pressing harder against her; it was spinning her in circles into the center of the tank. The water in the enclosure had turned into a whirlpool that was pulling her into the dead center of the box. Pretia swam harder. She kicked her legs frantically. But the water was winning, trapping her in the middle of the whirlpool. Her grana was blocked—waterlogged. Her shadow self wouldn't appear.

The whirlpool let up, and she tried to rein in her thoughts. She needed to concentrate. Before she could make a plan, the swirling in the bottom of the tank resumed. Pretia swam as hard as she could, fighting the current that spun her in tighter and tighter circles until it nearly held her in place.

If I don't split, are they just going to watch me drown? she wondered.

Then it came. A weak, flickering version of her shadow self. She saw it emerge. It took a few lame strokes, then crashed back into her. She couldn't sustain it.

The current died down. She swam at a regular pace, trying to figure out how to maintain her shadow self the next time.

When the whirlpool started up, Pretia was ready. Her mind was still, her nerves calm. She swam hard until her shadow self emerged. But just like the previous effort, no sooner had her shadow self appeared and taken three or four strokes than it crashed back into

Pretia, and she was her regular old self, barely managing to fight the whirlpool.

After two more attempts, the whirlpool and the regular current died down altogether.

"You may get out of the tank," the tribunal leader announced.

Pretia hauled herself from the water and climbed down the ladder. She wrapped herself in a towel, teeth chattering.

"That will be all," the leader concluded.

The entire tribunal stood and exited the viewing theater, leaving Pretia alone on the cold, harshly lit stage. She shivered and pulled the towel closer.

The door to the room opened and a man entered. Pretia recognized him as one of the Phoenician guards Rovi had pointed out in the stadium earlier that night. "I'll take you back to the Dreamer Village."

"That was it? That was the entire test?" Pretia asked.

The guard didn't answer.

"Did I pass?"

"Please come with me." He held the door open.

She pulled on her tracksuit and sneakers.

"When will they tell me the results?"

"This way," the guard said, leading Pretia to a side exit from the court building. She followed in silence.

Pretia felt hollow. Her body was exhausted, but worse, her soul felt crushed. The games were off to a horrible start. First the protests, then the tribunal. If this kept up, she'd never make her parents proud. She'd never be able to prove to them she'd been right in running away to Ecrof and then to Phoenis.

She climbed into the van and slumped against the window. She closed her eyes, not even caring about the dazzling city outside.

◆

12

R O V I

AN OLD FRIEND

THE SORNA HORN ECHOED THROUGH THE Junior Epic Village, marking the beginning of the first day of the games. Rovi paused outside his residential tower, taking it all in.

The village was buzzing with athletes who mobbed the kiosks, stocking up on flags, T-shirts, noisemakers, and sparklers to support their teams. The grana temple was filled with silent competitors lighting flames before their events. The anthem of House Somni blasted from every speaker, while clusters of Dreamers chanted their fight song as they marched through the immaculate rows of buildings.

Last night when Rovi returned from the opening ceremony, he'd found his event assignment slipped under his door. He'd be competing in the 800, the 4x400 relay, and the Epic Mile—the 1,500. The 800 was the leadoff event on the track, which meant he'd be in the spotlight in the Crescent Stadium right away. But his happiness at his selections was tempered with anxiety.

What had happened to Pretia? Where had she been taken?

Rovi chose the outdoor cafeteria for breakfast, where he could soak in the sights and sounds of the village. He filled his tray and ate slowly, keeping an eye out for his best friend. His eyes wandered from the walkways to the fountains bursting with purple water. Pretia never appeared.

On his way out of the cafeteria, he bumped into Virgil and a crew of divers from Aquiis. "Have you seen Pretia?" Rovi asked.

"No," Virgil said, tossing his long blond hair. "I heard she got in some sort of trouble, though." Rovi didn't appreciating the diver's gossipy tone. Before he could craft a snippy reply, the sorna horn announcing the imminent departure of the event transport sounded.

Rovi hurried toward the Grand Concourse just in time to board the Epic Coach—a special bus for competitors that carried them to the stadium in extreme comfort. It was outfitted with screens and grana gadgets to measure anxiety, review past performance, and aid visualization. On board, he found a crew of Dreamers all wearing their game faces. He slid into a seat and immediately felt a tap on his shoulder. Eshe had taken the place next to him.

"Looks like it's you and me today striving for Dreamer and Ecrof Glory," she said. "We need to lead off strong for House Somni and Ecrof."

"Looks that way," Rovi replied. He pressed his nose to the window, scanning the village. "Have you seen Pretia?" he asked.

"No," Eshe said. "She's probably going with the spectators. This coach is only for competing athletes. As you can tell."

"But did you see her this morning?" Rovi asked.

Eshe shook her head. "Maybe she's training with Vera. You know, Vera is in every one of my events but this one."

"That's not surprising," Rovi said.

"Do you think she's going to do it?"

"Do what?" Rovi was growing irritated. It was hard enough to try to focus on his event instead of worrying about Pretia without Eshe babbling in his ear.

"Tie Farnaka Stellus."

"Maybe. Who knows."

Rovi closed his eyes. He needed to focus. He pulled his Memory Master out of his pocket and slid it on over his forehead. Soon he was watching himself execute a perfect 800.

Thankfully, Eshe slid on the Mensa Crown dangling from her headrest and let him concentrate in silence for the rest of the ride to the Crescent Stadium.

After a while, Rovi realized he wasn't actually paying attention to the Memory Master. He'd opened his eyes and was once more scanning the streets of the Upper City for Star Stealers. He was so distracted by searching for Issa on the sparkling streets that he didn't notice the coach come to a halt.

"Rovi." Eshe was shaking him. "Let's go."

He looked at her blankly.

"We're here."

The stadium was even more impressive in the full light of day than it had been under the silvery moonlight the night before. The bronze arches glittered and seemed to emit a warm glow. Rovi felt his heart flutter as he stepped from the van.

The Realist convoy had pulled up at the same time, and an equal number of serious-faced Realists were disembarking. Rovi spotted two Epic Elite upperclassmen from Ecrof. They acknowledged each other with a stiff wave. But that was it. Everyone knew the importance of academy glory fell far below house victory and personal triumph. As Rovi saw it, he was a Dreamer first, an individual second, and an Ecrof student third.

Thirty runners had been selected for the 800. They would compete in heats until they were down to the top ten finishers. Then it would be, as always, a single race for the three podium positions. Rovi followed the Dreamers to a desk where they were instructed to sign in with a race official and receive their heat assignments.

The stands were filled to capacity and crackling with excited electricity. Blue and purple banners fluttered from every seat. Rovi could see a group of young Phoenician Dreamers blowing sorna horns. Nearby, a bunch of Realists from Hydros or possibly Megos were waving blue sparklers. As he walked past, someone threw a stuffed Dreamer Pegasus from the top of the stands. Once more the eyes of fifty thousand spectators were on Rovi. But it didn't make him nervous this time. Instead, he was filled with confidence. He was on home turf. He was ready.

He began his warm-up, jogging several laps of the track, and finished with some half-paced sprints. He'd been drawn in the third heat. To stay warm, he continued to jog off the track so as not to be in the way of the race.

He touched his toes. He did a few fast-feet drills. He kept his mind on his own movement, never once letting his eyes stray to the action on the track. Whatever his competitors were doing was immaterial. This race was his and his alone.

With his back to the action in the starting blocks, he put on his Memory Master, then stepped forward into a lunge.

"Pssst, Rovi!"

He stood, pushed back his Memory Master, and glanced around. Seeing no one, he replaced his Memory Master and continued lunging.

"Rovi! Rovi Myrios!"

He righted himself and took off his Memory Master again, dialing in the stadium instead of his visualization.

"Rovi! Over here."

He looked into the stands. It took him a moment to figure out what he was seeing. In the front row someone was extending an arm into the air with the palm raised skyward and the fingers cupped as if plucking a star from the heavens—the Star Stealer salute.

"Or do you not talk to Star Stealers anymore?" the person said.

Issa! His Star Stealer brother dropped his arm as Rovi dashed over to where he was sitting with five members of their gang, three girls and two boys. The old gang looked a little thinner and more ragged than when he'd left them. But their garb was unmistakable and marked them as Star Stealers—loose tan pants and ragged tunics with no house colors in sight.

Issa put a finger to his lips, his dark eyes twinkling. Then he reached over the barrier to give Rovi a high five.

"You're here!" Rovi exclaimed.

"Where else would we be?" Issa replied. "There's no way in the world I'm missing Swiftfoot in the Junior Epics."

"But I thought—" Rovi began. "Aren't you all in hiding or something?"

"We have our ways," Issa said. "As long as we keep a low profile, we're golden. This is a proud moment for Star Stealers across the land. Everyone, not just our band, is pulling for you."

Rovi beamed, then felt himself blush.

"And I hear you're pretty good," Issa continued.

The announcer delivered the results from the first heat over the megahorn.

"I have to get ready," Rovi said.

"Make us proud," Issa urged.

Light on his feet, his heart happy and full, his mind certain and confident, Rovi went through his final preparations. He shed his tracksuit and Memory Master. He retied his Grana Gleams and leaned into a few last stretches.

It was time for the third heat.

Rovi positioned himself in the starting blocks.

The stadium disappeared.

The noise from the crowd evaporated.

He was barely aware of the other racers uttering the Grana Prayer in their different dialects.

His lips moved unbidden: *May the gods grant us the fortune to compete with grace and the grana to excel beyond our expectations.*

Then it was just him and the track.

◆

And *go*.

His legs were in charge.

They led the way.

He felt no strain.

No pain.

No effort.

He didn't look back.

He didn't think about his competitors. The track was a blur beneath his feet. He ran with his arms tucked to his sides. He glided through the turns on an angle, taking them easily. It felt like he was moving effortlessly, barely touching the ground. It was as if he wasn't racing at all, just flying forward wrapped in the familiar warm Phoenician air and kissed by his hometown sun.

He crossed the finish line ahead of the pack, posting his best time ever.

Rovi jogged to a halt. He had come to rest in front of his Star Stealer gang, who were all on their feet cheering wildly, their arms extended skyward, fingers plucking invisible stars in celebration, while Issa tried to calm them down so they didn't attract undue attention.

"You did it!" Amrav, Rovi's old rival in the gang, cried.

"Hey," Rovi said. "It's just a heat. The real work is yet to come."

"Good job," Issa said quietly. Then he turned to get his gang under control. "Go focus on your race, Rovi. I'll find you after."

"Where?" Rovi wanted to know.

"You know better than to ask," Issa said with a grin. "I turn up where I turn up. And I always turn up."

Rovi laughed. Issa never failed to keep his word. He was the most steadfast and reliable person Rovi had ever known. He was also the most daring and loyal, willing to sneak into the best-protected places of the Upper City if he knew it would help his gang.

"Then I'll see you when I see you," Rovi said.

"You'll see me," Issa replied.

Rovi floated back to await his assignment for the next heat.

He was drawn in the second group. He jogged lightly to stay loose. Then just as before, when it was his turn, he took to the starting blocks, serene and confident.

Once more his feet did the work.

Once more he moved effortlessly.

Once more he glided across the finish line ahead of the pack. Another personal best.

He jogged to a halt, arriving at the same spot where Issa and his gang had been sitting—but their seats were empty. Rovi searched the stands.

It didn't take him long to find his leader, his brother, the boy who'd been his best friend when he'd most needed one. Issa was running, darting this way and that through the crowd, cutting a haphazard path. Rovi instantly recognized what he was doing. Rovi had done the same thing countless times when he was a Star Stealer. Issa was trying to escape the Phoenician guards.

Rovi scanned the crowd for the telltale red hats. He saw three of them spread across the crowd. They weren't chasing Issa. They had each seized a different member of the gang, including Amrav, and were forcefully leading the captive Star Stealers away. The kids thrashed and kicked against their captors. They fought fiercely. And worse—the crowd was booing them. Rovi watched in stunned silence as the crowd parted to make the guards' job easier.

In the commotion, Issa and a few other Star Stealers had vanished. But that didn't make up for the three who had been captured.

The hubbub settled down. The spectators returned to their seats. And when the Phoenician guards returned, the crowd applauded them.

◆

Rovi's breath caught in his throat. He walked to the end of the stands and waved his arms, trying to summon a nearby guard. Eventually the woman noticed him and came down to his level.

"What happened?" Rovi said.

Never in his life did he imagine he would be talking to a Phoenician guard like this, face-to-face without fear.

"It was handled," the guard replied. "You're safe."

"Of course I'm safe. But what happened to the kids who were sitting down here?" Rovi indicated the part of the stands where his fellow Star Stealers had been sitting.

"You mean the gang of Star Stealers?"

"Yes, them," Rovi said, trying to keep his cool.

"They are not allowed in the Upper City. They were causing a disturbance."

"Who was disturbed?" Rovi demanded. "They were just watching."

"They were congregating," the guard said.

"What's that supposed to mean?"

"Star Stealers have always been a problem in Phoenis. But recently they have been gathering in larger groups and causing trouble. It is now strictly against Phoenician Law for Star Stealers to appear in a group larger than two. And they broke that law."

Rovi couldn't believe what he was hearing. "They broke a law because there were more than two of them?"

"Young man," the guard said in a tone that Rovi hadn't heard since he'd been a Star Stealer, "you might be here as a visiting athlete, but I should warn you that voicing such public support for Star Stealers in Phoenis is a violation of our code of ethics."

"But I was a—" Rovi began, and then stopped himself. He took a deep breath. "Where are you taking them?"

"To Hafara, where they belong. At least until the games are over. We can't afford trouble during these important weeks."

"Hafara has been abandoned for ages!"

"Special circumstances have caused it to be reopened," the guard said. "So don't worry about Star Stealers anymore. That's my advice." And with that, she returned to her post.

Rovi stood there stunned. Hafara Prison was rumored to be deep underground in one of Phoenis's tunnels left behind by the River of Sand. Long before Rovi had been born, Hafara had been closed when the Phoenician officials deemed it too gloomy even for prisoners.

Star Stealer tales said Hafara was a large, lightless subterranean complex below the Upper City. It was rumored that prisoners who'd been taken to Hafara when it was still in use were forever changed by the time they spent underground devoid of light and human contact. There were other stories too—ones that were only spoken of in whispers—that the remains of the River of Sand could be used to chase down any prisoner who attempted escape. Rovi shuddered as he thought of his friends locked away deep underground. What could the Star Stealers possibly have done to make the Phoenician authorities reopen Hafara?

"There you are!" Eshe was tugging on his arm. "They've been paging runners for the final race. This is it. You and I are taking that podium."

Rovi stared at her blankly. It took him a moment to register where he was and what he was supposed to do.

"What's wrong?" Eshe asked. "You look like you've seen a ghost."

"Not a ghost," Rovi said.

"Whatever it is, think about it later." Eshe tugged on his arm again. "If you don't get to the starting blocks soon, you'll be disqualified."

In a daze, Rovi followed her around the track. As a Star Stealer, he'd always been on the lookout for the guards. It wasn't uncommon for some of his crew to be rounded up from time to time. Usually they were just told to move elsewhere, but if they were caught stealing, they would be sentenced to a period of time making the sand bricks he'd described to Pretia before being released back to the streets. Hafara Prison was a whole different story.

"Hurry," Eshe said. She yanked him toward the starting blocks. Finally, she let go and rushed ahead herself, calling out over her shoulder that she'd meet him there.

He made it just in time, the moment the starter called, "On your marks."

Rovi crouched. All he needed was two minutes of mental space not to think about the captured Star Stealers. All he needed was two minutes of focus.

He tried to say the Grana Prayer, but it came out twisted and wrong—a mangled mash of words.

He willed himself to forget about the guards leading his friends away.

He couldn't.

"Get set."

His mind wouldn't obey. He saw them being dragged through the stands. He saw them fighting back against the guards.

"Go."

Rovi was late out of the blocks.

His gait was unsteady. His breathing uneven. He was aware of everything—the length of the track, the roar of the stadium, the position of his competitors.

He tried to calm his mind. He tried to find his zone. But the race was passing him by.

On the last stretch, Rovi made a final push, an ungainly, panicked effort. He moved from last place into fourth, just missing the podium.

To his surprise, it was Eshe who won. A Dreamer from Dynami had come in third. Even Eshe seemed shocked by her own performance. Rovi knew what he had to do. He gave her a huge hug.

"Congratulations, recruit." He hoped he sounded happier than he felt.

"What happened to you this time?" Eshe asked through the broadest smile Rovi had even seen.

"I lost," Rovi said.

"You were crushing it in every heat," she said.

"I should have saved the best for last," he replied. "You were the smart one."

Eshe ducked her head. "I thought it would be both of us up there." She indicated the podium.

"Hey, two out of three podium positions for House Somni is pretty good. And you scored us some Ecrof Glory, too." He held up a hand for a limp high five, which Eshe returned exuberantly before heading off for the medal ceremony.

He watched Eshe mount the winners' podium. Three flags rose: two purple, one blue. The green and gold Ecrof colors had been pinned to the top flag. The Dreamer anthem blasted across the stadium, followed by the Ecrof fight song. These should have inspired Rovi. Instead, he felt dead inside. He'd failed. He'd let himself be distracted. He wasn't the Dreamer hero he imagined himself to be. He didn't feel at all like the pride of the Sandlands.

Rovi didn't join the raucous celebration on the bus ride back to the village. He took a seat alone near the back. The Dreamers were chanting Eshe's name and singing their fight song at the top of their lungs.

"Are you upset about your performance?" Rovi looked up to see Satis slipping into the seat next to him.

"Among other things," Rovi grumbled.

"I saw what happened," Satis said. "In the stands. Your friends were chased away."

"My friends were *arrested*. The guard told me they would be taken to Hafara Prison."

Satis looked serious. "Rovi, I know that's disturbing. But you are here to compete for House Somni and Ecrof. You can't afford distractions. You are a Dreamer now, not a Star Stealer."

"No one knows about my past?"

"No," Satis said. "And we shall keep it that way. I'm sorry, but I have to remind you that you cannot go check on your friends. Being found off the Junior Epic premises would result in dismissal from the games."

Rovi gritted his teeth. "I know."

"Was Issa one of the ones who was taken by the guards?" Satis asked.

Rovi brightened slightly. "No," he said. "Issa always escapes."

"That's good," Satis said. "The Star Stealers will need him. He'll take care of them. What *you* need to do now is to put your friends out of your mind. I know it's hard, and I admire the compassion I see in you. But you are charged to bring honor to the Dreamers. You won't help the Star Stealers or anyone else by falling short. Do I have your word you will focus?"

"Yes," Rovi said.

Satis held his gaze. "No more distractions?"

"None," Rovi promised. But his heart wasn't in his vow.

13

PRETIA

A PROTEST

WHEN THE BREAKFAST SORNA HORN SOUNDED
two mornings after Pretia's ordeal at the tribunal, she decided it was
time to confront her fellow athletes. Until then it seemed impossible
to leave the room and face the outside world. She'd told Vera about
her experience, but besides permitting her to tell Rovi, Pretia swore
her friend to secrecy. She couldn't let anyone else know that officials
on both sides were concerned about her grana. That would only
throw fuel onto the protesters' fire and make them believe even more
deeply in their cause.

Vera understood. She brought Pretia her meals and even wrote
out some training regimens Pretia could do in their room.

In the last thirty-six hours, Pretia had taken four showers, hoping they'd scrub away the memory of her ordeal. But standing under
the water, she was reminded of the eyes of the tribunal members
boring into her, watching her thoughts emerge as she struggled to
summon her shadow self.

What had they seen?

What had she shown them?

She knew she was being a bad teammate and a worse friend,
missing Rovi's 800 and two of Vera's jumping events. She felt even

worse when Vera told her about Rovi's performance in the 800, how he'd totally flubbed the final race.

But now she knew she had to rejoin the games. She rolled over and picked up the paper with her event assignments. She'd been chosen for the marathon, the 100, and the 4x400, on a team with Vera, Eshe, and Rovi.

She tossed the paper aside. She couldn't imagine competing. What was the point? If she split herself, people would say her victory was tainted. If she didn't split herself, she wasn't living up to her full potential.

The second horn sounded. In the other bed, Vera rolled over and stretched. She'd returned last night wearing two medals, a gold in the long jump and a bronze in the triple jump.

Pretia had tried to apologize for missing Vera's competitions. But Vera had shushed her, telling her that after her ordeal, Pretia certainly deserved a day to herself.

Suddenly Vera was up like a shot. "It's a new day," she said, bounding to the side of Pretia's bed. "Are you ready?"

"For what?" Pretia grumbled.

"The marathon!" Vera said brightly. "We have two hours to prepare."

"I'm not competing," Pretia said.

"You don't know that," Vera replied. "Anyway, you can't spend *another* day hiding out in the room." Vera began pulling her out of bed. "Get dressed. Running clothes. Tracksuit." She went to Pretia's closet and began throwing her competition gear toward the bed. "Let's go!"

Pretia sat up. "I would have heard if there had been a decision from the tribunal. So I'm probably not allowed to compete."

"We'll figure it out. But you need to prepare as if you are going to run today."

Pretia turned over her singlet. "How can you be so motivated all the time?"

"How can you *not* be motivated?" Vera answered. "Come on, we've got races to win! Get dressed!"

Pretia sighed. "Okay, but only because I'm dying for some fresh air." She knew there was never any arguing with Vera. She dressed in running shorts, a tank, a headband, and her favorite gold Grana Gleams. She pulled on her tracksuit and, arm in arm with Vera, headed for the dining hall.

The Dreamer anthem echoed through the village. Dreamers in their competition gear were everywhere. Pretia passed a kiosk offering purple face painting and another that did semipermanent purple hair coloring. A line of athletes was filing into the grana temple.

Pretia spotted a leaderboard that displayed the running medal count. There were a total of 150 medals at stake in the games.

House Somni was leading by a single medal.

Ecrof and Dynami were tied for most school medals.

Vera was in a four-way tie for most individual medals with two. The imperious, golden-haired Rex Taxus also had two medals.

"Ugh. Rex Taxus," Pretia groaned. "Please don't let him be the star of these games."

"He won't be," Vera assured her. "I'll see to that. But he'll probably hold his lead through today, since I only have one event and he has several. How about you, Pretia? Are you feeling like a win for House Somni today?"

Was Vera trying to kill her with positivity? "I don't even know if I'm allowed to race."

"Hmm," Vera said. "Well, they didn't tell you that you *weren't* allowed to race, did they?"

"Not yet," Pretia said glumly.

"Let's eat as if you're running the marathon," Vera said. "You want to be prepared."

They headed for the interior dining hall, which was usually less crowded than the open-air one, and filled their trays with lavender oats, which would fuel them but not weigh them down.

Pretia was pouring honey into a bowl when she felt a hand on her shoulder. She turned and saw Satis standing over her, a serious look on his face.

At the sight of the kindly Visualization Trainer, her heart sank.

"I failed," she said. "I failed the test."

"No, Pretia," he said. "There's been no decision as of yet."

"What does that mean?" she said.

"Well, it's up to you, really. You are free to compete, of course. You are also free to withdraw."

"So the test wasn't about whether or not I could compete? It was just about whether or not I could use my grana?" Pretia hung her head as she found a seat at an empty table. Satis and Vera joined her.

"Right," Satis said. "With no official decision, what you do is your decision. But my fear is that if you split yourself in the marathon and the decision comes down that you will be forbidden from doing so in the future, there's a significant chance you'll be banned from the rest of the games."

"What?" Pretia cried.

"You would be found in violation of Granic Law, and that's an automatic disqualification. So I'd err on the side of caution."

"You mean compete but not split myself?" Pretia stared at her food. She didn't have any appetite.

"The choice is yours," Satis said.

"It's not always a choice," she said. "Sometimes it just happens."

"And you can't control it? You can't restrain it?" Satis said.

Pretia angled away from Vera on the long bench so her friend couldn't hear her. "Yes," she said. "I can stop it when it's happening. But it costs me."

"You are a fearsome competitor even without splitting yourself, Pretia," Satis assured her. "I would certainly love to see you out there for Ecrof and Somni."

Pretia closed her eyes to think. No sooner had she done so than the picture in her Grana Book popped into her mind. A long twisting road that foretold both difficulty and success. She knew this image pertained to many things, not just the marathon. But what was a marathon if not a long road? If it had to be difficult, so be it. And maybe, just maybe, that explosion of golden light at the end of the road as shown in her Grana Book meant there was a chance she could win.

"I'm not sure I can win without my grana, so what's the point?"

"The point is to run in a Junior Epic race," Vera said.

"I don't know," Pretia replied. "I can try, but it's like I'm being set up to lose."

"Maybe you'll surprise yourself," Vera said.

"Fine," Pretia said. "I'll do it. But I'm not happy."

"Of course you're not," Satis agreed. "But perhaps if you do this, it will work in your favor with the tribunal."

"Let's hope," Pretia grumbled. She took a bite of her breakfast.

Satis sighed. "I wish you could be free to do your best," he said.

"When will the tribunal make a decision?" Pretia asked.

"They are deliberating. They—" He broke off without finishing.

"What?" Pretia asked.

"There have been more protests. They are under a lot of pressure."

"I'm planning a counterprotest," Vera announced, throwing down her fork. "Tonight on the Grand Concourse." She bounced out of her seat. "I'll show Julius and his gang. And that stuck-up Rex Taxus, too."

"The Dreamer Trainers have discussed this. We decided it would be best if you all stayed focused on your competition. We opened the games well. We're leading. Let's work on that."

Vera looked from Satis to Pretia.

"Vera," Satis said, "wouldn't it be better to prove yourself to Rex Taxus on the field than during a protest?"

"I can do both," Vera said, competitively. "I'll—"

Pretia held up her hand. "It's okay," she said. "I know you're all on my side. Even some Realists are on my side. At least my uncle is." She sounded more confident than she felt. She couldn't shake the memory of running and swimming in those cold glass chambers, watched over by the forbidding tribunal. She couldn't believe her fate was in their hands—a group of adults who were so clearly against her.

"All right," Satis said. "I'll tell the race officials that you'll participate in the marathon. And I'll let the tribunal know that you've voluntarily offered not to split yourself."

"Do you think that will help my cause?" Pretia said.

"It can't hurt," Satis replied. "Good luck today."

When the Visualization Trainer had left, Vera leaned over her plate toward Pretia. "You understand what's about to happen, don't you?"

"What?" Pretia replied warily.

"You," Vera said, patting her on the shoulder, "are about to compete in your first Junior Epic Games! Nothing can change that. From this moment on, you will always be a Junior Epic Competitor."

A smile broke across Pretia's face. Vera was right. Finally, after all the setbacks, after all the people who tried to prevent her from doing so, she was about to compete in the Junior Epic Games. Sure, the marathon wasn't exactly her favorite event. She was much more excited about the 100 and the 4x400 relay. And sure, she couldn't split herself today. But she was about to represent House Somni and Ecrof.

No matter what happened in the race, she would enjoy this honor.

After breakfast, Pretia and Vera joined a line of Dreamers filing toward the Epic Coaches to the various venues. Virgil chatted with some friends ahead of them, a crew of willowy divers from different academies. They passed Eshe, who had, to her delight, been substituted at the last minute for shot put and was pantomiming her throw as she boarded her coach.

"She's a little intense, don't you think?" Vera said.

"She reminds me of someone," Pretia said.

"Who?"

Pretia laughed. "It'll come to me."

They took their seats as the coach began to roll out of the Junior Epic Village. Pretia had yet to see the decked-out interior of an Epic Coach, and she admired the luxurious seats complete with grana and visualization gadgets, not to mention the galley kitchen well stocked with Power Snacks and Spirit Water. There were also screens hung throughout the coach that played previous Junior Epic events. Despite the spectacular interior, Pretia was more interested in what was going on outside the coach—the miraculous city unfolding before her eyes.

She kept her gaze trained on the window as they passed the stadium and began to wind their way through the Upper City into the Lower City. The streets were lined with spectators cheering on the Dreamer coach as well as the Realist one that was following behind.

A delegate from the Kratos Academy in Chaldis stood up to address the athletes.

"The coach will take you out of the city gates to the edge of Phoenis," he said. "The race will commence at the Moon Palace. You will run along the Phoenician Road toward the city of Ur for ten miles. Then you will double back, returning along a different road—the Tunis Road. You will enter the city through the gates and run up the road we are on now. The route crosses the river Durna and proceeds into the Upper City. Then you will head for the Tile Palace, run one circle around the Temple of Arsama, and head into the Crescent Stadium for a final lap of the track before crossing the finish line. Remember, the road on this race will not always be smooth or paved. Compete well and thoughtfully. Take caution and do your best. Here's to dreams that never die!"

The athletes returned the cheer in one voice.

With that, the delegate sat back down.

As the coach approached the Moon Palace, the athletes grew silent, suddenly confronted with the enormity of the task ahead of them—a twenty-six-mile race through an unforgiving desert.

It was still morning, and the white-and-silver tile of the Moon Palace remained in shadow. The Dreamers filed off the bus. Pretia and Vera signed in and got their race numbers.

"You have fifteen minutes to warm up," a delegate bellowed through a megahorn. "Then the race will start. There will be Power Snacks and Spirit Water stations along the way. A race van will patrol the course in case of emergencies."

Pretia and Vera peeled off from the pack to complete some paired stretches, followed by a light jog. They shed their tracksuits.

"Runners to the start!"

A throng of fifty Junior Epics assembled between two poles. Pretia glanced ahead, out over the desert. She shaded her eyes, peering into the vast nothingness ahead. She would run into that emptiness and then back while the sun rose, the air warmed, and the day stretched on bright and hot. All she had to do was run her best—and keep her shadow self reined in. She pushed down her resentment.

"Go!"

The athletes started at once, a mass of bodies jolting forward. It took a few moments for them to fan out and give each other space. Soon Pretia found her stride and fell in beside Vera.

At first the athletes ran in a packed group, trying to keep up with one another. But after a mile, they stretched out along the course. Some had sprinted on ahead, trying to establish a lead they hoped to hold the entire race. Others hung back, clearly pacing themselves, waiting until later to make a move.

Pretia and Vera stayed in the middle, keeping the leaders in sight but not pushing too hard yet.

After two miles, Pretia could run without feeling hemmed in by her competitors. She and Vera spread across the road, keeping pace with one another.

The desert was no longer in shadow. The sand shone a light gold color that Pretia knew would darken to bronze as the day lengthened. On either side of the road was nothing but an expanse of sand, now and then interrupted by an oasis of date palms or a single, lonely building or a crumbling altar smudged with ancient ash.

The road beneath their feet was hard and cracked, baked by the relentless sun. There wasn't a cloud in the sky.

They ran through the first water station, where attendants handed out cups. Pretia didn't break stride. She poured some cool water on her head, and more down her throat, and kept going.

Six miles into the race, a wind picked up, sending sand swirling. Pretia spat it out of her mouth and rubbed it from her eyes.

They approached a tiny village. The elders had come out to bang drums as the athletes ran through. The children, about Pretia's age and younger, with scarves over their head and eyes to protect from the sand, ran along the road until they tired. A young boy unwound his own scarf and held it out for Pretia. She accepted it and covered her head and mouth.

"Like a true Sandlander," Vera said approvingly.

They kept on. Pretia's arms and back were slick with sweat. Now there were no more villages. Just sand and sand and sand.

And then the road turned into a bridge, a high overpass over a deep valley of—what else?—sand. Pretia let her eyes wander briefly, tracing the path of the sandy valley flowing to the east.

The Phoenician Road stretched on ahead. In the distance, she could see the the city of Ur shimmering against the horizon—a black silhouette of dome-shaped buildings flickering in and out of focus. They had almost reached the turnaround.

In two more miles they came to the outskirts of Ur, a small city compared to the glory of Phoenis. The marathoners were now firmly divided into two groups, with Pretia and Vera at the back of the lead runners.

The citizens had come out to support the racers. The Dreamers of Ur lined up on the right side of the road, the Realists on the left. They banged drums and shook shakers filled with beads. Children blew on small toy sorna horns and danced along the road. At odd intervals, small temples popped up, simple structures of unadorned sand bricks strewn with offerings to the gods—fruits, flowers, and pieces of pottery.

Three race officials stood by a water station at a curve in the road, directing the runners. Instead of heading north into the city, the competitors veered to the west in front of a small altar at a cross-roads and doubled back along the Tunis Road.

Here, as the Dreamer delegate on the bus had promised, the road grew rougher, completely broken in patches and sometimes entirely covered in sand. Pretia was tempted to take off her shoes, but she knew she'd need them for the run through Phoenis.

Again, the road crossed a bridge over a deep, dark, jagged depression in the sand. But this time, instead of running off into the distance, the sandy crevice curved and began to follow parallel to the Tunis Road, mimicking each of the road's twists and turns.

Pretia tried to point this out to Vera, but Vera was deep in her zone and didn't acknowledge her.

Pretia took her mind off the exhaustion seeping into her legs by watching this strange crevice that followed the road, sometimes veering off slightly into the desert, but often returning and running alongside it.

The road twisted and turned with the valley mirroring it—less like a road than a river. A sandy river. And then Pretia knew what she was seeing: the famous River of Sand.

Now that she knew what it was, it was so obvious. The valley running alongside the Tunis Road wasn't a valley at all, but a deep, cratered depression left behind when the River of Sand had been dammed by the people of Phoenis. She shaded her eyes again, marveling at how wondrous and terrifying it must have been to see a massive current of sand moving through the desert, twisting and turning. It must have looked like a living thing, a giant snake rushing through the land.

She understood why the people of Phoenis had decided to dam the river. Imagine if all of that sand was allowed to rush through the desert, wild and dangerous? Certainly, only the gods would have been able to control such power.

Pretia was tiring. Her mind wandered. She was still in the leader pack but falling off the back. She suspected that if she split herself, she could watch herself move on ahead smoothly. But she knew she shouldn't.

Finally, she could see the Moon Palace outlined in the distance, marking the outside edge of Phoenis. She was reaching the homestretch.

The dried-up River of Sand, which had been a faithful companion to the Tunis Road, vanished, diving underground just before the Moon Palace. Vera and the leader pack had pulled away slightly, leaving Pretia. She knew if she didn't use her exceptional grana, she wasn't going to win.

She passed the Moon Palace, the tiles glowing yellow in the brilliant sun, where the Tunis Road joined the Phoenician Road. More and more spectators lined the course. Some patted the runners on the back as they passed. Others ran alongside.

The gates that admitted them to the Lower City were hung with purple and blue streamers. Only four more miles.

Pretia's stride adjusted as she hit the cobblestones. She ran through the marvelous chaos of the Lower City—the warrens of side streets, small markets. The sweet smells of the hawker stalls and the bells and drums of the street musicians.

The road ran on an incline, up and up toward the Upper City.

Pretia's legs burned. She could barely keep the leaders in her sight.

She crossed the river Durna and arrived at the plaza where the Alexandrine Market was held. Today the plaza was turned into a festival for the Junior Epics, filled with stages and kiosks celebrating the athletes.

At the far end of the plaza, spectators jumped the race barrier and mobbed the course, only parting each time a runner passed. They were cheering and waving signs. Pretia's legs ached but her heart soared at the encouragement up ahead. They were urging her on.

But were they? The closer she got to the crowd, the more the voices of those spectators sounded angry, not supportive. They weren't cheering. They were protesting.

The guards had carved a path through the protest for the runners to pass, but still the crowd of angry spectators remained thick.

Pretia faltered. She stutter-stepped. She wanted to turn back or leave the course. But that would only make things worse. She had no choice but to head straight for the thick of the protest.

They were Realists of all ages—current competitors and people decades past their athletic prime. They shook signs with Pretia's picture on them—her face doubled, with one of the images crossed out. She could hear them shouting.

"Stop the Self-Splitter!" they cried.

"Only one princess!"

"*Real* athletes stay together!"

At the forefront of the group was someone Pretia instantly recognized—Julius Renovo. She broke stride. She wanted to scream at him and tell him to stop. She wanted to announce herself proudly. But the words caught in her throat. She found her footing and ducked her head, bracing for the insults that she was sure would be rained upon her.

To her surprise, the Realist protesters parted for her as she approached, as if they didn't know who she was. And then Pretia realized that the scarf she wore to protect her from the sand provided the perfect disguise. The protesters had no idea that the person they were protesting was in their midst. She knew she was safe until she passed, when they might glimpse the name on her singlet.

When she was through the group, she turned. The protesters weren't looking in her direction. Instead, the protesters faced the oncoming runners behind Pretia, while chanting and waving their signs again.

She exited the market and ran into the heart of the Upper City. A few runners had fallen off the leader pack and were struggling in the final miles, allowing Pretia to improve her position in the race. She knew it wasn't enough to make the podium, but still, she was pleased. She hadn't used her grana, and she'd done better than she expected.

She was coming up on the Tile Palace, larger and more extraordinary than the Moon Palace down below. Now she could see the Temple of Arsama, its triangular point reaching impossibly high into the blue sky. All that was left for her to do was to run one circle around its base, then head into the Crescent Stadium.

Up close, Pretia couldn't believe how large the pyramid was. She could barely see from one end of each side to the other. It took her much longer than she'd imagined to make her circuit of the massive building. On the final side she passed a faltering Dreamer from Dynami.

Now she headed for the stadium. At the entrance she passed an older Realist from Ecrof who had cramped in the homestretch.

Pretia hit the track. She was shocked to discover there were only three runners ahead of her—Vera and two Realists.

She took a deep breath, ready for a final exertion. She would sprint the final lap. She would do what it took to catch the runners ahead. It was possible. It was if— She was about to accelerate when she stopped. She could feel herself starting to pull away, to split. Her shadow self was about to emerge. She felt a wavering, a momentary separation. Her shadow self *wanted* to win. It told her she could win. She could catch the pack and pass them. She could snag Junior Epic Glory and prove to her parents that she had been right in coming to Phoenis. She could write herself into the record books. She could achieve the dream of nearly every child in Epoca.

But actually, she couldn't.

Not with the stands packed with spectators. Not with everything that was at stake.

She could feel her shadow self separating. It was going to take off. "No," she muttered. But it was too late. She had split. She had stepped outside herself.

"Stop!" And then Pretia did the only thing she could think of in the moment—she tripped herself, diving onto her side with a painful crash. She didn't worry about the humiliation of falling in front of fifty thousand people. All she wanted to do was recall her shadow self.

To Pretia's relief, her selves collided. She rolled over. A race official had sprinted to her side. "Are you all right?"

"I'm fine," Pretia assured him.

"That was a nasty tumble," he said. "I'll take you to the medics."

Pretia dusted the dirt from her knees. "I'm going to finish." She might not win, but she was not going to be disqualified for failing to cross the finish line. And before the race official could object, she dashed toward the end.

She was too late for the podium. She watched Vera cross in first place and raise her arms in an exhausted victory salute. The two Realists followed. Pretia came in fourth.

After she crossed the finish line, she found Vera and hugged her. "You won gold!" She held up her hand for a high five.

"Did my stupid brother and his friends cost you a podium spot? Did they slow you down?"

"No," Pretia said. "They didn't even know who I was with my headscarf."

"I wanted to kill Julius. If I hadn't been in the middle of a race, I would have." There was fire in Vera's eyes. "Right after the medal ceremony, I'll find that pompous gang of Realists and give them a piece of my mind."

"No," Pretia said. "No way. And you don't have to do that— you just won the marathon! That's amazing. Focus on that."

Vera's face relaxed. "Okay, but I *am* going to show Julius."

"Show him by destroying his record," Pretia urged. "Now go get your medal."

Pretia stood on the sidelines and watched Vera climb to the winners' spot. The smile on Vera's face was as wide as the sea between Cora and the mainland. Pretia felt her heart swell as the flags rose and the anthems played.

When the medal ceremony ended, Vera stepped off the podium still grinning from ear to ear. "I'm beat," she said to Pretia.

"No recovery training?" Pretia teased.

"By the gods no," Vera sighed. "Just rest."

"Not so fast, Ms. Renovo." The race official who had come to Pretia's aid on the course now stood in front of them. "Do you know that you're the youngest winner of the marathon in the history of the Junior Epic Games?"

Vera gave him a slightly smug smile. "Yes, and I'm only the second *female* winner, too."

The race official looked impressed by her knowledge.

"And now the Dreamers have won the marathon three more times than the Realists," Vera continued. It was clear that she had more to say, but the official interrupted.

"You must attend a press conference at the village immediately," he said. "Yours is quite an accomplishment. Unless you are too tired, of course."

"Not at all!" Vera said. "I'm ready."

"I'll go with you," Pretia said.

Satis was waiting by the Epic Coach to escort them. A few eager Phoenician kids stood by the door, holding out memorabilia for Vera to sign.

"Really?" she said, taking a pen. "You want my autograph?" She inked her signature on a few hats and programs.

"That was wild," she said as Satis ushered the kids away.

The coach sped away to the Dreamer village. When they disembarked, a crowd of athletes was assembled to greet Vera, chanting her name.

"Wow," Vera said. "It was just the marathon."

"Well, it was historic," Satis said. "And it's put you on the map as *the* athlete to watch."

Vera beamed at her fellow Dreamers.

"Are you ready to face the press?" Pretia asked, relieved that she wasn't the one who would have to answer questions from a bunch of adults.

"I can't wait!" Vera gushed.

They cut through the village swiftly, heading right for the media center. Pretia watched as Satis led Vera to the front of a crowd of reporters. Behind her, on a screen, a clip of her crossing the finish at the marathon played on repeat.

The reporters all spoke at once. The room was noisy and chaotic, with everyone trying to be heard over each other.

"What does it feel like to be competing for a different house than your family's?"

"How do you feel being the youngest person to win the marathon?"

"Did you always plan to follow in your brother's footsteps?"

Vera answered all their questions with her usual brand of assured confidence. She was a Dreamer. That's all that mattered. She was thrilled to win the marathon. She was here to break records and exceed expectations.

"Are you planning on breaking Julius's medal record?"

At this Vera's eyes lit up. "I will totally break my brother's record medal haul. But I have a larger goal."

"And what's that?" the reporter who was questioning her asked.

"I'm going to break the record number of medals won by Farnaka Stellus."

Suddenly the room fell silent.

"What did you say?" the reporter asked.

"Did she say *Farnaka Stellus*?" another reporter demanded.

Vera opened her mouth to repeat her answer. But in an instant, Satis was at her side, pulling her away from the podium.

"What's going on?" Vera demanded.

"I believe that's enough questions," Satis said. "This interview is over." He held up a hand to the reporters.

"But I was just telling them about—" Vera said as Satis led her out of the room with Pretia on their heels.

"If you want to chase records," Satis said, "you need to rest and not chat to reporters. Focus on the upcoming events instead of what has already happened."

"But why?" Vera protested.

"Just listen to your Trainer without contradicting," Satis said in an uncharacteristically sharp tone.

"Okay," Vera mumbled. She didn't sound all that convincing.

But Pretia considered Satis's advice. She couldn't dwell on her frustrating finish to the marathon. She was going to need to find a way to make these Junior Epic Games worthwhile, or all her sacrifice and risk was for nothing. And doing that meant looking toward the future.

◆

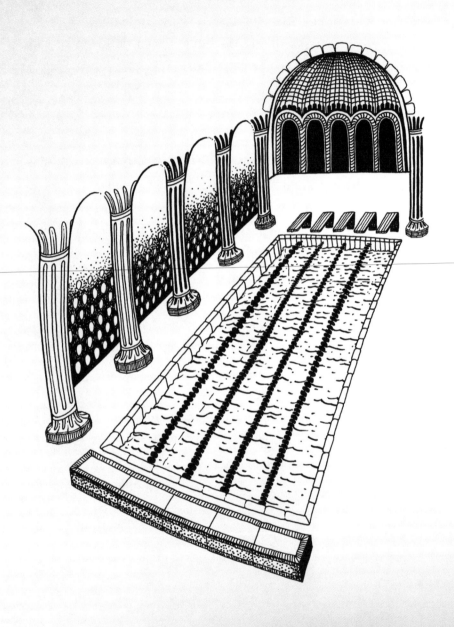

14

R O V I

A REQUEST

ROVI WAS GRATEFUL THAT HE HAD ANOTHER DAY off before his next event—the Epic Mile. He needed to regroup and get his head back in the game. But he still couldn't shake the image of his fellow Star Stealers being led off like serious criminals. And he hadn't been sleeping well. His dreams had been filled with disturbing images of the subterranean Hafara Prison.

At least today wasn't a competition day for him. But it was for Vera. She had two events in the pool—one in the morning and one in the evening—and he and Pretia were going to watch.

They met, as they had agreed, at the Grand Concourse, where spectator transport took non-competing athletes to the various venues. Pretia was glancing up and down the concourse nervously.

"Still no decision?" Rovi asked.

Pretia shook her head. "Not yet."

"It's so unfair," Rovi said, "keeping you waiting like this."

"Tell me about it," Pretia replied. "I'm starting to wish I'd listened to my parents in the first place and never come."

"Don't say that," Rovi implored. But he had to admit, she had a point. Her Junior Epics weren't exactly all fun and games.

The spectators' van pulled up, and a crew of Dreamers bearing flags and signs supporting their friends and teammates got on board.

"Let's sit in the back," Pretia suggested.

Rovi followed her to the rear and settled in, once more, to watch the Upper City of Phoenis pass by.

It took Rovi a moment to realize where they were headed, as he gazed out at the genteel and colorful streets of the Upper City. He knew, of course, that they were going to a pool. But as they drew near, he recognized the exterior of the Royal Baths where he had spent his last moments as a Star Stealer.

He and Issa and the gang had snuck into the Upper City and the pool—a place to which only the most elite members of Phoenician society had access. They'd braved the possibility of detection by the Phoenician guards to swim in the delightful waters and forget for an instant that nothing so nice was ever allowed them. But when the guards had noticed, they had rushed for the Star Stealers and would have caught Rovi had Satis not appeared and whisked him away to Ecrof.

The Dreamer spectators exited the van and entered the baths. The familiar steamy eucalyptus scent hit Rovi right away. He closed his eyes and breathed deeply.

The pool was as spectacular as Rovi remembered—wide and deep, surrounded by arches and colonnades on all sides where, during a normal day, affluent Phoenicians lounged. Today these areas had been converted into stands for spectators. On one end of the pool were the starting blocks for the swim event and at the other the high diving boards and the springboards. In order to make use of the whole pool, the swimming and diving events were staggered.

The vaulted ceilings were trimmed in gold and painted with the constellations of the Phoenician sky. The pool looked less like a place for serious competition than it did like a luxurious playground. But Rovi knew better. He knew that today's races were going to be fierce, especially with Vera taking part.

The Junior Epic Athletes who'd come to watch were instructed to sit on one of the longer sides of the pool facing supporters from Phoenis and elsewhere. Pretia found seats near the swimming blocks so they could watch Vera take off.

"We can move later if we want to watch diving," she said.

But Rovi had no interest in moving closer to the diving boards. He winced at the memory of skirmishing with a Realist boy, only to belly flop off the high diving board.

His confrontation with the Realist and the resulting scuffle had caught the attention of the Phoenician guards, who had swooped in and tried to capture the Star Stealers. Because of Rovi, his gang had been imperiled. Knowing now what the Star Stealers were up against, Rovi felt doubly sickened by the memory.

An announcer's voice echoed through the swim complex. The first race was about to start—the kickoff heat of the individual medley. Rovi and Pretia got to their feet and cheered as they saw Vera shed her enormous swim coat, snap her swim cap over her puff of wavy hair, and step onto the block. Rovi watched her mutter the Grana Prayer under her breath. Then the bell went off and the swimmers dove in.

Vera won easily, finishing half a pool's length in front of the second-place swimmer.

Rovi and Pretia watched the remaining heats. The only other swimmer they knew in this race was Cyril. Except for Vera, all the other swimmers who'd qualified for the next round were Rhodan Islanders or students at the Aquiis Academy.

There was another race—the backstroke—after Vera's to give the swimmers in the medley time to recover before their next heat. Pretia and Rovi didn't know any of the athletes but cheered loudly for House Somni.

"Hey," Pretia said when the first round of heats was over, "I think there's someone in the stands on the far side of the pool waving at you."

◆

Rovi shaded his eyes and stared across the starting blocks to the facing spectators. "I don't see anything," he said. "Just a bunch of Phoenicians cheering for their houses."

"I could have sworn—" Pretia began. "Never mind."

When Vera's second round began, Rovi and Pretia got to their feet to cheer her on. *"Vera! Vera!"* Rovi chanted. He knew she was in the zone and couldn't hear him—or rather shouldn't hear him. But maybe she'd feel his support.

Then he felt Pretia tug on his arm. "There," she said over the melee. She was pointing across the pool. Rovi followed her finger. There was one figure on the opposite side who wasn't cheering. But before Rovi could get a good look, the person vanished.

"They were definitely waving at you," Pretia said.

The friends turned their attention back to the race. Vera swam well, but the other swimmers were equally strong. Rovi and Pretia remained on their feet, cheering her on. After two laps, she was in fourth place.

"Oh no," Rovi said, "what if she doesn't make it out of this round?"

"I hope she's not distracted," Pretia said.

"What on earth could distract Vera?" Rovi wondered. Her focus was usually so razor sharp that he couldn't imagine anything taking her out of the moment.

"Well," Pretia began. "There was this thing at the media center. She was telling the reporters about Farnaka Stellus, and Satis practically yanked her away from them."

"Probably because no one wants to hear about some guy no one cares about," Rovi said. "It's much more interesting if she's chasing her own brother's record."

They watched Vera close in on the two leaders.

"You're probably right," Pretia said.

Vera was catching up. Rovi and Pretia cheered louder, so loud and forcefully that Rovi nearly toppled into the row in front of him. To their delight, Vera touched the wall in second place.

Rovi waved his arms and shouted her name as loudly as he could as she pulled herself out of the pool. She'd made the finals.

"There!" Pretia said.

Someone was standing in the shadows of one of the bleachers. Rovi could feel eyes on him, boring into him from across the pool. He stopped cheering and watched. But again, the person vanished.

Throughout the following heats Rovi scanned the area surrounding the pool. He could feel someone watching, but he couldn't pinpoint the spy.

Next up was the second round of the backstroke. Rovi paid no attention to the race, hardly even bothering to cheer for House Somni. When that heat was over, Pretia tapped him. "Okay," she said, "here she goes."

Rovi glanced over at the starting blocks in time to see Vera utter the Grana Prayer.

The bell rang out.

The swimmers hit the water.

Everyone's focus shifted to the final race.

And that's when the figure who'd been watching Rovi stepped out of the shadows, revealing himself fully. He raised an arm straight up in the air, palm upward, fingers pressed together as if to pluck a star. It was Issa. He dropped his arm and began beckoning Rovi across the room, an urgent look on his face.

Pretia cupped her hands around her mouth and shouted, *"Ver-aaaaaaa!"* Then she looked at Rovi. "How come you're not cheering?"

Rovi called Vera's name. But he wasn't focused on the race. He was tracing Issa's path so he could find him later.

The next thing he knew, Pretia's arms were around him. "She did it! She did it!"

"She won?"

"Were you even watching? She came in second! But that's still a medal. And a Dreamer came first, so we did great overall. Vera is up to four medals. Almost halfway to what's his face's record." She held up a hand for a high five, which Rovi returned distractedly.

"Pretia, cover for me."

"Do what?"

"Cover for me. Don't tell anyone where I'm going."

"Where *are* you going?"

"I need to find someone."

Pretia gripped his arm, trying to restrain him. "Wait! You're not going to leave the grounds, are you? You can't! It's not allowed!"

But before she could ask any more questions, Rovi slipped away through the crowd.

For a moment, he wasn't Rovi Myrios of Ecrof, a Dreamer, but Swiftfoot the Star Stealer. He slipped through the crowd like a ghost, past teammates, competitors in their puffy swim coats, rivals, Trainers, and delegates from different academies. It was as if he weren't there at all—a shadow no one saw. He slid into the colonnade. He knew where Issa had gone—toward the hallways that led from the pool through which his gang had snuck into the Royal Baths more than a year ago.

He didn't have much time. After the medal ceremonies he'd have to rejoin his group on the van or risk being thrown out of the Junior Epic Games. If that van left without him—Rovi didn't like to think about the consequences.

But right now, what he needed to do was find Issa. He slipped along the corridor, away from the cheering crowds. The eucalyptus scent from the steam room and recovery bath got stronger as he went deeper into the complex. Heady vapor wafted down the hall. Rovi waved his hands in front of his face to clear the air.

Then he felt someone grab his arm.

"Swiftfoot!" Issa pulled Rovi into a hug.

Issa was a few years older than Rovi. But up close Rovi suddenly realized that now *he* was stronger and healthier than his friend. Beneath Issa's ragged tunic, Rovi saw that he was all skin and bones.

"Are you all right?" Rovi asked. "After my race, I couldn't find you."

"We had to hide because of what went down in the stadium. We almost always have to hide now." Issa took a deep breath. "It's not safe anymore. You saw what happened. The guards keep rounding us up."

"Why?"

"They claim we're plotting something. It's not true, of course. The only reason the gangs are banding together is to find a way to survive. We've been trying to organize ourselves, but it's getting harder every day. Ever since it was announced that the Junior Epics were coming to Phoenis, life has been almost impossible for the Star Stealers."

"Issa, I'm so sorry," Rovi said. He hated to hear that the games he loved so much were causing his friends trouble.

Issa gave Rovi a crooked smile. "It's not *your* fault. Anyway, you're a fancy Dreamer now. And hopefully a Junior Epic Champion."

Despite himself, Rovi smiled. He couldn't help being proud of how much he had accomplished in a year. "Not in that last race," he said. "I—I got distracted by what happened to you and the gang. But I'll make up for it next time."

"You better," Issa said, "oh great Sandlander hero!" He punched Rovi in the arm playfully. Then his voice changed. "Except you're not really from here, are you?"

"Um, well, I mean—" Rovi stammered. Issa *knew* his story. So why was he asking?

"If anything, you're a Star Stealer at heart, not a Sandlander, right?"

"I guess," Rovi said. He was lots of things. A Star Stealer, a

Dreamer, an Ecrof student, a Junior Epic Athlete. But Issa would never understand that. Star Stealers disliked labels. They hated authorities and conventions like academies and houses.

"Rovi, you saw what happened at the stadium. You saw what happened to Amrav, Sheva, and Ester. They were taken."

Rovi bit his lip and looked at the ground, thinking of his friends thrashing against their captors. "I saw."

"You know where they were taken? It's not like the old days when they sent us to make sand bricks at one of the work sites. They go to Hafara Prison," Issa said.

"One of the guards told me that."

"Once they are taken," Issa went on, "once *we* are taken, we don't get out."

"Never?"

Issa shook his head. "Not yet. Not one Star Stealer who has been taken this year has been seen again."

"How many are in Hafara?" Rovi asked.

"Some entire gangs are gone. The group Tarik led and Gita's, too," Issa said.

Rovi stared at Issa through the steam. All those Star Stealers deep underground, far from the light of day. "But that's not fair," he said.

"Of course it isn't. They're making an example of us because we don't fit into the pretty Dreamer versus Realist picture of the Junior Epic Games." Issa stepped closer to Rovi. "We need *your* help, Rovi."

"Me? What can I do?"

"You can be our voice. You can speak about what's happening to us. When you're on the medal stand, you can let people know you're a Star Stealer and advocate for the Star Stealers. If you win a medal and are given the chance to speak, you can explain about our plight."

"But—but—I can't."

"Why not?"

"They'd never let me. I'd be disqualified."

Issa gritted his teeth. "How do you know that if you haven't tried?"

"There's—" Rovi took a deep breath. He knew that Issa would have no interest in what he was about to say. "There's a Junior Epic Code. The games are about the glory of sport, not personal agendas." He could feel Issa staring at him unpleasantly as he summarized Janos's words from their first day in Phoenis. "That's *why* the gods granted us grana. It's the Epocan Way."

Issa sighed. "But what if you don't have sports? What if sports are off-limits to you because of who you are? What if you aren't allowed to be part of the *Epocan Way?*"

"But I do—" Rovi began before he realized what his old friend was asking. Now that he was a Dreamer and no longer a Star Stealer, Rovi had this option available to him. But Issa and his gang didn't.

"You don't understand," Rovi said. "I wouldn't be able to compete anymore."

Issa held his gaze. "Is that all that matters?"

"Yes," Rovi said. Then he clapped his hand over his mouth. "That's not what I meant. But I'll lose everything if I do something that gets me kicked out of the Junior Epics. Everything. I need to honor my school and my house. They're all I have."

"I see," Issa said. A sad look passed over his face.

From the cavernous pool room, Rovi could hear the Dreamer anthem come to a close. The medal ceremony was ending. He needed to hurry so as not to miss the van back to the village.

"I have to go," he said.

"Rovi," Issa said, reaching for his hand. "Please think about it. Think about helping us."

"I don't know if I can," Rovi said.

"I guess the risk is too big," Issa said. "You wouldn't want to lose everything you've been given."

Rovi felt tears in his eyes. "I'm sorry. I'm so sorry."

◆

"Don't worry," Issa said. "I understand. And—" He paused. "I'll be there for your next event. But this time, you better win." He pulled Rovi back into an embrace. "I don't want it getting out that Swiftfoot is second best to anyone. Now go." He released Rovi.

"But—" Rovi wanted to say more. He wanted to explain better. He wanted to tell Issa that *after* the games he'd do whatever he could for the Star Stealers. For now, however, the games were too important. There was too much at stake.

He wanted to explain all of this. But he was too late. Issa had disappeared.

◆

15

PRETIA

A JUDGMENT

PRETIA EXAMINED THE LEADERBOARD IN THE center of the Dreamer Village. The Realists were now ahead by four medals, twenty to the Dreamers' sixteen. Vera was tied for most individual medals with five after making the podium in both her events yesterday. Aquiis and Ecrof were tied for most academy medals.

Pretia looked at the daily competition schedule. None of the meets she wanted to watch were until the afternoon, which gave her the morning to train. And she certainly needed to train, especially if the tribunal decided that she couldn't split herself. Then she'd have to compete better than ever.

Pretia was about to head to the cafeteria when she heard a commotion rippling through the Dreamer Village. From up above on the walkways, Dreamers were pointing at someone or something.

Watch out for the opposition, she heard. *Realist coming through.*

As quickly as they'd started, the comments stopped. She glanced toward the fountains, and through the spray of purple water she saw Janos and another Realist delegate making their way toward her.

"Uncle Janos," Pretia said. She stopped herself short of hugging him. Suddenly she was overcome by cold terror. Had someone seen her momentary split at the end of the marathon? Had Janos come to remove her from the games?

"What's wrong, Pretia?" Janos asked. "Afraid of the opposite team? You of all people can't hate Realists that much."

"What? No." Pretia's mind was racing. "I just . . . Did I . . . did I do something wrong?"

"I don't know, did you?" her uncle asked in a serious voice.

Pretia took a deep breath. "No," she said. She hadn't. She hadn't meant to reveal her shadow self at the end of the marathon. It had been a mistake that hadn't harmed anyone. At least she hoped so.

"That's good," her uncle said. His eyes were kind, but his voice was all business. "But I *am* indeed here about a question of right and wrong. There's been a decision."

Now all Pretia's nerves tingled at once. She took a deep breath and exhaled loudly. "What did they decide?"

"You'll need to come hear it yourself," Janos said.

"Can you just tell me?"

"Even I don't know what has been decided. The rules of the tribunal state that all decisions must be heard in person."

Pretia shuddered. The thought of all those adults staring down at her again, deciding her fate for her and coldly judging, made her heart race and her palms sweat. She felt as if her knees were going to give way.

Janos lowered his voice and met her eye with a serious but confident gaze. "Pretia, you must face this like you will face all challenges going forward as ruler."

"I don't want to rule," Pretia said. "I just want to compete."

Janos put a hand on her shoulder. "I, too, had no interest in statecraft. But I don't think you are going to be able to make the same choice I did. I don't see a future in which you don't rule Epoca."

Pretia sighed. "Ugh. Why not?"

"Because of who you are—the Child of Hope."

"I told you, I hate that name," Pretia moaned. "It's like everyone hopes I do something they want, but no one cares about what *I* hope for."

A thoughtful look crossed Janos's face. "I believe that is the wisest thing I've ever heard from someone your age. But all of this is such a long way off. Today a different challenge awaits. And you must face it with dignity, no matter the outcome."

"Uncle, can I bring someone with me? Just for the ride to the tribunal. I'm happy to stand alone for the decision but—"

"Of course," Janos said. "Be at the Grand Concourse in ten minutes. Satis and I will accompany you."

Pretia sprinted to the outdoor cafeteria, searching for Rovi or Vera. Both had already finished eating.

She checked her dorm.

She checked the training track.

She ducked into the grana temple, where shadows from purple flames to the seven blessed gods danced on the walls.

Time was ticking away.

She had three minutes to make it to the Grand Concourse.

Pretia sprinted away from the indoor training track through the village. She passed the leaderboard. She passed the cafeteria again. She could see the van idling in the distance.

"Pretia!" A hand grabbed her as she raced past. "Where are you going?"

"I can't—" Pretia started to say before realizing it was Vera who was holding her. "Vera! I've been looking for you. Come with me."

"Eshe and I are about to do some relay practice." Pretia noticed that Eshe was standing behind Vera, a baton in her hand. "We were looking for *you*, since you're on our team."

"Not now," Pretia said.

"This is important," Vera began. "The 4x400—"

"Vera!" Pretia cried. "There's been a decision. I don't have time to explain. Just come with me."

"We're training," Eshe said in her best imitation of Vera.

"Please!" Pretia insisted.

"Of course," Vera said. "Let's go."

"But we need to practice," Eshe said. "We need to—"

Vera and Pretia were already sprinting away. They raced to the van, not stopping until they were in their seats.

"Okay," Vera said as the van pulled out of the village, "what's going on?"

"I need to appear in front of the tribunal to find out their decision. I didn't want to go alone."

"We've got this," Vera said, taking her hand. "And, more important, *you've* got this."

Pretia smiled, although she didn't feel too sure that things were about to go her way.

As before, the ride passed in silence. This time, however, Pretia's anxiety was different. She knew where she was going and who she would face. What she didn't know, of course, was what was going to happen.

She watched the city pass by—the massive stadium, the towering pyramid of the Temple of Arsama. She wondered if she would get to enjoy these as a competitor permitted to unleash her grana in its most glorious state, or if she would be hindered, forever holding back and restraining herself.

When they arrived at the Phoenician High Court of Sports Fidelity, Pretia and Vera mounted the steps hand in hand. Janos held open the door for them. Then he pulled Vera aside. "This is where you leave her. She must go alone."

"Can't I watch?" Vera asked.

"Only officials may attend the tribunal," he explained. "You must wait here." He pointed at a bench.

"But—" Vera protested.

"It won't take long," Janos assured her. Then he led Pretia solemnly down the corridor.

Pretia clenched and unclenched her hands as she approached the door to the tribunal. Before they entered, Janos placed a hand on her arm and squeezed. "No matter what happens, you are still who you are. Don't forget that. You can do something special that no one else can do."

"Even if I'm doing it for the opposite team?"

"Pretia, you are both a Dreamer *and* a Realist. I keep telling you that. For you, there are no teams. Denying this essential part of yourself hurts both houses in the long run."

"Pretia Praxis-Onera!" Pretia heard the familiar voice of the tribunal leader. "Please stand before us." Janos stepped back so she could enter. Then he followed and took his own seat.

Everything was exactly as it had been before—rows of Dreamers to her left, Realists to her right, and up ahead, on their elevated dais, the imposing members of the tribunal.

The room reminded her of something—why hadn't she noticed it before? The layout was strikingly similar to the image in her Grana Book. She was the path between the two houses, represented by the mountains in the picture. They would be steadfast. She would have to twist and turn if she wanted glory.

"Step forward," the leader commanded. His loose skin shook as he spoke.

Pretia looked at the faces of the tribunal members above her. The woman with the severe features and white hair—how had she voted? And the youngest member, the Dreamer, surely he'd been on her side. But how could she be sure? Even some of the Dreamers had seemed wary of her at their last meeting.

The woman with the white hair spoke first. "Do you have anything to say before we begin?"

◆

Pretia looked her in the eye. But as usual, she had no words. "No," she said. "I'm ready to hear your decision."

Now the tribunal leader took over. "You are here not because of your rank but because of your ability," he thundered. Pretia marveled that such an elderly person could have such a powerful voice. "And our decision has nothing to do with your parentage. Our only considerations came from what we witnessed during your testing."

Pretia shuddered at the memory.

"The tribunal of the four hundred ninetieth Junior Epic Games has found that—" The leader, undone by the volume at which he was projecting his voice, was consumed by a fit of coughing. "The tribunal of the four hundred ninetieth Junior Epic Games has found that for the course of this competition and all competitions going forward, in any and all events, Pretia Praxis-Onera—"

Pretia held her breath. She wanted to close her eyes. She wanted to look anywhere but at the man about to pronounce her fate.

"May use her grana to its fullest."

Her mouth fell open. "Really?"

"Without impediment or hindrance," the leader concluded. Then he stared at her with a sour look. "Consider yourself lucky. This was not an obvious judgment, and it could easily have swung the other way."

Relief coursed through Pretia. She didn't realize how much tension she'd been holding inside. And now that it was gone, she felt as if she might collapse to the ground. She looked toward the Dreamer side. Satis and Cleopatra gave her subtle signals of victory. She glanced toward the Realists. Everyone, including Janos, sat stone-faced.

The tribunal leader banged on the desk, ending the session. The doors swung open. The adults filed out first. Pretia followed slowly. Before she was out the door, Vera tackled her.

"Congratulations," she cried, her voice echoing too loudly in the marble hall.

"How did you know?" Pretia asked.

"I listened through the door," Vera said with a conspiratorial grin, and hugged her again. "Now we have something important to do!"

"What?"

"We need to train, silly."

Pretia groaned. "First I need to eat," she said. In the rush to the tribunal, she'd forgotten breakfast.

"You sound like Rovi," Vera laughed. "Speaking of which . . . let's go find him."

Before the van came to a complete stop on the Grand Concourse, Pretia and Vera bolted from their seats. Pretia was itching to get her breakfast and move on to training. She couldn't wait to finally use her grana to its fullest in Phoenis.

"Wait, girls!"

They turned at the sound of Satis's voice. "Not so fast, you two." The Visualization Trainer was scrambling to get out of the van.

"You won the battle, Pretia," he said with a smile as they stepped outside. "But I'm afraid you haven't won the war."

"What's the war?" Vera asked. "The Junior Epics? Because Pretia is totally going to medal."

"The war is the endless resistance against what you can do. Just because a tribunal ruled in your favor doesn't mean they changed everyone's mind," Satis said.

"So there will still be protests?" Pretia asked, looking over toward the Realist Village.

"Perhaps," Satis said.

"I wonder . . ." Pretia began. "I wonder if it would have been different if I'd decided to compete for House Relia when I first got to Ecrof."

"I like to imagine my fellow Dreamers would be above protesting," Satis said, his hand flying to the purple ribbon on his uniform. "But we are all given to mistrusting and resenting talents that don't belong to us. If you ever, when you are older, decide to represent House Relia, I'm sure you'll see that Dreamers, too, have their shortcomings."

"Pretia would never do that!" Vera exclaimed. "Would you, Pretia?"

Pretia shrugged. She had given up trying to guess her future.

"So be prepared," Satis said. "For anything."

"I am," Pretia said. "But now I actually need to *prepare*, you know, train. So—" She looked anxiously toward the cafeteria. She was genuinely starving now.

"And one more thing," Satis said.

It was all Pretia could do to stifle a groan. She loved the Visualization Trainer, but she'd had enough of adults for one day.

"Not for you," Satis said, looking at Pretia. "For Vera. I know you have set yourself an impressive goal for these games," he said.

"Yes," Vera chimed in brightly, "I'm going to tie F—"

Satis put a finger to his lips. "Perhaps it would be better to focus on breaking Julius's record instead."

"But Farnaka Stellus won more medals!" Vera exclaimed. "He won nine. Julius only won eight."

"Keep your voice down," Satis said.

"What's wrong with saying that?" Vera demanded. "I read it in an Epic Text."

Satis sighed. "There's more to the story than what you read." He led them to a quiet corner of the village. "I'm going to tell you the truth, but when I do, you must promise that you'll stop talking about Farnaka Stellus."

Vera and Pretia exchanged curious glances.

"You are correct. Farnaka Stellus *was* the most decorated athlete in the Junior Epic Games. That was the final year that Janos competed, in fact. They were contemporaries. So that should give you an idea of how good he was."

Pretia looked at Vera, whose eyes were so wide it looked as if they'd doubled in size.

"He was a Dreamer and Sandlander—from Phoenis, in fact. The only Epic Games he competed in as an adult took place here, too."

"I know that." Vera sounded impatient.

"He quit in the middle of the games."

"That's why he's not in any of the record books?" Vera asked.

"That's only part of the story. His main event was the 100, like yours, Pretia. It was the opening event that year. Farnaka won, beating Janos. But on the podium during the medal ceremony, he shocked everyone by switching his Dreamer singlet for a Star Stealer tunic. He threw off his medal. Then he raised his arm in the Star Stealer salute and declared, *No sports for any until there are sports for all.*"

"What does that mean?" Vera asked.

"It means," Satis explained, "that until Star Stealers and any of the other Orphic People are allowed to participate, Farnaka wouldn't compete. But it means something more than that. It means that he challenged the Epocan Way of Dreamer versus Realist. He dismissed the importance of the two factions that make up our society. He came out against *the very purpose of the games themselves*, which is to decide who rules between Somni and Relia. And that is a high crime against Epocan Order."

"Was he a Star Stealer?" Pretia wondered.

"No," Satis said. "He wasn't. But he was a Sandlander, and must have known them, to be so concerned about their fate."

"So why—?" Pretia's head was filled with questions. Who would give up sports? Who would toss away an Epic Medal?

Satis continued without letting her finish her questions. "Rumor had it that he went to live with a gang of Star Stealers. Some even say that he tried to convince the Star Stealers to act against the authorities to disrupt those games and future games. The only thing everyone is sure of is that no one ever saw him again."

"So that's why he didn't show up at the parade," Vera said.

"Yes," Satis said. "What he did was a major violation of Epic Code. Our nation is founded on the principle of sports being the highest authority. Sports take the place of conflict. To speak against the sacredness of sports, especially on the Epic Podium, was a national disgrace."

"I take it that's also why he's not in the record books," Vera said.

"The historians did what they could to erase him, yes," Satis answered. "But now you understand, Vera, why you must not mention his name. You want to chase greatness, but you don't want to align yourself with someone who spoke against sport and the fundamental tentpole of our Epocan system."

"I don't," Vera said quietly.

"Good," Satis replied. "Better than chasing someone else's history is making your own, Vera. And you are well on your way."

Vera's smile shone as she watched their Trainer walk away.

When he was out of earshot, she turned to Pretia. "That was . . . interesting, but I'm still going to surpass Far— I'm still going to surpass him."

Pretia clapped her friend on the back. "I know," she said.

But something in Satis's story irked her. Pretia also didn't adhere to the Epocan model of Dreamer or Realist. She was not from either house; she was from both—the Child of Hope who was supposed to unite Epoca. But what if it didn't work that way? What had Janos said? For her there were no teams. Didn't that imply that being both Dreamer and Realist meant she belonged to *neither* side?

Maybe she had more in common with Star Stealers than she thought.

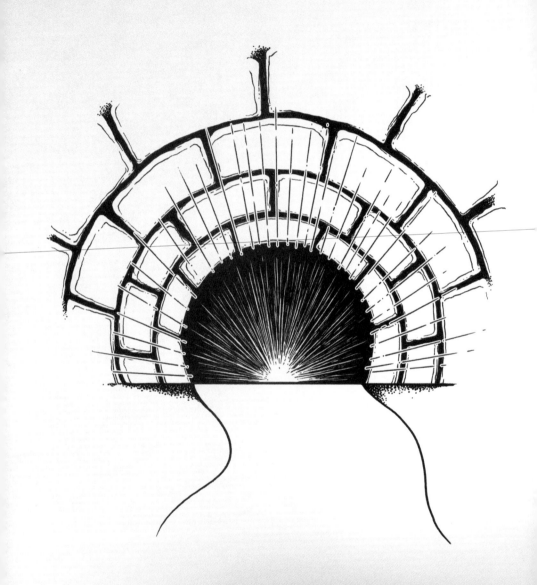

16

ROVI

A NO-SHOW

WHAT ISSA ASKED WAS TOO MUCH. THERE WAS NO way Rovi was going to risk his new position as a celebrated Dreamer. There was no way he was going to risk his future at the games by championing the Star Stealers from the podium. What he *was* going to do was make the podium. He wouldn't let Issa down in that respect.

Issa had promised to be there for the Epic Mile, and Issa never broke his promises. With Issa risking everything to be in the stands, Rovi vowed to do whatever it took to win.

He knew that his first task would be to block out the world for the duration of the race—for five minutes he couldn't think about the protests against Pretia and her grana, the memory of the Phoenician guards leading his friends away, and his recurring nightmares about Hafara Prison.

For five minutes or so, all he could do was run.

Run first. Think later.

He spoke to no one as he walked to the dining hall for breakfast. He forced himself to eat light—enough to fuel him for the 1,500 but not weigh him down. He went to the indoor track and did a light jog, an Epic Mile at less than half pace. He stretched. He went back to his room, showered, and put on his race gear.

He was ready. He would do Issa proud. He would do his father and mother proud. He would do Ecrof and the Dreamers and the Star Stealers proud. But most of all, he'd do himself proud.

Usually, mile events were held at the same track as all other short- and middle-distance events. But Phoenis provided an alternate venue, one even more unusual than the magnificent Crescent Stadium: the Temple of Arsama, whose four sides measured exactly a quarter of an Epic Mile each. There were no heats. All twenty runners would run at once. One lap of the temple to victory. That was all.

Cornering would be different than on the track. But Rovi was confident. If there was one thing his feet knew how to do, it was run on the streets of Phoenis.

After signing in, the athletes were allowed to walk or jog a single tour of the course. Rovi decided to walk. He had already tested his legs that morning and he felt good. But he had another agenda. Walking would allow him to check the stands for Issa. He knew this meant taking his head out of the game for a moment, but he figured it was worth it. Knowing Issa was there would give him an extra boost.

At each of the four corners of the pyramid the officials had erected a tower of bleachers for the spectators. Rovi walked briskly, his Memory Master on his head to keep track of the course so he could review it once more before the race started.

He rounded the first corner and glanced into the stands. There were guards everywhere, blocking the spectators from reaching the racecourse, more Phoenician guards than Rovi had ever seen in his life. Behind them, the stands were filled with Junior Epic Competitors and games officials. He kept on. The stands in the next corner were filled with Dreamers flying purple flags and waving purple banners. Still no Issa. The third set of bleachers was filled with a sea of blue Realists.

Rovi made the final turn. One more set of bleachers. One more chance to check for Issa. Then he'd have to put his game face back on.

The final set of stands was filled with a mixed crowd—officials, fans from both houses, family members of the competitors, waving homemade signs. He paused, combing the bleachers, trying to look at the spectators one by one.

No sign of Issa. Perhaps he was lost in the crowd, or perhaps he was keeping a low profile. But it wasn't Issa's way to not make his presence known to Rovi.

Rovi took a last look, scanning the shadows and the more obscure places. But all he saw were guards. Guards, guards, and more guards.

A horn blasted. He needed to hurry to the start.

Rovi took one last look behind him. Issa had promised. He'd *promised*! He'd never let the guards stop him before. But Rovi had promised Satis something, too—no more distractions. He wouldn't let his favorite teacher down.

"Runners!"

There was no time to worry. There was no time to think. Rovi had to put everything behind him—family, friends, and Star Stealers. For five minutes—or less, if all went well—there would only be the race.

"Last call, runners!"

Rovi shed his warm-ups. He got into position. He muttered the Grana Prayer.

Now there was only the race.

"Go!"

Rovi took off. Steady. Calm. Confident.

Halfway down the first side of the pyramid, he found an inside lane. He could feel the sun bouncing off the golden bricks. He could sense the tremendous temple rising above him. He ran.

He made the first turn, dimly aware of Dreamers chanting the Dreamer chant.

Someone was calling his name. Not Issa.

But it didn't matter. Not now. Not for another few minutes.

He rounded the next turn. He could feel the crowd of runners around him thinning. There were five, maybe six, of them in a break-away pack.

One more turn. Then the homestretch. He wanted to pause, to break stride, to hear if someone special was calling his name. But his feet wouldn't let him. They moved unbidden, finding a surer, quicker path around the great pyramid, leading him forward, until—until Rovi realized he was in the lead. He sensed this, but he knew better than to check.

Now it was just him alone, flanked by the pyramid on his left and the crowd that had gathered to watch the conclusion of the race on his right. Just him and the familiar ground of Phoenis. Just him and his feet.

And then, without Rovi knowing exactly what had happened, it was over.

He crossed the finish line.

First.

Suddenly everyone was all around him at once—friends, strangers, classmates, schoolmates, fellow Dreamers, Phoenician Dreamers, delegates, officials, Trainers.

"Rovi! Rovi! Rovi!" they chanted.

Then he heard a familiar voice—two familiar voices. "You did it!"

Vera and Pretia were standing in front of him, looking as happy as if they had medaled themselves. "Epic Gold!" they cried in unison.

He'd done it. He'd medaled, and not just any medal—a gold medal. Rovi, the former Star Stealer. Rovi the orphan. Rovi the Dreamer!

In a daze he was led to the medal podium and instructed to mount the highest platform. He heard the Dreamer anthem followed by the Ecrof fight song. And then, to his surprise, the anthem of Phoenis. This brought him back to earth. He wasn't Phoenician. His parents were from mainland Epoca. If he was anything besides a Dreamer from

Ecrof, he was a Star Stealer. But there was no Star Stealer anthem, and there had been no Star Stealers watching the race.

He sat quietly on the bus ride back to the village. Instead of celebrating with his teammates, he kept his nose pressed to the window, searching for a sign of his friends or of any of the other gangs of Star Stealers. Although Star Stealers were prohibited from the Upper City, they were usually around. And even a former Star Stealer like Rovi could always spot another Star Stealer lurking in the shadows, haunting the edges of the market, slipping through the Upper City on a risky errand.

But he saw no one. Not a single Star Stealer was out on the streets. As they approached the gates to the Junior Epic Village, Rovi saw a sign he'd never noticed before. It forbade anyone not affiliated with the games from entering the village. But at the bottom it read: *Any Star Stealer seen near the games or the village will be instantly arrested.*

Rovi waited until dark. After the final sorna horn of the day sounded to announce the sleeping hours, he slipped out of his residential tower. He knew he couldn't leave through the entrance to the village. That would be too dangerous. But he was familiar with another Phoenis—a city of secret passageways and back alleys. Under the cover of darkness, summoning all his skills as Swiftfoot, he stole through the sleeping village away from the gate toward the back, where a high wall protected the Junior Epics from the rest of Phoenis.

He had to find Issa.

Rovi was skilled at climbing. His hands and feet found footholds, and in no time he was up on top of the wall, slinking along it like a cat. Then he was slithering down the other side, loose in the Upper City.

The city smelled like jasmine at night. The velvet-purple expanse above him glittered with stars. The Tile Palace glowed. The Temple of Arsama towered—the point at its apex piercing the night sky. Rovi stared over the desert to where the Moon Palace caught the silvery lunar light in its hundreds of thousands of tiles.

He moved quickly through the sleeping streets of Phoenis, past the Alexandrine Market, where the Junior Epic kiosks were shuttered for the night. He passed opulent homes and fine restaurants. He picked up his pace, hurrying from the market down a set of crumbling stairs that led to the Lower City.

The Lower City didn't sleep like the Upper City did. People were always shuffling about the twisted, narrow streets. Light and music slipped from houses. Even a few vendors remained open.

Rovi darted from alley to alley, trying not to attract attention. Finally, he arrived at the banks of the river Durna, at the Draman Bridge, where Issa's gang always camped. He paced back and forth beneath the bridge's protective shelter, then crouched down, checking the shadows close to the wall. Last year, thirteen kids had made their home down here. Now it was abandoned. There were no pallets, no blankets, and no signs that there had ever been anyone there at all.

Rovi cupped his hands over his mouth. "Hello," he called in a low voice that bounced back at him with an echo.

No answer.

"Issa?"

Nothing. Surely there must be some sign of his gang—a piece of clothing, a fruit rind, a sandal.

Then a figure stepped out of the shadows. Rovi jumped. It was a man. In the moonlight, Rovi could see that he wasn't dressed in Star Stealer garb, but in heavier clothes that looked uncomfortable in the Phoenician heat. Rovi couldn't see his face, which was in shadow. All he could make out were a number of gold rings on both of the man's hands that glittered in the moonlight.

Rovi turned, prepared to run.

"It's not safe for you here," the man said. "You shouldn't linger by the river."

It took Rovi a moment to realize he'd been mistaken for a Star Stealer.

"You should hurry before the guards come," the man continued. "They've been patrolling the river every night."

Rovi stepped back toward the wall, on the off chance that the man would recognize him as a Junior Epic and turn him in. "Where should I go?"

"The other river."

Rovi gulped. The River of Sand. He did not want to venture into the dried-out tunnels. They gave him the creeps. Even though it had been more than two thousand years since the quicksand had flowed, the idea of walking in its former path terrified him.

"Go," the man said, "or I'll have to turn you over to the guards if they show. I can't keep all of you safe."

"Where in the tunnels are they?" Rovi knew there was an entrance close by, but the tunnels were extensive, stretching for miles beneath the city.

Footsteps echoed above. "Hurry," the man said. "I hear the patrol."

A flash from a hand lamp cast into the river, sending a yellow glow into the water. "Go," the stranger hissed. Then he tossed the lamp at Rovi.

Rovi caught it and began to run. He feet flew over the pathway along the river. His eyes probed the dark wall to his right, searching for the tunnel entrance. Where was it?

He glanced quickly at the water. He could see the streaks from the guards' hand lamp from the bridge behind him. Soon the light would find him, if it hadn't already.

And then he saw the entrance. Quick as he could, he folded himself in half and ducked into the tunnel. He stepped into the hollowness left behind by the River of Sand.

Rovi tried to catch his breath. The tunnel seemed massive. The hand lamp cast a weak glow only able to illuminate the small area directly around Rovi.

Now what? Now where? He had to find Issa, but how?

Rovi stood and stifled a shudder at the thought of the tunnel roiling with quicksand as it had during the time of the gods. Phoenicians and Star Stealers alike used to whisper that the river wasn't simply the work of the gods, but the work of Hurell himself. They used to say there was something dark, dangerous, and uncontrollable in the quicksand that was the work of the Fallen God. Rovi had always dismissed these rumors as silly legends. But now, standing in the tunnel, he felt a chill.

He took a deep breath and hoped his feet would guide him.

The tunnels were a maze, but unlike the corridors at Ponsit, which closed around Rovi, muffling his grana, at least there was space to breathe and think.

Five minutes.

Ten minutes.

Twenty minutes he walked through the tunnel. It twisted and turned, running back and forth through the city.

He heard a noise and froze. Was the river coming?

Rovi turned and rushed back the way he'd come—except he no longer knew which way he'd come. This was a bad idea. No, this was a *terrible* idea. His feet hammered the ground. His footsteps echoed loudly off the tunnel walls.

What if he couldn't find his way out? He'd be disqualified from the Junior Epic Games. Stripped of the medal he'd won only hours before.

There was that noise again. It wasn't the river. It was *voices*.

"Someone's there," he heard. "There's someone in the tunnel."

He squinted and saw a flicker of light coming from a gap in the tunnel wall. A little further up, he saw an opening.

Suddenly a figured jumped out, holding a hand lamp. "Who's there?"

"It's—it's—" Rovi sputtered.

"Swiftfoot?"

Rovi's heart leaped as he recognized Gita, a leader of a rival gang—a gang whose members, according to Issa, had all been taken to Hafara. She held up the lamp higher.

"Yes," Rovi whispered, afraid of the echo of his voice that the tunnel might throw back at him.

"This way," Gita said. She beckoned him down the passage and through the door.

Rovi followed Gita's brighter lamp, then stepped into an alcove off the main tunnel filled with a mismatched gang of Star Stealers, some of whom he knew and some of whom he identified only by their attire. They were worn and thin. Their faces were lean and shadowy with hunger. In their midst was Issa.

Rovi rushed to his friend and hugged him so hard he nearly toppled them both to the ground. "You're all right!" Rovi exclaimed. "When I didn't see you today, I thought—I thought the guards had gotten you."

"I'm sorry I missed your race," Issa said. "I tried to come, but there were guards everywhere. It wasn't safe."

"I saw," Rovi said, his heart heavy.

"I got close. But one spotted me and chased me through the Lower City. I barely made it back into the tunnels."

Deeper in the alcove, Rovi could hear a few of the remaining Star Stealers let out nervous sighs.

"I couldn't risk it. You've seen the signs?"

"You mean the one at the Junior Epic Village?"

"Yes," Issa said. "I tried to find you there first before the race. But there are more. They're all over Phoenis, warning us away from places like the Alexandrine Market. We're not allowed to be *anywhere*."

"Why?" Rovi asked.

"We're not sure," Issa said. "They say we are a threat to Phoenis. It started when they began to prepare for the games, and it's gotten worse in the last two months. Now there are so few of us left. The group needs me." He gestured to the twelve or so Star Stealers gathered in the room. "I couldn't take the risk of being caught."

"Wait," Rovi said, "these are *all* the Star Stealers who are left?" When he'd left for Ecrof, Issa's gang alone had twelve members, and that had been one of ten Star Stealer gangs in Phoenis.

Issa glanced around the alcove. "They've rounded up everyone else."

Rovi looked at the faces staring at him. Would he have been one of these lucky ones, or would he have been caught and taken to Hafara Prison? "How long have you been down here?"

"We started using the tunnels to get around not long after you left. We were permanently chased from the riverbank about a month ago. So this hideout is our home now."

Rovi shivered. He didn't think he could sleep in the dried-out bed of the River of Sand. "Aren't you worried about the river? It's down here somewhere, right?"

"It's deeper in the tunnels," Issa said. "I've never seen it. And hopefully I'll never have to."

"But what if it breaks free?" Rovi said.

"It hasn't for two thousand years." Rovi glanced over his shoulder as if the river might be in the main tunnel. "And if it does," Issa continued, "there are the warning sirens. Hopefully that will give us enough time to reach the river Durna."

"Hopefully?"

"What else can we do?" Issa said.

Rovi sighed. But before he could say any more, a shadow was cast from the tunnel into the hideout. Rovi felt someone standing behind him and stepped aside.

The new arrival wasn't a kid like the Star Stealers, but an adult. Rovi tensed. Star Stealers usually stayed clear of adults, who often turned them in to the guards.

"I believe you have something that belongs to me." The man held out a hand to Rovi. He spoke in Epocan with a heavy Sand-lander accent.

Rovi hesitated. Then he saw the rings. He held out the hand lamp.

"Thank you," the man said. "I see it got you where you needed to go."

"Who are you?" Rovi asked.

"My name is Fortunus," the man said.

"Fortunus has been helping us for the last month," Issa explained. "He came to Phoenis to unite the Star Stealers. Fortunus, this is Rovi."

"Rovi Myrios," Rovi said. He was instantly ashamed of using his last name. Star Stealers, who were orphans and outcasts, didn't have family names, and if they did, they shed them. To his own ears he sounded as if he was bragging.

Fortunus didn't seem to mind. He smiled and looked Rovi over. He was small but powerful. He looked like a Phoenician or a Sand-lander of some sort, with naturally tan skin. But he had a strange pallor about him, as if he hadn't seen the sun much recently.

Up close, Rovi could see that the strange clothes he'd noticed aboveground were indeed foreign to the Sandlands—leather pants and a woven T-shirt that looked to be made of wool or some other heavy fabric. Fortunus's black hair was shaggy and short. And he had a smile that lit up the room like a glowing crescent moon.

"Rovi Swiftfoot," he said. "The hero of the day."

Rovi couldn't help but smile.

"Wait," Issa said. "You won?"

"Of course he did," Fortunus said, taking a seat on a rough-hewn bench. "I've been trying to get back here to give you the news. But I had some scouting to do." His voice became serious. "It's worse up there than ever, Issa. There is double the normal amount of guards. Soon we won't even be able to scrounge food. We will need to make our move."

"Okay," Issa said with a meaningful look at Rovi, "I understand."

"But," Fortunus said, patting the spot next to him so Rovi could sit, "let's put that aside for a moment. We have a legend among us. They'll be singing songs about him someday."

Rovi tried not to blush as he joined Fortunus on the bench. "If they're going to sing songs about anyone, it's going to be my friend Vera Renovo. She's making history at the games. She intends to break the record held by Farnaka Stellus for most Junior Epic Medals."

"Does she now?" Fortunus said, sounding impressed. "That's *very* ambitious. But I predict Epic greatness for you, too, son," he added. "I'm proud to know you."

"Really?" Rovi beamed. "Me?"

"You ran one of the fastest Epic Miles in the history of the Junior Epics. Your reputation precedes you, even underground," Fortunus said. "Tell me more about yourself. Although I already know quite a lot. I've been following your exploits."

"My what?" Rovi asked.

"Your adventures—from the streets of Phoenis to the holy hills of Ecrof. News travels in all circles. If the rumors are true, you are a champion in the making," Fortunus said with a serious smile. "And you are destined to do great things."

"Hopefully," Rovi said.

"Only if you want to," Fortunus said.

"I do," Rovi assured him.

The man clapped him on the back. "That's the spirit. I see why you were on the Scrolls of Ecrof. I'm sure your family would have been proud."

Rovi bit his lip. The thought of his family made him sad, but he didn't want the Star Stealers to see. They were tougher than that.

"I also know how proud *this* family is of you," Fortunus said. "It's not often a Star Stealer rises to Junior Epic Glory or becomes the pride of House Somni."

An enormous smile broke across Rovi's face.

"You are many things to many people," Fortunus said. "That's a blessing."

"Tell us about the race," Issa broke in.

"Yes, tell us," Fortunus said. "I wish I could have seen it."

Rovi described the course and how he'd barely realized he'd won until his friends told him. Now that he knew Issa wasn't in Hafara, he finally allowed himself to enjoy his victory.

But as he neared the end, he broke off. "I'm sorry," he said to Issa. "I didn't do what you asked. I didn't mention the Star Stealers on the medal podium." He felt his cheeks burn with shame.

"Forget about it, little brother," Issa said.

"Yes, forget about it," Fortunus echoed cheerfully. "You've just had your first Junior Epic win—you can't be expected to shoulder the burden of others. This is your time to shine." He winked at Rovi.

"You're not mad," Rovi said, looking at Issa.

"No," Issa said. "You should enjoy your victory."

Fortunus reached into a leather bag and offered Rovi a hunk of honeyed bread. "If I were your father, I would take you out for a proper celebration of your victory. But this is all I have to offer."

Rovi hesitated. He didn't want to accept food in front of the hungry Star Stealers, but it felt rude to refuse. "Go on," Fortunus urged. "A small celebration on your behalf."

Rovi took the bread.

"And one more thing." Fortunus reached back into his bag. "A true Phoenician fig."

He handed it to Rovi. "Now, I should leave you and your friends to catch up." He stood.

◆

"No!" Rovi blurted, suddenly realizing how badly he wanted the older man to stay. For in all his victory celebration that afternoon and evening, something had been missing. He'd had no mother or father to share his joy with, no parents to celebrate his win and to let him know how proud he'd made them. When it was all said and done, Rovi was alone. In fact, if not for Pretia and her family, who didn't feel like family to him at all, he'd have had nowhere to go between terms at Ecrof. "I just—" Rovi continued.

Fortunus and Issa exchanged a glance. "Stay," Issa said.

"If that's all right with our honored guest," Fortunus said.

"Of course," Rovi exclaimed through a mouthful of bread and fig.

"You know," Issa said, "Fortunus wasn't just a Star Stealer. He was a gang leader, like me. His group lived behind the Moon Palace out in the desert."

"Really?" Rovi asked. He always wondered what happened to Star Stealers when they grew up. He knew they left their gangs, but that was it.

Issa's eyes grew wide. "But now he lives in the outlands, which is where a lot of us wind up. And he's been traveling from the Snowy Mountains to the Ice Continent and down through Epoca's major cities to gather together Orphic People such as ourselves."

"Why?" Rovi asked.

"So that anyone who lives beyond the designations of Dreamer and Realist might have a safe haven—a country of their own," Fortunus said. "We need to band together before we are forced to disappear or turn ourselves over for a life of servitude in one of the mines simply because we are neither Dreamers nor Realists. It is no longer safe for any Orphic Person to live in mainland Epoca, Star Stealers in particular. The Phoenicians have grown intolerant of our gangs over the years. But imagine a country composed of all of us: Moon Jumpers, Sun Catchers, Star Stealers, and the rest. A place where we can live and thrive without fear of the Dreamer and Realist authority."

"So you're the one gathering the Star Stealers together," Rovi said.

"I am. But it proved harder than I thought. Every time I gathered the leaders, the authorities thought we were planning something dangerous. And they started to crack down. But now it's time to act. We must leave."

"Issa, you want to leave Phoenis?" Rovi asked. He was no longer a Star Stealer. He no longer slept on the streets of Phoenis. He no longer stole food from the market or the Upper City. But he also couldn't imagine Phoenis without Star Stealers in it.

"We have no choice," Issa said. "Look around. This is who is left. They will get us soon if we don't leave. It's our last chance."

The other Star Stealers clustered in the alcove nodded at Issa's words.

"So—when? When are you going?" Rovi felt himself begin to tear up. What if he never saw his friend and brother again?

"Ah," Fortunus said sadly, "that is the difficult part. I wanted to leave soon, but we can't."

"We can't leave the others behind," Issa explained. "There are close to a hundred of us in Hafara Prison."

Rovi shivered at the thought of all those Star Stealers abandoned underground.

"You see, Rovi, that's the problem," Fortunus said. He offered Rovi more bread. But Rovi found he no longer had the stomach for food.

Issa sighed. "I'm not leaving without my gang, and the other leaders feel the same."

Rovi could feel a pit opening in his stomach. "What will you do?"

"There's only one thing to do, Swiftfoot," Fortunus said, placing an arm on Rovi's shoulders. Rovi stared at him expectantly. "We need to free your friends."

◆

"From Hafara?" Rovi's mouth hung open.

"Yes," Issa said. "Fortunus has a plan."

Rovi studied Fortunus as he took a deep breath and smoothed his leather pants.

"Even after I was a Star Stealer, I spent years underground in Phoenis. I learned many of the city's secrets. A great city always has plenty of secrets." He winked. "And one of the things I learned was that there is a key that opens all the locks in the city. It was buried two thousand years ago." His voice was grave and excited at the same time.

"We need that key," Issa said, "to get into Hafara Prison."

"Where is it?" Rovi demanded.

"It's buried in the Temple of Arsama," Fortunus explained. "It's called the Key to Phoenis. But only the best thief will be able to steal it."

And before he knew what he was saying, the words were out of Rovi's mouth. "*I'm* the best thief."

Fortunus's eyes twinkled. "I like that competitive fire. House Somni is lucky to have you."

Rovi didn't have time for the compliment. "If you need that key, I'll get it for you."

"Rovi!" Issa exclaimed.

"I'm not just Rovi. I'm Swiftfoot," Rovi said. "And what's more, I've been training my grana for a year. It's made me even faster than I was when I lived here. I know what I can do. And I can do this."

"I didn't dare hope you would help us," Issa said softly. "I would try it myself, but Star Stealers can barely travel aboveground. We are confined to the River of Sand tunnels now. So there is no way for me to access the temple. And even if I could, I am getting older. I'm not as nimble as I once was."

"I said I'll do it," Rovi declared. He'd just medaled in one of the premier events in the Junior Epic Games. And he hadn't even had to work that hard to do it. He'd also slipped out of the Junior Epic

Village undetected. Plus, he'd found Issa in the tunnels of the River of Sand. If he could do all that, he could steal a key from a temple. By the gods, he could steal anything.

Before he could say anything more, Issa pulled him into a powerful embrace. "I love you, little brother," he said. "Thank you."

Rovi returned the hug.

Then he felt Fortunus encircle them both with his arms. It reminded Rovi so much of being hugged by his father that he had to swallow hard.

"I'll steal the key," he assured them. "We have to free our friends."

◆

17

PRETIA

A CONFRONTATION

PRETIA COUNTED SILENTLY IN HER HEAD, then again out loud: "One, two, three, four, five, six, seven, eight, nine, ten, eleven, twelve." Twelve seconds—the length of her fastest 100-meter sprint. That's all she needed to do. Twelve seconds over several heats. Then she could make the podium.

She turned the counting into a beat, a rhythm that kept her going all morning. She heard it in her footfalls as she descended the stairs of the residential tower. She heard it in the sound of Spirit Water flowing into her cup in the cafeteria, the footsteps of the athletes overhead on the elevated walkways, the rhythm of the purple water falling back into the fountains, and the noise of the wheels of the vehicles rolling down the Grand Concourse. Twelve seconds to Junior Epic Glory.

In the late morning, Pretia and Vera boarded the Epic Coach to the Crescent Stadium. The first heats would take place before midday and the final race when the golden sun had reached its full height.

Pretia's heart skipped in her chest. This was her time to shine. This was her moment to show the world that she was more than a princess, more than the Child of Hope. She could show everyone who she really was—a Junior Epic—and what she was capable of.

The gate to the Junior Epic Village lifted. Vera reached over and squeezed Pretia's hand.

"Are you excited?"

"I can't believe this is actually happening. I mean, the marathon was one thing. But this is so much better." Pretia had been walking on air since the tribunal's decision.

"You got this," Vera said. "If I have to lose to someone, I'm glad it's you."

"We'll see," Pretia said.

"It's going to be you or me with the gold," Vera continued. "I just know it. Julius holds the record for this event at both the Epic and the Junior Epic Games. Hopefully one of us beats his time."

"It'll be symbolic either way," Pretia said. "He can protest all he wants, but we'll have the record."

Vera gave her a wide smile. "Well, I was thinking it would be *more* symbolic if you did. But you know, taking down Julius's record in this event would be pretty awesome. Snooty Realist."

"Here's to dreams that never die!" Pretia said. They slapped hands.

The entrance to the stadium was mobbed. A dozen eager kids swarmed up to Vera, demanding her autograph. She gladly signed caps, programs, T-shirts, even sneakers and water bottles.

"It's going to be you whose autograph they'll want after this race," Vera said.

"I've signed enough autographs," Pretia laughed. "I'm happy it's someone else for once!"

Vera took her by the shoulders and spun her around so they were face-to-face. "No joke, Pretia. I want you to promise me that you'll show everyone what you can do."

Pretia met Vera's eye and felt a warm rush of gratitude for her fiercely loyal friend. "All right. I promise."

The stands were packed when the athletes entered. Pretia grinned when she saw the crowd speckled with signs bearing Vera's name and cheering her on. She glanced at the royal box to make sure it was empty, that her parents hadn't turned up to watch her race—or, worse, stop her from racing. To her relief, flags from their respective houses occupied the seats reserved for the king and queen.

She began to warm up by running three laps of the track. She passed Vera and nodded. She passed Eshe, who waved and tried to tag along with Pretia. On the final turn, a runner sprinted past her, knocking into her slightly.

"Watch yourself, Princess." It was Rex Taxus, the Realist who'd challenged her at the first protest.

"You watch out," Pretia retorted.

But Rex was out of earshot. Well, she'd show *him* on the field. She'd heard he was great, but he was certainly no match for her shadow self.

Pretia sat in the grass and stretched.

The stadium roared. Banners flapped. Pretia tuned it out as best as she could.

"Runners!" a voice boomed across the stadium. "Assemble at the start."

Pretia joined her fellow competitors as an official drew them into heats. She was in the second heat with Eshe. All she needed in this round was to make the top five. Then she'd be in the semifinals. And there, once again, all she needed would be a top five finish. In the finals, however, it would be different. She wanted that gold medal for her place in the record books.

Pretia took a deep breath. Top five. She could do *that*. No reason to worry just yet.

Rex Taxus was kicking off the opening round. He strode to the starting blocks as every Realist in the audience rose to their feet, clapping and chanting his name.

"He's amazing," Eshe gushed. "If only he wasn't a Realist."

"Which means," Vera retorted, "that he actually isn't amazing."

"All I'm saying is that he's an amazing runner. The best I've ever seen." Then Eshe shot a bashful glance at Pretia. "I mean, almost."

"Well, this is his chance to prove it," Pretia replied.

The starter's horn sounded. Rex took off like a cheetah. He moved effortlessly, like he was flying or gliding. He crossed the finish line before Pretia had time to process what was happening. The other runners were so far behind, it seemed as if they were in a different race.

"Wow," she said, despite herself.

"He reminds me of my brother," Vera said.

"He's *really* good," Pretia said.

When it was her turn, she lined up in the starting blocks. She had an outside lane, which made chasing down opponents slightly more difficult, but she didn't let it faze her. She crouched down. She uttered the Grana Prayer. She heard the other athletes do the same—most in traditional Epocan and others in their local dialects. The horn sounded, and she was out of the blocks. "One, two, three, four, five," she started to count. But it was unnecessary. Her feet found a rhythm ahead of her mind. They flew faster than she could count. And before she had time to process the race, she was across the finish line. She checked the result. Fourth. Not bad.

She had barely exerted herself. She'd conserved energy. She could push harder in the semifinal and final stages.

She exhaled the tension she hadn't realized she'd been holding all morning. She was finally doing what she had set out to do ever since she'd made the decision to run away from Ponsit Palace. She was competing unhindered by others' judgment. She was allowed to be herself—to be her best self.

She took a deep breath and looked into the stands. A mass of purple flags was waving. Purple banners were flying. And people were chanting her name.

Pretia's heart swelled. She would make them proud.

Eshe ran over and hugged her. "We made it." Eshe finished fifth in the heat, just sneaking into the next round.

"Not so fast," Pretia said. "This was just the first step." The sun glowed fierce and beautiful overhead. The sky was faultless blue. But there was a cool breeze that rippled across the field. It was perfect weather to run her heart out.

Pretia jogged in place as she waited for Vera's heat to start. Vera took to the starting blocks to thunderous applause. Her fame as a breakout star of these games was spreading. People waved signs with her name painted in Dreamer purple. A few had even drawn pictures showing Vera's trademark puff of hair flying behind her as she raced. But Vera didn't even notice. She was a pro, stone-faced as she said the Grana Prayer.

She went off like a shot, dusting the competition to win her heat by a full second. She checked her time, then trotted over to Pretia and gave her a fist bump.

When the whistle blew to start the semifinals, Pretia and Vera moved to the blocks. Rex Taxus and Eshe were in the second heat.

"Top five," Vera said.

"Consider it done," Pretia promised.

Pretia got in position. She said the Grana Prayer and heard it echo up and down the line of runners. And they were off. Once more, before she knew it, she was across the finish lane. Fourth place again. She'd made it, barely. Vera had bested her by a millisecond.

In the other semifinal, Rex Taxus once more beat the rest of the field. Eshe finished sixth.

"If I'd been in your heat, it would have been different," she said when Vera and Pretia went over to console her. "It's so unfair that I had to race with Rex Taxus."

"Well, now *we* have to," Vera said.

"Yeah, but in the final," Eshe moaned. "That's not fair."

◆

"Who told her sports are fair?" Vera asked when she and Pretia walked off.

"You still don't think she reminds you of anyone?" Pretia asked.

Vera gave her a confused look. "No? Why do you keep asking me that?"

Pretia put on her tracksuit to stay warm during the round of javelin that took place before her final race. She walked to the far end of the field, away from the competition, her footsteps hammering a twelve-second count. This time Pretia knew she'd need to pull out all the stops. She lay on the turf, closed her eyes, and visualized the race. She went deep into her mind, drawing out her shadow self, seeing herself splitting apart. Over and over and over she made herself split. Each time she saw herself win.

She was dimly aware of the javelin contest unfolding somewhere else on the field—the roar as the contestant hurled the javelin, followed by the applause as his or her distance was announced. Pretia was barely conscious of the stadium, the crowds, the flapping banners, the golden sun hanging in the azure sky. But she *was* conscious of her small and important part in all of this—the special talent she held inside her that would take her to the top of the race.

Suddenly a different sort of cheering erupted. Pretia opened her eyes and sat up. She could see a group of people racing around the track. But there was no scheduled race. She squinted across the stadium. They weren't even dressed in racing gear.

"Pretia!" She turned. Vera was dashing toward her from the other direction.

"Vera, slow down!" The last thing Vera should be doing between races was running. But Vera didn't slow down.

The crowd on the track was drawing close, too.

In an instant, Vera yanked her to her feet, pulling Pretia away from the track, toward the center of the field.

"What's happening?" Pretia exclaimed.

She glanced over her shoulder. She could see the group on the track comprised five people in Realist blue who were now being chased by a phalanx of Phoenician guards. They were coming right for her. Over the roar of the audience, she could hear what they were chanting:

"Stop the princess."

The guards tackled three of the runners. But two had started cutting across the field, closing in on Pretia, who was frozen watching them. "Pretia!" Vera shouted. "Come on!"

Pretia could hear that some people in the stands had taken up the chant.

"Stop the princess."

As the two protesters closed in, Pretia could see that one was a tall girl with flaming red hair. The other, unmistakably, was Julius Renovo.

"Julius!" Vera shouted, skidding to a halt. Her voice was thick with fury. She looked from Pretia to her brother, then reversed course and began to run full tilt at Julius. She didn't slow down as she drew near to him. The siblings were on a collision course. Vera held her hands out in front of her as she ran.

Then, with all her strength, she shoved Julius to the ground.

The famous track star twisted on the field, struggling to stand.

Vera cupped her hands over her mouth. "Guards! Get this protester off the field. He's interfering with the race."

While Pretia watched Vera face off with her brother, the red-headed girl had run an exaggerated loop and was now rushing at Pretia from behind, with a guard in pursuit. If Vera could stand up to her famous and powerful brother, Pretia could address this flame-haired stranger. Pretia wanted to back away, but she willed herself to stay put. She had to face her accuser.

The girl was almost on top of her. Her face was contorted in anger. "*Cheater!*" she screamed at the final moment before the guard tackled her. "*Cheater!* This is Rex Taxus's race!"

Pretia's heart was galloping, but she tried to stay calm. She needed to speak. "I use my gods-given grana," she said. "That's all."

"We will erase you from the record books," the girl spat. The guard dragged her to her feet and began to haul her off the field. "You won't race again. You won't rule. Your grana is unholy. It's unnatural. *You* are unnatural."

Pretia was shaking, but she tried her best not to let it show. She had so much more to say. She wanted to tell the girl that her protest was unfair—that judging anyone for their grana wasn't right. But she feared she'd said enough. She didn't want to draw more attention to the situation.

A few feet away, Julius was picking himself up. "Don't you know who I am?" he said to the guard trying to haul him off. "I'm Julius Renovo. I won this race in the last Epic Games without the aid of cursed grana," he added with a dark look at Pretia.

Vera stared her brother down as she came to put an arm around Pretia's shoulders. "Pretia's grana is as natural as the sun and the sand—as natural as yours or mine," she said. "Tell him, Pretia. Tell my snobby, snotty brother."

Pretia could no longer control her trembling limbs. She took a deep breath, trying to regain her focus.

"Vera's right," she said.

Julius snorted. "Is that all you have to say for yourself?"

"No," Pretia said. "I—"

"You are as unholy as my misfit sister. If people ever witness what you can do, they will understand how unnatural it is," Julius announced.

The guard, obviously impressed by the status of his prisoner, started to escort Julius away from Pretia.

Pretia watched him stride off the field, the guard's arm linked through his, to a mixed reception of cheers, boos, and timid applause.

Vera took her hands. "Shake it off. Shake it off and show them," she said. "Now it's more important than ever."

Pretia clutched her arms around herself to still her shaking body. Everyone in the stands had seen that confrontation.

"Pretia, snap out of it!"

"Sure, um, okay," Pretia mumbled.

"You don't sound sure," Vera said. "Remember what you promised before we entered the stadium?"

Pretia nodded numbly.

"Even the tribunal was in your favor. This is your race. Look." She pointed at the stands. "Look at all those people. At least half of them are on your side. Maybe even more, since you're half Realist. You need to show them what you can do."

Pretia was trembling. "I don't know—"

Vera gave Pretia a small shake. "Yes. You do know. You know what you can and will do. You have risked *everything* to be here. Do *not* let them see they can get to you." Vera was staring right into Pretia's eyes. Suddenly the stadium vanished; the crowd silenced. "It's just you and me here," Vera said. "You and me. I got you and you got this. Okay?"

"Okay," Pretia said.

"Just you and me," Vera repeated.

In a trance, Pretia followed Vera to the starting blocks. The whistle to start the final 100 meters of the entire Junior Epic Games sounded. Vera was on the inside, the lightning-quick Rex Taxus to her left, and Pretia next to him.

On your marks.

Pretia crouched down. She muttered the Grana Prayer, aware of Rex Taxus doing the same next to her. She heard Dreamers chanting her name and Vera's. She could do this.

Get set.

Vera was right. She *had* risked everything for this.

Go.

And they were off. But not before Pretia heard "Stop the princess," crashing through the stadium like a tidal wave.

Pretia's feet hit the track. One, two, three, four—

She was aware of Rex Taxus at her side. Then he pulled ahead. There were only a few meters to go.

She needed to act. *Faster.* Pretia willed herself. *Faster.*

She was back next to him. She could feel her shadow self trying to break free, but something was restraining it. It was as if it could sense her reluctance.

Five-six-seven. Her feet raced. Her mind fought to keep up. It was now or never. She needed to split. She needed—

Pretia tipped forward, flinging herself over the line. She hadn't split herself. She'd missed her chance.

She ran until she came to a halt, then turned to check the results. Even though she hadn't summoned her shadow self, maybe there was a chance she'd made the podium. But before she could determine where she'd finished, she was tackled by a pack of Dreamers—including Vera, Eshe, Cyril, and Virgil. They were slapping her back and trying to high-five her.

"What happened?" Pretia asked, catching her breath.

"You won!" Virgil screamed.

Eshe and Vera were on top of her. "You *won*!"

"For real?" Pretia asked.

She looked over and saw Rex Taxus sitting on the ground with his head on his knees. "I beat *him* without splitting myself?"

Cleopatra Volis rushed over and swooped Pretia up into her arms. "You sure did. You are a Junior Epic Champion!"

"You beat everyone," Vera said, exuberant.

For a second, Pretia's joy vanished. "Did *you* medal, Vera?"

"No," Vera said. "I finished fourth."

Pretia's heart sank. "But your record!"

"Don't worry about me," Vera said. "This was your race. And you were *amazing*!"

It hit Pretia all at once. Vera had been too anxious about Pretia's performance to run her best in the 100-meter final. "I'm so sorry," Pretia said. "You were too focused on me."

"Don't be ridiculous," Vera said. "I've got a few more chances to hit ten medals, including our 4x400 relay. And with you on my team, that's basically a done deal." She held up her hand for a high five.

"Now that *will* be epic," Pretia said, slapping her hand, "in every sense of the word."

"And since you didn't split yourself, no one can even threaten to challenge your record," Vera said. "Not that I'd let them."

Pretia wrapped her arms around her friend. She felt as if she were floating. She couldn't feel the ground beneath her feet as she moved through the crowd of congratulatory Dreamers. She was in a daze as she climbed to the podium for the medal ceremony. She kicked dust from her gold Grana Gleams. How had she won without splitting herself? There was no longer any question that she belonged at these games. Her medal was won on the same terms as anyone else's.

Her heart lifted when she heard her name announced as the winner of the 100. All her nerves tingled as the official placed the gold medal—*the gold medal!*—around her neck. She looked into the stands at all those purple banners waving for her and was filled with a happiness such as she'd never felt before as the Dreamers' flag was raised for her. She put her hand on her heart for the Dreamer anthem and sang the Ecrof fight song. This must be what Rovi had felt when he won the Epic Mile—like he was on top of the world.

But . . . wait. Where was Rovi?

The second the singing ended, Pretia jumped from the podium and tugged on Vera's arm. "Was Rovi here?"

"He must have been in the stands somewhere," Vera said as they headed for the Epic Coaches.

"But wouldn't he have come to find us?" Pretia said.

"Well, you did miss his first event the day after the tribunal," Vera reminded her. "Maybe something important came up for him."

"So he's paying me back?" Pretia asked. "I didn't even know he was mad at me."

"No, that's not what I meant. I'm sure he's here somewhere."

Pretia wasn't so sure. There was no way Rovi wouldn't congratulate her after her first Junior Epic Victory, especially after all she'd risked to achieve it.

The Epic Coach had hardly stopped when it arrived back at the village before Pretia was racing toward the boys' residential tower. Rovi wasn't in his room. And he wasn't hanging around the fountains or on the training track.

She figured if she was going to find him anywhere, it would be in one of the two cafeterias, but he wasn't in either. She checked all the food kiosks. No Rovi.

She checked the grana temple and the media center. She was about to give up and return to her room when she heard someone call her name.

"I've been looking everywhere for you," Rovi said, rushing toward her. He glanced at the gold medal hanging around her neck. "I wanted to congratulate you in person."

"You were there?"

"Of course. You were amazing. It must feel incredible!"

"Standing up on the podium was so unreal," Pretia said.

"And it must have been amazing to finally use all your grana."

Pretia eyed him curiously. "How so?"

Rovi shook his head slightly and shifted from foot to foot. "You know, to split yourself."

Pretia could feel the anger rising up inside her. "What do you mean, *split myself*?"

The friends stared at each other. Then Rovi looked down at his feet.

"You weren't there, were you?" Pretia said. "You missed the race."

"I—I—kinda," Rovi muttered.

"You *kind of missed it*?" Pretia tried to control her voice. "And then you lied to me?" She could have forgiven him for missing her event if he hadn't lied. But the lying was too much.

Rovi took a deep breath. "There was something I had to do."

"What in the world did you need to do in the middle of the Junior Epic Games?" Pretia snapped.

"Not everything revolves around the Junior Epic Games," Rovi said.

"Right now it does."

"No, Pretia. There are other things."

Pretia put her hands on her hips. "Like what?"

"Like family," Rovi said defiantly.

"What family? You don't have family." She regretted the words almost immediately. But she was too mad to take them back.

"I do," Rovi said. "Just not in the same way you do."

Pretia eyed him. "You mean the Star Stealers."

Rovi nodded.

"You missed my event because you were with the Star Stealers?" she asked incredulously. "You left the village?"

"Last night."

For a moment, Pretia was speechless. "You spent the entire night off-site? What if you'd been caught?"

"I wasn't," Rovi said, a little too proudly. "I know this city. And I wanted to spend the night with my friends."

Pretia bit her lip to keep from screaming at her friend. "Rovi, first of all, you could get in so much trouble I don't even want to think about it. But more important, you know the Star Stealers are the whole reason I wasn't supposed to come to Phoenis in the first place. They're dangerous."

"You don't actually think that, do you?" Rovi sounded shocked.

"I do," Pretia barked. It was only partially true. She knew what her parents had told her—that the Star Stealers had somehow threatened her safety and the rule of Epoca. She didn't quite believe it herself. But she was so mad at Rovi for skipping her event and lying about it that she wanted to wound him.

Now Rovi's eyes flashed with anger. "You have no idea what you're talking about. You don't even understand them. No one does. Ever since the Junior Epic Games were announced for Phoenis, their lives have been ruined."

"Because *they* were trying to ruin the games."

"No. Because they were trying to survive. And now they need my help."

Pretia was stunned. "Rovi, you're not serious? You can't do anything here besides compete. That's the Junior Epic Code."

"We'll see," Rovi said.

"What are you planning?"

"Nothing. You wouldn't understand."

Pretia lowered her voice to a stern, furious whisper. "You'll get disqualified. They'll take away your medal if they find you sneaking away. You could be the reason the Dreamers lose the games. If they take your medal and we lose, it's on you."

Rovi looked shocked by her tone. "Pretia, that's not going to happen. You really wouldn't understand. You have everything. They—we—have nothing."

"*We?* Since when are you a Star Stealer again? Last I checked, you were Rovi Myrios of House Somni."

Rovi looked at her sadly. "Pretia Praxis-Onera, I thought you of all people would understand being two things at once. I guess you don't."

And with that, Rovi marched toward his residential tower. Pretia remained outside, trying to calm herself down. She could hear a marching band approaching through the Dreamer Village, playing their fight song. Purple sparklers shot into the air, celebrating the day's victors. She was one of those, but she didn't feel like celebrating anymore. Her victory was soured by Rovi's accusations.

She looked down at the medal hanging on her neck. The purple ribbon told her she was now a Dreamer hero, but she didn't feel like one. Instead, she felt as if she was always letting someone down.

◆

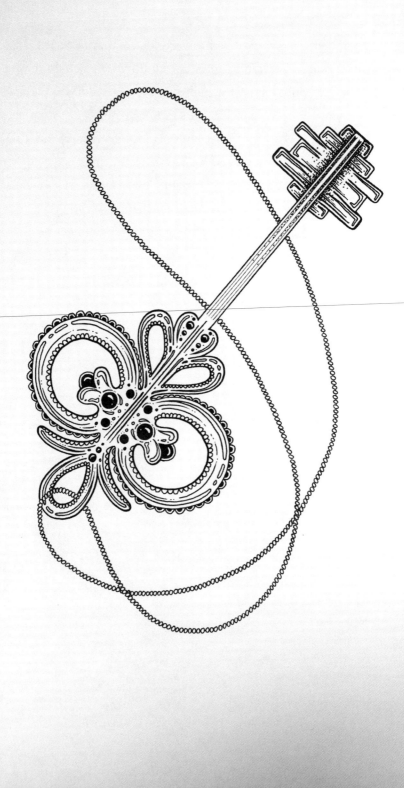

18

ROVI

A TOMB

TODAY ROVI WASN'T A DREAMER. TODAY HE wasn't an Ecrof student. Today he wasn't a Junior Epic Medalist.

He was a Star Stealer.

And to do what he had to do, Rovi needed to keep the games at a distance. He didn't attend any events. He stayed out of sight all day. He didn't train. He hid in his room from dawn until dusk, dressed in his everyday clothes: no sports kit, no Ecrof insignia. He slipped his Memory Master into his pocket for good luck. When darkness fell, he snuck back to the wall behind the village, and just like before, he slipped away.

The Temple of Arsama was behind the Crescent Stadium. To avoid passing too close to the stadium, Rovi would have to take the long way around the Upper City. And he had to move quickly. According to the plan he, Issa, and Fortunus had worked out when he'd spent the night with the Star Stealers, Fortunus would be waiting for him behind the temple in thirty minutes. Rovi would make it if he didn't dawdle or run into trouble.

The streets were busier than the last time he'd snuck out. Stragglers hurried to the stadium, waving banners. Restaurants overflowed into the plazas. Vendors dismantled their stalls.

Rovi glanced at the sky toward the triangular top of the temple that was pointing directly at the moon. He paused for a second. The temple seemed imposing and forbidding—a relic from another time. It didn't seem like a place a little Star Stealer could invade. He shook off these thoughts. He had to keep his mind on the imprisoned Star Stealers. He couldn't afford to second-guess what he was about to do.

He moved like mercury, keeping his head down and sticking to the shadows. Just another young Phoenician going about his business in the Upper City. From a distance, he could hear the roar from the stadium as first the Dreamer anthem, then the Realist anthem rose into the air. The decathlon finals were about to start.

He ducked into a narrow side street. Was someone following him? Was someone watching? Or was his mind playing tricks?

Rovi headed away from the stadium, toward the outermost edge of the Upper City. He used the shadow of the wall as cover as he approached the temple.

The Temple of Arsama, an imposing silhouette against the night sky, loomed even larger than in daylight. The dark mass of towering brick blocked out the entire Upper City of Phoenis behind it.

It was far and away the largest building Rovi had encountered in his life. And somewhere deep inside the temple was a key—an impossibly tiny object in comparison to the building that housed it—that would free the Star Stealers.

He'd never find it.

He'd get lost.

He'd—

"Rovi!" He heard his name whispered in the dark. Then he saw a flash of gold from Fortunus's rings as a hand reached out and pulled him away from the wall. He exhaled, happy to see a familiar face.

"Hurry. The guards have just finished their patrol." Before Rovi knew what was happening, they were heading toward the Temple of Arsama.

"I was worried you wouldn't come," Fortunus said. "I knew you would try, but I was concerned you'd be prevented."

"No one can stop me," Rovi said, sounding a lot more confident than he felt.

"I'm glad," Fortunus whispered. "If I were your age and still had your agility, I'd do this myself. But like all Star Stealers, I've aged out of the trade."

"I'm still Swiftfoot," Rovi said.

"I know you are. That's why you are perfect for this assignment."

Perfect. No one had ever called Rovi "perfect" before.

Fortunus patted the brick. "This temple is a relic. But it's also a vault. There are treasures and secrets everywhere. You just need to know where to look and how to find them. As I said, you were made for this task because of your talents both as a Star Stealer and as an athlete."

Fortunus leaned against the wall. "Now, this temple was built for the last Phoenician ruler before the Age of Grana: Queen Arsama. The pyramid has three main chambers: the Grand Gallery, the king's chamber, and the queen's chamber."

"So I need Arsama's chamber?"

"Yes," Fortunus said. "It's the third chamber down. You will enter the Grand Gallery first, a museum to the glory of ancient Phoenis. Below that is the king's chamber. And below that, the queen's. If the legends bear out, she will be holding the Key to Phoenis in her hands."

"You've been inside? You've seen all this?"

"No one has actually seen Arsama's chamber since ancient times. The only place open to the public is the Grand Gallery, and the noble vaults just outside where important Phoenicians continue to be buried. But I've seen the layout of other similar temples up close. If this one follows the same pattern, you just need to work your way down from the Grand Gallery. The chambers open into one another as you descend."

"How do I get to the Grand Gallery? The temple is closed."

"There is the main entrance for tourists and so forth. But that is closely guarded day and night."

"Is there another entrance?"

"There is indeed. Which is why this is *your* mission, Rovi Myrios, the swift-footed Dreamer." Fortunus looked up at the temple admiringly. "These things are masterfully built. You would think that the interiors would be stuffy and stale, but they are cool. That's why everything is perfectly preserved. The ancient Phoenicians did this by letting in no light and only a very precise amount of air to preserve all the artifacts, paintings, and bodies perfectly. You'll get in the same way the air does."

Together they gazed upward. The temple's wall rose up into the night at a treacherous incline. "Up there," Fortunus said, pointing toward the top of the pyramid, "is an air shaft. There's one on the north side and one on the south. You can access the Grand Gallery through the shaft. You will have to find your way down to the rest."

"And how do I get to the air shaft?" Rovi asked, eyeing the steep wall uncertainly.

"You climb!" Fortunus said with a confident laugh.

"You want me to climb this?" Rovi indicated the slope of the temple.

"You are a Dreamer *and* a Star Stealer. You can do anything. I have faith in you. Now go," Fortunus said. He handed Rovi a rope and a small hand lamp the size of a relay baton. "Tie this rope to the top of the air shaft before you drop into the Grand Gallery. You can shinny up it to escape."

Rovi took the hand lamp and tucked it into his pocket.

"When you have the key, bring it directly to your brother Issa and me. We will be waiting in the tunnels exactly where you found us last time." Fortunus gave Rovi a firm handshake. "Here's to stars that can be stolen. Do us proud, Swiftfoot." And with that, he slipped away in the dark so quickly that Rovi didn't have time to say goodbye.

In an instant, Rovi was climbing up the side of the pyramid. His feet found footholds, his hands did the same. The ancient, crumbling brick made his progress easier than he had imagined. In a few minutes he was up so high that he was afraid to look down. In a few more minutes he wasn't sure he'd even be able to make out the ground below.

He had to keep climbing. Rovi glanced ahead. He could make out the pyramid's point drawing closer. Where was the air shaft? In fact, what *was* an air shaft? A hole, right? A hole in the building to let the air in. Something darker than the dark wall he was scaling.

Then he saw it—slightly above him to the left. A few more feet. He scrambled sideways and hauled himself into the opening. His legs dangled down into the nothing below. He felt around with his hands, trying to get a sense of the air shaft. It seemed solid, rounded with a downward slope, and not much larger than Rovi himself. A small brick jutted up at the lip of the air shaft. It wasn't much to secure the rope to, but he'd have to try. Rovi tied the best knot he could, then let the rope unfurl. He listened to it descend into the depths below.

Now he had no choice—he had to descend. Down he went, gripping the rope as he slid through the air shaft.

When he thought he couldn't slide any further, the shaft ended six feet above the floor. Rovi let go of the rope and hit the ground with a loud, echoing thud. He hurried toward the closest wall in case his graceless entrance had made enough noise to attract the attention of the guards Fortunus told him were stationed somewhere outside this very room.

When there was no movement besides the rapid fluttering of his own heart, he began to take stock of his surroundings. He could see the Grand Gallery, a museum of ancient Phoenician treasures, by the glow of the small hand lamp. There were golden statues, masks, and treasures too numerous to count—goblets, crowns, and all sorts of fancy-looking knickknacks. Coffins bearing murals of the long-dead rulers of the Sandlands were propped up against the walls—dozens of unblinking faces staring out at him, watching the young Star Stealer trespassing in their temple.

Rovi ignored these faces. He needed to find the way down. He made a tour of the gallery, checking the walls for a passageway or a door. It took him three rounds before he saw it—an opening between two coffins that an adult would have to slip through sideways. He stepped in. Immediately the closeness of the walls made his pulse race and his chest constrict. He had to move quickly.

The narrow passage twisted as it descended before it opened into a wider hall that let him into a room slightly smaller than the Grand Gallery. In this room there was only a single coffin displayed horizontally on a pedestal in the center of the room—the king. The sight raised the hair on his neck. The room was lined with shelves, all filled with the king's relics. Rovi peered closely at a golden platter. It was too beautiful not to touch. He picked it up and turned it over in his hands. It would be easy to take it with him. But that's not why he was here. He replaced the platter carefully. Even so, the sound of the metal hitting the shelf summoned an echo that bounced back and forth in the chamber like a scream from the dead.

Rovi jumped and stifled a cry. He needed to get out of here. He spun around, looking for the door. Where was it?

There, diagonally opposite the door he'd entered through. Rovi hurried into the passage. Like before, it was narrow, twisting and turning as it led him deeper into the temple. Around and around. He stumbled a few times, banging into walls until he finally reached the queen's chamber.

This room was smaller than the king's but more ornate. A large gilded statue of Arsama stood in the center of the room. Her black hair was sculpted into an impressive tower. She was depicted with her hands pressed together in front of her in the old prayer style, her

◆

eyes slightly downcast. Her statue stood at the foot of her coffin as if watching over it, daring anyone to defile it.

Like the king's room, the walls were lined with shelves. Here the treasures were even more impressive—more gold and jewels than Rovi had ever seen. As Rovi surveyed the treasure, he heard a creaking noise—or did he imagine it? He glanced over his shoulder at the statue. Arsama's eyes had moved. They had been staring straight ahead. He was certain of it. And now they had shifted to the side, tracking him.

Rovi darted to the opposite side of the room. The eyes followed. He could *feel* them tracking him like a hunter. He shivered, beginning to sweat. He needed to open that coffin, although it was the last thing he wanted to do.

He took a deep breath and put his hands on the lid. He closed his eyes, uttering a pointless prayer, asking to be forgiven for what he was about to do. Then he slid the coffin open. Inside was a mummified woman dressed in the remains of what looked to be a simple flaxen robe. There were no riches, no ornaments, no treasures alongside her. Rovi took a closer look. There was nothing between her wrapped hands.

All this work for nothing. Fortunus had been wrong.

Rovi took a step back. Once more, he considered the riches in the chamber. What a contrast they provided to the humble contents of the coffin. The mummified woman seemed to have been entombed more like a servant than a queen.

Then it hit him. What had Pretia told him back at Ponsit when he'd stumbled across a royal coffin? Servants were often buried in the place of royals to confuse grave robbers. Royals were hidden deeper belowground, where thieves wouldn't find them.

This wasn't Arsama at all.

Rovi pumped his fist silently. Now all he had to do was find the actual queen's chamber somewhere deeper in the temple.

He began to search for another door. It wasn't in any of the walls. Rovi checked several times over, but he couldn't focus with that statue staring at him—watching him.

Focus. He had to focus. Where else could it be? It couldn't be in the ceiling. So that left the floor.

Suddenly Rovi knew exactly where to look. He lined himself up with Arsama's statue and directed his eyes to where her gaze had been when he'd entered. Straight ahead and slightly down.

And there it was—a lighter square on the floor. A trapdoor. Rovi got on his knees and traced its outline with his fingers. To his relief, he felt a catch. He pressed down, and when the floor gave way, he lowered himself legs first. He only felt empty air. But he had no choice. He jumped.

The fall wasn't far—no more than ten feet. When he stood, he was in a much narrower passage than he'd been in before. He cast the hand lamp about. He couldn't see much; the walls were so close together. He wiped his slick palms on his shirt and tried to calm his racing heart.

He moved down the passage, which was so tight that the light didn't penetrate far. He lost his footing, crashing into the wall on his right. In a few more steps, he lost his footing again. The passage turned sharply, then doubled back, and finally headed downhill so steeply that Rovi tumbled, skidding on the descent, tearing his shorts and scraping his hands.

He picked himself up at the bottom. The passage forked here, he realized, holding up the lamp.

He dashed in one direction.

And then in another.

He was sweating profusely. He reached into his pocket and found the Memory Master headband to wipe his brow. But the sweat kept coming. He put the headband on to keep the sweat out of his eyes.

The passage twisted and turned, sometimes splitting, sometimes

◆

reconverging. Rovi darted this way and that, harried and unfocused. He didn't feel like Swiftfoot. He didn't feel like a Junior Epic Medalist. He felt like—he felt like . . .

He'd felt this way once before, back in the Ponsit Palace's labyrinthine halls. The labyrinth had blocked his grana. And that's what was happening now.

Was *this* what Pretia had felt like all last year at Ecrof when she had forcibly restrained her grana? No wonder she had struggled so much in competition. It was dreadful.

Rovi's breath came fast and ragged. He was panicking and he knew it. But there was no choice but to go on. All mazes led somewhere and if they didn't, then you'd eventually find yourself back at the beginning.

Okay, Rovi told himself, *okay.* He closed his eyes, trying to find somewhere calm and still inside himself, trying to forget how deep underground he must be and how lost he potentially was.

He had to find the chamber. He could do this. He had to. He would walk, not run. That would keep him calm.

But he wasn't calm. His mind raced. He needed to focus, yet he couldn't.

He wiped away the sweat that had slipped below his headband and froze, his hand on the cloth.

The Memory Master! Rovi couldn't focus, but the Memory Master could focus for him. It could remember when he couldn't and create a mental map of his actions and replay them. He didn't have his grana, but he had something almost as good. He had his father's help.

Just thinking of Pallas Myrios at his side calmed Rovi. He adjusted the Memory Master and got to work. *Take it slow,* he told himself. *Take it easy.* There was no need to rush. He'd get there when he got there. He'd find the final chamber if he stayed calm.

He walked down the narrow hall, not minding for once that the wall brushed his shoulders. When he came to a fork, he went left. When he came to another fork, he went right. When the passage descended, he followed. And when he was forced to climb back up and wound up where he had started, he replayed his last movements and started over.

The only thing Rovi knew for certain was that the general direction he needed to head was down. Every time he took a wrong path and began to climb, he replayed his steps until he figured out how to go down again.

Without grana, it felt as if some part of his brain was numb. He didn't feel like himself. It was as if he were forced to compete without one of his senses, as if he were suddenly rendered deaf or blind. But he was making progress. He felt it.

For a while the passages coiled tighter and tighter, so he was forced to shimmy sideways. Twice he had to begin this section again. Each time he worried he would be unable to breathe, but he made it.

And finally, the maze ended. There was only a single way forward—a long ramp. Down he slid, into the dark, until he hit solid ground. He held the hand lamp up and cast its light into the room.

He'd expected a final challenge. But the next step was simple. There was only one coffin. It was unadorned and made of plain wood. If Rovi was right, inside he'd find Arsama's mummy surrounded by riches. He calmed himself once more and reached his hands out toward the wooden lid. He rattled it, and it slid to the side. He raised the hand lamp. Inside was a woman—or the preserved remains of one—wrapped in rich purple silks. Arsama had been a Dreamer! All around her were treasures, cups and jewels and finely wrought metals. But Rovi was only interested in what was between her folded hands—a big, brass key.

He did not want to reach in and take that key. He did not want to touch the dead queen. But he'd come this far. Carefully he eased the key from its two-thousand-year-old home. "Sorry," he whispered, "but I need this."

He palmed it and waited. Surely something would happen.

Nothing.

Rovi took off his Memory Master and wiped his brow. And as he did, the ramp—the only way out of the chamber—began to rise and retract. Rovi jammed the key in his pocket and grabbed on to the ramp before it was out of reach and he was stuck underground. He caught it just in time and shinnied onto the ramp as it ascended.

His breath was harsh in the tight space. That had been close—too close! But now all he had to do was follow the Memory Master in reverse. He reached for it, only to come up empty-handed.

It was gone.

The Memory Master must have fallen in his mad rush to catch the closing ramp. Rovi gulped air, trying to make a plan. What would Satis tell him? What would his father tell him? What would Vera and Pretia tell him?

He took a breath.

They'd tell him he could do it. They'd tell him he was ready. They'd tell him he'd trained for this.

And he had. That's what the Memory Master was for: training. Now it was time for the event. He put his hands to his temples. The headband had trained his mind. It had trained his feet. He *was* ready. He didn't need the full strength of his grana. He had his talent and his memory and that was enough.

Rovi took off through the maze. He twisted through the passages. He didn't stumble. He didn't misstep. He just flew forward, unsure of where he was going but certain of the outcome. In fifteen minutes, he'd made it to the queen's chamber. In another ten, he was in the king's.

Finally, he reached the Grand Gallery and rushed to the air shaft. At the base of the opening he tripped on something. The rope lay coiled at his feet. It had fallen from where he had tied it.

He had no method of escape.

In a panic, Rovi surveyed the Grand Gallery. There was only one exit, Rovi realized. It would take him straight past the guards and out through the main entrance of the temple where visitors were admitted during opening hours.

Rovi paced the gallery once more. Either he could be discovered by the guards when the temple opened and definitely get in trouble, or he could risk it by running past them now and at least have a chance at delivering the key.

He tiptoed to the door and peeked out. A well-lit hallway led to the temple entrance. He could see two guards seated on either side looking out over the Upper City. He knew he could outrun any guard—he was a Junior Epic Gold Medalist.

There was no door or gate to bar his progress. But there was no place to hide, either. He had to hope that his speed and agility were enough.

On your marks.

Get set . . .

He tore away, as fast as he could down the hallway, past maps and diagrams on the walls for the visitors to examine, past replicas and dioramas. He ran faster than he ever had. He put everything into this effort, every millisecond he'd spent training at Ecrof, every single technical instruction he'd received. He kept his arms pinned close, his fingers tight together. He held his chest upright.

Faster. Faster. Faster.

He blew past the guards.

He could sense them behind him, initially too startled to move, too stunned to realize what had just happened. Someone had run *out* of the Temple of Arsama.

But their inaction was short-lived. Too soon, Rovi heard footsteps sprinting behind him.

Down the sandy steps from the temple entrance he ran, his feet never missing a beat. In the open air, his grana was restored to full strength. He knew his feet would lead him as they always did. He flew over the cobbled avenue, the grand approach to the pyramid. He ran for the heart of the Upper City. He knew better than to glance over his shoulder. But his senses told him the guards were at his back, doing their best to keep pace with him.

He needed to accelerate. He needed to escape.

Now he was all Star Stealer, dodging and darting at remarkable speed, finding alleys he didn't know existed and taking them to unknown destinations.

The guards were good—better than the ones who patrolled the Alexandrine Market. Rovi could maintain his distance but he couldn't shake them.

Usually Rovi could rely on the chaos of the busy market and the crowds of the Lower City to aid his escape. But now it was nighttime and the city was empty. All he had to rely on was himself and his grana.

His footsteps echoed loudly, as if they were summoning the guards, alerting them to exactly where he was headed.

He sprinted through plazas and courtyards. He climbed balconies. He swung from balustrades and zigzagged through colonnades. His grana was helping—but it wasn't enough.

He could feel the guards at his heels. They were closing in.

He raced out of the market and tried to form a plan. He would cross the bridge over the river and then take the steps down on the far side to get to the water level. Then he'd sprint along the narrow towpath and duck into the entrance to the River of Sand he'd used when he'd found Issa. He hoped the total darkness by the river would hide where he was going.

He left the market and hit the Draman Bridge.

The two guards were close behind. The quickest way down to the river was if he jumped. But he didn't want to risk losing the key in the water.

◆

He took the stairs, the guards on his tail. They were too close. He ran through his old, abandoned camp. He was closing in on the tunnel entrance. But if he took it, he'd lead the guards right to the Star Stealers.

Rovi continued past the entrance and took the next flight of stairs up to the streets. Then he doubled back, racing for the Upper City.

Faster, faster. Through the market again. Up another flight of stairs. Soon he could see the back wall of the Dreamer Village. Returning the key would have to wait. He scrambled up the wall, scraping his knees and hands.

He flung himself down into the village and lay panting against the wall. When his breath was quiet, he slunk to his residential tower. He dragged himself up the stairs to his room. He took the key out of his pocket and slid it between the pages of his Grana Book, where no one would see it. Touching another person's Grana Book was forbidden. Then he rinsed his face and slid into bed just in case anyone checked on him.

But he was too full of adrenaline to sleep. His mind raced. He hadn't delivered the key. And that meant he'd have to escape from the village once again, risking discovery to bring it to Issa and Fortunus.

Rovi had had enough of adventures. He could still feel those guards on his tail. He wanted sleep to come so he could escape the memory and the fear. But his eyes wouldn't close. Instead, they were drawn to the window that overlooked the village, where he could suddenly see two Phoenician guards patrolling the grounds with their hand lamps, peering into every corner.

And he knew exactly what they were searching for.

◆

19

PRETIA
AN ARRIVAL

VERA'S BABBLING WOKE PRETIA UP. "I'M going out to check the scoreboard. I need to make sure Rex Taxus didn't take a medal in the pool last night. I heard he might have been a late entry in the freestyle. Do you want to come? You should come."

Pretia rubbed her eyes.

"Because if he got a medal, that means he's closing in on me, but if he didn't, that means—"

"Vera," Pretia grumbled, "slow down."

"I don't want that stuck-up Realist to be the star of the games," Vera continued. Then she clapped a hand over her mouth. "That came out wrong. What I mean is, if someone else has to set records and get attention, I don't want it to be a guy who's leading protests against my best friend."

Pretia yawned and stretched. "Vera, I want you to set that record for *your* sake, not because of anything to do with me."

Vera had moved to the window and was peering out as if she could see the leaderboard from where she stood.

"Okay, okay," Pretia said, taking the hint. "I'm coming."

It took them some time to make their way out of the residential towers. Every Dreamer they passed had a word of encouragement or support for Vera. People held doors for her, stood aside as she passed. They stared and whispered.

"Why can't they just treat me normally?" Vera said. "It's making me anxious."

"Now you know what it's like being Princess of Epoca," Pretia laughed, grateful that someone else was getting all the attention for once.

As they passed through one of the plazas in the village, they saw that a swap meet had been set up, where kids from different academies were trading their kit.

"I bet your shirts would be a big-ticket item," Vera said. "Who wouldn't want a Praxis-Onera jersey?"

"I think Renovo is going to be a collector's item," Pretia replied.

"Trade you," Vera teased.

They picked their way through the ad hoc market until they reached the leaderboard. Pretia watched Vera's eyes fly over the numbers and stats.

"Phew," Vera said. "Either Rex didn't swim or he didn't medal. I'm still ahead of him."

Pretia checked Vera's medal count. Vera had participated in so many competitions that Pretia couldn't keep up with them all. She sat on top of the medal leaders with eight, the record-setting number of medals that Julius had won in the last games. As she'd said, Rex Taxus was nipping at her heels.

"Rex is only signed up for one more event," Vera said. "So no matter what, he can't pass me. Now all I have to do is get two more medals and I can pass Far—" She lowered her voice. "You know, that old guy's record."

"If no one remembers him, why does it matter to you so much?" Pretia asked, curious. "Can't you just aim for Julius's record?"

"It's personal," Vera said. "I set this challenge for myself and I plan to meet it."

Pretia turned back to the board and looked at the overall medal count. "The Realists are ahead by three medals. We can pass them."

"If it comes down to the final relay," Vera said, "you're going to have to split yourself no matter what sort of protest or distraction my brother organizes. We'll need that podium position."

"I know," Pretia said. "I'll do whatever I need to."

"This is going to be close," Vera said. "Somni can't afford any missteps."

A wave of anxiety passed over Pretia. The Dreamers also couldn't afford to have any medals taken away. That's exactly what would happen if the officials discovered Rovi had snuck out of the village.

She glanced over her shoulder. "Have you seen Rovi?" she asked.

"I've been with *you* all morning," Vera reminded her. "Why? You want to look for him?"

"No," Pretia answered a little too abruptly. She was still annoyed at him for lying to her.

"Whoa," Vera said. "Everything okay?"

Pretia breathed deeply to settle herself. "I mean, I don't want to find him right now." She busied herself by checking the leaderboard. She knew she had been unfair to Rovi the last time they talked. She needed to apologize but wasn't entirely looking forward to the conversation. "Okay, so today there are swimming relays in the pool and high jump and discus at the Crescent Stadium. That's you and Eshe in the high jump, right?"

"Yes," Vera said. "Are you sure everything is okay?"

"Of course," Pretia replied, not meeting Vera's eyes. "I'm hungry and sore. Not splitting myself really did a number on my calves. I think I'll hit the health center after breakfast. I want to be in perfect condition for the relay."

Rovi wasn't at breakfast, which relieved Pretia, since she didn't want to confront him, but it also filled her with anxiety, in case he was off doing something risky. She ate quickly and rushed off to the health center, hoping to get there before it got jammed with athletes wanting to soak their ankles in the ice baths, submerge in the healing pools, roll out their muscles on the bubble racks, and slide into the soothing suits.

The health center was empty except for one athlete who'd fearlessly plunged both her ankles into an ice bucket: Eshe. She looked delighted to see Pretia.

"Sore or injured?" she asked as Pretia entered the room.

"Sore. It's not bad. I'm going to roll on the bubble racks for a bit," Pretia replied, heading toward the rolling ladders with rotating, soft bubbly balls on them that contoured to an athlete's body and worked out muscle stiffness. "Ready for your event today?"

"Totally," Eshe gushed.

"I better see you and Vera on the podium," Pretia said.

"You will."

Pretia envied the recruit's confidence.

Eshe looked around to see if anyone was listening. "Is it true?"

"Is what true?"

"Are *they* here? Am I going to get to race in front of them?"

"In front of whom?" Pretia asked.

Eshe gave her a strange look. "Your parents. The king and queen."

"My parents? In *Phoenis*?" Pretia couldn't hide the panic in her voice.

"A delegate was just here. She told me that those of us competing today have to acknowledge the royal box before our event and from the podium if we medal."

"I haven't been told anything," Pretia said, trying to hide her mounting anxiety.

"No one back home will believe it. Imagine winning gold in front of the king and queen! I'd even settle for silver."

Why wouldn't Eshe be quiet? Pretia needed to think. *Should I hide? Should I find Janos?*

"Can I meet them? Will you introduce me? Pretia!"

An ice cube hit Pretia in the arm. "What?" Startled, she glared at Eshe.

"You weren't listening," Eshe said. "I asked you if I can meet your parents."

Before Pretia could respond, four burly adults stepped into the health center.

They weren't dressed like delegates or officials from the games.

"Princess Pretia Praxis-Onera, there you are." A strong woman with arms like a shot-putter's strode toward her. One glance told Pretia she was a royal guard.

"Yes," Pretia said.

"You need to come with us."

"I'm busy," Pretia said. "I'm rehabbing my calves." She was tired of adults bossing her around and making her do things besides focus on the games.

In four strides, the woman had crossed the room and taken Pretia's arm. "It's for your own safety," she said.

In silence, Pretia followed the guards out of the village. They formed a barrier around her as they went—one in front, one in back, and one on either side.

A royal van was waiting on the concourse. Pretia got in without being told.

The van drove through the Upper City in the direction of the Tile Palace. Instead of stopping in front, it pulled around back. The door opened and two guards hustled Pretia inside so quickly she didn't have time to admire the magnificent building close-up.

Once inside, she was marched down a series of corridors, deeper and deeper into the palace. Her anxiety grew with each step. What would she say to her parents? How could she apologize for disobeying them? They would be furious.

Finally, the guards stopped in front of a single, heavy bronze door. One of them knocked. Pretia heard a bolt slide back. Then the door swung open. She felt a hand on her back urging her inside. She stepped into the room.

Her parents were dressed not in official garb, but in the casual clothes they reserved for long voyages.

The king stepped toward his daughter and embraced her. "You're safe!"

"Of course I'm safe," Pretia said warily. "Why?"

Her mother rose. "Pretia, you disobeyed us."

The king let Pretia go, and the joy in his face at seeing Pretia was replaced by anger. "We were very disappointed," the king said sternly. "We are still disappointed."

Pretia hung her head. "I'm sorry."

"It's a little late for sorry," her father said. "You knew that when you got to Ecrof's protected island, you would be beyond our reach."

"And you also knew," the queen added, "that when you were selected for the team, it would be your duty to compete. You planned this so well, Pretia."

"Along with your brother," the king said with a meaningful look at his wife.

"Your uncle has always put sports above all else," the queen said, her voice disapproving, "even if it contradicts our wishes. Did he plant this idea in your head?"

"He doesn't always consider what's best for the kingdom," King Airos added. "Don't think this act of defiance on his part will go unpunished. He takes too many liberties with his position."

"Don't blame Uncle Janos," Pretia pleaded. "It was my decision. I just couldn't imagine life without sports."

"Well," the king said, "that is exactly what you will have to do. From now on, there will be no more sports for you."

Pretia inhaled sharply.

"You are the Child of Hope before anything else," the queen said. "Your duty is to your kingdom, not to a team."

"My duty is to House Somni, at least for a few more days."

"Not anymore," the queen said.

Pretia looked at her father. "Don't you want the Dreamers to win? If I run in the 4x400, I can almost ensure them a medal. And Somni is going to need that medal."

The king sighed. "Then they will have to win it without you."

"Is this all because I ran away?"

"No," the queen said. "It has to do with safety."

"But the games *are* safe," Pretia pleaded. "There are guards everywhere."

The king held up his hand for Pretia to stop talking. "And there will be more guards from now on. Something very alarming has happened here in Phoenis."

Pretia looked around the room, taking in her surroundings for the first time. The room was small, more like a bunker than royal quarters. In the center was a sturdy table and six chairs, everything inlaid with tile. Even the floors and walls were covered in mosaic. The only surface that was unadorned was the heavy bronze door. She'd seen doors like that before—they were designed to block out noise from outside and keep whatever was said in the room secret.

The king spread his large hands out on the table. "Pretia, we think it's time you begin to understand and be consulted on some matters of state."

"Someone has broken into the Temple of Arsama," the queen said, taking a seat at the table. "We have reason to believe it is the work of the Star Stealers."

"We think," the king continued, "they are planning to hold the games hostage."

"How?" Pretia blurted.

◆

The queen folded her hands and stared at her rings. "We aren't sure. All we know is that they stole something very important to Phoenis. An ancient key. The most important key in Epoca."

"Why would the Star Stealers want an old key?" Pretia asked.

"This key opens every door in Phoenis. If they have it, they can do anything with it. They could take control of the city," the king explained.

"They are outsiders," the queen added, "and they threaten our natural order, since they are neither Dreamers nor Realists."

Pretia folded her arms over her chest. "Well, neither am I!"

"Pretia!" Queen Helena gasped. "*Never* say such a thing. You are both. That is the point of you."

Pretia had to work hard to control her tone. "The point of me?"

"Your birth united this county with a new future," the queen continued.

"What if that's not what I want for my life?" Pretia asked.

The king lowered his voice. "You have no choice. It's who you are. It is why you were born." He cleared his throat. "Now that the Star Stealers have this key, there's no telling what they will do with it. We need to get you out of here as soon as possible."

"You mean I have to leave the games before they're over?" Pretia exclaimed.

"Yes," the queen said. "Immediately. Tonight."

"But it's my Epic Duty to compete."

King Airos sighed. "And you have done your Epic Duty already. You competed, and won. Janos will select a suitable alternate. And this time he will do as I command." Pretia was taken aback by the fierce tone in her father's voice. "There is no shame and no prohibition against you leaving now. Athletes leave the games for many reasons—illness, injury."

"But I'm not ill or injured," Pretia objected.

"No," the queen said. "You're something worse. You are unsafe."

"How?" Pretia demanded. "Why?"

"If the Star Stealers managed to get that key from deep in the Temple of Arsama, there is no telling what they are capable of," Pretia's father explained. "And no telling what they will do."

"The Phoenician guards have told us that only the best thief could have pulled that off and not gotten caught. Someone swift and nimble," the queen said. "We need to be very cautious."

Pretia's mind caught on the word *swift*. Her gut churned. Hadn't Rovi's nickname as a Star Stealer been Swiftfoot? And hadn't he bragged on the day he arrived in Phoenis that he'd never been caught stealing by the guards?

The king looked at Pretia meaningfully, unaware of her roiling thoughts. "Don't you see how dangerous the situation is? The Star Stealers could use that key to open the gates to the Junior Epic Village. Phoenis will not be safe until the key and the Star Stealer who stole it are found."

Pretia's mind was racing. If Rovi had indeed stolen the key, surely the Star Stealers weren't planning to do anything bad with it. Rovi wouldn't have anything to do with something that endangered her. But this was an argument she couldn't make to her parents. She had to tread carefully.

"The guards have been doing their best to round up the Star Stealers for the last year," the queen continued. "They have been making the streets safer for the games. But as we feared back at Ponsit, their efforts have not been enough."

"What do they do with the kids they've rounded up?" Pretia asked.

The king and queen exchanged glances. "We leave that up to the Phoenician authority. It has always been the right of any province in Epoca to mete out their own punishments," Queen Helena said.

"I assume they are being sent to make sand bricks as usual," Pretia's father added. "It's not such a bad punishment."

"But they're kids," Pretia objected.

"That doesn't mean the law doesn't apply to them," Queen Helena said sternly. "Whatever the law may be. And as for you, you are not above our authority, no matter what my brother says. You will return to Castle Airim with us," the queen said. "Last year, I thought Ecrof might be good for you. But I see that even a short time spent learning sports has distracted you from the essential work that lies ahead. It has made you reckless and careless."

"What essential work?" Pretia asked.

"Whether you like it or not, you are the Child of Hope," the king answered. "And we brought you into this world so you could unite Dreamers and Realists." His face softened. "What's more, we love you beyond all imagining, Pretia. You are *our* hope. Not just the hope of Epoca. If something happened to you, we would never forgive ourselves."

"We hope one day for a world without so many boundaries between houses," the queen said.

Pretia stared at her parents. "And that's my job?"

"Yes," her father said. "A world of Dreamers and Realists without friction. A world where the houses might blend."

"What if I want—" Pretia began. Suddenly she didn't feel like speaking anymore. There was nothing more to say, no more objections to make.

"We've already seen what happens when you do what you want," her mother said. "You will come with us when you've packed. Janos will be disappointed, I know. But then again, I'm very disappointed in him."

Janos wouldn't be the only one. Pretia could only imagine Vera's reaction. Vera wanted to make history. And Pretia could assure her that she would. She knew she might also be the one person who would guarantee a win for House Somni if it came down to that. But her parents had made up their minds.

◆

"The palace guards will take you back to the village," the king said. "When you've finished packing, we will depart."

Pretia drew in a long, slow breath. She stood up and looked directly at each of her parents, meeting their eyes in turn.

Then, without a word, Princess Pretia Praxis-Onera left the chamber.

In a daze, Pretia walked through the Dreamer Village for the last time. She ignored the leaderboard and the athletes getting ready for the final days of competition. She blocked her ears to the music pouring from the speakers and the glorious purple water in the fountains. Without a word to her teammates, she headed straight for her room. Thankfully, Vera was out. Pretia couldn't imagine how she'd explain to her friend what was happening.

She pulled her duffel out of her closet and began stuffing her gear inside. A few weeks ago, these clothes had been her most prized possessions. But now they were just a reminder of everything she'd never do again. She put her gold medal in last. At least no one could take that victory away from her.

She looked for a pen and paper to leave Vera a note, but when she found them, getting the words out was too difficult. Word would travel around the village soon enough that Pretia had been taken away.

She gathered up her Grana Book and opened it to the image that had told her to go to Phoenis. She must have read it wrong. There was no reason for her to have come here. She snapped the book shut and stuffed it in her bag.

Pretia took a final look around the room, then opened the door. Instantly, she was bowled over by Vera. "My laces!" Vera shouted.

Pretia rolled over on the floor.

"I need backup laces. Mine snapped," Vera panted. Then she took in Pretia's backpack and duffel. "Wait, where are you going?"

"Nowhere," Pretia said.

"Are you *leaving*?" Vera gasped.

Pretia stared at her friend.

"Hold on," Vera said, her eyes blazing. "I heard your parents are here. Eshe was babbling about it. Are they . . . did they . . . ?"

Pretia could almost hear Vera's mind putting it all together.

"They're taking you home?"

"Um—"

"They're taking you home!"

Pretia sighed. "It's complicated."

"No it isn't," Vera said. "Not at all. You're not going."

Pretia stood and shouldered her backpack. "I have to."

"What you have to do is secure victory for House Somni," Vera said. "That's why you came. There are only two days left."

"My parents are worried because someone broke into the Temple of Arsama and stole an ancient key." Pretia didn't want to go into details about the Star Stealers. "They think I'm in danger."

"Who cares about some old key?" Vera said. "Can't they just keep you somewhere safe until the 4x400 at least?"

"They won't."

Vera bit her lip. "Well," she said, "if they won't, maybe we can."

"What do you mean?" Pretia asked.

"Do you want to race?" Vera asked her. "Do you want another Junior Epic Gold? Do you want victory for House Somni?"

Pretia was silent for a moment. One more race. What harm could it do? It'd be her last for sure. But she'd love one more medal. And beyond that, she'd love to help Vera write her way into history. "Yes," she said slowly. "More than anything," she added in a whisper.

Vera's face brightened. "Then we'll just have to hide you until the relay."

"Where?" Pretia asked. A guard was waiting at the entrance to the residential tower to take her back to the car that was idling on the Grand Concourse. Her heart beat quickly. If there was any chance that she could compete in one last race for the glory of House Somni, she would take it.

"I don't know," Vera said.

Pretia's heart sank. But before Pretia could say any more, a broad smile erupted on Vera's face. "But I know someone who does. Rovi! No one knows how to hide better in Phoenis than Rovi. It's how he grew up."

"My parents have guards," Pretia said. "They're watching me."

Vera was already rummaging in her closet. She pulled out her giant swim coat and handed it to Pretia. "Put this on, hood up. It will conceal you."

"Then what?" Pretia asked.

"Pack your backpack with whatever you need for a few days. Then we'll go to the boys' tower and you'll wait for Rovi. It's totally forbidden for girls to go in there. So no one will check."

"So how are we going to get in?"

"Just walk in. Hood up, head down, like you belong."

"And then?" Pretia asked.

Vera shrugged. "Who knows. But he'll figure something out. Two days from now, you and I are going to take gold."

"Okay," Pretia said. She could feel her cheeks glowing. Her parents would be so mad. Again.

Pretia stuffed a few things into her backpack. Then she put on Vera's coat and lifted the hood. It was warm but hid her face from view. Vera was already racing down the stairs. "Rovi will know exactly what to do," she called over her shoulder.

Pretia sprinted after her, bulky and awkward in the enormous coat. Her adrenaline was surging. She didn't have the heart to tell Vera she was mad at Rovi. Right now, Rovi was her best option to hide. Even if she strongly suspected that his swift feet were responsible for the reason her parents wanted to whisk her away.

20
ROVI
A FAVOR

ROVI STOOD IN THE BACK OF A CROWD OF Dreamers at the Crescent Stadium, watching Vera as she prepared to make her final attempt in the high jump. If she cleared the bar, she'd make the podium and surpass Julius's medal count. The kids from House Somni chanted her name. Their cheers were echoed by the Dreamers in the stands. Rovi lent his voice but kept at a slight distance from his teammates.

He was nervy. Was it him or were there more Phoenician guards than usual? Each time he saw one of the telltale red hats, his heart stopped. News had traveled quickly that someone had robbed the temple. How long before he was discovered? He knew he'd been close enough for them to tell that the thief was a kid. Were they looking for him even now? He had escaped the guards, but his getaway hadn't been entirely clean. He'd left the Memory Master behind. The thought of it sitting in the Temple of Arsama terrified him. If the guards knew the key was missing, then they had been in those hidden tunnels and might have chanced on his headband. The key was in his pocket. He couldn't risk leaving it in his room. Although he knew touching someone's Grana Book was off-limits, he worried that given the circumstances, an exception would be made if they searched his room. It felt safer—although not that comforting—to have the key on his body. Worst-case, he could toss it if the guards were closing in on him.

But he knew he had to get rid of the key as soon as possible. Every moment that passed was another moment he could be caught red-handed.

"VE-RA! VE-RA!" The crowd stomped their feet as she stepped up to the line. The stands were filled with people holding signs with GO, VERA, GO painted on them.

Rovi cupped his hands over his mouth, calling her name along with his fellow Dreamers.

How many guards were patrolling this event? Fifty? Sixty?

Vera began her approach to the bar. She leaped, arching her back, lifting her legs, rising up and over the bar without touching it.

She crashed onto the mat, then bounced up to her feet, her arms raised in ecstatic victory.

All the Dreamers in the stands leaped to their feet at once. The Crescent Stadium was rocked by thunderous applause louder than anything Rovi had heard before. He cheered along with the crowd.

Vera had broken her brother's medal haul! She now had nine Junior Epic Medals. Rovi watched as a group of Dreamers lifted Vera onto their shoulders and began to parade her around the Crescent Stadium.

Rovi nearly leaped out of his skin at a touch on his shoulder, but it was only Satis.

"Are you okay?" the Visualization Trainer asked.

"Yeah," Rovi replied, struggling to control his nerves. "I was just anxious . . . for Vera."

Satis gave Rovi a curious glance. "Vera is the last person I'm ever anxious about." He beckoned Rovi a little way off from the crowd. "I need to ask you something in confidence."

Rovi's heart was pounding.

"A very important relic has been stolen from the Temple of Arsama," Satis said.

"What does that have to do with me?" Rovi asked. He was sure the Trainer could hear his heart thumping through his chest.

"The guards know that it was a Star Stealer who took it."

"How do they know that?" Rovi asked. His knew his voice sounded strained.

"The thief led them on a chase toward an old Star Stealer camp under the Draman Bridge," Satis said seriously. "Rovi, I know that's where your gang slept."

Rovi didn't trust himself to speak. He just nodded. He curled his hand around the key in his pocket. He wanted to kick himself. He hadn't been caught, but he *had* pointed the blame directly at the Star Stealers, which was almost as bad.

"If you are contacted by any of your old friends, you must immediately report it. This is a serious matter. Do you understand?"

Rovi could barely speak. He felt as if his throat were closing. "I do," he squeaked.

"I know how much you love Issa and your old friends," Satis said. "But what they have done is a danger to the Junior Epic tradition and to Phoenis. It will not be tolerated. And it would be a great loss to the Dreamers, Ecrof, and your future if you got caught up in anything they are doing." The Visualization Trainer sighed. "Rovi Myrios," he said kindly but firmly, "you have distinguished yourself for House Somni. Focus on that. This is your only duty in Phoenis."

"I understand," Rovi said.

"Now go celebrate Vera's historic win. Join your teammates and friends."

Rovi managed a genuine smile. The group carrying Vera had rounded the track and was approaching. Rovi raised both arms in the air. "Here's to dreams that never die!" he shouted.

Vera was paraded around the stadium on the shoulders of two

burly Dreamers until the medal ceremony began. Fans showered her with streamers and hurled plush renditions of the Dreamer Pegasus.

Over the megahorn, the announcer kept repeating: "Vera Renovo has set the record for most Junior Epic Medals! We have a new record holder: Vera Renovo! History has been made."

But it was all a blur. The only thing that mattered to Rovi was getting rid of the key as soon as he could.

Rovi scanned the crowds. So many guards. But it was their job to keep Star Stealers and other unwanted people out, not to keep athletes in. He just needed to look confident, like he was on official business.

He approached three guards blocking the athletes' entrance to the stadium. His heart pounded so hard and quickly, he worried they could see and hear it. "Excuse me," he said. "I need to get a box of muscle bands from one of the vans for my teammate."

The guards looked at him. Rovi smoothed his tracksuit jacket, making sure they saw the Ecrof insignia.

"Hurry," a guard said.

"Of course," Rovi said.

He darted to the vans. The guards didn't check where he was going. He took off his jacket and turned it inside out in case any Junior Epic officials saw him. Now he was a Sandlander Dreamer out in the Upper City. Not an athlete. Not a Star Stealer.

He hurried away from the stadium through the wide, genteel streets of the Upper City. He crossed the Alexandrine Market, where you were usually guaranteed to see a few Star Stealers plying their trade. Now that it was a market for the Junior Epic Games, he knew he stood little chance of seeing an old friend or a member of a rival gang.

He kept his hand clenched around the key as if it might fly out of his pocket. He fought the urge to check over his shoulder at every turn.

At the far edge of the market, he descended a flight of stairs to the Lower City. Rovi relaxed a little. It was easier to hide here, and he felt less conspicuous. But still he needed to be careful.

He wasn't going to make the same mistake twice, so he overshot his old camp on the river Durna and passed a few different bridges until he came to the far reaches of the Lower City. Only then did he allow himself to descend to the path at the water's edge. From there it was a mile back to the tunnel entrance.

Rovi jumped down into the tunnels carved out by the River of Sand and, just as before, he shuddered. The idea of this massive space flooded with quicksand, as it once had been, terrified him. He took a deep breath and continued on into the darkness. He didn't have the Memory Master anymore, but his feet remembered the path to the alcove hideout.

Issa, always vigilant, knew Rovi was there before Rovi had announced himself. In an instant, his old friend had pulled him into the cozy chamber. "Where have you been, Swiftfoot? We've been waiting for you."

"The guards chased me from the temple," Rovi said. "I had to run all over the city before I lost them. It wasn't safe to come directly here."

"But you have the key?" Issa asked.

"Yes." Rovi reached into his pocket, desperate to hand the thing over and be done with it.

Issa sighed, his entire body sagging with relief.

"Issa, here." Rovi held out the key. But Issa had already turned his back and ducked into the alcove.

Only a few days had passed, but the assembled group of Star Stealers looked significantly more ragged than before. A few crusts of bread and some bruised fruit lay on a tattered blanket on the floor.

"Our Swiftfoot has succeeded!" Issa announced, his black eyes sparkling.

The remaining Star Stealers cheered quietly.

◆

"Sit, brother," Issa said. "I'm afraid we have little to offer you."

"I'm good," Rovi said, thinking guiltily about all the food he could have back in the Dreamer Village. Once more he offered Issa the key. Issa reached out but, instead of taking the key, closed Rovi's fingers around it.

"Hold on to that for the moment," he said.

"I don't want it," Rovi said. Before he could say any more, a shadow was cast across the entrance to the alcove. Rovi looked up and saw Fortunus's compact figure in the doorway.

"Our hero," Fortunus thundered, his voice echoing through the chamber.

Despite himself, Rovi blushed.

"I heard you led the guards on quite a chase," Fortunus said.

"I almost led them to you accidentally," Rovi admitted. "I had to take the key to the village. Here it is." This time he held it out to Fortunus.

"Let's have a chat, Swiftfoot," Fortunus said. "Or shall I call you by your real name, Rovi Myrios of House Somni?"

"Either," Rovi replied. "They're both . . . me."

"You have done well, Rovi Myrios, very, very well. I'm not sure there's another kid—another person—in all of Epoca who could have done what you did. I am impressed." He put a hand on Rovi's shoulder. "Without you, the captured Star Stealers would remain locked up in Hafara Prison, possibly forever. But now they have a chance to escape with the rest of us."

"Where are you going?" Rovi asked.

"We will travel to the outlands of Epoca," Issa said, "perhaps even as far as the Winterlands, where Epocan Rule cannot touch us. But we must leave soon, while people are still distracted by the games."

"Which is why the imprisoned Star Stealers need your help," Fortunus said.

Rovi looked from Fortunus to Issa and back again. "I already helped. I stole the key. Here." He offered it again.

"Ah." Fortunus squeezed his shoulder. "But now you need to use it. Why don't we sit and talk about it." He sat on the rough-hewn bench and beckoned Rovi to sit next to him.

"You mean they need me to open the prison?" Rovi asked.

"Exactly," Fortunus said.

"Wh-why me?" Rovi sputtered.

"Because," Issa said, sitting down next to him, "just as you said: You are both our Swiftfoot and Rovi Myrios, Junior Epic Champion from House Somni and the famed Ecrof Academy. You can do things none of us can."

"What kind of things?" Rovi said uneasily.

Issa shook his head sadly. "You see how we live now, Rovi. We can't be seen by anyone without running the risk of being locked away. Once they manage to get rid of the Star Stealers, the Orphic People in other cities don't stand a chance. But even if you got caught, they'd be more lenient with you. You're the pride of the Sandlands and no longer a Star Stealer. You wouldn't be sent to Hafara."

"The prison is underground," Rovi said. "Can't you just take the tunnels? You wouldn't have to risk being seen."

"There are places, especially near the prison, where the tunnels are guarded," Fortunus explained. "We wouldn't be able to pass. But there is a way to get into the prison from the Upper City."

"Rovi," Issa said, "you know what Hafara is, right?"

"A prison," Rovi replied. "Everyone knows that."

"It's not just a prison. It's an arena," Fortunus explained. "A blood sports arena from ancient times."

"The prison is a games pit?" Rovi asked.

"It *was* a games pit," Fortunus continued. "A secret place for those who wanted to witness deadly spectacles between prisoners of Phoenis. What's most important, though, is *where* it is, not *what* it is. It was located exactly where people in Phoenis go to watch sports today."

"What do you mean?" Rovi asked slowly.

"Hafara is directly below the Crescent Stadium," Issa explained.

Rovi's mouth opened, but it took a moment for the words to emerge. "You mean I've been competing *on top* of my fellow Star Stealers?"

"Exactly," Fortunus said.

This revelation turned Rovi's stomach. He slumped forward. "I knew there had been a place for blood sports. My friend Vera and I even talked about how it was below the stadium. But I didn't know that place was *Hafara*."

"In the time of Hurell," Fortunus explained, "they built a replica of the Crescent Stadium underground for that purpose. Hafara is the mirror image of Crescent, except that at its center, instead of a grassy patch for field events, there is a sunken pit for blood sports. When they turned it into a prison to hold Hurell's followers at the start of the Age of Grana, the ancient Phoenicians redirected the deadly River of Sand so that it would surround the pit at its center."

"I can't believe this," Rovi said. "While I've been celebrating in the open air, my friends have been suffering under my feet."

"Precisely," Issa said softly. "That's why we need *you* to free them. While it is possible to access the prison through the tunnels, the risk of running into guards is too great. But *you* can get there easily, through the stadium."

Rovi looked from Issa to Fortunus. "You knew this all along, that I'd have to open the prison—didn't you?"

"We weren't sure," Issa said. "A week or so ago, I could have gone myself. But now it's too risky. If I were caught with the key, everything would be over. Also . . ." He trailed off.

"What?" Rovi asked.

"The last months have been hard," Issa said. "I'm not as

strong as I used to be. I don't have the stamina to do what needs to be done."

"Opening the prison?"

"That," Issa said. "But also crossing the River of Sand."

"Oh, no," Rovi said. "No way. Even if I did do this, wouldn't the authorities release the river to chase down the escapees?"

"The warning siren should give you time," Issa said.

Fortunus placed a hand on Rovi's shoulder. "It has to be you, Swiftfoot. You are the only friend to Star Stealers who is both strong enough and able to access the prison through the stadium."

"What about you?" Rovi said. "Why can't you go to the stadium?"

"I'm afraid that would be impossible," Fortunus said.

"Why?" Rovi demanded.

"None of us are allowed in the stadium," Issa cut in. "But you will be right there—you won't even have to sneak in."

Rovi winced at the thought. How could he have been enjoying victories in the stadium when there was such suffering below him?

"And you will be perfectly positioned to save them," Fortunus added. "There is a stairwell on the bottom level of the stadium that leads down to the prison. If you follow the tunnel at the base of the stairs, you'll reach the quicksand moat."

"The River of Sand," Rovi said.

"Yes," Fortunus said. "That will be difficult. But remember, you are a hero. A Junior Epic Champion."

"I thought it was so powerful only the gods could control it. How do I cross it?" Rovi demanded.

Fortunus looked concerned. "I have to admit that I don't know. I would be lying if I told you I had a solution. But I seem to remember that with visualization, nearly anything is possible. And from what I've heard, your father was a leader in the field."

"You know how to *visualize*? Were you an athlete?"

"I have had many lives, Rovi Myrios." Fortunus stared into his eyes. "For someone of your talents," he said, "this will be a piece of cake."

"I don't know," Rovi said.

"The river is an advantage for us, Rovi. It's so powerful that it makes it unnecessary for the guards to remain at the prison all day. They cross it once in the morning to feed the prisoners using a bridge that only they can lower, and then they leave. If you time it right, they will be gone."

"I don't know," Rovi said. He'd taken too many risks already. He couldn't sneak out again. Not after his conversation with Satis, who had so much faith in him. He had taken this final risk, but he couldn't take any more. Pretia was right. He owed it to House Somni to obey Epic Code. He couldn't lose his medal. "I can't," Rovi said.

"If you can't," Issa pleaded, "no one will."

Rovi hung his head. "I'm sorry," he said. He held out the key. "Please take it. It will only cause me trouble."

Fortunus took the key. "We understand," he said. "It is too much to ask."

There were tears in Issa's eyes. Rovi tried to overlook them.

He hugged Issa and Fortunus. He didn't want to say goodbye to them, but he knew, after the way he'd just disappointed them, he couldn't stay. Without another word, he ducked into the tunnel. His heart was heavy as he wound his way back to the river and then through the Lower and Upper Cities, heading back to the stadium.

By the sun, he guessed he had just enough time to make it back before the discus had wrapped up.

With every step, he tried to put the Star Stealers further from his mind. He had to remember that he was Rovi Myrios of House Somni. His first duty was to the Dreamers and the next to Ecrof. For two more days, he had to refocus on the games and his teammates. That was his calling. That was his obligation.

He made it to the spectators' van just in time. He let out a relieved sigh as the door closed behind him. No one had noticed that he was missing. And more important, he had turned over the key. Even if the guards searched him, they'd find nothing. He might not have been able to help the Star Stealers further, but he was in the clear.

Luckily, he had a seat to himself. He didn't want to speak to anyone. He tuned out the chatter of his fellow Dreamers as they rolled through Phoenis. The minute the van came to a stop, Rovi bolted for his residential tower.

Swiftly he climbed the stairs to his room, eager to be alone. He put his hand on the doorknob, but the door was already ajar. He was certain he'd closed it.

Someone was in his room. A guard? An official? Rovi gulped, then clasped his hand over his mouth. Had they found his missing Memory Master?! If so, he was done for.

Rovi pushed open the door. "Hello?"

No one was there. They'd come and gone, whoever they were. He shut the door.

"Rovi!"

He nearly jumped out of his skin as someone stepped out of the shadows behind him.

"Where have you been?"

◆

21

PRETIA

A HIDEOUT

"PRETIA?" ROVI LOOKED AS IF HE'D SEEN A ghost. "What are you doing here?"

"I didn't mean to scare you," she said. She'd been waiting in his room for hours. She heard the other athletes return from the stadium, filling the village with the sounds of celebration for Vera's historic victory. Several times she'd had to jump into the closet, worried that searchers were coming for her. But thankfully no one had thought to look for her in the boys' tower.

"You're hiding in my room, in the dark," Rovi said. "How is that not scary?"

Pretia hadn't thought about it like that. She'd been so desperate to see him that she'd jumped out of the shadows without thinking. Pretia took a deep breath. "I need your help."

"Aren't you mad at me?" Rovi asked

"I was. I am. But . . ." Her voice trailed off. "You must have had a really good reason for sneaking away, right?"

"I did," Rovi said slowly.

"Then I guess that's all that matters," Pretia said.

Rovi shook his head. "Not exactly. What matters is that you

refuse to see that Star Stealers are equals. You're too much like your parents and everyone else when it comes to my friends."

Pretia flushed. She hung her head. "I'm sorry."

"It's not enough to be sorry. You have to *think*." Rovi tapped his head. "If you're going to be the ruler of Epoca, you need to worry about *everyone* in the kingdom. Not just Dreamers and Realists. I know you hate the name, but the people of Epoca need the Child of Hope—all the people of Epoca need her. House Somni, House Relia, and anyone who doesn't fit those boxes, too."

This accusation—this reality check—hit Pretia like a punch in the stomach. Rovi was right. The hope her parents were always talking about was for Dreamers and Realists alone. Not for the Star Stealers or any of the Orphic People. "I'm sorry, Rovi. I really am. I never thought of it that way. I never considered what it might be like to be neither Dreamer nor Realist." She felt the tears coming and didn't do anything to stop them. She didn't have to be a noble princess in front of Rovi. "But I should have," she said. "Especially because I don't feel like *I* belong to either house. I don't feel like I belong anywhere." She was crying harder now. "I'm so sorry. I acted like a spoiled princess."

Rovi gave her a hug. "You did. Kind of. But you also acted like a supportive Dreamer. You had a right to be worried about what would happen if I cost House Somni a medal."

Pretia wriggled out of Rovi's arms. "About that," she said, wiping away tears. "How hard was it to sneak out of the village?"

"What?"

"I need your help. And . . . well, it's for the exact same thing that I got mad at you for."

Rovi looked at her, an expression of total disbelief on his face. "*You* want to sneak out of the village?"

"I need to hide," Pretia began, "and Vera thought you'd know where to hide me until the final race." Then, in one breathless rush, she explained her dilemma, all about the stolen key and her parents' arrival in Phoenis and their concerns over the temple break-in. She concluded with how they were going to end her games and take her away from Phoenis immediately.

"Are you sure you want to race?" Rovi asked. "We need you, of course. But aren't you risking too much?"

"No," Pretia said confidently. "I want to race." She paused. "I want to split myself. I've been too scared, even after the tribunal's decision. But just once I want to show Epoca who I am." She lowered her voice. "I might never get the chance again."

"What do you mean, *never*?"

"My parents aren't just taking me away from these games. They're going to stop me from playing sports for good."

"Forever?!"

"Apparently, my duty is to unite Epoca, just not by competing." Just saying this aloud filled Pretia with unfathomable sadness. It wasn't only that she'd miss sports. The knowledge that her future wasn't her own weighed on her. She'd always known it, to some extent, but it all felt real now.

"That's ridiculous," Rovi said. "Your talent honors the greatness of Epoca—isn't that why we use sports to determine our ruling household?"

"That's Epocan tradition. We have sports instead of war. But that doesn't mean I'm going to be allowed to participate."

"But you have the most amazing grana I've ever seen," Rovi said.

"Well, my parents and a whole bunch of Realists don't seem to want me to use it."

"For different reasons."

"What does it matter?" Pretia groaned. "Either way, I can't compete anymore."

"It matters," Rovi said. "A lot. And I want to see you use it in the 4x400. So does more than half of Epoca."

Pretia sighed. "Perhaps my parents are right," she said. "Sports *haven't* made me as happy as I'd imagined. Everything has been so confusing and difficult since I got to Phoenis. I thought this was going to be one of the most amazing experiences of my life. But it's been one of the most challenging, and not just on the field. I still want one more chance, though. And I want to win the Junior Epics for the Dreamers, if it comes down to that."

"Well, that would change your parents' minds," Rovi said brightly.

"I doubt it," Pretia said. She'd already won Junior Epic Gold, and her parents were still taking her away from the games.

Rovi drove one of his fists in the opposite palm. "This is all my fault."

Pretia considered her friend.

"Did you break into the Temple of Arsama?" she asked carefully. "Did you steal the key that's missing?"

Rovi nodded. "Yes," he said quietly. "I did. I'm sorry. It's my fault your parents are here. And it's my fault they want to end your Junior Epic Games. I promise I wouldn't have broken into the temple if I had known they'd do this to you. But it was necessary. I had to do it."

"What are the Star Stealers using the key for?" Pretia asked.

"It's not what your parents think," Rovi replied. "They're not trying to ruin the games or hurt anyone. For the last year, the Phoenician guards have been rounding up all the Star Stealers."

"Why?"

"They've always thought Star Stealers were a nuisance, and they're using the games as an excuse to get rid of them."

"Where are they taking them?" Pretia asked.

"To a place called Hafara. It's an underground prison made out of an old games pit that was used for blood sports during the time of Hurell. It's right under the Crescent Stadium." Rovi paused. "Pretia, we have been competing on top of my captured friends and old gang members."

Pretia shuddered.

"You're not going to open the prison yourself, are you?"

Rovi shook his head. "No way. I don't even have the key anymore."

"You've risked enough," Pretia said.

Rovi's eyes sparkled. "Well, there's one more risk I have to take. We need to get you hidden."

Pretia beamed. "You know a place?"

"I do. Star Stealers are experts at hiding."

"Where?"

"Underground," Rovi said. "With the Star Stealers themselves." An anxious look came over his face.

"What's wrong?" Pretia asked.

"Nothing," Rovi said. "I'll take you to see my friends, or what's left of them. But I wonder if they'll be happy to see me again."

"Why wouldn't they?"

"Well," Rovi said sadly, "there are some things I just can't do for them."

Pretia felt her anxiety rise as she and Rovi stole through the less-traveled paths of the Dreamer Village. She burrowed deep into Vera's enormous swim coat, pulling the hood over her face. At Rovi's instruction, they kept to the shadows, although no one seemed to take notice of them anyway.

They darted between the utility buildings and storerooms. The deeper they went into the village, the fewer people they passed. But Pretia couldn't shake the feeling that they were being followed.

Soon they were nearing a wall where the village ended. It was dark, and the lights of the Dreamer complex were hidden behind the buildings that abutted the wall.

◆

Pretia hesitated. "Rovi," she whispered. "Do you hear someone behind us?"

"I don't think so," he replied. "You're just nervous. Stick with me. I've been sneaking around for days."

Pretia tried to laugh to cover her nervousness, but she couldn't quite manage. She was about to follow her best friend down into the tunnels below Phoenis, into the former River of Sand. If they were caught, she'd be in direct violation of Epic Code.

"Now, we need to scale this wall," Rovi said. "We crawl along it for a bit, then there's a place to drop down on the other side."

"Wait." Pretia was certain this time that she'd heard footsteps. "Someone's here."

"Come on," Rovi hissed. "You're imagining it." He placed his hands on the wall, ready to boost himself up. "Hurry."

Pretia followed his lead. "One, two—"

"What are you two doing?"

Pretia let go of the wall and fell back onto the ground.

"Are you *escaping*?"

"Vera?" Rovi said. "What are you doing here?"

"Um," Vera said, "that's pretty obvious. I'm following you. Pretia, did you think you'd go off and hide without me?"

"Sort of," Pretia said. It hadn't even occurred to her that Vera would want to come. "But why are you here? You can't risk leaving the village—you'll jeopardize your record. You're so close."

"I broke Julius's record today. Now I only have one more medal to pass Farnaka Stellus."

"Exactly," Pretia said.

"I'm still coming with you," Vera said. "You two are not having an adventure without me. Especially not one that was my idea."

"Absolutely not," Pretia said.

"This is my decision," Vera replied firmly.

"Okay," Rovi said reluctantly. "But hurry."

"So where are we going?" Vera asked.

"To the Star Stealers," Pretia explained.

"Wait." Vera pulled on Pretia's arm. "Didn't the Star Stealers steal that key that's the whole reason your parents want to take you from the games?"

Pretia shot a glance at Rovi. "Tell her," he said.

"That wasn't exactly the Star Stealers. Or rather it wasn't a *current* Star Stealer."

Vera's eyes widened. "Rovi! You did that?"

"Yeah," Rovi replied cautiously.

"Wow," Vera gasped. "Everyone is saying the thief led the guards on the most amazing chase all over Phoenis. And escaped! That was *you*." She cocked her head to one side. "That's incredible."

"So can we go now?" Rovi asked.

"Sure," Vera said, scrambling onto the wall. "I'm really impressed. I'm—"

"Vera," Pretia asked, "you're not jealous, are you?"

"Not at all," Vera said. "But *everyone* is talking about that chase. Everyone. You better tell me everything about it. Let's get Pretia out of here first, though."

Pretia followed Vera onto the wall. And soon they were out of the village and in the heart of Phoenis.

It was clear to Pretia that Rovi understood every inch of the city. Under his guidance, it was almost as if Pretia and Vera had turned invisible. In no time, they'd passed through the stately streets and organized plazas of the Upper City and descended into the narrow, boisterous chaos of the Lower City.

It was easier to go unnoticed here, with the clamoring vendors shutting up their shops for the night, the noisy tumult in front of the food stalls, and songs and sounds of the buskers. Rovi led them through a maze of streets. Pretia had never moved through a city so unguarded.

She always had too many people watching her and protecting her.

They moved in silence until they came to the river Durna.

"I left the Star Stealers in an alcove in the tunnels a few hours ago when I brought them the key," Rovi said as they slunk along a narrow footpath beside the riverbank. Then Rovi vanished. It took Pretia a moment to realize he'd slipped into an opening in the wall that flanked the river. She and Vera followed him in.

They were in a huge tunnel that stretched out, dark and vast.

"Is this the River of Sand?" Vera asked, awestruck.

"It used to be," Rovi explained. "It's been diverted. Let's go."

Pretia's feet wouldn't move. "Why are you standing still?" Rovi asked.

"The river," Pretia began. "It's still somewhere underground, right?"

"The river hasn't flowed in more than two thousand years," Rovi explained. "I just heard it circles Hafara Prison like a moat. And that's miles away. Anyway, there's an early-warning siren in case . . . in case anything bad happens."

"Yeah, Pretia," Vera added, "you saw what it looked like out in the desert. Just a dry riverbed."

"I've been down here a bunch," Rovi said. "Just tunnels. No quicksand."

"Fine," Pretia said, giving herself a shake. "Let's go."

Rovi led the way. He navigated the tunnels as if he had carved them himself. After twenty minutes of twisting and turning in the dark, he darted to the left and tapped on a wall. Pretia could just make out the faintest sliver of light.

"It's me, Rovi," he said, beckoning Vera and Pretia into a gap in the tunnel wall.

They entered a small alcove in which a handful of haggard, hungry-looking people dressed in the tattered, flaxen clothes of Star Stealers had clearly made their home.

A scrawny boy with shaggy black hair, slightly older than Rovi, greeted them. "Swiftfoot, you're back!" He sounded delighted. "You changed your mind."

"Not exactly," Rovi muttered. He sounded ashamed. "I'm sorry. I've come for a favor."

The Star Stealer looked at Rovi sadly. "There's not much we can do for you."

"Issa," Rovi said, "these are my friends, Pretia and Vera. Pretia, Vera, this is Issa."

The Star Stealer glanced quickly from Pretia to Vera and mumbled a greeting, then stepped aside to let them into the little chamber.

"Pretia needs a place to hide out until the end of the games," Rovi said.

Issa glanced at her warily. "She'll be comfortable here?"

Pretia looked around the alcove. It was pretty sparse—just a few blankets on the floor and a couple of crude benches. But it was cozy in its own way. Most important, it was a place where no one would find her.

"I don't need much," Pretia said. "I won't eat much, either. And I promise I won't cause you any trouble." She glanced behind Issa to the ragtag group of kids in the hideout. Some waved, while others looked at her with mild interest.

"Then be our guest," Issa said. "Any friend of Rovi's is a friend of ours. But I have to warn you. We have very little food left. I'm going to have to risk a run to the outside world soon. I can't promise much, though."

"It's all right," Pretia said.

"Gita was aboveground scrounging for us," Issa explained. "I expected her to return with supplies, but she hasn't come back. I suspect she was taken by the guards."

"Oh no," Rovi said.

"She's a strong leader," Issa said. "At least she can comfort her gang in Hafara." He glanced behind him. Then his voice grew more serious. "Rovi," he said, "are you sure there's nothing you can do for us?"

"I can get you food if necessary," Rovi said.

"Not *that*," Issa replied.

Pretia saw Rovi shoot Issa a warning glance. She felt some unfinished business hanging between the two friends.

As she was wondering about this, an adult stepped out of the back of the room. He was short but sturdy, as if he'd once been an athlete but had taken up more rugged pursuits. His black hair was pulled back into a small ponytail, and his olive complexion seemed pale in comparison to those of the rest of the people gathered in the alcove. "Rovi," he said, "you've brought us friends, but you haven't changed your mind about helping us?"

Pretia gave Rovi a worried look. Surely this man wasn't talking about opening the prison. "Perhaps there is still time to convince you," the man said. Then he held out his hand, first to Pretia, then to Vera. "I am Fortunus." He mentioned no last name, like a Star Stealer. But his clothes looked to be made of heavier material than Pretia would have thought comfortable in the heat of Phoenis.

"Are *you* a Star Stealer?" Vera asked the man bluntly. "You look too old."

"In another life," he said.

"I'm Vera Renovo," Vera said.

"Renovo," Fortunus said. "That is a famous name."

"My brother is famous," Vera said, "but soon I'll be the more famous Renovo."

"So I've heard," the man said.

"You *have*?" Vera sounded delighted.

"Even down here I keep tabs on the games. You have nine medals. That is a record. Almost." He smiled.

Vera cocked her head to one side. She was looking at the man strangely. "What do you mean?" she asked.

"Just what I said. That's almost a new record."

"Vera, we don't have time to talk about some old athlete no one cares about," Rovi said. "Pretia will be safe down here. Let's go."

"Pretia will be as safe as the rest of us," Issa said. "I'm not sure how much longer we can stay, though. We are going to need to move soon. We've heard the guards may raid the tunnels."

"What happens then?" Pretia asked.

"Then we move. We flee the city," Issa said sadly.

"Wait," Rovi said. "You'd run without the rest of the gang? You'd leave them in Hafara?"

"If we get chased out of the tunnels before we can figure out a way to get into the prison, we'll have to," Issa said. "But I hope it won't come to that."

Pretia looked over at Vera, who was still studying the older man like he was part of a larger puzzle. "I thought Star Stealers didn't care about sports. How come you know so much about Junior Epic records?" Vera asked.

"There are things about the games that still interest me," Fortunus replied. "But I have long believed that there should be no sports for anyone until there are sports for all." He swept an arm around the alcove. "And that is not yet true, as you can see."

"What did you say your name was?" Vera asked.

Pretia nudged Vera. Why was she bothering this man?

"Fortunus."

"But that's not a Phoenician or Star Stealer name," Vera insisted.

"What's in a name?" Fortunus said lightly.

"A lot, I think," Vera said. "Rovi, what's the Phoenician word for *fortune*?"

"His name is Fortunus, not Fortune," Pretia said. She glanced nervously at Fortunus. But he was smiling knowingly.

"I don't speak Phoenician," Rovi said.

"*Farnak*," Issa said. "Or *Farnaka*."

A triumphant smile broke across Vera's face. "It's nice to meet you, Farnaka Stellus."

"Very clever," Fortunus chuckled, inclining his head.

"I knew it the minute you said that thing about *sports for all*. That's what you said on the medal podium right before you disappeared," Vera crowed. "*Farnaka*," she said almost to herself. "I've been hearing that word every day, over and over again when Sandlanders say their Grana Prayer: *May the gods grant us the fortune to compete with grace.* It never occurred to me that you might have changed your name."

"You didn't have much to go on. They removed almost all trace of me from the record books, and I removed all trace of myself from Epoca. I'm Fortunus now, no last name. No house. No heritage. No loyalty to kings or queens. No obligations except of my own choosing."

"And no interest in sports," Vera said, "even though you were the best."

"The best doesn't matter if what you are best at is not something everyone can at least attempt to do. It doesn't feel powerful or satisfying," Fortunus said. "We cannot live in a world guided by values that don't apply to everyone. The Orphic People have no place and no rights in Epoca."

Pretia looked at her feet. Her parents had guarded and upheld this tradition. Sure, they wanted to use her birth to unite the people of Epoca in new and deeper ways, but that unification didn't apply to Star Stealers and all the groups like them.

"But you were a superstar," Vera continued. "How could you give it up?"

"Talent and fulfillment don't always go together," Fortunus said. "The more I saw that sports don't solve all of our problems, as much as we are led to believe they will, the more I started to understand that perhaps sports aren't the answer to everything in Epoca. They give us the skills we need to survive and thrive. They teach us many important and indispensable things. But there are limits to what sports can accomplish. And they don't help everyone. Which is why I threw my lot in with the Star Stealers. They are not allowed to play sports. And they don't believe in the sanctity of sport."

"But I do!" Vera said.

"I don't expect everyone to try and change the world," Fortunus said. "If you break my record, you will have done your part."

"How?" Vera asked.

"Epoca puts too much faith in labels—Dreamer and Realist. You are the first Replacement to win Junior Epic Gold. You have made your own history. Once you are in the record books with all those medals, you can continue to make more. Especially if you cast off your label as a Dreamer. Deep down you are both things, Vera. It's what makes you great. And you, too, Rovi. You are two things as well." Then Fortunus clapped his hands. "Now, you two should go. Leave your friend with us. We will keep her safe."

"I can't believe it," Vera said. "I can't believe I actually met Far-naka Stellus."

"There is no Farnaka anymore," Fortunus said.

"For me there is," Vera said. "Maybe not for anyone else. But I'll remember him. And," she said, lowering her voice, "I also remember what he did."

"Now *that* is important. When they erased me from the record books, they took my reasons for quitting sports with them. So remember it. And one day, maybe you will be able to tell the real story."

"But first, I'm going to break your record," Vera said, grinning.

"The record is yours if you can manage it. And think about what you will do in the future, when you have the eyes of the entire nation of Epoca on you."

"I promise," Vera said. "But right now I'm all about sports."

"May they serve you well," Fortunus said.

◆

Vera turned to Pretia. "Okay, Pretia. Don't get too stiff down here. Maybe jog in the tunnels or something."

"I'll try," Pretia assured her.

"And we will see you in two days," Vera continued. "The 4x400 is the last race of the games, at nightfall. I'll meet you by the athletes' entrance to the Crescent Stadium fifteen minutes before the race. It's cutting it close, but we can't risk your being seen."

"Deal," Pretia said.

"You'll be safe here," Rovi said. "Issa takes care of everyone."

Pretia watched the boys hug.

"See you in two days," she said as Vera and Rovi headed for the door.

Before they ducked into the tunnel, Fortunus called them back. He shook Vera's hand like an equal on the field. Then he pulled Rovi into an enveloping embrace. When he let go, Pretia's friends trotted off, leaving her in the alcove with the Star Stealers.

Pretia stood in the center of the dim room, feeling out of place. Issa shuffled off to a corner and sat on a blanket with a girl about Pretia's age. Only Fortunus remained at her side.

He lowered his voice so only Pretia could hear. "They don't know who you are, Princess, but I do. And I know that, like Rovi and Vera, you are also two things at once, but in an even more remarkable and important way. You have greatness in you that transcends your talent on the field. There is so much you can do with it."

Pretia glanced nervously at the Star Stealers. "If they knew, they would hate me."

"Not necessarily," Fortunus said. "You are in a position to help them simply by understanding them. Try to see the world through their eyes. You are more like them than you know. There is a depth and power in you that perhaps you have yet to understand. You can see the world through two sets of eyes. You can be the one to understand those who have never been understood. But you are afraid."

"What do you mean?" Pretia asked.

"You are hiding from something," Fortunus said in a whisper. "What is it?"

"My parents," Pretia replied. "They don't want me to compete. But I want to run one last race. I need to."

"Are you sure that is all? Are you sure you are not hiding from something in your nature and in the nature of the land you are meant to rule?"

The mysterious man held her gaze.

"No," Pretia said. She knew this stranger was right, though. She *was* hiding from more than her parents this time. That was the reason she'd originally run away, to Ecrof. But now she was hiding from her duty to Epoca, from the burden of her birth. She wasn't just hiding because she wanted to help House Somni, she realized, but because she was starting to suspect that she might not be able to do the precise thing she was born to do. At least not as her parents imagined she should.

◆

22

R O V I

A   P R O B L E M

"JUST ACT NORMAL," ROVI WHISPERED TO Vera as they entered the dining hall the next morning. He zipped up his Ecrof track jacket and brushed off the sand and dust that he'd acquired from scaling the back wall of the village one last time. "And whatever you do, do *not* mention Farnaka whatever his name is."

"Game face," Vera replied. "Promise."

Rovi filled his tray, and he and Vera moved to a quiet corner of the cafeteria. Was it his imagination or were people looking at him strangely? He turned his back to the room and began to shovel lavender oats into his mouth.

"They're staring," Vera said. "Everyone is staring."

"Ignore it," Rovi said. "Just keep eating."

He forked up another mouthful of oats.

"Is it true?"

Rovi nearly choked with surprise as Virgil appeared at his side.

"Yeah, is it?" Eshe was suddenly standing next to Vera.

"Is *what* true?" Vera asked dismissively.

Eshe lowered her voice to a whisper. "Is Pretia *missing*?"

"That's what *everyone* has been saying," Virgil added theatrically.

Rovi shrugged. "I have no idea. I've been busy training."

"Yeah," Vera added. "Me too. Aren't you guys aware that these whole games might come down to our final race?"

"I am," Eshe said. "I'm on your team. Pretia's on the team, too, remember?"

"Of course," Vera said. "So is Rovi, and no one is worried about him."

"So *is* it true?" Eshe demanded.

Vera stood and picked up her tray. "My advice? Less worrying about rumors, more focusing on the relay."

She hurried toward the exit. Rovi followed. "Chill out, Vera," he said. "We're supposed to play it cool."

"Ugh," Vera sighed. "Eshe is just so—so *intense*. I mean, is winning all she cares about?"

Rovi couldn't suppress a laugh. "Vera, have you looked in the mirror?"

"No, why?"

"Uh, never mind. Let's check the leaderboard."

Together, they crossed the village. The leaderboard, which had been totally empty weeks ago, was now almost entirely filled with scores and stats. Vera was firmly in the lead with her nine medals. Ecrof and Dynami were tied for most academy medals. And House Relia led House Somni by three medals, 72–69. There were only three events left—the mile swim, the hurdles, and the 4x400. That meant nine medals. The Dreamers would need as many of those as they could get.

Vera stepped closer to Rovi. "Do you think she'll be okay?"

He glanced all around him before answering. "Pretia will be fine. I trust Issa. Now remember what we agreed on: Keep a low profile. Train, eat, and act as normal as possible." They exchanged a low five.

"Got it," Vera said.

"And if anyone asks about Pretia," Rovi added, "the last person we know who saw her was Eshe in the health center when the royal guards took her away."

"Perfect," Vera agreed.

The village was teeming with guards. There were guards in the cafeteria. There was a guard on the van to the pool. There were guards surrounding the Royal Baths.

Rovi had to work hard to appear calm. He cheered wildly for the Dreamers in the mile swim. Vera did the same. The Dreamers took two of the medals.

"What happens if there's an overall tie between the houses?" Rovi asked Cleopatra Volis on the van ride back to the village.

"Victory goes to the house with the athlete who has won the most individual medals—which is us," Cleopatra explained. "Unless something miraculous changes. Or Vera's medals get taken away for some reason."

"Rex Taxus can't catch me," Vera said. "He has seven but is only entered in one more race. I have nine already."

"If there's a tie, you're the tiebreaker," Cleopatra said. "So stay out of trouble!" she added jokingly.

Vera and Rovi exchanged a worried glance. Vera *would* be in trouble if the officials found out that she'd snuck away from the games. It would put her medals in jeopardy.

"Only one more day," Rovi whispered.

"I wish we could check on her," Vera said.

"She'll be at the stadium tomorrow as promised," Rovi said. There was no chance he was risking another trip into the tunnels. Not with all the guards crawling everywhere.

That night, Rovi slept badly. He was certain someone was outside his room. He tossed and turned until the first sorna horn sounded. He took a long shower to wake up and loosen his limbs. He needed to focus on the event at hand, the relay. The torrent of hot water provided a momentary distraction from all his anxieties. Today was the last day of the games. At noon the hurdles would kick off the day's events, which would finish at nightfall with the final heat of the 4x400. Rovi knew he could only relax when he finally saw Pretia again and they had run their last race.

Rovi toweled off and dressed in his tracksuit, then headed back to his room.

No sooner had he closed the door than someone knocked. "Rovi, are you in there?" It was an adult's voice. Rovi's heart skittered. *Breathe,* he urged himself. *Breathe.*

He opened the door.

Satis stood outside. Behind him were two Phoenician guards. And behind them was Janos.

"May we come in?" the Visualization Trainer asked.

Rovi nodded. The adults stepped into the room.

"Rovi," Janos said, "you have heard Pretia is missing?"

"I—um—there were rumors."

"You haven't seen her?" Satis asked.

Rovi could feel his palms start to sweat. What if they had found his Memory Master? "No."

Janos eyed him curiously. "And you haven't thought it odd that you haven't seen your friend? Now is not the time for heroics or lies, Rovi."

"I've been busy—um, training," Rovi said. He didn't sound remotely calm.

"When was the last time you saw Pretia?" Satis asked.

Rovi looked from the kind face of his favorite teacher to the stern faces of the guards. Frantically he counted backward in his head.

"I saw her . . . when was it? The days sort of blend, with so much going on." *Think. Think,* he commanded his rattling brain. "I saw her the morning Vera broke her brother's record. She was on her way to the health center." He hadn't seen her, but Eshe had mentioned to him that she'd seen Pretia rehabbing her calves.

"Now, Rovi," Janos said, "you know Pretia has run away before. Do you think she'd do it again?"

Breathe. Think. Focus. What was he supposed to know and not know?

"Why would she run away *after* winning gold?" Rovi said. "She's a Junior Epic hero. Anyway, I'm sure she wouldn't do anything to risk our final event. She wouldn't do that to me and Vera." He paused. "Or to Ecrof or House Somni."

Satis and Janos exchanged a glance. Had he fooled them?

"So you can think of no reason she might run away?" Satis asked.

"No!" Rovi insisted a little too emphatically. "No way," he added more quietly. "Pretia loves the Junior Epic Games. She's probably just lying low and getting focused or something."

Janos stepped forward. "Do you know of anyone who might want to harm Pretia?"

This time Rovi didn't have to lie. "What? No! Of course not."

Was Rovi imagining it or did Janos look a little sheepish?

"Not any of your—er—associates?"

"Associates?"

Satis cleared his throat. "He means the Star Stealers. Do you think any of them would try to hurt Pretia?"

"Definitely not. And they're not my associates—I'm a Dreamer, as you know. But in any case, Star Stealers don't hurt people," Rovi said. "Why doesn't anyone understand that! They're just kids, remember?"

"Well, Rovi, they might not want to hurt Pretia, but they might want to harm the games, and kidnapping Pretia could be a way to do that," Satis said calmly.

Rovi's jaw dropped. No Star Stealer would ever do a thing like that. But his heart was racing faster than before. Pretia was with the Star Stealers, and if she was found there, there was no doubt that Issa and the rest would be blamed.

"The Star Stealers *have* been disrupting these games," Janos said. "We're certain that they are behind the theft of a very important object from the Temple of Arsama. No matter what, there will be repercussions for them. Do you understand?"

Rovi swallowed hard and nodded.

"And anyone found to be helping them or hiding information about them will also be punished. For instance, that person could have a medal stripped away if they are a Junior Epic Athlete. Consider very carefully where your loyalties lie." Janos looked stern.

Rovi shrugged, pretending to be calm and collected. "With Ecrof and the Dreamers," he said.

Janos gave him a long look. "Very well," he said. "Good luck tonight. And let's hope your teammate turns up."

Then the visitors turned and left, shutting the door. Rovi stood rooted in place staring at the door. He'd done it. He'd fooled them and protected Pretia.

Today, she would come out of hiding and help House Somni to victory, and after that, what happened to her was up to the royal family. Rovi had done his part. He'd hidden her to help the Dreamers. He was done with adventures—no more tunnels, no more mazes, no more temples, and no more key. All he had left was the final relay—one more chance at gold for the Dreamers.

He jammed his hands into the pockets of his track jacket. One of them hit something cold and hard that he didn't expect. He felt his stomach drop. He didn't want to look. He suspected he knew what it was. Slowly he pulled his hand from his pocket. In it was the Key to Phoenis.

As cold dread crept over him, he remembered Fortunus's embrace before Rovi left Pretia with the Star Stealers. Rovi started to sweat and to shake.

He'd had the key in his pocket the entire time Janos and the guards had been in his room. He had been holding all the evidence they needed to punish him and the Star Stealers.

As these thoughts were flooding his head, there was another knock on the door. His heart stopped.

Maybe he hadn't fooled them after all. Maybe they knew all along that he knew where Pretia was and they were just testing him.

He jammed the key back in his pocket and opened the door.

It was only Satis.

"Rovi," he said quickly. "There's something else I need to tell you. It's about your friend Issa."

Rovi stomach flipped. "What is it?"

"He was caught by the guards this morning and brought before the games officials. They didn't call him by name, but I was there and I recognized him."

"What was he caught doing?"

"He said he was just stealing food," Satis began.

Before he could stop himself, Rovi spoke. "Then that's what he was—" He abruptly shut his mouth.

Satis looked at him quizzically. "How do you know that?"

Rovi's pulse was racing. He'd made a misstep. "That's all Star Stealers ever take."

"They take shoes," Satis said meaningfully, reminding Rovi that he himself had seen Rovi steal his precious Grana Gleams. "And valuable keys. Anyway," Satis continued, "the officials claim he wasn't stealing food, but that he was trying to disrupt the games. They've taken him to Hafara."

Rovi's hand clenched around the key in his pocket. He held the answer to Issa's freedom.

"I thought you deserved to know," Satis said. "Both because you love him and because I don't want you to get distracted searching the stands for him today."

Rovi hung his head. "I won't," he said.

Satis took Rovi by the shoulders. "I know how hard this must be for you. But remember, you are a Junior Epic Champion and a pride of House Somni and Ecrof. That is what you must focus on. One more race. That's all."

"I'll try," Rovi said.

"Good," Satis said. "I'll see you at the stadium later for the hurdles and then the 4x400. Let's hope Pretia shows."

"I have faith in her," Rovi said.

"Here's to dreams that never die."

"Yeah," Rovi said, "to that."

When Satis left, Rovi fell back on his bed. His mind was spinning. He had the key. Fortunus had tricked him. It almost hadn't worked—if Rovi had discovered the key a day ago, he might have returned it or even discarded it. But now that Issa was in Hafara, he knew what he had to do. He *had* to save his brother. There was time, but barely. The 4x400 wasn't until evening. He had the entire duration of the hurdles to enact a plan.

The morning passed in a panicked blur. Rovi counted the minutes until it was time to head to the Crescent Stadium for the hurdles, when he could slip away and search for the entrance to Hafara, somewhere beneath the field.

He rode in silence to the stadium, pretending to be immersed in some intense visualization. But his mind was on anything but his race. When he followed his fellow Dreamers to the field to watch the hurdles, he was only dimly aware of the proceedings. He felt Satis's eyes on him, watching him as if he knew Rovi was planning something. Rovi did everything in his power to look nonchalant. He tried to cheer when he was supposed to and urge on his fellow Dreamers. But he was really looking for a chance to escape.

He watched the first heat, trying to keep track of the Dreamers' progress. The only thing he could think about was Issa. Issa in

Hafara. Issa trapped directly below the stadium, below the stampeding footfalls of careless Dreamers celebrating their victory in a heat. Issa lost in the bowels of Phoenis. Issa imprisoned in a deadly pit formerly used for blood sports.

The third heat concluded. The only athletes to progress were from House Somni. When a swarm of Dreamer athletes raced onto the field congratulating their teammates, Rovi saw his chance. He checked for Satis. The Visualization Trainer seemed focused on the next racers lining up, at least momentarily. As the voice over the megahorn thundered for all non-competing athletes to leave the field, Rovi slipped away into the interior of the Crescent Stadium.

The ground level was mobbed with spectators buying souvenirs and refreshments. Rovi moved stealthily, quickly but not so fast that he'd attract attention. Three times he ran through the interior passage on the ground-level colonnade. There were kiosks and vendors, merchandise booths, snack bars, viewing stations. He pulled open door after door. One led to a machine room. Another to a medic office. One was to a room for stadium personnel. Another was for games officials. Another was a press office.

Rovi began to panic.

One door was storage.

Another was broadcasting.

And then one was locked. Rovi knocked. No answer. He rattled the door handle. It didn't budge.

Then, checking from side to side, he took the Key to Phoenis out of his pocket. He slipped it into the lock. It turned easily.

The door opened into blackness.

"Hello?" Rovi called, stepping inside the pitch-black room. He waved his arms about, trying to get a sense of his surroundings. "Hello," he repeated. His voice echoed back at him. He slid the lock into place behind him in case anyone had noticed where he was going.

He took a tentative step forward, then another. Then his foot hit nothing. Rovi stepped back and crouched down. Was he standing next to a drop-off, a cliff, a chute? He lay on his stomach and felt for the edge with his hands. Then he reached down. A few inches below he felt solid ground. And then again, a few inches below that. Stairs!

He had to hurry. He flew down the steps. They went on forever— down and down and down. The stairs twisted and turned as they descended in a never-ending zigzag that disoriented Rovi.

The sounds of the stadium disappeared. Soon the only noise was the echo of his footsteps on the stone steps.

He had to move carefully because of the many switchbacks. The stairs reminded him of the Infinity Steps back at Ecrof that changed and reversed course of their own accord. Soon he'd lost any sense of which direction he was facing. Was the stadium behind him or in front of him? How far down had he gone? Was he facing north or south? East or west?

When he thought it would be impossible to descend any further without hitting the center of the earth, the stairs stopped.

Although he couldn't see, he could sense that he had arrived in a large chamber.

"Hello?" Rovi called again.

This time there was no echo. Something was absorbing the sound.

He would have to pick a direction. He had no idea which way Hafara lay. Left? Right? Straight?

Rovi took a deep breath. Straight. He set off cautiously in the dark. Small stones skittered from his feet. He held his breath. Would something reveal itself—some sign that he was approaching the prison?

And then it did—his foot hit something wet, heavy, and loose. Not the solid ground. Not the dirt and dust. But something sandy. Something moving.

Rovi had stepped into the River of Sand.

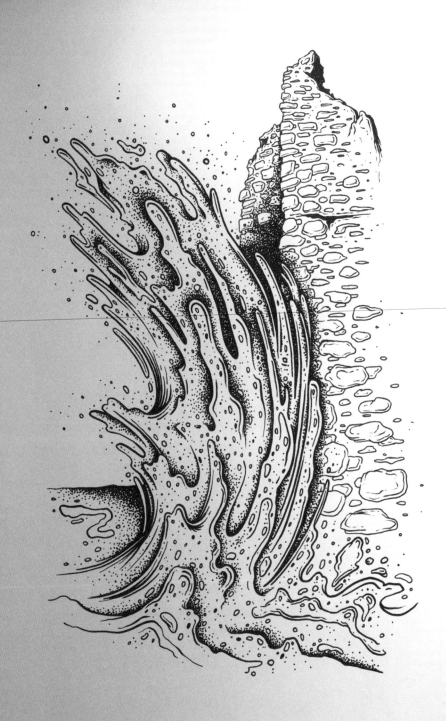

23

PRETIA

A RIVER

PRETIA SAT CROSS-LEGGED ON VERA'S SWIM coat in the back of the alcove. The atmosphere was tense. Issa had left early that morning to scrounge food for the hungry Star Stealers who were down to three stale loaves of bread. He'd been gone for hours. Everyone knew what that meant, but no one dared say it aloud. Hafara.

The remaining Star Stealers paced back and forth, sometimes darting out to the tunnels to check for Issa. He never came. They huddled in a nervous cluster. They were so thin and frail. And something else—they were frightened.

Pretia wanted to turn invisible. She wrapped her arms around her middle to silence her rumbling stomach. She'd eaten a little bread, but it was nothing in comparison to the lavish, overstuffed plates she was used to.

She hated to see the suffering around her. She felt it was her fault somehow. She, or her parents, could do something to help these innocent kids, but they hadn't even tried. She wondered how much her parents even knew the extent to which the Star Stealers were suffering. Surely, the king and queen wouldn't stand for such extreme treatment. Sadly, from her last conversation with her parents, she knew that helping the Star Stealers was the furthest thing from their minds. But if they knew, surely they would do something.

She felt helpless. She drew her knees into her chest, then reached into her backpack and pulled out her Grana Book. She closed her eyes and framed her question: *How can I help the Star Stealers?*

She flipped through the pages as always, until one just felt right. Pretia let the book fall open on her lap. She prepared herself to confront the image. To her surprise, it was the exact same image she'd turned to back at Ponsit, the twisty road through the mountains that had told her to run away to Ecrof.

She'd been so sure of herself months ago, when she'd interpreted the picture as saying her best course was to sneak off to Ecrof and then Phoenis. But now it was providing the answer to a different question.

"I haven't seen one of those in a long time." Pretia looked up to see Fortunus standing over her. "May I sit?"

Pretia made room on the swim coat.

"I'd like to look if you don't mind," Fortunus said. "Of course, I know not to touch."

Pretia inclined her Grana Book so he could see the image. "You must have had one, right?"

"Yes," Fortunus said. "I was born into House Somni. I gave up my Grana Book when I gave up my house affiliation. It seemed silly having a book tell you what to do."

"I don't think it's silly," Pretia said.

"Sometimes it's easier not to have to rely entirely on yourself," Fortunus said. "What do you see in that picture?"

"I'm not sure. Several months ago, this picture guided me to defy my parents and run away. The mountains were my parents." She pointed to the page. "See? One is bluish and the other purple. I'm the road between them. I'm supposed to move away from them. I thought that meant running away. But I'm not sure running away is the answer this time."

Fortunus folded his hands, waiting for her to explain.

"I asked the book how I can help the Star Stealers," Pretia said.

"And?"

She took a deep breath and looked at the image again. "It's odd. I think it's telling me the exact same thing as it did before but in a slightly different way. The mountains are still the two houses, my two sides, Dreamer and Realist. So I am the road." Her finger traced the squiggly road between them.

"And what are you supposed to do as the road?"

Pretia sighed. "The easy answer seems to be that I should unite the houses, because the road touches both mountains. But that feels wrong. That's simply what my parents have been telling me to do."

"And what do you think your book is telling you to do?"

Pretia hesitated.

"Let me rephrase that," Fortunus said. "What is it that you *feel* you are supposed to do?"

Pretia bent over the page again. "Let's see. I feel I'm supposed to move but also stay put. I don't quite understand it. The road signals movement away from the two mountains—the two houses—but it also means bringing them closer together."

"And what about that fire at the end of the road? What is that?" Fortunus asked.

"When I first saw it, I assumed it meant Junior Epic Victory. But this time I asked about the Star Stealers, so I can't quite figure it out." Pretia slammed the book. "It's so confusing."

"It will come," Fortunus said.

"But that's impossible. How can Junior Epic Victory be the same as helping the Star Stealers?"

"Nothing is impossible," Fortunus said. "The only thing that stops you is your own fear. The answer is inside you. It always is."

"You sound like my uncle Janos," Pretia said.

Fortunus laughed good-naturedly. "I remember him well. In

another world he and I would have spent our best years fighting for Epic Glory. But our paths took us in different directions. Now we fight our individual battles for the soul of Epoca."

Pretia opened her mouth to ask what he meant. But before she could, their conversation was interrupted by footsteps in the tunnel.

"Issa!" one of the Star Stealers at the entry exclaimed. "He's coming!"

The footsteps approached hard and fast. The glow of a hand lamp drew nearer, bouncing off the tunnel walls. The group near the entry backed away, making room for their friend to enter. But when someone rushed through the doorway, they immediately saw that it wasn't Issa at all. It was Vera.

Pretia bolted from the swim coat over to her friend. Vera was panting. Her puff of black hair was loose and wild.

The Star Stealers glared at her. "Where's Issa?" one of them demanded.

"Where's Rovi?" Vera gasped.

"Rovi?" Pretia said. "He's not here. Why would he be here?"

"Because," Vera panted. "Because Issa."

"Because Issa what?"

Vera gulped air. "Satis was looking for Rovi after the hurdles."

"Why?" Pretia asked. Her nerves were jangling.

"I'm not sure exactly," Vera explained. "He didn't tell me precisely. He just asked me if I'd seen Rovi. And urged me to find him. He said he was worried because Rovi seemed upset that Issa had been arrested."

"So it's true," Fortunus said sadly. "Issa is in Hafara. I knew Rovi would go to save him if it came to that."

For a moment, Pretia was too stunned to speak. "But that key he stole, he turned it over to you, right?"

"Rovi has the key," Fortunus explained. "It's useless to us. Hafara is right below the Crescent Stadium. We could never reach it."

"But tunnels must lead there," Pretia said. "These are the old paths of the River of Sand, and the River of Sand surrounds the prison."

"What?" Vera exclaimed. "Rovi is headed for the River of Sand?"

"The tunnels do lead there. But they are patrolled by guards," Fortunus said. "The Star Stealers can't risk that. Rovi has the best chance to access Hafara."

"But it's *surrounded by the River of Sand*," Pretia said. "There's no way to cross that."

"We need to stop him," Vera said.

"Or help him," Fortunus suggested.

Pretia looked from Vera to Fortunus. Either way, stopping Rovi or helping Rovi meant getting to Rovi first. "We need to find him," she said. "You said we can get to Hafara from the stadium?"

"Yes, it's directly below it. But you don't have time," Fortunus said. "You'll have to take the tunnels. The prison is about two miles from here."

"What about the guards?" Pretia asked.

"They patrol irregularly," Fortunus said. "But be very careful."

Vera cleared her throat. "I'll take care of them. If Rovi could lead the guards on a chase from the Temple of Arsama and lose them, I can do the same." She paused. "Or better."

"I admire your spirit, Vera," Fortunus said.

"And," Vera added, "I'll still have enough energy for the 4x400 tonight," she said. "I'll still beat your record, Farnaka."

"So what's the plan?" Pretia asked.

Vera thought for a moment. "We head toward the prison together. If we meet any guards, just follow my lead." Vera turned to Fortunus. "We need another hand lamp if you have one. And I need something to tie back my hair. It's a mess."

Pretia was shocked. "You're worried about your hair at a time like this?"

Vera ignored her. "Does anyone have a scarf? Preferably one of those Sandlander ones."

A young Star Stealer girl in a torn mud-colored tunic came forward and offered Vera an olive-green scarf. Vera got down on one knee. "Hey, that's really nice of you," she said. "I know you guys aren't big on the Junior Epic Games. But how do you feel about taking my track jacket in exchange?" She pulled off her silky purple jacket, revealing a simple white T-shirt, and handed it to the young Star Stealer. Then she wrapped her head in the scarf. "That's better. This hair was making me crazy. And it's too identifiable, if anyone sees us." She turned to Fortunus. "And now a hand lamp."

Fortunus rummaged in his bag and handed Pretia a small light. She switched it on and shouldered her backpack.

"Good luck," he said.

"We don't need luck," Vera announced. "We have talent."

"You've got a good friend there, Pretia," Fortunus said. "You two are a perfect team."

And with that, Pretia and Vera dashed into the tunnels.

The hand lamps bounced erratically. Pretia tried not to stumble on the unfamiliar ground without sacrificing speed.

"Vera," Pretia said, "what's your plan with the guards?"

"I told you not to worry about it," Vera replied. "And maybe we won't even see any guards."

"Let's hope," Pretia said. Guards would surely recognize her and take her back to her parents.

They ran on in silence. The only noise was the hollow echo of their footsteps.

After ten minutes they saw the glow of a hand lamp on the ceiling up ahead. Pretia skidded to a stop. She clutched Vera's arm, pulling her back.

Vera broke free. "Let go," she hissed.

"Wait," Pretia urged.

But now Vera had grabbed her hand and was dragging her forward, yanking her down the tunnel.

"What are you doing?" She'd spoken too loudly. Her words boomed in the tunnels. No doubt the guards, or whoever was up ahead, had heard them.

"Just follow my lead," Vera hissed.

"Who's there?" came a deep male voice.

"Hide!" Pretia said frantically. But Vera seemed determined to keep going. In an instant they were face-to-face with two Phoenician guards. Vera twisted her fingers around Pretia's arm, making the skin burn. "Stop it. Let me go!" Pretia yelped.

"Trust me," Vera said under her breath.

"Who are you?" one of the guards thundered.

"Tell them," Vera said calmly.

"I'm—I'm," Pretia stammered. What was her friend doing? "I'm . . ."

"This is Pretia Praxis-Onera."

"And who are you?" the guard demanded of Vera.

"Her kidnapper," Vera replied.

"Let her go," the other guard ordered.

The first guard looked at Pretia. "Princess? Are you okay?"

Pretia nodded. She wasn't sure what Vera was up to.

"Let us pass," Vera commanded.

The guards snorted with laughter. "You have to be joking," said one. "You're just a kid."

"Really?" Vera said. Pretia heard the familiar competitive note in her voice.

The first guard stepped toward them. "You cannot escape," he said.

"I can and I will unless you let me pass with the princess. I'm the fastest runner in Phoenis. I'll outrun you easily."

Vera was going to outrun the guards?

Suddenly Vera's plan started to make sense to Pretia.

"Hand her over," one of the guards insisted. "This is your last

◆

warning. Otherwise we will handle this with force."

Vera dropped Pretia's wrist. "You'll have to catch me first," she said. "I'll beat both of you." And then, quick as a flash, Vera was racing back in the direction from which they'd come.

The two guards hesitated for a moment. Then the first one chased Vera. The second guard looked at Pretia deferentially. "I'm glad you are safe, Princess."

Pretia stood up as straight as she could, thinking fast. "Guard," she said, in her most regal voice. "That girl, whoever she was, is faster than you think. She's the one who led those guards on a chase from the Temple of Arsama. She'll get away a second time." She summoned her most authoritative tone. "As Princess of Epoca, I order you to give chase and catch her."

"And leave you here?" the guard asked.

Pretia stared him down. "What did I say?"

"But . . . but, Princess," the guard sputtered.

"Go!" Pretia pointed in the direction Vera had departed.

The guard stutter-stepped, then sprinted off after his partner.

Pretia didn't waste a moment before racing in the opposite direction, deeper into the tunnels toward Hafara.

By her calculation and the Star Stealers' estimation of distance to the prison, she was more than halfway there. If she hurried, she could reach the dreaded River of Sand in less than ten minutes.

She picked up the pace. Eventually, the sound of her echoing footsteps changed. The tunnel had widened into an enormous cavern that seemed to be the exact size of the Crescent Stadium—an underground replica, a deep, dark mirror image. She cast her lamp around. She stood on what looked like an old running track. Around its inner edge ran a sludgy black mass—the River of Sand. And on what seemed to be an island in the center of roiling quicksand rose stadium seats that reminded Pretia of the Games Pit at Ponsit.

She shuddered. Below those seats were the imprisoned Star Stealers.

She shone her lamp into the river. It moved with a current so powerful that it sent actual waves of sand crashing over the edge by the prison. Only the gods could have created something so remarkable and monstrous.

A voice broke the muffled silence. "Help!"

"Rovi?" Pretia cried.

"Pretia? Is that you?"

She scanned the track with her hand lamp. "Where are you?" Pretia called.

"I'm in the river," came Rovi's voice. He sounded panicked.

"Where?" Pretia screamed.

"I'm holding on to the edge. But the current is so strong."

"Keep talking, Rovi. Keep talking." Pretia tried to focus on the direction from which his voice was coming.

Although the cavern distorted sound, she sensed that Rovi was off to her right. Moving quickly but carefully, Pretia hurried along the edge of the old track, keeping an eye out for her best friend.

"I can't hold on much longer," Rovi said. Pretia could tell that he was near tears.

"Sing," she said. "Sing the Ecrof fight song."

The cavern was silent for a moment. And then the familiar words of their school song filled the chamber. With each step Pretia took, Rovi's voice grew stronger.

Rovi stopped singing. "Where are you?"

"Almost there," Pretia assured him.

"I'm sinking," Rovi cried. "Hurry!"

Pretia cast the lamp into the darkness. There was Rovi—or what she could see of him. He'd sunk up to his waist in the river. His hands clung frantically to the edge of the crumbling track.

Instantly, Pretia threw off her backpack, fell to her knees, and grabbed him under the arms. She couldn't even manage to free him by an inch. She tried again. He sank deeper.

◆

"Stop!" Rovi said. "It's no use."

Pretia shone her lamp across the quicksand river toward the prison. "What were you planning to do?"

"I didn't have a plan. I just wanted to get to Hafara. Issa's there. In that games pit."

"I heard," Pretia said. "Vera told me."

"You saw Vera?"

"She found me in the tunnels and we came straight here. She had to lead some guards on a chase so I could make it to you."

"I think you're too late," Rovi groaned. He twisted desperately in the quicksand.

"Don't," Pretia said, placing a hand on his shoulder. "Struggling seems to make it worse."

"What are we going to do? What if—?"

"Don't worry." She sat down on the track next to Rovi and placed a hand in his hair. "I'll think of something. I promise I will."

But her thoughts were blank.

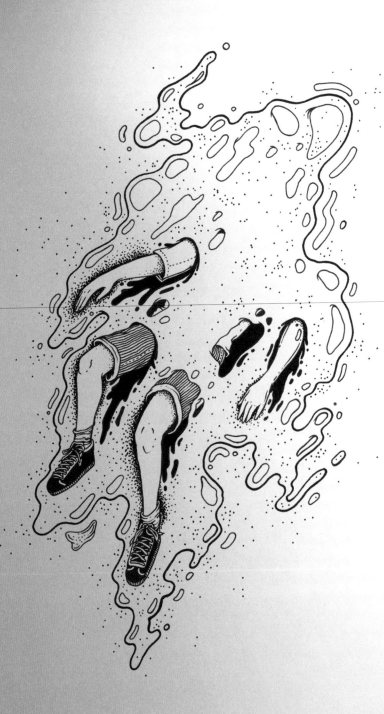

24

ROVI

A GAMES PIT

ROVI COULDN'T FIGHT BACK HIS TEARS ANY-more. Thankfully, it was dark enough in the cavern that Pretia couldn't see him cry. This was it. He was stuck and there was no escape. He'd tried to save Issa, at least. There was comfort in knowing that he had tried to do whatever he could for his friend. He hadn't been selfish or a coward. But he had failed.

"Let's sing something again," he said. "Please." Anything to take his mind off what was happening.

"The Dreamer anthem," Pretia suggested.

"All right." They sang, but Rovi's heart wasn't in it. His voice kept cracking. And he could detect the note of false cheer in Pretia's voice.

She broke off singing and stood up. "It's going to be okay."

"No," Rovi said. "It isn't. I'm sinking. I can feel it. It's over. I've ruined everything. I can't save the Star Stealers. I'm going to get us disqualified from the 4x400, and I'm going to lose my medal for House Somni."

"Rovi, stop." Pretia herself was near tears. She squatted down and looped her hands under his shoulders. He heard her take a deep breath and felt her tense, preparing for a last try to save him. "One . . . two . . ."

"*Stop!*"

Someone was approaching them, carrying a hand lamp. "What are you doing?"

"Vera!" Pretia exclaimed.

"Let him go," Vera shouted. "That's quicksand."

Rovi felt Pretia release him. "I know it's quicksand," she said.

"Don't pull him. Each time you tug, the quicksand will pull in the opposite direction. And it's stronger than you are," Vera said.

"Get me out of here," Rovi pleaded.

Pretia braced herself, ready to grasp him again.

"No!" Vera said, stepping between them. "We have whole deserts of it in Alkebulan. I've seen it swallow animals. *Big* animals. Lions and elephants. Fighting it is the worst thing you can do."

"Do you have a better idea?" Pretia demanded.

"Not yet," Vera admitted.

Suddenly Pretia bolted upright. "But I do. We're going to swim."

"Swim?" Vera asked.

"No way," Rovi protested. "You don't know what it's like in this stuff. It will drown us."

"I don't think so," Pretia said. "It's not going to be fun, but I think it can work. When I was tested by the tribunal, they put me in a water tank that turned into a whirlpool. The motion of this quicksand river is sort of like that whirlpool. Look how it's crashing on the opposite side."

She pointed to where the powerful river was sending waves of sand up over the edge by the prison.

"You have no idea how powerful those waves of sand are!" Rovi exclaimed.

"We need those waves," Pretia said. "We're going to use them. You can feel the sand moving, right?"

"Of course," Rovi said. "I can barely hold on."

"Well, it's just like a whirlpool. And whirlpools pull you to the center. We *want* to go to the prison—the center, right?"

Rovi didn't like the sound of this. There was no way to *swim* in the quicksand.

"I thought we wanted to get out of here," Vera said. "We need to get back for our race."

"Not without the Star Stealers," Pretia said. "We can't leave them."

"I know," Vera said. "Let's do this. Rovi, the river has you because you're struggling against it. You need to relax and become part of the quicksand. Technically, you're supposed to lie back and float so it carries you along."

"I'm not so sure about floating in a whirlpool of quicksand," Rovi cried. "There has to be another way."

"No," Vera replied. "Pretia's right. There's no other way."

"We're going to work with the sand," Pretia chimed in. "It will carry us to the prison."

And before Rovi could protest further, both his friends had kicked off their shoes and were entering the river. They slid into the sand up to their waists, then their shoulders, so they were even with Rovi.

"Now let go of the edge," Pretia said.

"No."

"Just relax," Pretia instructed.

Rovi was anything but relaxed.

"If we go under," Vera said, "let the quicksand take you. It's pulling us to the left, inward toward the prison."

This was not remotely comforting. "What if we can't get back to the surface?" he asked.

"Remember," she said, "struggling will make quicksand pull you down, but if you relax, it will bring you back to the surface. Trust me."

Rovi thought his heart was going to explode.

"The waves should help, too," Pretia added. "They'll lift us up over the far edge."

The idea of being carried by a quicksand wave did nothing to calm Rovi's all-consuming panic. "Are you sure?"

Out of the corner of his eye he saw Pretia and Vera exchange a covert glance. "Yes," they said in unison. But neither sounded as confident as Rovi would have wished. Vera took one of his hands while Pretia took the other.

Once he had let go, he could immediately sense the powerful quicksand carrying him to the left. Rovi hadn't realized how tired he'd grown from clinging to the edge. He couldn't relax. The heavy sand and its strength was terrifying.

How had he held on for so long? The current was faster and stronger than he'd allowed himself to realize. It threatened to pull him away from his friends. He linked his fingers tightly through theirs.

No one spoke. The River of Sand created its own sort of noise—a mighty silence that roared.

Rovi could tell the current was winding them closer to the looming prison. The sand tickled his chin. "We're sinking!" he said.

"I know," Pretia replied, her voice tight and tense.

"We're not going to make it to the prison before it pulls us under," Rovi said.

Vera tugged on his hand. "Relax. You have to relax."

"How?" Rovi said. But he wished he hadn't spoken. The sand was in his mouth. He jerked his head upward and spat just in time. The next thing he knew, a blanket had been thrown over his senses. He couldn't see. He couldn't hear. He couldn't smell. He couldn't breathe.

Every cell in Rovi's body told him to fight, to tense, to panic, but somehow he resisted. He let his limbs grow loose and his thoughts float.

He could feel the whirlpool circles tighten. They were closing in on the prison.

But Rovi could feel himself growing dizzy. His mind was going black.

He was spinning away.

But before he did, he felt himself being lifted. The quicksand was raising him up. He was cresting one of the waves as it broke over the landing near the prison.

Rovi gasped. He could feel his breath returning. The wave broke, leaving him on solid ground. He rolled onto his back. He rolled again and again, until he rolled clear of the River of Sand.

They'd made it.

25

PRETIA

A RESCUE

PRETIA FELT SOMEONE TUGGING AT HER ARM and she reached up to rub sand from her eyes. She cleared it from her nose and mouth. Rovi was pulling her to her feet. "Move, before you slip back in."

She was dangerously close to the river. Waves of sand crashed onto her legs.

"Pretia! Get up," Vera shouted.

Pretia rose and combed her fingers through her hair. "Now what?"

"Now we enter the prison," Rovi said.

Pretia fumbled for her hand lamp in her pocket where she'd stored it just before she'd fully submerged in the quicksand. It took a moment to flicker back to life. She cast its glow upward, where it hit the looming wall of the prison.

"Hafara is an old games pit," Rovi explained. "That sloping wall above us must be the bleachers, and below them should be the pit. So there's got to be a door at our level where they let the spectators in. Fortunus said that the guards come and go once a day using a bridge that they can lower from the far side," he continued. "The door must be somewhere near where the bridge comes down."

"Let's hope we can use that bridge to cross back," Vera said. "I don't feel like another trip through the quicksand."

They brushed as much sand as they could from their clothes. Pretia took the lead, dashing around the towering wall of the underground stadium. She bounced the light from her hand lamp up and down.

Suddenly Vera skidded to a halt, a finger in the air.

Pretia held the hand lamp up. Forty feet overhead was a metal walkway.

"And here's the door," Rovi said. He banged on the wall. "Pretia, give me the lamp."

She handed it over and watched as Rovi took a brass key from his pocket.

"You're sure that key works?" Vera asked.

"It worked to get into the stairwell," Rovi said.

They all held their breath while Rovi fit the key into a rusty brass keyhole. He jiggled it. Nothing. He jiggled it again. And then, with difficulty, it turned. The lock clicked open.

Together, Pretia, Rovi, and Vera pressed their shoulders against the door. It opened easily, admitting them to Hafara.

They were in a stadium, but it was unlike any stadium Pretia had seen before. It was cold and forbidding. They stood on a circular stone walkway. Rising above them were bleachers, and more than twenty feet below, in a pit, was the remains of the fighting arena. Pretia shuddered at the thought of the blood sports that had taken place down there.

"That's a long jump," Rovi said, peering over the edge.

"Yeah," Vera said. "That's going to hurt."

"Take off your scarf," Pretia said, holding out a hand to Vera. "Hold on to it and lower me and Rovi down."

"What about me?" Vera asked.

"You stay up here. Look for somewhere to secure the scarf. We're going to need someone to pull us up somehow."

"Got it," Vera said. She looped the scarf around her wrists and braced herself. The cloth dangled down toward the prison floor. It took about five feet off the jump. It wasn't much, but it would help.

"I'll go first," Pretia said.

Before Rovi could object, Pretia had sat down on the edge of the walkway. Rovi went to help Vera brace herself against Pretia's weight. Pretia shinnied down the scarf and then let go, landing with a grunt on her feet.

Then Rovi took the scarf from Vera. "Are you sure you can hold it?"

"I can do it," she answered.

In an instant, Rovi was standing next to Pretia in the pit.

Pretia turned and faced the open prison—no walls, no cells, no beds, just pallets on the floor. The space was illuminated by a handful of flickering yellow Helian lamps. It smelled of rot and mildew. Stains and smears from long-ago blood sports marked the stone floors. She looked up into the looming, unreachable stands.

"Where is everyone?"

Rovi cupped his hands over his mouth. "Issa?"

The name echoed horribly off the walls.

"Hello?"

There was a shuffling from the back of the prison. A voice called out in the dark. "Swiftfoot?"

Suddenly it looked as if the walls of the prison were coming to life. Kids began to emerge from the shadows. Some of them were so gaunt and skinny they looked like no more than shadows themselves.

"Issa!" Rovi cried.

"Did they get you, too?" the voice asked.

"No," Rovi said. "I'm here to free you. Come out. It's safe."

◆

Pretia watched as Issa stepped into the weak light and embraced Rovi.

"I can't believe you came," Issa said.

"I almost didn't make it," Rovi said. "Without Pretia and Vera, I wouldn't have."

"Pretia?" An older girl had joined their group. She was tall, with long black hair that hung in two dirty-looking braids. "Gita!" Rovi exclaimed. Gita gave Rovi a cautious look, then turned to Vera and Pretia with a mistrustful stare.

Pretia could feel Gita's eyes boring into her. "That's the Princess of Epoca's name," Gita said.

"I *am* the Princess of Epoca," Pretia said.

"The royal family doesn't care about Star Stealers," Gita said, her voice heavy with disdain. "Why are you here?"

"I came to help Rovi," Pretia insisted. "To help you."

"Is this a trick?" Gita asked Rovi.

"Gita," Issa said, "Pretia is Rovi's friend. We can trust her."

Gita folded her arms over her chest. "Maybe you can, but I can't. I won't."

"We don't have any choice," Issa declared. "If she and Rovi have a way to get out of here, we need to follow them. We need to get out of the city as soon as possible. Phoenis is no longer our home."

"So, *Princess*," Gita said in a snide tone, "how do we get out of here?"

Pretia glanced at Rovi. What was their plan?

"You have no idea, do you," Gita said scornfully.

"Hey!"

Pretia and Rovi turned at the sound of Vera's voice calling across the pit. "What's going on down there?"

"Who is that?" Gita asked.

"That's how we get out," Pretia said confidently. "We'll make a rope out of clothes and whatever else we have, and Vera can secure it up there. Then Rovi or I will climb up and pull the rest of you out one by one. How many of you are here, Issa?"

"About a hundred," he said.

"That's doable," Pretia replied.

Issa put his fingers to his lips and blasted a loud whistle, summoning the rest of the Star Stealers from the shadows.

"But how are we going to get back across the River of Sand?" Gita asked. "In fact, how did you cross it in the first place?"

"We swam," Pretia said.

"I'm not sending my gang into the quicksand," Gita said forcefully. "That's certain death."

Pretia glanced behind Gita and Issa at the Star Stealers slowly coming out into the open. They looked weak and thin. There was no way they could swim.

"Of course not, Gita," Rovi said. "Don't worry."

He pulled Pretia's arm, hurrying her back toward where Vera stood above them. "Ignore her," he whispered.

"But what are we going to do?" Pretia said. Her brain and body had worked tirelessly to get to this point, and she was all out of inspiration.

"We always think of something," Rovi assured her.

"Did you see those kids?" Pretia whispered. "They can hardly walk."

"They'll be able to walk if their freedom is on the line," Rovi said. "Star Stealers are stronger than you think."

"Let's hope so," Pretia said. She called up to Vera, overhead, "We have to make a rope of clothes." She took off her jacket. "We can start with this."

"Gotcha," Vera said. "I have this scarf, and I can sacrifice my track pants. I have running shorts on."

"We can use my entire tracksuit," Rovi added. "Now we only need a few more things to make it long enough." He turned back to the Star Stealers. "Issa!" he shouted. "Did you find any spare clothes?"

Issa ran out of the shadows with a handful of scarves and tunics. Rovi shot him a grateful smile and sat down on the ground to begin tying their clothes together. Soon he had a rope that would reach Vera.

"Now throw it to me," Vera called.

Rovi tried to toss the rope to Vera, but it fell way short. He tried again, then handed the rope to Pretia.

"Nope," she said, shaking her head and giving it back. "You do it."

"I can't throw that well," Rovi said. "You just saw me fail."

"Remember what you did back at the decathlon trials?" Pretia asked.

"You mean what you told me to do," Rovi reminded her.

"But you *did* it. Now you're actually in Phoenis with your Star Stealer gang." Pretia paused. "Throw like your happiness depends on it. Which it does."

She stepped back, making room for Rovi. She glanced up at Vera, who was on her hands and knees leaning over the edge, ready to catch the rope.

Rovi's next throw fell short. So did the following one. He kicked the ground in frustration.

"You got this," Pretia said.

"I can't do it," Rovi insisted.

Pretia thought for a moment. "Maybe this time you should pretend that you're back in Ecrof at the trials."

Rovi shook off her suggestion. "That game isn't working anymore."

"What if this throw is the difference between you making the Junior Epic Team or Castor taking your spot?"

A small smile broke across Rovi's lips. "That might work," he said. He rearranged the rope of clothes in his hand. He pulled his arm back over his shoulder and threw. The rope sailed up and up, right into Vera's waiting arms.

"Woo-hoo!" Rovi cried.

Pretia high-fived him.

"Great throw," Vera called. "I've secured the scarf to a nasty-looking iron hook up here. I don't even want to think what it was used for. Now I'll tie this to the scarf and we're good."

"I'll go first to test it," Pretia said, "just in case it doesn't hold."

Vera lowered the rope. Pretia tugged on it. It felt strong and secure. Bracing her feet on the wall of the pit, she began to climb. It was hard but manageable if you were healthy and strong—which most of the Star Stealers weren't.

She pulled herself onto the walkway next to Vera. "Some of those kids down there are really weak," she explained. "We'll have to haul them."

"Well," Vera said, "let's get going. Rovi, start sending them up."

It was slow work. Some of the Star Stealers, like Issa, who were older and stronger or who had spent less time in Hafara, could climb themselves. But many others had to be pulled up by Vera and Pretia.

When half of the Star Stealers were out, Pretia fell back on the ground. "I need a break," she said.

"Let me," Issa said, taking the rope.

"And me," Gita said, joining him. "We wouldn't want a princess doing all the work."

"Lay off her, Gita," Issa hissed.

"Only when her family lays off us," Gita snapped.

Pretia was glad it was dark enough in Hafara that no one could see the angry flush on her cheeks.

Gita and Issa pulled out the remaining Star Stealers. Rovi climbed up last.

"Okay," Pretia said, "let's go. I can't think in this place."

Issa put his fingers to his lips and whistled. "Everyone out!"

As a single mass, the Star Stealers made their way out of the horrible stadium and stood in front of the roiling River of Sand.

"Now what?" Gita asked. "Any more ideas, or was that it?"

"I'm thinking," Pretia barked. She looked up at the bridge they'd seen on their way into the prison. It was at least forty feet overhead, but she, Rovi, and Vera had faced down worse challenges. "We need to figure out a way to get the bridge down."

"No!" Issa cried. "There's an alarm. If you lower the bridge from this side, it will let the guards know that the prison has been breached. If that happens, they could release the River of Sand from the moat as punishment."

"And flood the tunnels?" Pretia asked.

"Exactly," Issa said.

Vera wrapped a hand around Pretia's wrist and pulled her to the side. "Whatever we do, we've got to act fast. Once those guards stop looking for me, they'll come check here. One way or another, they're going to figure out we broke into the prison."

Pretia felt her own eyes widen. "And one way or another they'll have reason to release that river."

Pretia's mind was racing. There had to be a way across. She looked at the waves of quicksand. Something was nagging at her. She might not be able to cross the river, but part of her could do things that the physical Pretia couldn't, a part of her that was stronger. Now, more than ever, she needed her shadow self.

But how? She couldn't just summon it. It only came when her body was straining and needed it to help her. She tiptoed over to the edge of the river where the quicksand waves were crashing.

"Get back," Rovi called.

Pretia didn't listen. She held up a hand to shield herself from the waves of sand. Then she put a foot in deep enough that she felt the river grab her.

"You'll get stuck!" Vera screamed.

But that was exactly what she wanted.

"Stop!" Rovi rushed to pull her back.

"I know what I'm doing," Pretia said.

"What *are* you doing?" Vera demanded.

Pretia felt the quicksand grip her as it tried to pull her in. "I'm going to walk across."

"You'll get trapped. You're already trapped." Vera was nearly hyperventilating.

"I can do this, Vera," Pretia said. "My shadow self can. It's always been able to do things my physical body can't. It's stronger than I am. It emerges when I need it, not when I want it. And right now I need it more than anything. I need to get across that quick- sand." With all her might, she tried to yank her foot out and dash across the River of Sand. It was stubbornly and completely stuck.

She faced the sandy waves as she tried to will her stuck foot out of the sand. *Run,* she told herself, *run.*

She focused. She tuned out the panicked conversation behind her, straining against the sand, willing her trapped body to sprint forward. *Now!*

Finally, she felt her self begin to split. There was her shadow self taking off, dashing across the quicksand. In no time, Pretia had watched herself cross to the other side. Then she felt the curious shock that came when her two selves collided again.

"Whoa," Vera said.

"She just—you just—" Issa stammered. "What did I just see?"

"You saw the Princess of Epoca cross the River of Sand on foot," Rovi said, his voice full of wonder and pride.

Gita had come to stand with the group near the crashing waves. "It's great that *she* can cross. What are the rest of us supposed to do?"

"I'm going to carry you," Pretia said.

"That's impossible," Vera said.

"No," Rovi said. "No it isn't. I've seen her do it." He and Pretia locked eyes.

"I did it before and I can do it again," Pretia said.

"I don't know," Vera said.

"But I do," Rovi insisted. "I know she can do it. I've seen it and I'll go first."

"Rovi's right," Pretia added. "My shadow self can carry more than I ever could, move faster than I can. It's the only way." Pretia beckoned Rovi over. "I'll take Rovi and when I've brought about thirty more people across, he can start to lead a group to Fortunus and the rest in the hideout. I'll take you a bit later, Vera, so you can follow Rovi with a second group. I'll come last, when everyone is across."

She looked from Rovi to Vera and then to Gita. "Unless anyone has a better idea."

No one spoke.

"Let's go," Pretia said firmly. "Rovi, get on my back."

Rovi edged up to the quicksand waves and climbed on Pretia's back. *Go*, she urged. Her shadow self took off, sprinting across the sand as if it were carrying nothing at all. Pretia watched it deposit an astonished-looking Rovi on the far side, then collide back with her physical body. "You're next," Pretia said to Issa. Once more, she split herself and crossed before allowing her selves to collide again.

One hundred crossings. It would take a while, but she had no choice. She was the only one who could help.

"Gita," Pretia said, "get everyone lined up. Explain what's happening."

"I don't need a princess to tell me what to do," Gita said.

"Can't you see I'm trying to help?" Pretia pleaded.

"Can't *you* see that I don't trust anyone in the royal family?" Gita replied. "Since when has doing what they say done a Star Stealer any good?"

"It's not just what I say. It's what has to be done," Pretia said calmly.

Gita looked torn, but finally she turned and began to explain the situation to the larger group. Pretia said, "Vera, you keep count.

When I take you across, lead your group to the alcove or find Rovi in the tunnels."

It was time to go to work.

One by one, the Star Stealers climbed onto Pretia's back. Many of them were older than she was, but their lifestyle and their time in Hafara had made them terrifyingly light.

After ten crossings, she slipped into a rhythm. The crossings became routine. Her muscles grew accustomed to the strain on her back. And she learned to anticipate the exact moment of release and relief as her shadow self took the burden of the crossing off her shoulders.

When she'd carried just over thirty Star Stealers across, Rovi signaled that he was heading into the tunnels. "Vera, are you ready?" Pretia asked.

"Let's go," Vera said, climbing on.

Pretia went back to work, mechanically running back and forth across the quicksand. With Vera's group halfway assembled, a small boy in a ragged tunic climbed on Pretia's back. His ratty hair was long and dirty, a sure sign he'd been underground for a while. He was younger and lighter than most of the Star Stealers.

Pretia watched herself split. But when her shadow self was halfway across, Pretia's physical body lurched, and she staggered to the side. Her foot, still stuck in the quicksand, twisted uncomfortably. She fell to the ground, yanking her ankle. She glanced up, grateful to see her shadow self had made it to the other side and deposited the small, shaggy-haired boy safely.

Gita took Pretia by the elbow and helped her stand. "Are you okay?"

"Yes," Pretia said. What had just happened?

"Do you need a break?" Gita asked. Her voice was filled with genuine concern.

Pretia could feel her physical body tiring, but her shadow self never tired, at least not that she knew of. "We don't have time," she said. "I'll be fine."

"Are you sure?" Gita asked. "You've been working really hard."

"There's more to do," Pretia said through gritted teeth.

The next Star Stealer climbed on. The crossing went off without a hitch. Then, while carrying a girl her own age, Pretia's physical self lurched again. Once more, her shadow self carried the Star Stealer to safety.

But Pretia took a deep breath. Her lungs felt raw, her limbs heavy. She was exhausted.

"Pretia," Gita said. "Are you *really* okay?"

"Yes," Pretia said.

Gita gave her a doubtful look.

"Listen," Pretia said, "I told you I wasn't going to let you down."

"I . . . I know," Gita said. "I can see how hard you've been working."

"I said I'd get all of you across," Pretia said, "and I will."

"But are you going to be all right?" Gita said. "I can't believe I'm saying this to a member of the royal family, but I'm worried about you."

"I'm fine," Pretia said. "Are you ready to cross? Unless you object to getting on a princess's back."

"I don't," Gita said carefully. "Not after what I've witnessed here."

"I should take you now so you can look after the younger ones on the other side in case you need to get them out of there quick."

"Good idea," Gita said.

She got on Pretia's back. For the first time, Pretia fully felt the weight of the person she was carrying. She staggered once before her shadow self took over and made a smooth crossing.

But each passage grew progressively harder. Her shadow self didn't show any strain but Pretia's body was fatiguing fast. Her legs shook. Her back ached. If she couldn't stand and attempt to run from the quicksand, her shadow self wouldn't know to help her. She had to keep going.

Pretia glanced over her shoulder. Five more Star Stealers to go. She could do this. She had to.

After she carried the first one across, she couldn't stand upright. She had to rest her hands on her knees for support. By the time she got to the third to last, she was no longer able to help her passenger onto her back.

Finally, she was down to a single Star Stealer. The last to go was a girl so young it made Pretia sick to think of her in Hafara. She had the biggest eyes Pretia had ever seen. She looked at Pretia in wonder. "Are you *really* a princess?" she whispered as she climbed on Pretia's back. She couldn't have been more than seven years old.

"Yes." Pretia could barely get the word out.

"So why are you helping us?" the girl asked.

"Because," Pretia rasped. Then she cleared her throat. "Because," she said in the clearest voice she could manage, "nobody should suffer the way you have. If the Junior Epic Games require that innocent people be treated this way, then they are not a true celebration of the glory of Epoca."

"I've heard the games are spectacular," the little girl said. "I know they are not for me," she continued, "but still I'd like to see them someday."

"I promise," Pretia said, "one day you'll be able to see the games. Maybe even compete. What's your name?"

"Raki." The girl pressed her lips to Pretia's ear. "Thank you," she said. Pretia could not even reply. Suddenly the ache in her body was so great that she thought she would collapse under the girl's insubstantial weight.

She stumbled forward and nearly fell into the roiling quicksand. Raki cried out. Pretia righted herself in time.

Pretia felt Raki lay her small head on her shoulder.

"Are we going to be stuck?" Raki asked.

Pretia dragged in a ragged breath. Her lungs burned.

"I don't want to be stuck here."

She could feel Raki beginning to cry. She had to do this one last time. She couldn't let the tiniest Star Stealer down.

Pretia forced herself upright again.

Run, she urged her shadow self. *Please.*

For a single horrible moment, she thought she wouldn't be able to split. But then her shadow self emerged. It wavered at first, before taking off for a final trip across the quicksand.

Pretia tried to watch from the prison side of the river. But everything was going black. Before she saw her shadow self deposit Raki safely, her head began to spin. And slowly, oh so slowly, she fell backward, crumpling into an unconscious heap in front of the looming wall of Hafara Prison.

◆

26

ROVI

A SIREN

ISSA KNEW THE WAY TO THE STAR STEALER hideout, so Rovi let him take the lead. Rovi wanted to run, but the enfeebled Star Stealers couldn't move very quickly. So they set out at the briskest walk they could manage. Still, the two miles to the alcove was taking way too long. With each step, Rovi grew more and more anxious.

By Rovi's count, half an hour had passed since he'd left the cavern and Hafara. The line of Star Stealers stretched out through the tunnels. Some of the younger ones were falling behind.

"Are we close?" he asked Issa.

"Almost there," Issa replied.

"I'll bring up the rear," Rovi said, and raced off to the back of the line to make sure no one had been left behind.

When he reached the back, he discovered a small, shoeless boy struggling to keep up. Rovi scooped him up and piggybacked him through the tunnels.

Eventually, Rovi saw a light cast into the tunnel up ahead. "Issa!" Fortunus's voice called. "Issa and . . ." The rest of Fortunus's exclamation was lost in the clamor of the rescued Star Stealers greeting the few left in the alcove.

"But where are the rest?" Fortunus asked when Rovi arrived at the head of the line.

"Vera is bringing one group. Pretia will follow with the rest."

Concern crossed Fortunus's face. "I wish you were all together. We need to hurry. Once the guards realize that the prison—"

"I know," Rovi said, "they might release the river to chase us from the tunnels. Issa said."

"Let's hope it doesn't come to that," Fortunus said.

"I'm going back to help," Rovi said.

Fortunus looked over the group of Star Stealers. "We need to act fast to get as many to safety as possible. We can't wait for the others. I will lead this group to the mouth of the tunnel. We will wait for you there. But if you don't come soon, I must head out at dusk. Once we make it to the Moon Palace, we are at the edge of the city limits of Phoenis and we will be safe." Fortunus looked at Rovi. "You have done an incredible thing, Swiftfoot. Star Stealers and the Orphic People all over the outlands will tell the tale of this night for years to come. Your name will be a legend." He took both of Rovi's hands in his and looked him straight in the eye. "*You* will be legend. But I wonder if you would consider joining us."

Rovi broke away from Fortunus's gaze and glanced at Issa. Then he turned to take in the Star Stealers gathered in the tunnel. "I can't," he said. "I can't let my school down. I can't let the Dreamers down. I've already done too much to endanger their victory at the games. I have to go back when you're safe."

He'd done everything Issa and Fortunus had asked him to do. And he was proud of that. They had drawn him out of his comfort zone as an elite Dreamer and challenged him to help others and to do what was right. But now it was time to return to House Somni. That was where he belonged. That was where his father would have wanted him to be.

◆

"I'll run back to help Pretia and Vera, and we'll bring the rest of the kids to the tunnel entrance."

"We will see you there," Fortunus said.

No sooner had he spoken than a wail resounded through the tunnels.

"What is that?" Rovi cried.

"The siren!" Issa exclaimed.

Rovi's heart began to race. Their escape had been discovered. The river had been released.

The siren was a steady wail—earsplitting and terrifying. Fortunus turned to Issa. "When we get to the end of the tunnel, you go on ahead. Get these kids to the Moon Palace. It's too risky to wait. I'll bring the rest to you."

"Okay," Issa agreed.

"We can't lose another second," Fortunus urged. "Rovi, go tell the others to hurry. Issa, let's move out."

Rovi spun around and was about to sprint off.

"Wait!" Issa called.

Rovi stopped. Issa ran and flung his arms around him. "I didn't get a chance to say this last time. Goodbye, brother," he said.

Rovi had to shout to be heard over the siren. He dropped his head to Issa's shoulder. "Goodbye."

"And thank you," Issa said. "You risked more than anyone else ever would have for us."

"That's what you do for family," Rovi said. He bit his lip. "And don't worry, brother. One day I'll find you again. Now go."

Rovi didn't waste an instant. He raced back through the tunnels. It took him ten minutes to reach Vera and her group, who were stretched out in a long line through the tunnels. Like the Star Stealers he'd led, many of these kids were lagging and exhausted.

Vera broke away from her group and rushed to Rovi. She cupped her hands over her mouth. "That must be the warning siren, right?"

Rovi nodded vigorously.

"How much time do you think we have before they release the river?"

"Not much," Rovi answered. "You need to get these Star Stealers to the tunnel mouth as quickly as possible. Fortunus—Farnaka—whoever he is will meet you there."

"Okay," Vera replied over the insistent wail. "Go help Pretia. I'll meet you both at the tunnel entrance, and then we'll head back to the stadium."

They slapped hands.

"Hurry," Rovi said, and ran off. He picked up his pace, figuring it was about another mile until he reached the prison. In a few minutes, he heard voices up ahead in the tunnels. When the tunnel turned a corner, he collided with Gita.

She had a small girl on her back. "You guys made it!" Rovi yelled. But his heart plummeted when he saw the look on her face.

"The quicksand is overflowing the moat," she called over the noise. "It's bubbling up. The river is coming."

"Fortunus is waiting at the tunnel entrance. Get there as fast as you can. The guards could be on us at any minute." He paused. "And if they aren't, that could be bad, too."

"Why?" Gita asked.

A horrible realization was dawning on Rovi. They hadn't encountered any guards in the tunnels, which meant the guards could be purposely *avoiding* the tunnels. "Because they could be releasing the river," he said.

"I'll hurry," Gita said.

"Vera is bringing her group there, too, and Issa has already led a group out of the city," Rovi added. "They're all heading for the Moon Palace. If anyone gets separated, that's where to go. Make sure everyone knows."

As Rovi had been talking, the final group of Star Stealers had gathered around Gita. Rovi scanned the crowd.

"Where's Pretia?"

"She wouldn't—she couldn't come," Gita said. "She couldn't stand up, or answer. I couldn't help her, Rovi." She paused. "I tried. Believe me, I did."

"You *left* her?"

"She's still by the prison. You'll see. There was nothing I could do. I was wrong about Pretia," Gita continued. "Without her, we'd still be stuck in Hafara. But we had to go."

It seemed as if the siren was getting louder. It was inside Rovi's head, rattling his teeth, making his brain shake. The Star Stealers flinched against the sound and clustered tighter around Gita.

Rovi's stomach clenched. "Go!" he barked. "Get to safety."

His legs led him through the tunnels as if they had memorized every twist and turn on the outbound journey. In a few minutes, the tunnel opened into the circular track, where the noise from the siren was almost deafening. He hurried toward the spot where Pretia's shadow self had deposited him after the crossing.

He was almost there when he saw her lying on the track near the edge of the river next to her discarded backpack and her gold Grana Gleams. Had Gita lied to him? Or had Pretia made it across since Gita had left?

He glanced at the river. Gita was right. It *was* rising. He needed to move Pretia immediately.

Rovi rushed to Pretia's side and dropped to his knees. "Pretia! Get up." He shook her shoulder and rolled her over. Her face was expressionless, slack. She was listless—like she was hardly there at all. "Pretia!" he screamed. "Wake *up*."

She didn't move. He was near tears, but he knew tears wouldn't help.

"Pretia, please." He wrapped his arms around her and tried to lift her. Her body felt strange, as if it wasn't a body at all. Rovi looked at the sand. It was rising higher and higher, swallowing the track.

Then, beyond the moat, something caught his eye—a figure holding a hand lamp, lying on the opposite side by the prison. Pretia!

But if that was Pretia, who was this? Rovi stared at the figure in his arms.

It could only be her shadow self. Suddenly Rovi felt as if he was touching something he shouldn't, something more sacred than a Grana Book—a deep part of his best friend's soul. He laid Pretia's shadow self gently back on the ground, away from the encroaching quicksand. Then he cupped his hands over his mouth and screamed as loudly as he could, "Pretia! Get over here!" But it was futile to try to make himself heard over the wailing of the siren.

He had to wake her up. But he couldn't reach her.

"Pretia," he called again, although he knew it was pointless.

The siren was making it impossible to think. Rovi crouched down next to Pretia's shadow self. "Please," he said, "please do something. Help her."

He waited. Pretia's shadow self remained motionless.

"Pretia needs you. You need each other."

The siren was growing louder and louder. Rovi cupped his hands over his ears to dull the noise, but it was no use.

Then he felt the figure next to him stir. He scooted back. Pretia's shadow self was moving!

Rovi's eyes widened as this other Pretia, a more ethereal version of his friend, her actual soul, stood up. And then, as he watched in disbelief, Pretia's shadow self began to walk back across the River of Sand. It reached the other side, stepped through the crashing quicksand waves, and squatted down next to Pretia's motionless body.

Then the shadow Pretia scooped up the physical Pretia in its arms and began to carry her back across the river. Pretia looked like a deadweight. Her head dangled limply and her feet swung back and forth.

The shadow Pretia moved easily across the River of Sand, as if she were carrying nothing at all, as if the surface below her feet were solid ground, not roiling and rising quicksand.

Rovi watched as Pretia's shadow self carefully laid his best friend at a safe distance from the approaching river. Pretia's physical body seemed drained of something vital. She had no vibrancy, no energy. Then it hit Rovi—she looked exactly like the kids he'd seen last year back at Ecrof, the ones whose grana had been stolen by the deadly strangler fig.

Rovi clutched his stomach. The thought of her grana being gone nearly made him sick.

Pretia's shadow self stood over her motionless body.

"Wake her up!" Rovi cried. "Please."

Suddenly the shadow self seemed to waver and flicker as if it were melting in front of Rovi's face. And before Rovi could say anything else, it collapsed on top of Pretia's physical body. The minute the two Pretias collided, the shadow self vanished, leaving Rovi alone with the motionless body of his best friend.

He fell to his knees and took Pretia gently by the shoulder. He bent over her so he could be heard above the siren. "Pretia, please. Please get up."

Nothing.

How much longer did Rovi have before he had to flee the cavern? He glanced nervously at the River of Sand. Three-quarters of the track was gone.

He took Pretia under her shoulders and dragged her farther away from the approaching quicksand.

"Pretia, the river is coming fast. Wake up, please."

Now a new sound filled the cavern, a booming noise. The waves of sand had started breaking on *this* side of the prison. Towering waves, twice as high as Rovi, were crashing one on top of the other, spraying him and Pretia with sand.

There was no doubt. The river was rising faster and faster.

"Rovi?"

Pretia's voice was so faint Rovi nearly missed it over the siren and the sound of the waves. He looked down. Her eyes were fluttering open. "What happened?"

"You were stuck on the prison side of the river," Rovi explained. "Your shadow self carried you back across. Can you stand?"

"I'm so tired," Pretia said.

"You have to try."

"What's that noise?" Pretia asked.

"The river is loose. It's rising. That's what the siren's for. We need to go."

"I can't," Pretia said.

"I am not leaving you. Get on my back."

"You can't carry me," Pretia said.

"I can and I will," Rovi said. He pulled Pretia to her feet and then crouched down so she could climb on.

Rovi struggled back to his feet. Pretia's tired body was heavier than he'd imagined. He looped his arms under her muscular legs and started for the tunnels. There was no way he could run. He could just manage a swift walk, which meant at least half an hour to meet up with the rest of the Star Stealers.

The tunnel twisted on ahead of him. Pretia grew heavier with each step. Pretia's head lolled on his shoulder. He could feel her ragged breathing on his neck. But Rovi didn't let up. To keep his spirits up, he whistled the Ecrof fight song and the Dreamer anthem.

Suddenly he could hear footsteps coming in his direction. Rovi flattened himself against the wall in case it was the guards.

"Rovi!" Vera's voice echoed through the tunnels.

"I'm here," he replied. "I've got Pretia." A few seconds later, Vera came into view.

"Is she okay?" Vera gasped.

"She's exhausted," Rovi said.

"Let me help," Vera insisted.

Rovi could feel Pretia stirring.

"It's okay," Pretia said. "You can put me down. I think I can walk."

Rovi helped Pretia to stand. He and Vera held her up.

The tunnel was rocked by another thunderous crash.

"The river is rising fast," Rovi said. "It's going to flood the tunnels."

"Let's go," Vera said. "Pretia, are you sure you can do this? We can carry you if you can't walk."

"I'm good," Pretia said. Her voice sounded stronger. "I think being separated from my shadow self for so long while I was carrying the Star Stealers destroyed me. But now that I'm whole, I'm feeling better."

"Still," Rovi said, "let us help you."

As a trio, their arms looped around one another, they began to make their way out of the tunnel. With every step, Pretia seemed to be coming back to herself. But it was slow going.

Now a new sound could be heard over the siren, the unmistakable roar of the approaching quicksand.

Rovi flinched. There was no doubt that the river was close by, flooding the tunnels at their backs. He and Vera exchanged worried glances.

"Hurry," Vera urged. The three friends, still linked together, broke into a jog.

The roar grew louder. The sand was closing in. Rovi could feel it—a cool and looming pressure behind him.

He and Vera let go of Pretia as the three of them sprinted full tilt through the tunnels. They were in lockstep for the first few minutes, but then Pretia began to lag. Rovi reached back and grabbed for her arm, pulling her along with him. After a hundred feet, she fell back again.

Rovi looked over his shoulder and stopped to let Pretia catch up. The instant he did so, he saw the River of Sand crashing around a corner of the tunnel.

"Run!"

The friends ran. Rovi could see Vera in front of him, sprinting away at full speed.

He could see a circle of light up ahead and the glimmering water of the river Durna.

Vera had made it through the tunnel, with Rovi a split second behind her. His feet pounded the ground. He risked another glance over his shoulder, even though he knew it would cost him time. Pretia had fallen behind again. And the river was catching up. He could see it close on her heels.

He reached back. He grabbed Pretia's hand and began to pull her forward, dragging her the last ten feet to the mouth of the tunnel.

The river was roaring in his ears. He could feel it right behind them. The entrance was in reach, but Rovi knew he had to jump if he was going to beat the River of Sand out of the tunnel. With one final effort, he leaped clear of the tunnel, through the entrance, and free of the rushing quicksand. He tossed himself to the side, flattening himself against the wall along the riverbank at the precise moment the quicksand crashed through the tunnel's mouth.

Then he looked down at his empty hand. Pretia's fingers had slipped through his.

She'd been swallowed by the River of Sand.

27

PRETIA

A REALIZATION

PRETIA HAD GAINED STRENGTH AND MOMENTUM as she'd sprinted through the tunnel. The reunion with her shadow self had restored her, but it hadn't been enough. She could feel the River of Sand at her back. It was cold and clammy, but also powerful. She was aware of the sheer force that was chasing her. She also knew that she couldn't outrun it. She would be swamped by the quicksand, and there was nothing she could do.

Rovi had grasped her hand. But Pretia hadn't been able to hold on as she felt the wave of sand begin to close in. She held her breath, ready to be swallowed. The river crashed onto her shoulders. It broke over her body. But then she began to rise. Instead of sinking into the River of Sand and being drowned inside it, Pretia was rising to the top of it. She felt her grana working with the power of the river.

Before Pretia knew what she was doing, she was on top of the river, as if she were bodysurfing on the waves of the Rhodan Islands. She pulled herself up further, managing to get to her feet so she was standing on top of the river. She held her hands out to each side for balance and control.

And like that, standing upright, as if the river was under her command and not the other way around, Pretia rode the River of

Sand right out of the tunnel and into the fresh Phoenician air.

She barely had time to register what was happening. The tidal wave of sand carried her across the river Durna, where she slid off her improbable conveyance and onto the opposite bank. Then the wave she had been riding crashed down, flooding the river Durna, turning the freshwater river into a torrent of quicksand.

There was no river water visible anymore, just sand that was flowing fast and furious, roaring as it went. Pretia could easily imagine how it would continue out of the city and return to the dry riverbeds she'd seen in the desert.

Pretia stood stunned, unsure of how to understand what she had just done. How had she *ridden* the River of Sand? It had taken her breath away. It more than made up for all the times her grana had been restricted or questioned. Her grana had helped her do something impossible. No, it had helped her do two impossible things—rescue the Star Stealers and surf the River of Sand.

Pretia gulped the sweet night air. This was the first moment of pure joy and exhilaration she'd experienced since coming to Phoenis. In fact, this was the first moment she remembered enjoying using her grana since . . . since . . . well, she couldn't actually remember.

She looked across the flowing quicksand to the far side. Rovi, Vera, and Fortunus stood on the opposite bank with the last group of Star Stealers that Pretia had carried across from Hafara.

"Pretia!" Rovi was waving her over. He pointed at the nearby bridge that she could use to cross. "Hurry!"

To her surprise, Pretia found she could indeed hurry. Somehow, the river had mostly restored her. Or maybe it was her delight at using her grana that had restored her. Pretia sprinted to the other bank.

Her friends and the Star Stealers were looking at her with awe-struck expressions on their faces. Even Fortunus looked a bit stunned.

"How . . . how . . ." Vera stammered.

"I don't know," Pretia admitted.

"You made it," Gita said. "I'm so glad you made it." She lowered her voice. "I'm sorry I mistrusted you."

"No," Pretia replied. "*I'm* sorry."

"But you saved us." Raki, the youngest Star Stealer, had taken her hand. "What are you sorry for?"

A lump swelled in Pretia's throat as she looked down at Raki. Where to begin? There were so many things she needed to apologize to the Star Stealers for that it overwhelmed her. "I'm sorry for everything you have suffered as citizens of Epoca. You deserve more."

She looked at the group gathered around Fortunus. How could Phoenis treat kids this way? How could Epoca? How could her *parents*? The thought turned her stomach. When she was Queen of Epoca, nothing like this would happen.

"Pretia," Rovi said, taking her by the shoulders, "are you okay?" His eyes were wider than she'd ever seen, and he was nodding his head frantically as if willing her to answer quickly.

"That was *amazing*," Vera said, the awestruck look still on her face. "And I've seen you do some amazing things."

"That river was made by the gods, and *you* can control it," Rovi said. "Your grana is—"

"Don't." Pretia held up her hand. She'd had enough of people trying to describe or classify her grana. "Even I don't understand my grana." Whatever allowed her to control the river was the same thing that made her grana threatening to others.

"Pretia Praxis-Onera."

Pretia turned at the sound of Fortunus's voice.

"These Star Stealers tell me you have saved them in a way that not a single person, child or adult—in Epoca or anywhere else in the world—could have done. It seems that you are, indeed, the Child of Hope."

"I hate that name," Pretia said. "I don't want to bring my parents' sort of hope to the people of Epoca. They only hope on behalf of Somni and Relia."

"Well," Fortunus said with a serious smile, "you *have* brought hope to the Star Stealers. They will never forget that."

Pretia considered the group assembled around Fortunus, his praise echoing in her ears. She had lived up to her name. She had served her people.

"Now we have to go," Fortunus continued. "The river is loose and the guards will be on us soon. Gita insisted on waiting to make sure you were all right. By now Issa should be at the Moon Palace with the rest of the Star Stealers."

"Pretia!" Vera tugged on her hand. "We also need to go."

Pretia turned and looked at her friend. She had no idea what Vera was talking about.

"We can't be late," Vera insisted. "We have to get ready for the relay."

Pretia looked at Fortunus. "Where will you go?" Pretia asked.

"We will begin our journey to the outlands. There are people who will harbor us along the way. When it is safe, I will lead the Star Stealers to join a large group of Orphic People who have gathered in the outlands, where they can be free. My hope is that one day our people can be part of Epoca, welcome to participate in all your traditions," Fortunus said. "But for now we will build a life far away from the rule of Dreamers and Realists."

Pretia gazed down at the river Durna bubbling with quicksand. She could just make out the gates that led from the Lower City to the widespread desert. It would be an unforgiving journey.

"Vera's right, Pretia. You need to start heading back for the race. The people of Epoca are waiting," Fortunus said.

The race. The relay. The Junior Epics. All of it seemed so remote and distant since she'd rescued the Star Stealers. But now she had to shift her focus. She had risked everything for this race. Game time was approaching.

"We have to go," Rovi insisted. "We can't be disqualified."

"There's a whole stadium waiting to see what wonders you'll do next," Fortunus said. "A whole nation waiting on your performance. But, Rovi, your invitation to join us still stands."

"I'm sorry, Fortunus, I told you earlier: I'm a Dreamer now," Rovi said. "And I was a Dreamer before. It's what my father would have wanted. He left my Grana Book at Ecrof for a reason, so one day I might have the chance of being a Dreamer again."

"I understand," Fortunus said, a smile playing at his lips. "I foresee much Epic Glory in your future."

Pretia looked at her friends. She looked at Fortunus and the scraggly band of Star Stealers. She looked up, taking in the golden grandeur of the Upper City rising from the tangle of the Lower City. She looked in the opposite direction, watching the released River of Sand flowing away from Phoenis into the wild desert.

"I wish I could go with you," Pretia said. "But I have a duty to my house and my teammates." She paused, and for the first time she understood how she might actually live up to her name: the Child of Hope. "And I have a duty to you to make Epoca a better world for Star Stealers—and for all the Orphic People."

Suddenly, ruling Epoca didn't seem so bad. Her rule didn't have to be like her parents'. She could rule with her own important mission, her own goals. If she returned to the games and raced, she would have to eventually submit to her parents' command that she return to Castle Airim and give up sports. But at least she could do that knowing that she could work to make Epoca better for people like Raki and Gita, who'd suffered so much.

Gita took Pretia's hand. "You have a race to run," she said. "I hope you show everyone the amazing things you can do." Then she wrapped her arms around Pretia. "I hope we meet again sometime."

"Me too," Pretia said.

Vera tugged on Pretia's arm. "We have to go," she urged. "Now."

Pretia backed away from the Star Stealers. Fortunus clapped his hands, and the scraggly band began to head out of the city. Pretia and her friends watched them for a moment. Just before they disappeared from sight, she saw Fortunus raise his hand toward the heavens as if plucking a star from the sky. Rovi returned the salute. And then the Star Stealers were gone.

"Okay," Pretia said. "Let's do it. One last race." At the moment, it seemed impossible to summon the emotional energy to compete. But she had risked everything for this final event. She would dig deep for a reserve of inspiration.

"For Junior Epic Glory," Vera said.

"For Dreamer Glory," Rovi said.

"And," Pretia added, "for personal triumph. I want to see what I can do—and I want everyone else to see it, too."

"I think I can get us up to the stadium undetected," Rovi said, "but then what? How do we get Pretia into the race without her parents discovering her?"

"You guys are going to have to stay hidden, while I find Eshe," Vera said. "She can sign in for all of us, and we'll just show up on the starting line at go time."

"That's a huge risk," Rovi said.

"Do you have a better idea?" Pretia asked.

Rovi shook his head.

In silence, he led them out of the Lower City and into the Upper City. Despite having recovered since being separated from her split self across the River of Sand, Pretia's body was still tired. Her legs felt leaden, and her breath sounded ragged in her ears. She tried to hide her condition from her friends and keep pace. But it was a struggle.

Soon they could see the Temple of Arsama and the Crescent Stadium rising in the distance.

"Let's hide by the Epic Coaches," Pretia said. "That way we can enter quickly through the athletes' entrance."

"I'll find Eshe and then keep an eye on the races so I can signal you two when it's time to line up," Vera said. "But do me a favor," she added. "Don't just sit around and wait. Try and warm up."

"Vera," Pretia said. "I think I'm *warm* enough. I've been exercising for the last two hours straight."

Vera thought for a moment. "Well, okay. Don't get cold, then."

Rovi and Pretia locked eyes and tried not to laugh.

They had almost arrived at the stadium. Pretia's heart was racing as they drew closer to the coaches parked near the athletes' entrance. She pivoted her head this way and that, hoping no one noticed her presence.

This was it. This was her last chance to race and demonstrate her grana. This might be her last chance to prove herself as an athlete. She needed to push herself to her limit and beyond.

They slipped between a row of coaches. Rovi tapped on their doors, searching for one that was unlocked.

"I'll force one open if I have to," he said. "But I'd rather not."

"Hurry," Pretia said. She was growing more and more anxious around the sounds and cheers from the Crescent Stadium. She was so close to being able to reveal herself . . . but also in the most danger of discovery since she'd run away.

Rovi was rattling the door of a smaller van. "This one is locked but improperly. I think I can get it open."

Pretia watched, her anxiety rocketing, as Rovi jimmied the door open. "Got it," he said.

"Get inside, you two," Vera commanded.

Rovi stepped into the van.

Pretia prepared to follow.

◆

"There you are!"

Pretia jumped, knocking into the side of the van. The game was over.

"I've been looking *everywhere* for you guys."

Pretia's heart was racing so fast it took her a second to process that it was Eshe who had appeared in front of her.

"We're about to be disqualified! You weren't on the transport. Where have you been?"

"It doesn't matter," Vera said.

"Yes it does," Eshe snapped. "We have ten minutes to sign in, or we'll be disqualified. Tell me where you were."

"We were somewhere we weren't supposed to be, Eshe, and the less you know about it the better."

"You're not acting like teammates," Eshe grumbled.

"We're here to race, aren't we?" Vera said.

"I guess," Eshe said.

"And we're here to win," Pretia added.

"Then I guess you'll need these," Eshe muttered. She held out a small sports bag. "I grabbed racing gear for you and Vera. I had a feeling you would need it."

"Wow!" Vera cried. "Good thinking. I hadn't even considered that."

Eshe couldn't hide how pleased she was with Vera's praise. She turned to Rovi. "Sorry, I couldn't snag yours. I didn't want to risk sneaking into the boys' residence. Unlike you guys," she said with a pointed look, "I'm not comfortable breaking the rules and jeopardizing my team's outcome."

"I have some extra clothes in my backpack," Pretia offered.

"That's okay," Rovi said. "I'm wearing my race gear. It's a little dirty and sandy, but it will do."

"Thanks, Eshe," Vera said. "Now, you and I should go register. Pretia and Rovi are going to wait here until the race."

A confused look passed across Eshe's face.

"My parents don't want me to race," Pretia explained. "If they know where I am, they'll pull me."

"And we need Pretia to guarantee victory," Rovi added.

"Oh," Eshe said. "I was just wondering how you two are going to warm up sitting in this van."

Pretia and Rovi exploded into laughter.

"What's so funny?" Eshe asked.

"I have no idea," Vera said. "But let's go. I'm sure they'll figure out how to stay loose." She looked at Pretia. "Keep your eyes on the athletes' entrance. When you see me wave, hurry into the stadium and head straight for the starting line. Do not stop for any reason."

"Got it," Pretia said.

She and Rovi got into the van and watched Eshe and Vera head inside. Rovi kept watch out the window while Pretia changed into her competition gear. "I need to relax a little," she said. "All right?"

"Are you going to be okay to race?" he wondered.

"Of course," Pretia said. She slouched in the seat and closed her eyes. She was exhausted both mentally and physically. She needed to sleep. But she would take what she could get until game time.

As she drifted off into a light doze, the image in her Grana Book danced behind her closed eyelids—the twisting road through the two mountains, one of which represented each of her parents. She saw the slight cloud cover on each mountain, the blue and purple hues muting their peaks, and the brilliant, golden fire at the end. She imagined that gold meant victory was waiting, but what if it meant something else? What if she had been wrong about what awaited her?

"Pretia!"

Rovi was shaking her awake. "It's time."

She could have slept for hours—even days. Instead, Pretia pulled herself to her feet, shook her head, arms, and legs, and followed Rovi off the van.

"Just walk in like you own the place," he said.

"How about we jog in?" Pretia said.

"Or run?"

They took off, down the line of vans and coaches. They waved at the guards like they had every right to be entering the Crescent Stadium, which they did. They dashed past athletes preparing for their heats, coaching their friends, warming up and cooling down. Pretia could hear a voice coming over the stadium's megahorn announcing the start of the upcoming heat—their heat. She heard the announcer thunder, "From Ecrof Academy: Vera Renovo, Eshe Sonos, Rovi Myrios, and Pretia Praxis-Onera." She heard applause followed by silence.

Once more the announcer introduced her team, "From Ecrof Academy: Vera Renovo, Eshe Sonos, Rovi Myrios, and Pretia Praxis-Onera." The silence from the stands was deafening. She and Rovi picked up their pace.

"Last call for Vera Renovo, Eshe Sonos, Rovi Myrios, and Pretia Praxis-Onera. Runners line up."

As the announcer finished speaking, Pretia and Rovi burst onto the field and raced to the starting line, where Vera and Eshe were waiting. At their appearance, the strangled tension in the stadium evaporated, and the Dreamers in the stands burst into applause.

"Phew," Vera said. "Let's get into position. I'll lead off, then Eshe. Rovi will run third. Pretia, you clean up. We need you to run last in case we fall behind. We just need a top four finish in our first two heats to make the finals. But that's no reason to hold back."

The four of them put their hands together and fist-bumped.

"We got this," Pretia said. But she was nervous. What if she was too tired to do her part?

"Racers, take your places."

Rovi pulled Pretia to the side. "Don't think. Don't look in the stands. Don't worry. Just run."

"I got it," Pretia said. She was less worried about her mind than about the fatigue in her limbs.

Vera crouched into the blocks. Eshe, Rovi, and Pretia stood off to the side, readying for their turn with the baton. Eshe jogged in place as Vera crouched down alongside the seven other leadoff runners in their heat.

The starter's horn sounded. Vera was off. She seemed calm and confident as she sprinted down the track. At the halfway point she had a clear edge over the other runners. The officials had whisked the blocks away, in preparation for the next leg of runners. Eshe got into place and starting jogging while looking over her shoulder for the handoff.

Vera passed the baton to Eshe, letting go at just the right moment—and Eshe raced away. Three-quarters of the way around the track, she was passed by a Realist from Dynami who handed off to his teammate first.

Rovi was in third place when he received the baton. Pretia readied herself. She began to focus as she watched Rovi round the track. If he pulled into the lead, there was a chance, despite her overall exhaustion, that Pretia could race without exerting herself fully. She knew she needed to conserve energy for the later, more competitive heats. It was a risk, but one she felt she had to take.

At the 300-meter mark, Rovi's quick feet had put him in second place. Pretia began her jog and held out a hand behind her. The baton hit her palm just after the Dynami Realist to her left received his.

She ran, the stadium a blur around her. She tried to focus on her form, on making herself as aerodynamic as possible. She was aware of the heaviness in her legs and the raw scraping in her lungs with each breath. But she was moving and not losing ground. At the halfway point she was still behind the Dynami runner. A hundred meters more and she could rest.

Pretia could feel her legs slowing and a tightness in her back, probably the result of carrying all the Star Stealers. As she tried to lean into the final turn, her rhythm broke. Her steps grew erratic. Just before she crossed the finish, a Realist from Aquiis passed her, pushing Pretia into third.

She staggered to a stop, then doubled over, her hands on her knees, desperate to catch her breath. In an instant, her teammates surrounded her.

"Are you okay?" Vera asked.

"I'm fine," Pretia said.

"You looked . . ." Vera began.

"You looked tired," Eshe said.

"I said I'm fine." Pretia righted herself.

"You can always split yourself if you need to, right?" Vera asked anxiously.

Pretia drew a deep breath. "Don't worry, Vera. I'll do what needs to be done." Then she glanced around the stadium, taking it all in for the first time—the crowd, the banners, the noise. "Now what?"

"What do you mean?" Rovi asked.

"Well," Pretia said, "we can't hide anymore. Everyone knows I'm here now."

"I guess we wait with the rest of the Dreamers. What else can we do?" Rovi flung his arm around Pretia, and they walked off the field to where the athletes from House Somni were gathered.

No sooner had they arrived than Satis Dario and Cleopatra Volis appeared in front of them. Satis's usually kind, placid face was a mixture of relief and anger.

"Your parents have been looking everywhere for you." He lowered his voice. "Please tell me you didn't leave the village."

"Satis," Pretia pleaded, "I want to do my best. And Somni is going to need two podium positions. I really have to concentrate."

Satis glanced around the stadium. "You are going to have to answer a lot of questions," he said. "But I suppose it will have to wait."

"I promise I'll tell you everything after we win," Pretia replied.

"Okay," Satis said with some reservation.

"Thank you. I need to focus on this race." Pretia paused. "My last race ever."

"If this is going to be your last race ever," Cleopatra cut in, "I expect you to do better in the next heat. Your last one hundred meters were subpar."

"I know," Pretia said.

"I expect more from you," Cleopatra said. "You looked worn-out, and it was only the first heat. Haven't you been training?"

"I'm fine," Pretia said for what felt like the one hundredth time in the last hour.

Cleopatra shook her head. "You didn't look fine. Do better next time."

Pretia flopped on the ground and started to stretch to hide her exhaustion. Satis squatted down next to her. "Your parents are going to find out, you know. I'm sure word has already reached them—they're probably on their way."

Pretia sighed. "I guess they'll see my final race, then," she said.

"Better make it a good one, in that case," Satis said.

He moved away, allowing Pretia to keep an eye on the subsequent heats. When the first round was complete, there was a break, allowing runners to prepare for the semifinals. Vera kept up a running patter about their competitors in the next heat. Pretia tuned it out. She knew her only competition was herself.

During the break, her eyes kept drifting over to the royal box. "Stop," Rovi urged when he saw what she was doing. "If they come, they come. Don't let it affect you."

"They'll come," Pretia said. "And they'll be mad. But right now my focus is on Dreamer Glory."

"That's the spirit," Rovi said. He glanced over his shoulder to check that no one was around. "What was Satis asking you?"

"He was wondering where I've been," Pretia replied.

"What did you tell him?"

"Nothing, but he suspects I left the village. And when people find out the truth, they'll strip our medals."

"Maybe not," Rovi said. "And all anyone will ever find out is that we went to Hafara, which is *below* the Crescent Stadium. So technically we didn't leave the site of the Junior Epic Games. We were here all along."

"Brilliant!" Pretia said.

"But don't worry about any of that now. We have a race to run." The royal box was still empty when the leadoff eight runners got in the blocks for the first semifinal. Vera was in the outside lane. Rovi, Eshe, and Pretia stood to the side, waiting for their turns. On "Go" the runners took off.

Vera was in command through the halfway mark, but then a few of her competitors picked up their pace and passed her. Vera crossed in third.

The handoff to Eshe was smooth. Eshe maintained her position for the entire lap of the track, crossing in third like Vera and passing the baton to Rovi.

"Go, Rovi, go!" Vera cried as Pretia got into position. Then she shot Pretia a knowing look. "Don't be afraid to do what you need to do."

Halfway around the track it seemed that Rovi was going to gain ground, but he stagnated and was still in third place when he passed to Pretia. It was a fluid transition. She didn't break stride as the baton hit her hand. But Pretia felt sluggish from the get-go. It seemed as if she were running through mud.

She was tiring. She was aware of the weight in her legs, the distance that remained to run, and the runners at her back. She was aware of too many things at once. She despaired as a Dreamer from Aquiis passed her. She tried to accelerate, but she had nothing in reserve. She was staring at the backs of three jerseys as she pounded the track. The runners ahead were pulling away. Catching them was getting harder and harder with every passing millisecond. She needed to stay where she was or all would be lost.

Pretia could feel someone else right on her heels. She knew better than to look—it would cost her more time. But she could feel the runner closing in. She tensed.

There was only one way to ensure her team would qualify for the next round. Pretia needed her shadow self. *Split,* she urged herself. *Split!*

The finish line was in sight, but she had fallen significantly behind the lead three runners.

Now the runner who'd been on her heels had pulled even. Pretia could not afford to lose another millisecond, another millimeter. If she did, she'd cost her team a spot in the finals.

But where was her shadow self? Why wouldn't it come? She needed it more than ever. *Split, please, split.* Nothing happened.

There were only a few feet between her and the finish.

Come on, she commanded her shadow self.

But it was too late.

She'd crossed the finish in tandem with the runner at her side.

Her teammates swarmed her. Rovi patted her back. "Good job," Vera said. But Pretia could hear the reservation and disappointment in her voice. Had she held on to fourth, or been pushed back to fifth?

"I'm sorry," Pretia said.

"It was *really* close," Eshe said. "There's going to be a review."

Pretia glanced at Vera's face. She could see the tension in her jaw. Pretia's failure to split might have cost Vera breaking Farnaka's record and the team's chance at gold.

"It's okay," Rovi said.

Pretia turned so her back was to Eshe. "I couldn't do it," she whispered. "I couldn't split myself. I think my shadow self is exhausted."

◆

Rovi looked at her, concern in his eyes.

"I'm so sorry," Pretia said again, panting.

"You have nothing to apologize for," Vera said. "You've done so many heroic things today."

"But what if that means the Dreamers don't win the Junior Epics?" Pretia said under her breath. "What if you don't break Farnaka's record?"

Before Vera had a chance to reply, Eshe wheeled around and forced herself between them. "We made it," she cried. "Pretia finished fourth. It's official."

A wave of relief broke over Pretia. She pulled away from her friends. "I need some space. I need . . . I need to rest up." She headed for the sidelines of the track.

"Is she okay?" she heard Eshe ask Rovi.

"She's fine," Rovi replied.

Pretia sat down at the edge of the stadium. She knew she should stay loose, but she was too tired. She understood what had happened out there. Her shadow self was exhausted from carrying the Star Stealers and even more from the time her two selves had been separated on either side of the River of Sand. She didn't know if she could summon it for a final effort.

Pretia was dimly aware of the other semifinal heat. All she knew was that a team led by Rex Taxus had made it into the final round.

During the break before the last race, Rovi joined her. "Listen," he said, "no matter what happens out there, we've accomplished so much. Just do what you can. Vera, Eshe, and I will try to go the extra mile."

"I don't want to let you down," Pretia said. "Or House Somni."

Rovi didn't meet her eye. Instead, he glanced around the stadium, something clearly on his mind.

"What?" Pretia asked. "What are you not telling me?"

"I don't want to pressure you. Everything you did in Hafara is more than enough for one day—you know I believe that. But there are only two Dreamer teams in the finals."

Pretia groaned. "So both our team and the other Dreamer have to medal in order for Vera to break the tie, right?"

"Exactly," Rovi said. He looked apologetic. "Maybe I shouldn't have told you."

"It's fine," Pretia said. "I needed to know." She got to her feet and began to jog. "I needed to know," she repeated. "And now I need to warm up."

As she jogged and stretched, Pretia was aware of the thousands of Dreamer eyes on her all wondering the same thing—would she let her team and her house down? She was the weak link on the field. Everyone knew it.

The announcer summoned the racers to the starting line for the finals.

Pretia took a deep breath. It was now or never.

Vera crouched down in the blocks. Pretia leaned over and clapped her on the back. "We got this," she said, demonstrating a confidence she didn't have.

Vera nodded. She was in the zone. Pretia wished she could join her there.

Just before the start, there was a commotion in the stands. Pretia looked up. The crowd rose to its feet as a hush fell. She heard the announcer over the megahorn: "Everyone, please face the royal box to acknowledge our king and queen."

Along with the entire stadium, athletes and spectators alike, Pretia faced the royal box and saluted her parents. It was surreal, standing on the field and acknowledging her parents as if she were a regular citizen of Epoca and not their child. But perhaps, for the next few minutes, that's exactly what she could and should be. Maybe they'd be able to see her that way: just another runner in an important race, instead of their cherished Child of Hope.

◆

"On your marks," the announcer said.

Vera got back into position.

"Get set."

Pretia was aware of Eshe visibly vibrating with excitement at the arrival of the king and queen.

"Go!"

Pretia willed herself to ignore the royal box and devote her focus to the events on the field.

This was it—the Dreamers' last chance to claim the Junior Epic Games, Vera's last chance to break Farnaka's record, and Pretia's last ever chance to race, to compete, and to medal.

Vera burst into the lead, dusting her competitors as she raced down the track. At the final turn she was in complete control. She passed the baton to Eshe, who sprinted away. For much of her lap Eshe maintained Vera's lead, but at the third turn, a Realist from Rex Taxus's team pulled even. On the homestretch he passed Eshe. But Eshe held him close. She extended the baton to Rovi's waiting hand.

But before Rovi could grasp it, Eshe dropped it. A gasp went up from the crowd.

The baton fell to the track, where a runner from Dynami kicked it. The baton shot off the track into the grass. Rovi dodged incoming runners, weaving around them in order to retrieve it. By the time he did, all seven other runners were well past the first turn.

He returned to the track. "Go, Rovi, go," Pretia screamed.

"Go!" Vera echoed, her hands clenched in anxiety.

It was an impossible task. The runners were spread widely across the track, but the leaders were well out of Rovi's reach. He was working harder than Pretia had imagined he could, straining with every step. But Eshe's mistake had cost him too much ground. Rex Taxus's team was in the lead. The other Dreamer team from Dynami was in second. Rovi was half a track length behind the leaders.

Pretia got into position for the handoff.

One by one, the other seven runners received their batons and sprinted away. When the baton hit Pretia's hand, Rex Taxus had already passed the halfway mark and was closing in on the 300-meter line.

The time had come for one last, desperate effort. If her shadow self had deserted her, Pretia would have to rely on her body and spirit alone.

Push.

She gave everything she had, despite the overwhelming exhaustion in her limbs. By sheer force of will, she raced around the track, trying not to think of the outcome and about how far behind she was.

She needed to enjoy this, to savor it, to make the most of this one final moment. She needed to drink it all in and remember it and let go of all the fears that could corrupt her last seconds as an athlete. She needed to race away from those fears, leaving them in the dust.

The stands vanished. The track vanished. Her competitors vanished. It was just Pretia out there, alone, racing for all that she was worth, running unburdened by all the anxieties that had led to this moment. And then her shadow self emerged, bursting from her with a jolt such as she'd never experienced before.

Pretia's shadow was a lightning bolt—a speeding bullet. It tore down the track, a blur of Dreamer purple and golden sneakers.

Pretia didn't pause to watch. She kept running, as if her physical self's exertion could drive her shadow self on.

One by one, her shadow self picked off the runners until it was neck and neck with Rex Taxus in the homestretch.

Pretia herself kept up her pursuit. They were doing this together, her physical body and her split self.

Only a few more steps. Only a second or less. That was all that remained.

And with one final exertion, Pretia's shadow self leaned forward, tipping over the finish line in front of Rex Taxus.

A few moments later Pretia felt that curious collision as her physical body crossed the finish line and her shadow self crashed back into it.

She had done it!

They had done it!

What's more—the Dreamers from Dynami had finished third.

The stadium exploded with purple fireworks, streamers, confetti, and banners.

Pretia wiped sweat from her eyes. She turned toward the royal box and saw her parents on their feet, clapping wildly for her.

It didn't matter that this was her last race. This was the best feeling in the world. Pretia's heart swelled—she felt as if she were floating above her body. Everything was so real and surreal at the same time.

Dreamers were swarming all around her, congratulating her on her win.

"My teammates—not just the ones from this race but all the athletes from House Somni—and I did this together," Pretia insisted. She reached for Vera in the crowd. "And without Vera Renovo's record-breaking medal haul, we never would have clinched Junior Epic Victory." Vera beamed as the Dreamers began to chant her name.

In the middle of the commotion, Pretia saw that Eshe was standing off to the side. She broke free of the jubilant Dreamers. "Hey," she said, hugging her teammate, "we ran an amazing race."

"I nearly ruined it," Eshe said.

"First of all, I nearly ruined it earlier," Pretia said. "But without your performance in previous heats, we'd never have made it. I was useless."

"I guess," Eshe said. "Everyone saw me mess up."

"Want to know what I think? If you hadn't dropped the baton, I could never have summoned my shadow self. You helped me."

"Do you mean that?"

"Absolutely," Pretia said, releasing Eshe. "Now let's celebrate."

The moment she'd let go of Eshe, Pretia felt a grip on her shoulders. "That's the athlete I always knew was in there." Satis's voice was in her ear. "I've been waiting for this moment since I first saw what you could do at Ecrof."

"So have I." Pretia looked up from Satis's embrace to see the stern face of her uncle Janos. "I knew you had it in you," Janos said warmly. And then he backed away, leaving Pretia to celebrate with her team.

The Dreamers hoisted her and her teammates on their shoulders for a victory lap around the track before putting them down to continue celebrating. Eventually, the crowd parted to allow Pretia and her team to approach the podium for the medal ceremony. When it did, she saw that Rex Taxus was standing stock-still, his mouth open. During the explosion of Dreamer joy, he hadn't moved to commiserate with his Realist teammates.

They locked eyes.

"That—that." His mouth opened and shut, obviously stuck on what he wanted to say. "That was simply incredible."

Many unbelievable things had happened to Pretia that day, but this was perhaps the most incredible.

"I have never seen anything like what you just did," Rex added. And then, with the stunned look still on his face, he slumped off to join the crowd of somber Realists. She stared after him for a moment before continuing on to the podium, where the teams lined up behind their respective podium positions.

The announcer came over the stadium's megahorn. "Today, in honor of the final event of the games, King Airos and Queen Helena of Epoca will present the medals to the victors and the runners-up. They will also award the Junior Epic Cup to House Somni, winner of these Junior Epic Games."

A deafening cheer shook the Crescent Stadium, followed by the Dreamer fight song.

◆

Several officials began to cross the field, carrying a table with the Junior Epic Cup and a megahorn on a stand.

Pretia's heart leaped into her throat. She'd known she would have to face her parents, but she wasn't prepared for it to happen quite so soon. She had hoped for a few more moments to drink in the wondrous atmosphere of the victorious end of the games before facing the consequences of what she had done.

Pretia looked toward the royal box. Her parents had left their seats and were being escorted down to the field.

Vera could clearly feel her tension. "Don't worry," she said. "You're a hero. They saw that. You just executed the most remarkable feat and comeback in the history of the Junior Epic Games. And I would know." Vera turned to Rovi. "Right, Rovi?"

Rovi nodded distractedly, his eyes fixed on the king and queen as they crossed the field.

"Rovi?" Pretia asked. "Are you okay?"

"Yeah, sure. Why?" His voice was distant, as if he wasn't aware of the momentous occasion.

Pretia's parents had reached the podium to begin the medal ceremony. The Junior Epic Cup, a glittering glass-and-gold trophy showing the faces of the seven blessed gods, stood in front of them next to a megahorn, presumably for House Somni's victory speech.

The stadium's announcer bellowed, "In third place, the Dreamers from Dynami."

The stadium was rocked by Dreamers' chants as the third-place finishers mounted the podium. They bowed their necks as the king and queen placed bronze medals around them.

"In second place, the Realists from Dynami."

Rex Taxus and his team stepped forward so the king and queen could place silver medals around their necks. The applause from the Realist camp was more muted than the Dreamers' reaction had been.

"And finally—" The announcer's voice was drowned out by

the Dreamer fight song once more erupting across the stands. "And finally, in first place, the Dreamers from Ecrof, as well as their flag bearer, Rovi Myrios, who will accept the Junior Epic Cup on their behalf."

Pretia, Vera, Rovi, and Eshe stepped onto the winners' place.

Pretia studied her parents. It was over. She'd run her race. She achieved what she'd dreamed of when she fled Ponsit Palace what felt like a lifetime ago. She had no idea what would come next, but part of her was relieved she didn't have to defy them any longer.

As hard as she tried, she couldn't read her parents' expressions—she saw that they were working hard to maintain their officially neutral faces. Were they angry or proud? Surely they wouldn't demonstrate their anger at Pretia in front of the entire nation, especially not after such a remarkable victory.

She watched them each take a gold medal from one of the attendants and approach the podium. They placed the medals over Vera and Eshe first, then received two more.

The queen stood in front of Rovi, the king in front of Pretia.

Pretia and Rovi bowed their heads to receive their medals. "Welcome back, my daughter," the king said in a low voice. "That was indeed impressive. Still, there are many things we have to discuss. You have presented us with some challenges."

He looped the medal around her neck and placed a kiss on her cheek that, despite his stern words, was full of warmth and love.

"And now, the Junior Epic Cup will be presented to Rovi Myrios as representative of House Somni," the announcer declared.

Together, the king and queen carried the cup to Rovi. He accepted it. An attendant drew the megahorn near so he could speak. He took the cup and held it with one arm.

Then he looked at Pretia, a strange expression in his eyes. He seemed at a loss for words. "Go on," she urged.

Suddenly Rovi raised his free arm toward the sky, his palm

upward, his fingers cupped together like he was plucking a star from the heavens. The Star Stealer salute.

Pretia's heart stopped. Her breath caught. He was risking everything they had just achieved against so many improbable—no, *impossible*—odds.

And then, bending slightly toward the megahorn and speaking in the most powerful voice Pretia had ever heard Rovi use, he proclaimed, "No sports for any until there are sports for all."

The stadium fell silent.

The queen's eyes widened in shock. King Airos, too, seemed stunned.

Pretia looked from Rovi's stoic stance to her parents' muddled confusion. The Junior Epic Cup glinted in the stadium lights, a brilliant flash of gold.

Then it hit Pretia.

This was the moment in her Grana Book.

This moment was why she had to run away to Ecrof and hide in Phoenis. Her suspicion that the golden fire at the end of the twisty road wasn't victory had been correct. She could see it clearly now. And what was more, she could feel it.

Her parents—their houses—were the murky mountains and she was the twisty path. But the golden fire at the end of the road wasn't winning; it was knowledge. It was enlightenment. That was her duty and her destiny. Her experience with the Star Stealers had shown her a new purpose: to lead Epoca into a brighter future, a future in which equality was paramount. A future in which Epocans would understand the Orphic People who lived among them, and accept them. She could see the way forward, and it was her duty to lead her people along that path.

Pretia extended her arm skyward. She raised her palm. She brought her fingers together.

And finally, she found the words she needed. "No sports for any until there are sports for all." Her voice rang out, clear and strong. "This victory is not just for House Somni, but also for the Orphic People, now and forever."

The king and the queen stared at Pretia.

"I am the Child of Hope," she continued. "This is *my* hope. This is the hope I bring to you. A united Epoca for Dreamers, Realists, and Orphics."

The stadium remained silent.

Then Vera raised her arm, joining Pretia and Rovi in their salute.

Every inch of Pretia was vibrating with excitement and tension. She knew she had done the right thing. She had saved the Star Stealers, but it wasn't enough. She had to proclaim herself their champion.

The king stepped forward. Pretia's blood froze. Would he strip her medal from her?

"So you have accepted your name at last," he said. "Though not without complications."

"Yes," Pretia said. "I have."

"You have come into your destiny as I knew you would," the queen said, "and made a statement as a future ruler. It's not one that I could have predicted. But I shall try and respect it. What you did on the field today was most impressive, but this gesture was even more so."

"You have stepped into your fate as future ruler whether you like it or not," the king said.

"I am ready," Pretia said proudly. She had saved the Junior Epic Games.

"Good," her parents said in unison. Then they raised their arms so the entire stadium could see and applauded Pretia and her friends.

The stands exploded in thunderous applause.

"You are indeed the Child of Hope. You always have been," the queen said.

◆

"But in my own way," Pretia replied.

"As it should be," the queen said, kissing her forehead.

Pretia's parents backed away, marking the end of the medal ceremony.

Overhead, the sky erupted with Dreamer purple fireworks. Pretia turned to her friends. "We did it," she said. "We did more than I ever imagined we could have."

"I think I made Issa proud," Rovi said. "I know I did."

"I sure made Farnaka proud, both on and off the field," Vera said. "I bet he never imagined I'd break his record *and* take a stand. And I made Ecrof proud, too."

"And you showed your brother what you're made of," Rovi said.

"Pretia showed my brother what she's made of," Vera echoed.

"You two made *me* proud," Pretia said. "Me and the whole of Epoca. No matter what happens next, we have done something incredible."

As one, the three friends looked up at the sky. A full moon hung above the stadium, watching over them, making the sky glow with soft purple light.

Who knew what dreams would come and what challenges would arise. A world of wonders and possibilities, hopes and fears stretched out vast and unknowable before them. But there was one thing Pretia was certain of: whatever came, they would be ready to face it.

She looped one arm over each of her friends' necks, hugging them close. "Here's to dreams that never die."

AFTERWORD

Kobe's imagination was as vivid and creative as it was unrestrained. His vision for the four, and possibly eight, books that would have formed the complete Epoca series began way before the first page of *The Tree of Ecrof* and extended far past the final page of *The River of Sand*. What you hold in your hands represents only a small part of Pretia's journey. But we feel that without Kobe's creativity and guidance, it is impossible to complete the series. And because the series is incomplete, we wanted to give you a sense of where the story was headed and reveal some of the secrets buried in the pages you have read.

You may have started to suspect that there is something unusual about Pretia's parentage. It's true: King Airos and Queen Helena are not her parents. She is in fact the daughter of Syspara, the Realist queen's sister, and her Dreamer partner Fortunus. Heartbroken over the death of several infant children, Queen Helena, with the help of her confidante, Anara, switched her sickly baby with that of her pregnant sister Syspara. Syspara, devastated over the death of her child and suspicious about her sister's actions, fled Epoca to the outlands, where she has been plotting her revenge.

Unbeknownst to her, Pretia has inherited her remarkable grana from her birth mother, and this is why her uncle Janos is her champion, despite her not choosing to compete for his house—he suspects that she is actually his favorite sister Syspara's child.

Speaking of Janos, you are probably wondering about his devotion to Hurell, the God of Suffering. This is one of the primary threads we were not able to satisfy in two books. It was Kobe's intention to take Pretia and the reader on a journey of discovery in which they would come to understand the God of Suffering as a positive force. Although Pretia's parents call her the Child of Hope, she is, in fact, the Child of Suffering stolen from a mother who was tricked into believing her child dead. Syspara, like Janos, is a devotee of Hurell and is raising an army in her outland kingdom to restore the Fallen God to prominence in order to bring the people of Epoca into greater understanding of his many facets.

As Pretia progressed on her life's journey, she would have discovered the truth about her parentage and the origins of her remarkable grana. She would have realized her destiny as the Child of Suffering, for only then, when she had recognized that through suffering we enter into hope, could she understand the extent of her powers.

But all of that we will leave to your imagination. We know Kobe would love you to continue Pretia's journey for her, to carry her with you and to imagine her adventures. He would love you to internalize its lessons—the necessity of drawing strength from fear and that success comes from a marriage of dreams and reality . . .

For now we will leave you with the Grana Prayer he wrote for each of the houses—the two sides of Pretia's self: "May your inspiration fly freely, toward a boundless sky and a sea of ideas, and lead you to wonders that never cease. . . . Guided by fear, led by thought, steered by confidence, may you never go astray." We hope you continue this journey in your minds and hearts and carry Kobe's stories with you forever and always.

THE MAMBA & MAMBACITA SPORTS FOUNDATION

is a nonprofit organization that was founded in loving memory of Kobe and Gianna "Gigi" Bryant and is dedicated to creating positive impact for underserved athletes and young women in sports.

To help continue Kobe's and Gigi's legacies, please visit MambaAndMambacita.org.

KOBE BRYANT was an Academy Award winner, a *New York Times* best-selling author, and the CEO of Granity Studios, a multimedia content creation company. He was also a five-time NBA champion, two-time NBA Finals MVP, NBA MVP, and two-time Olympic gold medalist. Above all else, he was a loving husband and a doting father to four girls. In everything he built, Kobe was driven to teach the next generation how to reach their full potential. He believed in the beauty of the process, in the strength that comes from inner magic, and in achieving the impossible. His legacy continues today.

IVY CLAIRE is a *New York Times* best-selling author, a former world-ranked athlete, and a national and collegiate squash champion. She spent a decade competing internationally before turning full-time to writing. She holds a degree in classics and in a parallel life is a literary novelist. She lives in Los Angeles with her family.

GRANITY STUDIOS, LLC
GRANITYSTUDIOS.COM

Library of Congress Control Number: 2020943464
ISBN (hardcover): 9781949520187
ISBN (eBook): 9781949520224

Printed in the United States of America
1 3 5 7 9 10 8 6 4 2

Book design by Karina Granda
Cover illustration by Debora Cheyenne
Interior and spine illustrations by Simona Bunardzhieva
Type design by Typozon
Art direction by Sharanya Durvasula